Praise for Kate Clayborn and her novels

"Kate Clayborn's writing is a study in syntax and rhythm; her storytelling is a perfect example of patience and pacing. With her trademark eye to detail of setting and scene, she has built a pitch-perfect love story, in a precious world-within-the-world setting, and honest-to-God the most delightful cast of characters I've met in ages. Tonally perfect, deeply romantic, and exquisitely crafted, Clayborn delivers a modern romance masterpiece."
—*New York Times* bestseller Christina Lauren on *Love at First*

"Kate Clayborn's luminously beautiful *Love at First* is playful, heartbreaking, wise, and wonderful. I adored this story about two souls finding their way out of loss and grief and forging their own paths to true love." —Ruby Lang, author of *Playing House*

"A novel of lush complexity, one bursting with humor, a tender melancholy, and meditations on love, friendship, and life, any reader can find solace and inspiration in. It's lyrical and engrossing, a novel that possesses all the colors, idiosyncrasies, and range of the alphabet. Like the pages Meg designs, *Love Lettering* is a novel bursting with hidden messages essential to discover—as long as we open our hearts to analyze the codes."
—*Entertainment Weekly*, A+ for *Love Lettering*

"Quirky and winning." —*USA Today* on *Love Lettering*

"Fresh, funny, clever, and deeply satisfying."
—*Kirkus Reviews*, STARRED REVIEW on *Love Lettering*

Georgie, All Along

Books by Kate Clayborn

Georgie, All Along

Love at First

Love Lettering

The Chance of a Lifetime series

Beginner's Luck

Luck of the Draw

Best of Luck

Novellas

"Missing Christmas" in *A Snowy Little Christmas*

Georgie, All Along

Kate Clayborn

KENSINGTON
PUBLISHING CORP.

www.kensingtonbooks.com

KENSINGTON BOOKS are published by
Kensington Publishing Corp.
119 West 40th Street
New York, NY 10018

All Kensington titles, imprints, and distributed lines are available at special quantity discounts for bulk purchases for sales promotion, premiums, fund-raising, educational, or institutional use.

This book is a work of fiction. Names, characters, businesses, organizations, places, events, and incidents either are the product of the author's imagination or are used fictitiously. Any resemblance to actual persons, living or dead, events, or locales is entirely coincidental.

To the extent that the image or images on the cover of this book depict a person or persons, such person or persons are merely models, and are not intended to portray any character or characters featured in the book.

Special book excerpts or customized printings can also be created to fit specific needs. For details, write or phone the office of the Kensington Sales Manager: Kensington Publishing Corp., 119 West 40th Street, New York, NY 10018. Attn. Sales Department. Phone: 1-800-221-2647.

The K with book logo Reg US Pat. & TM Off.

ISBN: 978-1-4967-3730-4 (ebook)

ISBN: 978-1-4967-3729-8

First Kensington Trade Paperback Printing: February 2023

10 9 8 7 6 5 4 3 2

Printed in the United States of America

This one's for the quaranteam

Chapter 1

Georgie

Well, well, well.

If it isn't yet another reinvention.

From the sweat-damp bucket seat of my old Prius, I stare in disbelief out my windshield at a storefront I hardly recognize. The last time I came to Nickel's Market and Deli, the red-orange sign above the door had read "N el's M et & D i" and the front window had been haphazardly adorned with white posterboard signs, each crookedly hung rectangle bearing a red-markered message about the week's sales on six-packs or pork rinds or paper towels.

In fact, that isn't just what it looked like the last time I came here.

That's what it looked like *every* time I came here. All throughout my childhood, all throughout my adolescence.

But Nickel's now is a different story, clearly—its once-dingy brick façade charmingly whitewashed, its new sign artfully vintage-looking and hung perfectly straight above the sparkling-clean front window. Instead of posterboard signs, there's an

Instagram-worthy display of seagrass baskets, each filled with fresh produce and rustic-looking loaves of bread, Mason jars full of jewel-toned preserves and jams.

"What the heck," I mutter to myself, even though I shouldn't be surprised. For months, it's exactly this sort of thing that Bel has been banging on about—the various transformations in our once-unremarkable, slightly shabby hometown of Darentville, Virginia. The shops, the tourism, the redevelopment of land along the river—they've all drawn my best friend back here for her own brand of reinvention: city to small town, child-free to mom-to-be, in-the-office workaholic to remote-work part-time consultant.

I should be happy seeing this transformed version of Nickel's—happy for Ernie Nickel, who's run the place forever, and happy for Bel, who probably loves this version of it. But I'm uneasy, and not only because the very specific strawberry milkshake I've stopped to order on a last-minute impulse probably doesn't even get served here anymore.

No, this uneasiness is bigger, more diffuse—a tide of frustration at being so bowled over by a storefront facelift, a looming doubt about my decision to come back here. My eyes drift to the rearview, and I wince at the backseat evidence of my haphazard departure from LA, my whole life from the last nine years shoved into two suitcases, a duffel bag, and four extra-large black garbage bags.

It's a mess back there.

It's a mess in here, I think, pressing my palms to my eyes, gusting out a heavy sigh. Twenty-seven hundred miles on the road and I'm not ruminating any less about what's happened to my life over the last month, a sort of slow-motion reverse reinvention that's left me jobless and homeless and entirely without a plan for myself. Every five minutes, I hear a phantom chiming from my phone, the tone I have set specifically for Nadia, as if I'm expecting that any second now, she'll call to tell me her own sudden, shocking plans for changing her entire life—giving up her hugely successful career, her hugely influential existence in LA, her absolutely *indispensable* personal assistant—were a total mistake.

"This will be so good for you, Georgie," she'd said to me, as the movers had packed up the last of her things. "You'll finally be able to do all the things *you* want to do."

I'd smiled and nodded and made a checkmark next to the *primary bedroom* entry on the moving list, and tried desperately to ignore the terrifying blankness in my head at that phrase: *all the things* you *want to do.*

I reach for my phone, too late remembering that I've already made more than a dozen pledges over the course of this cross-country drive to check it less, to stop treating it like it still needs to be superglued to my hand.

There's only one message, and it's from Bel: a string of emojis that represent her excitement over my imminent arrival. Exploding celebration cone, heart-eyes face, those two Playboy-bunny looking ladies standing in some kind of weird formation, a bunch of pink sparkle hearts. It's not the sort of frantic *can you do this immediately?* type of text that's dominated my life over the last few years, but still, it's a good reminder. If there's one thing that's cut through the terrifying blankness problem, it's the prospect of spending time with Bel.

I want that, at least.

I take a deep breath, gathering my resolve. Get in, get Bel's favorite milkshake, get over to her new house, and start helping her with whatever she needs. *You're good at that,* I tell myself, unhooking my seat belt. *You're used to that.*

Before I get out, I drop my phone into the center console, removing the temptation and recommitting to this new plan, the only one that's made even a hair of sense since Nadia rode off into the sunset of her reinvention-slash-retirement. I think of Bel on the phone last month, begging me to come, and it's the motivation I need to finally shove open my door and unfold my tired, tense body from the driver's seat.

Of course, my settled resolve lasts only until I catch sight of my reflection in that sparkling-clean front window, at which point I remember what I put on this morning in the last lousy hotel room of this trip: a threadbare white tank top that I'm pretty sure I spilled coffee on somewhere back in Tennessee and a pair of ankle-length linen overalls that very much have the appearance of having been pulled from a garbage bag.

I do not look like a grown woman who's managed to make a functional life for herself.

I look like the nineteen-year-old screw-up who left this town nearly a decade ago.

I check over my shoulder, relieved that the small parking lot is empty except for a lone, ancient pickup truck that looks as likely to be abandoned as it does to be waiting for the return of a Nickel's customer. Maybe it'll be some random teenager working in there today, someone I don't know and who doesn't know me. Maybe this will be as quick and easy as I need it to be—a win for all the losses I've been hit with over the last few weeks.

But almost as soon as I hear the old, familiar bells tinkle above the door, I know quick and easy isn't in the cards, because even though my first sight of the inside of Nickel's shows everything new—new layout, new lighting, new shelves, new products—my second sight is of something familiar: Ernie Nickel wheeling himself into view, his salt-and-pepper mustache a bit thicker and his hair a bit thinner, his smile warm and inviting and full of recognition.

"Georgie Mulcahy, as I live and breathe," he says, and I feel pretty good about that greeting until he adds a gentle, knowing chuckle. "You haven't changed a bit."

I silently curse my overalls, even as I stuff my hands into the deep, comforting pockets.

"Hi, Ernie," I say, stepping up to the counter and trying an old tack, familiar from my years of being a topic of conversation around here.

Deflection.

"I sure can't say the same for this place." I paste on a smile, trying to affect the confidence of a person who totally planned to appear in public exactly like this. I am suddenly extremely aware of the size of my hair, which is no doubt humongous from the wind I've been letting blow through it all day. "It looks great in here."

Thank God, Ernie—always a talker—takes the bait.

"Well now," he says, his smile growing wider as he maneuvers to the low-slung counter. "I've got all them tourists to thank for it! Them and the retirees. You wouldn't believe the money they've brought around. I sure gotta stock and serve different things."

He gestures to a chalk-lettered menu above him, full up with a list of soups and sandwiches that bear names with no resemblance to the "tomato" or "turkey and swiss" items I remember as favorites. I squint up at the Beverages section, stalling on a listing for a kale smoothie that makes me wonder if I hallucinated my whole entire road trip. Nadia loved a kale smoothie.

"Do you still make milkshakes?" I blurt, because it is not my job anymore to know what Nadia loves.

Ernie scoffs in mock offense. "Now you know I do."

I'm so relieved that I order two strawberry milkshakes, even though I've always preferred chocolate.

Ernie's in it now, a full-on thesis about how well Darentville's doing, property values on the rise and even a mention in a *Washington Post* article about up-and-coming destinations along the Chesapeake Bay. He tells me we're well on our way to being as good as Iverley, the town right to the southwest of us that's got more waterfront and so has always had more wealth. I can't say I'm in the mood for more talk of transformation, but at least this way, Ernie's not going to focus on my apparent lack of one.

But then the bells over the door ring out again, and as soon as I hear the voice accompanying them—a sing-songy, drawling, "Hey, Ernie!"—I know my reprieve is over.

"That *must* be Georgie Mulcahy," the voice calls, and I take a breath through my nose. What I wouldn't give not to be wearing a trash-bag outfit at this moment.

I send a nervous smile toward Ernie and turn to face the music.

In the form of my ninth-grade music teacher.

"I *knew* it," Deanna Michaels says, laughing. "I sure did see the back of you enough!"

Behind me, I can hear Ernie swallow a laugh, and I concentrate on controlling the heat in my cheeks. I laugh, too, all unbothered self-effacement, but my brain is doing a highlight reel of every time Mrs. Michaels sent me out of her classroom. Tardiness, talking too much, the time I made up a new set of lyrics to "The Circle of Life" and taught them to the rest of the alto section.

"Hi, Mrs. Michaels," I say, definitely trying not to dwell on those lyrics. "Nice to see you again."

"Well, I had no idea you were coming into town," she says, clasping her hands in front of her chest, a move so familiar it gives me flashbacks to standing on the risers in her classroom. "I ran into your mother last month, and she didn't mention a word about you visiting!"

"I didn't know I would be visiting last month," I say, but even as it comes out of my mouth I realize I've made a mistake, giving her the kind of information she can make use of.

Her eyes light in a way I recognize—the part-pitying, part-indulgent look that so many of my teachers gave me once I no longer had them in actual class—and she laughs lightly. "That's so like you, Georgie. You always were a fly-by-the-seat-of-your-pants type!"

It's a little unfair, this accusation; it isn't as if I decided to come yesterday or something. And also, my current pants are not even technically pants. But Mrs. Michaels isn't entirely wrong. I was impulsive, flighty back when she knew me, and I haven't really changed. It's just that I've put flying by the seat of my pants to good use. I've pretty much made a living off of it.

But now I don't have that living anymore.

"You know me," I say.

"Now, Georgie," Ernie says, something gentle in his voice, "tell us about that fancy job you've got! Your daddy says you went to the Oscars last year."

"Actually, I—"

"Ernie," chuckles Mrs. Michaels, "you know better than to believe anything Paul Mulcahy says!"

"I did go," I say, and for the first time I've let an edge of annoyance slip into my tone. It's good-natured, I know, this teasing about my dad's legendary tall tales and exaggerations, but it's always chafed me, enough that I'm willing to exaggerate a little myself. I hadn't *actually* gone, but I had worked that day, had done a flurry of complicated errands for Nadia, including delivering things to the hotel room where she was getting ready. Then I'd ridden with her in the limo over to the Dolby so she could practice the speech she didn't ultimately get to give.

So technically, I *had* gone. Sort of.

Mrs. Michaels raises her eyebrows, and I feel a fleeting moment of satisfaction. But there are limits to my own capacity for stretching the truth, and in a moment of absurd overcorrection, I say, "I'm in between jobs at the moment, though."

An awkward silence falls, and then Ernie—blessed, heroic Ernie—turns on the blender. I use the time to tally up things that there's no point in saying. *My boss decided to change her life. She said it's time to think about changing my own. I could pick up the phone and have a job exactly like my old one tomorrow, if I wanted it, except the problem is I don't know if I do.*

I don't know if I want anything.

The blender quiets. Is my face the color of a strawberry milkshake? Probably. Mrs. Michaels's eyes have gone more in the direction of pitying. She smiles kindly and says, "Well, a good idea to move back home! It's very expensive out there in Los Angeles, as I understand it!"

"Oh, I haven't moved home," I say, but I think I might've

swallowed those last two words a bit, imagining Mrs. Michaels walking past my garbage-bag-stuffed Prius out there. Embarrassingly, I have an extremely late-breaking realization: I *have*, functionally, moved home, since I don't have any solid plans beyond these couple of months I've promised to spend with—

"Bel," I blurt, because if there was ever a way to get Mrs. Michaels's attention deflected from me, it was by drawing it to my best friend. "I'm here to spend time with Bel."

It works like a charm.

"Oh, *Annabel*," she says with the kind of reverence reserved for a straight-A, perfectly behaved, always-on-time student. "Everyone is *thrilled* she's moved back. And with that lovely husband of hers! Have you met him?"

I want to roll my eyes, but refrain. It's a subtle dig, but a dig nonetheless. Bel and I were always unlikely best friends in the eyes of teachers.

"I was her maid of honor," I say.

This clearly is more impressive than (only sort of) going to the Oscars, judging by Mrs. Michaels's expression. I smile, maybe a tad smug, thinking of the dream of a bridal shower I threw for Bel three years ago, exploiting every connection, every favor I was owed to make it luxurious. A destination weekend in Palm Springs with a bank of hotel rooms, beautiful catering, gift baskets, and spa treatments. Bel says her friends still talk about it.

Take that, trash bags! I'm thinking, but the truth is, this fleeting, polite exchange with my former teacher has only served to bring back that parking lot doubt. I want to be with Bel, sure. But I don't want to be in this fancy new Nickel's, looking a mess. I don't want to be in this town, where people know me as a flake, a failure.

Where I spent a lot of years with the same sense of blank confusion about my future as I have right now.

That smug smile I'm wearing wavers, and before it can wobble completely off, I turn back to Ernie, who's moved over to a sleek iPad that rings my neurotic *better check your phone* internal alarm. I try to refocus on the milkshakes and on the reason I came all this way—Bel and her new home, Bel and the baby that's coming soon. That isn't a blank, at least.

"It's $8.42 for the shakes," Ernie says, and my smile firms up at the price increase. Counting out change at the counter like Bel and I used to do probably doesn't cut it for the kids in Darentville these days. Well, good for Ernie. And good for me, too, not to need to shake out quarters anym—

Shit, shit, shit.

I pat uselessly at my pockets—God, why do overalls have so many pockets!—and sense the self-satisfied stare of Mrs. Michaels behind me.

Typical Georgie, I can practically hear her thinking.

But when a throat clears in a low rumble behind me, it obviously hasn't come from Mrs. Michaels.

I lower my head and let my eyes slide shut. Two witnesses to my humiliation is bad enough; does there have to be a third involved? Am I going to turn around and find someone else who recognizes me, another person eager for a light, no-harm-meant laugh at my expense?

"Ernie," I say quietly, raising my eyes again. "I left my card out in the car. I'll just run—"

The throat clears again, and this time, I look over my shoulder to find a stranger watching me from beneath the brim of a weathered, olive-green ball cap that's pulled low over his eyes.

I narrow my own at him, at the way he's standing there with impatience clear in every line of his long, lean body, at the way he holds his dark-bearded jaw tight. If it weren't for how obviously irritated he looks, I might feel a kinship with him, since his clothes are in worse condition than my own—work boots and faded jeans that are both pretty well caked in dried mud, a T-shirt with a wide, dark stain along one side. Even Mrs. Michaels looks to be keeping her distance, but she's clearly still interested in what's coming next.

I face Ernie again, though something is tugging at my memory about the man behind me. *Is* he a stranger, or—

"Do you need to borrow some money, Georgie?" Mrs. Michaels chirps, her voice the kind of sweet that sets my teeth on edge.

"I have the money in the car," I say, only to Ernie. "It'll only take a second."

A basket thunks onto the counter beside me.

"I'll get it," says the stranger, his voice pitched low. So low that I'm certain he's also trying to shut out Mrs. Michaels.

I can't bear to look over at him yet. Instead, I focus on his basket, full of staples—milk, eggs, a bag of rolled oats, a bunch of underripe bananas, one of those loaves of fancy bread.

"I have the money," I repeat, my voice barely above a whisper. "I only need to—"

I break off when I notice his fingers curling tighter around his basket, his knuckles briefly going white, the muscles along his tanned forearm flexing.

"Ernie," he says tightly, not acknowledging me in the least. "I'm in a hurry. Put her stuff on mine."

I try to ignore his nice forearm so I can focus on his not-nice manners, in spite of the fact that he's offering to pay my bill. But when I finally look over at him, I find that his face—even in profile, even half-covered by the brim of his hat—is as distracting as that flexing forearm. The line of his thick beard is cut close along his square, set jaw, the slope of his nose is sharp, the fan of his dark eyelashes is lush enough to cast a small shadow on his cheeks.

"Sure thing," says Ernie, which at least snaps me out of my fixation on the most attractive, most irrelevant details about this entire situation.

"Ernie, wait," I try again, but he only gives me a small shake of his head, as if he's trying to warn me off any further challenge to this man's *I'll-pay-for-it* demands. Behind me, Mrs. Michaels has either gone mute or finally slinked off somewhere into the store, but I don't want to look either way.

"Pardon," the stranger mutters, reaching an arm past me and pushing his card into the reader. When he pulls it out, the edge of his hand grazes briefly across the front of my *ridiculous* overalls, and he grumbles out an irritated apology. I'm warm all over with embarrassment, with hyperawareness of how foolish, how *flaky* I must look.

"You're all set, Georgie," says Ernie, his smile soft and kind and forgiving.

I grab hastily at the milkshakes he's pushed toward me on the counter, try to focus on the weight of them in my hands instead of the whirring in my head. It suddenly feels so important, so telling that I've botched this. Not even a full week without my job and I'm a puppet with its strings cut. If my phone isn't pinging all day with to-dos, I'm lost, irresponsible. A blank, a mess.

"I'll pay you back," I say to the man beside me, pitching my voice louder this time. Whether Mrs. Michaels hears me doesn't seem to matter quite as much, though, when the stranger is determined to pretend he hasn't. He's unloading the contents of his basket as if he's trying to make up for the time he lost in having to say the fifteen words he's spoken over the course of the last minute and a half.

"I'll get cash and leave it with Ernie," I add, determined now, like paying back this random man is my best shot at reversing the course of this homecoming.

"Fine," he says, in a tone that says he just wants me to stop talking.

Well, fine *then*. I'm oddly and unexpectedly buoyed by his gruff dismissal. It's better, somehow, than the schoolroom-flashback spectacle of the last five minutes. It's no *Typical Georgie* for this guy; it's *Broke Woman Holding Me Up*. That, at least, simplifies things.

"Tomorrow," I promise Ernie, and the stranger who is still

ignoring me, and myself. It feels good to say it, like I'm gathering up some of my puppet strings, or filling up some of that blankness that's ahead of me. Tomorrow I'll be helping Bel. Tomorrow I'll pay back this bill. Tomorrow there'll be *something*.

I don't bother waiting for a reply. I raise my chin and turn to find Mrs. Michaels still there, too pleased by half. I send her what I hope passes for a confident, unbothered smile as I move past her, and I make myself an additional promise.

I am not going to spend the next two months this way—a topic of conversation or a target of well-meaning but rudely executed excuses. And I am not going to avoid that blankness anymore, the same one that chased me for almost the whole last two years I last lived in this town.

I'm going to fill it up; I'm going to figure it out.

What I *really* want.

Somehow, this time, when I leave Darentville, I'm going to be well and truly different.

Chapter 2

Georgie

Barely a half hour from the time I stepped onto the wide, white front porch of Bel's brand-new home, I decide it's a good thing I made that backup promise to myself.

Because honestly?

From the look of things, Bel isn't going to need that much help from me after all.

We're in the nearly done nursery, Bel sucking at the dregs of her milkshake and pushing her foot against the plush-carpeted floor to keep her brand new, top-of-the-line glider moving with hypnotic smoothness. She ended the house tour here, most excited to show me the crib she and her husband, Harry, assembled the day before yesterday, and even though I'm impressed by it, it's not any more impressive to me than everything else in this house—big windows with waterfront views and rooms that somehow seem both incredibly polished and incredibly lived-in, even though Bel and Harry have only been here for about three weeks. I pictured boxes lining the walls, disorganized closets, cabinets and drawers that needed stocking and systematizing. I pictured stuff for me to *do*.

Instead, I feel strangely extraneous, and now that we're done with the tour, the topic of conversation Bel's landed on—my unemployment—isn't exactly helping. I wish I hadn't left my phone downstairs, not that anyone's calling at the moment.

"I don't understand how she could up and *leave*," Bel says, the hand that's not holding her milkshake smoothing over her rounded belly. She looks serene and stylish—black cropped pants, black sleeveless top, a pair of delicate gold studs in her ears, her dark blond hair pulled into a low ponytail. When she showed me her home office, already set up with two monitors and a whiteboard calendar on the wall filled with her careful handwriting, she'd told me that she gets dressed for work every day, even in this new setup.

"I read that it's important to keep routines when you work from home," she'd said, and I'd gotten strangely stuck on the phrase. I'd worked from home sometimes, I guess—in Nadia's small guest house, where I'd moved only three months after I started working for her, I'd often made calls and travel arrangements and filtered through thousands of her emails. But I worked in the main house, too. I worked in hotel rooms when we traveled. I worked on sets. I worked standing against the walls of ballrooms and restaurants where events were being held. I worked anywhere, and there wasn't much of a routine to any of it.

"Bel," I say from my spot on the floor, my back pressed against the spindles of the recently assembled crib. "You *literally* left DC less than a month ago."

She furrows her brow, looking offended. "It's not the same," she says, but the thing is, it kind of is. On the face of things, Nadia and Bel don't have a huge amount in common. Nadia is a famed screenwriter and director, part Nora Ephron and part Nancy Myers; Bel is a quiet but powerful force in the world of

US education nonprofits. Nadia is a vortex of chaotic, whirl-wind creativity; Bel is a steady, organized problem-solver.

But however different they are, both of them have made big changes. Both of them are all about slowing down, living different lives.

And both of them are doing fine without my assistance.

I blow out a breath, annoyed with myself at dwelling on the comparison. *Nadia was your boss*, I scold myself. *Bel is your best friend.*

Still, the blankness yawns in front of me, and I'm desperate to change the subject.

"I saw Mrs. Michaels at Nickel's," I say. It's a sharp turn, and at first I don't think it'll work. Bel narrows her eyes at me for a split second, because she knows what I'm doing, deflecting this way. But she decides to give me a reprieve, I guess, because she tosses back her head and laughs.

"Oh my *God*, of all the people," she says. "Remember when she gave you detention for teaching us—"

"The new and improved 'Circle of Life' lyrics?" I say, smirking. It's not so bad to be reminded of my foibles in this context, since Bel has never made me feel like a flake. "Yes, it did cross my mind."

"She was a pedagogical terrorist," Bel says. "I still think of her when my posture slumps."

I do the sharp, quick double clap Mrs. Michaels used to do when she caught any of us slouching on the risers, and Bel laughs again before pressing her foot into the floor, stopping the motion of the glider, her eyes bright with excitement.

"Oh my God," she says, "This reminds me. I have something to show you!"

Is it another already unpacked, beautifully arranged room? I think.

I want to turtle right down into these overalls for the stray, snarky thought. In the twenty years of our friendship, I've never had this kind of reaction toward Bel—impatient, resentful, dangerously close to envy. And we've been through bigger shifts in our lives than this one, times when the differences between our situations were even more pronounced. The first time I'd driven up to Georgetown to visit her at college, I was splitting my time between my morning shifts as a cashier at the Food Lion and my evening shifts at a diner over in Blue Stone. I'd worried a little, as I made my way through the congestion on I-95, whether it would be strained between us, whether college would have already transformed Bel so completely that we wouldn't fit the same way we had for all the years of our friendship.

But it hadn't been like that; it'd been the same perfect fit it always was. A big hug at the curb outside her dorm, squealing happiness over being reunited. We'd taken walks around campus, gone to a house party with loud music and red Solo cups, had a bunk-bed sleepover, stuffed ourselves full of greasy cafeteria breakfast. I'd soaked up the atmosphere of her university experience without a trace of frustration over the knowledge that I'd never have a similar one of my own. And in the years after—after I moved to Richmond to waitress, after I got my first gig as a set assistant, and then as a personal assistant, after I settled into my full-time role with Nadia in LA—Bel and I *always* fit. Every phone call or FaceTime, every meetup we'd managed over the years of long-distance friendship, we fit.

And I know, deep down, that we still fit now.

"Well, let's have it," I say brightly, pushing to my feet and pushing off my attitude. I'm tired, that's all. Disoriented from all this recent change. Too much time in the car, in my own head, thinking about the blankness. I *do* want to see whatever she has to show me, even if it does have something to do with Mrs. Michaels's terrible double clap.

Bel braces a hand on the arm of her glider, giving me a smiling, self-deprecating eye roll at the way she has to heave herself upward a little. When she's finally standing, she frowns down morosely at her empty milkshake cup, and I hand mine over automatically. The truth is, I only managed to drink about a quarter of it. The fact that I couldn't pay for it has ruined the taste. It's become a shame-shake.

I feel an embarrassing echo of that handsome stranger's hand across the front of my overalls.

Bel takes a big, grateful sip and then says, "Okay, follow me."

We move down the hallway toward the guest room, which Bel had shown off on the tour with *great* emphasis, seeing as how she's still hoping I'll change my mind about staying at my parents' place instead of here. I'm about to tell her again that yes, I am still very impressed by the therapeutic mattress, but haven't changed my mind—*especially* since Bel has told me on many occasions what pregnancy has done to her sex drive—when she stops in front of a door across the hall from the guest room. If Bel shows me a perfectly arranged linen closet that Mrs. Michaels would quadruple clap in praise for, I'll probably cry.

"Don't judge me," she says, as she sets her hand on the doorknob, squeezing her eyes shut tight as she opens it.

"Haaaaaaa," I breathe out at the sight that greets me, a small room absolutely *packed* with stuff.

"I'm getting to it!" she says, defensively. But already I've taken a step into what is basically a wide center aisle, flanked on either side by haphazard stacks: some cardboard boxes, some plastic bins, and—I desperately try not to pump a fist in victory—a few garbage bags.

"Well!" I say, grinning. "I don't know what this has to do with Mrs. Michaels, but I am *delighted.*"

She scoffs and gently nudges me aside with her elbow, reaching for one of the plastic bins. It's got a strip of masking tape stuck to the top, and I recognize her mom's handwriting: *Annabel, Teen Years.*

I move closer to Bel, a clutch of sadness in my chest. Bel's mom died two years ago—a brutal, aggressive cancer that took her within months of her diagnosis. Nadia had given me three weeks off to be in DC, where Bel's mom spent her last days in a hospice facility.

"I've had all this stuff in storage since Mom," she says, her voice brisk, but I hear the grief in it, and I tuck even closer so she can lean some of her weight against me. "But since we have all this space now . . ."

"Totally," I say.

She takes a breath and sets her milkshake on another stack, moving to lift the lid on the bin.

"Wait," I say, taking over. I shift the bin to the floor, then set another sturdy one in front of it for Bel to sit on. It definitely doesn't look that comfortable, so I make a mental note as I crisscross myself onto the carpet that we'll need to move before too long.

"Look at *this*," she says, lifting the sweatshirt that's folded on top and shaking it out. It's dark green, our high school's official color, and across the front in big white letters it says, HARRIS COUNTY LOGGERHEADS. I know without her having to turn it around that there's a badly drawn turtle on the back. Somewhere I have this exact sweatshirt, which all of us got on the first day of our freshman year. At the time, it'd been a huge deal, a rite of passage—going to the county's high school meant you weren't just a Darentville kid anymore. You were in school with kids from Iverley, Blue Stone, Sott's Mill. You'd made it to the big time.

Bel pulls it on over her head, mussing her ponytail and stretching it over her belly. "Still fits," she says, and I obviously don't argue. "Eeeeeee, there's so much in here!"

Bel digs in excitedly, but I'm cautious, tense as I reach in. Of course I know that there's mountains of good memories in here, relics of the fun Bel and I had during those years. But I'm too close to that scene in Nickel's, the reminder that, separate from Bel, I was a disaster in high school—minor bad behavior, major bad grades, no ambition or plans for the future.

All the things you *want to do,* Nadia's voice echoes, collapsing somehow with every teacher and school counselor who prodded me with questions about college, vocational school, maybe even the military.

I never could see myself doing any of it.

Thankfully, I get a reprieve when the first thing my hand closes around is a synthetic, faded white sash—Bel's homecoming court souvenir from our senior year. Rough green glitter sticks to my hands as I lean across the bin and drop it over her head, laughing when she preens and smooths it against herself.

"I should've won," she says, and I dig back in, wondering if somewhere in here is the consolation construction paper crown my mom and I made for her the next day. Instead I find a photo of us, still inside the frame the parents' association sold at commencement—garish and thick, it's got our graduation year across the top and a line of puff-painted loggerheads along the bottom.

We're in our green robes, Bel's honor cords swinging between us, our caps off, our arms around each other, our cheeks pressed together, and our smiles huge. We look happy, twinned in celebration. But if I look close, I can see something else in my eyes—a fear at the ending of this, an uncertainty.

The same look I've seen in the mirror for weeks.

"Oh. My. God," Bel says, interrupting my thoughts. I look up to find her wide-eyed, a notebook open in her lap. "Oh my *Godddddddd,*" she repeats, and I lean forward to peek.

"What's—"

But as soon as I get close enough, the question trails off, because I *know* what this is. I haven't thought about it in years, but somehow, I'd know it anywhere.

Bel shrieks in excitement. "Our friend fic!"

"Oh my God," I echo quietly, taking it from Bel's lap without even thinking. I hold it with a strange sort of reverence, memories flooding me. I'd spent more time on this notebook at the age of thirteen than probably I did on any of the schoolwork

I was assigned for the next five years. I *loved* this notebook. I loved writing this fic.

"Look at your handwriting!" Bel says, and my eyes scan over the loopy script that I packed to the very edges of each page, pink and purple ink my medium of choice. When I skip a few pages ahead, I find an entry of Bel's, shorter and tidier and in a standard Bic blue, the same kind of pen she used for homework. It is possible that Bel thinks my handwriting has changed in some way, but honestly it still pretty much looks like this.

"I can't believe you still have it," I say, turning pages, barely registering what's written there. But even still, my head is full of the stories inside it, the scenarios Bel and I wrote with almost frantic excitement. We'd started it halfway through eighth grade, our minds constantly preoccupied with what awaited us in high school. Story after story of what we'd do once we got there, this new threshold of being *grown up*. Real teenagers.

"I didn't know I did," she says, scooting awkwardly forward. I set the notebook sideways atop the mess of stuff left in the bin so we can both look.

"Look at this," I say, pointing to one of her entries. "This is a whole story about you getting a powder-blue convertible when you turned sixteen."

Bel snorts. "*Extremely* fiction," she says. "My old Corolla must've had real impostor syndrome."

She flips ahead a page and my face immediately heats, seeing the huge hearts that decorate the margins. *Prom with Evan Fanning*, it reads across the top, and also I've made the *a* in his name a heart.

"Georgieeeeeeeeeee," Bel squeals teasingly. Maybe this is payback for me being delighted over her secret storage shame room. "You had *such* a crush on Evan Fanning!"

I groan in embarrassment. I *did* have a crush on him, and it lasted way longer than it should have, since he barely knew I existed. Evan Fanning was a year older than Bel and me, a golden boy from Iverley whose family owned and operated the local waterfront inn there. I'd met him once the summer before Bel and I had started this fic, tagging along with my dad to a job he'd had at the inn. Over the course of an introduction that probably lasted less than two full minutes ("This here's my girl Georgie, short for Georgie," my dad had joked goofily), I'd pretty much latched on to Evan's boyishly handsome face and good manners as evidence that he would be the perfect high school boyfriend. This fic is positively *littered* with his name.

"I wonder what happened to him," I say, but as I flip through the pages, really I don't. Instead, I sort of wonder what happened to *me*, because I can hardly believe what I'm seeing. It's the opposite of blankness, my newly teenaged brain fairly bursting with ideas about my future. Sure, it's a small-scale one, full of adolescent imaginings of local traditions and film- and TV-inspired teenage activity—*The Day We Jump Off Buzzard's Neck Dock, Sott's Mill Shopping, Hard Cider and Horror Movies*—but the point is, it's a *future*.

A future I wrote for myself.

My palms are sweaty, my face hot. I can't bear to look at Bel, because I know I'm having a way-too-serious reaction to what is meant to be a fun box of silly nostalgia. I am strangely desperate to be alone with this discovery.

From downstairs, I hear a door open and close, and like I've got thirteen-year-old muscle memory, I slam the notebook shut.

"Bel?" Harry's deep voice calls, and she excitedly calls back, "Up here!"

I transfer the notebook to my lap and quickly dive back into the bin, messily shoving things out of the way. *There it is*, I think, pulling out the folded-down paper crown. "Here," I say, shaping it back the best I can and handing it over to Bel. "Put this on, too."

She laughs and obliges, the faded-pink circlet crooked on her head. She stands and turns to the door right as Harry finds us, his face brightening into a smile as soon as he sees her.

"Well, look at you," he says, his eyes running over her, as

though his wife in a too-small sweatshirt and glittered home-coming sash is the best thing he's ever seen. Henry Yoon is a prince among men, the best person I could have ever imagined for my best friend to be married to, and I love him like a brother.

"Hiya, Harry," I say from my spot on the floor, and his smile transforms for me, familiar and friendly. He makes his way over, bending to accept my outstretched arms. He smells like fancy cologne, except not too much of it, and also whatever hair product he uses to tame his thick black hair back from his forehead. Except not too much of that, either. Harry always seems like he went to some kind of fancy school to learn how to be a very sophisticated man. He went to Stanford, but I'm pretty sure they don't teach you how to make cufflinks look totally normal there.

"Georgie," he says, giving me a light squeeze. "I'm so glad you made it safely. I'm so glad you could come."

He rises and stands beside Bel, draping an arm across her shoulders and lightly fingering the sash that's stretching across her belly. "Homecoming court, huh?"

"We've hit a gold mine," Bel says, gesturing to the bin. "Georgie was looking at—"

"The house is beautiful," I blurt, cutting her off, because that feeling of private desperation is persisting. I don't want to talk about the fic, not yet. I want to look at the whole thing; I want to dissect it. I want to roll around in its fullness.

"It's all Bel's doing," he says, and she presses onto her toes to kiss him on the cheek. For a second, they're in their own private, quiet world; he touches her bump and softly asks how she feels. She rests her hand over his and murmurs a reply that I don't catch, except for the word *daddy*, which I hope has to do with the baby and not the sex drive she keeps talking about. I use the time to tuck the fic more securely on my lap. I'd probably shove it down the front of these overalls if I thought Bel and Harry wouldn't catch me doing it.

"I tried to convince her to stay here," Bel says, her voice back to a normal volume, and Harry raises his eyes to mine.

"We'd be thrilled to have you," he says. "You could use some rest."

Bel nods. "Pampering," she says. "Time to think."

It's nice; of course it's nice, but it's also nearly Mrs. Michaels/milkshake-bankruptcy mortifying. The idea that I'm here to help somehow is dust in the wind; Bel and Harry stand across from me like a let's-help-Georgie team. Bel's pleas for me to come last month now strike me as a ruse I should've seen through—an effort to get me out of LA after such an unexpected change to my circumstances there. Suddenly it's not the prospect of sex noises that's putting me off the guest room, it's the idea of being a project for these two very successful people who already have most of their new house unpacked and who probably have been talking about me occasionally as they did it, wondering what I'll do now that I'm not working for Nadia. *Time to think,* I know, means *time to think about what's next,* and even though it's barely been an hour since I made myself a promise to do exactly that, I realize that doing it at someone else's coaxing—Nadia's, Bel's—simply doesn't appeal.

The fic fairly burns on my lap.

I shake my head, hoping my smile looks grateful. "It's like I said, Bel. I told my mom and dad I'd stay at their place. They want me to watch their plants while they're away."

This excuse would probably sound flimsy to anyone else, but my parents are super into their plants. They'd already had one of their lengthy, wandering road trips planned when I'd let them know I'd be coming, and I'd managed to convince them not to alter their schedule by assuring them of the serendipity of my availability as a house sitter. My parents are also super into things like serendipity.

"But you'll come over," Bel says. "Every day?"

"Of course," I promise, then sweep a gesture toward the boxes. "It'll probably take us that long to get through all this."

She nods, her eyes dropping briefly to the notebook, and when she looks at me again, I'm trying to tell her something silently; I'm trying to harness all our years of knowing each other, being close with each other, into conveying something about this unexpected find. Something about how I need to keep it private for now.

I made this promise to myself, I'm trying to say. *And I think this fic has something to do with it.*

There's no way she gets all that, but she gets something. She gets that I'll be taking this notebook with me tonight when I go, and she gets that I definitely don't want to talk about it yet. She gets that the let's-help-Georgie team needs to manage its expectations for now.

"Stay for dinner at least?" she offers, and I smile in relief—we still fit.

Dinner, I can handle.

"Absolutely."

Chapter 3

Georgie

I drive away a couple of hours later with Bel and Harry in the rearview, on the porch with their arms around each other, both of them lifting a hand to wave before I turn out of view. I honk once and stick a hand out the window, trying to convey my sense of total *fine*-ness through the casual gesture, but in spite of the impressive dinner—Harry's baked rockfish and roasted potatoes—I hadn't managed much to eat, my stomach fluttery with distracted anticipation ever since I first held the fic in my hands. All through cooking, eating, and cleanup, I could only keep a quarter of my brain on the conversation— more talk of Darentville's ongoing glow up (still needs more restaurants), discussion of the tense negotiations Harry is having with his financial planning firm about his hybrid telecommuting/in-office schedule (a nightmare!), *lots* of chat about the state of the birthing plan (underway, but not yet complete). At a certain point, I'd gotten the sense that Bel had managed some secret communication with Harry, warning him off any conversation that veered close to Nadia or LA in general, and while I'd been grateful, it'd only intensified my desire to be alone for a while.

I'm not even back on the main road before I put all the windows down again, letting the warm evening air renew my hair's hugeness, leaning into the knowledge that I don't have to put on a show for anyone else tonight. Beside me, the notebook sits on the passenger seat, and I already know I'm going to spend the next couple of hours reading it. That sense I had back in Bel's junk room hasn't lessened. If anything, it's intensified: This fic has some kind of answer for me.

The drive out to my parents' place is strangely familiar, more familiar than most of the Darentville sights I've seen today, and it's soothing to navigate my way through this side of town, where the changes don't seem so pronounced. I get farther from the riverfront and closer to the heavily wooded lots of the northeast side of town; I see rusty mailboxes I recognize and a crooked roadside sign that tells me to STOP FOR FARM-GROWN FRUIT, which means the Talbotts are still using the same mode of advertising they've used since they took over the place when I was twelve. It'd be a lousy business strategy, except that if you were in the know, you could also STOP FOR WEED, and I'd say a fair number of people from this area—including my parents—regularly did. Last year my dad told me that the Talbotts were taking their crop legal, now that state laws had changed, but my guess is that the county itself wasn't being as permissive about a sign advertising it.

It's another mile before I reach the barely visible turnoff to my parents' property, which at first sight looks less like a path to somewhere and more like a dirt-and-gravel dent in the woods. When I was growing up, it embarrassed me, this wild and hidden entry to our house, a contrast to the neatly trimmed, grass-lined asphalt driveways of other kids' homes, the ones who lived closer to the center of town. As I got older, I minded it less, growing into the understanding that my parents simply didn't abide by the same rules as everyone else—certainly not any rules that mandated lawn care—but I still rarely invited people other than Bel over. It'd be exhausting to explain how to look for that turnoff, and then there was the matter of what you'd see once you found it.

I see it all now, sprawling before me in all its strange, slightly hilarious glory, relics of my parents' half-formed habits and hobbies. There's a few more raised beds in the yard than the last time I was here, but the worn, crooked condition of the cedar is a reminder that I've mostly seen my parents in other places over the last five years—meetups we've made in other cities, an extended trip they'd taken to California for the holidays last November. Still, the beds are overflowing with plants—not the tomatoes or squash or herbs anyone might expect to find in planter boxes, but bee- and butterfly-attracting wildflowers only, tall and unruly, no real need for heavy watering or pest control. Beside the largest bed, there's a six-foot-tall metal rooster, painted blue and green and bright yellow, a homemade wooden sign around its neck reading: I LOVE YOU, SHYLA—the rooster and the sign both a gift from my dad to my mom on the twenty-fifth anniversary of the commitment ceremony they held not long after I was born. The rooster—my mom named him Rodney—isn't the only lawn ornament in the yard, just the biggest one, and as I bump down the rocky driveway, I see ones I remember and ones newly acquired: sculptures and bottle trees and wind chimes, brightly colored china mounted onto metal stakes to make a garden of porcelain flowers, hand-painted birdhouses, and hanging tree lights.

The small ranch house itself has always been unremarkable by comparison to the charming chaos of the outside, and it's got a real "a handyman lives here" energy, in that it bears all the signs of neglect that suggest the person living here does not often bring his work home with him. The white siding needs a power wash, the gutters are crooked, and there's a shutter missing from one of the front windows. It's not wholly dilapidated or neglected, but it is very well used, and the contrast to the house I just left is so sharp that I almost want to laugh.

I put the Prius in park beneath the rusty carport and breathe out a sigh of relief at this specific homecoming. All throughout my cross-country drive, I didn't think a whole lot about the prospect of being *here*, at this home—mostly I'd thought of the official job I didn't have anymore and the unofficial job I thought I'd be doing for Bel. But now that I'm here, I'm glad for it—this messy and crooked hideaway house that matches how I feel inside.

I forgo the trash bags and suitcases for now, grabbing only the duffel and the notebook for tonight. I may be glad to be here, but I sure can't say I know what I'll find once I'm inside, since my parents are historically hugely uneven about prepping for their trips. If my mom was feeling good in the days before, she would've straightened up, made sure laundry and dishes were done, maybe cleared out the fridge of anything that would spoil. But if she was having a flare, the process would've been slower, less pressured, her joints protesting too much effort.

Around back I fumble with my keys, ignoring a pang when I pass over the three I used most regularly when I worked for Nadia—office in Burbank, main house, my small guest cottage. The door here still sticks, especially in this summer humidity, my parents' many paint jobs over the years swelling up the wood past the point of comfort. But it's a fresh, sunny yellow now, the same color it was back when I moved out, and that, too, is a greeting.

Inside it smells like it always has—incense and Dr. Bronner's, which my parents use for cleaning everything from floors to linens. It is shockingly tidy—the kitchen I've walked into is clear of dishes, the dining room table I can see from here clear of crafts—so my mom must've been feeling better than good when they left. In the small living room, all of the plants—God, they have so *many* plants—look perky and well-tended. Still, I don't venture down the hall to the two bedrooms yet, fearing that things might be off the rails down that way. Instead, I take advantage.

By making a mess of my own.

I set the notebook on the coffee table and drop my duffel in the center of the living room floor, crouching to unzip it. Before I left Bel's, I shoved my phone inside here, fearing its siren song of phantom chimes, and I dig it out and put it facedown—points to me for not checking it—beside the notebook. The overalls I'm wearing are heavy now, damp with a day's worth of driving sweat, and while I probably should shower first, my more settled stomach is now nudging at me with hunger. I've got a real hankering for comfort food before I try washing the day off, and I know what I want to be wearing while I do it.

I rummage through the duffel, pulling out hastily rolled clothes and a couple of toiletry bags, all of which I leave on the rug while I search. Near the bottom I find a candle wrapped in a pair of running shorts and also three loose teabags, which is truly ridiculous, a sign of the chaotic, rushed state I was in when I finally—after putting it off as long as possible—packed up my few personal belongings. Finally, though, I find it: a thin, brightly colored, flower-patterned robe Nadia gave me during a closet cleanout a few years ago. It's got bell-shaped sleeves and goes all the way to the floor with a short train in the back, and it makes me feel like I'm on a soap opera. This is the kind of robe you put on when you've lost your job and your former teacher thinks you're pathetic, and also your best friend might think you are, too. This is the kind of robe you put on when you're about to eat snacks and read a diary of your adolescent fantasies. This robe is for *glamor*.

I unhook the overalls and let them fall to the ground, stepping out of them clumsily even as I perform the task of exhausted women everywhere—taking my bra off without removing my top. Once I've pulled it through the armhole of my tank, I fling it onto the old, slouchy couch, sending it the disgusted glare that all bras deserve after a long, hot day. Then, it's soap opera robe time. It's hideously wrinkled from its tightly rolled position in the duffel, but by some miracle it's still cool and smooth on my skin, which is excellent since my parents don't believe in air conditioning. I don't bother tying it at my waist; I just open a few windows and swan my way back into the kitchen, letting the lapels flap open and the train swoop—glamorously? pathetically?—behind me.

I prepare for slim or spoiled pickings in the fridge, but I'm surprised to find a fresh carton of eggs and a gallon of milk. I'll have to verify with a smell check later, but that's not what I'm looking for anyway. I know what I can count on in this house— there is absolutely going to be a jar of natural peanut butter in the fridge door (there!), and in the freezer I'll find (yep) a loaf of my mom's favorite gluten-free bread. In the pantry, I reach for the jar of honey and the box of raisins, and within five minutes I've made toast that is slathered in a truly inappropriate amount of peanut butter and honey mixture, topped with a sprinkle of raisins and sea salt. I've left crumbs on the counter, the peanut-buttered knife, too, but I can't make myself care. It's all part of the plan tonight, and the plan is me in my robe, eating this toast, and finding out whether it's wishful thinking for this fic to have an answer for me.

And at first, I'll admit—it *does* seem like wishful thinking. After all, young me struggled with the difference between *their, there,* and *they're,* so maybe answers will be more difficult to parse. Plus, there's the surplus of Evan Fanning (every *a* a heart; *why,* Georgie, *WHY?*), who I have placed in an embarrassing number of scenarios, including one where I blow him a kiss from the stands before his football game for luck (a whole two pages on this!).

And there's also the fact that I was *this* committed to the fic at all. Seventy percent of this notebook is filled with my writing, which is probably evidence of every lousy thing Mrs. Michaels was surely thinking about me today. If I would've made even half the effort on my classes as I made on this fic, at the very least I probably would not be twenty-eight years of age, sitting on my parents' couch in my underwear, a stained tank top, and a hand-me-down soap opera robe.

Except eventually . . . well, eventually, I get used to the clumsy grammar, the relentless crush, the sheer devotion I showed to this. I start reading, *really* reading, with the same set of eyes and the same stirring, curious hopefulness I'd felt back at Bel's when I'd first seen it. Sure, the fic is fantastical, but it's also full of what would have looked, to eighth-grade me, like perfectly reasonable plans for the years Bel and I had in front of us. Back then, I wasn't *only* a fly-by-the-seat-of-your-pants type. I was the type to have *intentions*. I *intended* that my first-ever summer job would be at the Fanning's inn in Iverley. I *intended* that Bel and I would jump off Buzzard's Neck dock the weekend before the first day of school, wishes for the year written, per local tradition, in Sharpie marker on our arms. I *intended* to shop for clothes at the trendy tourist boutiques in Sott's Mill, and I *intended* to get drunk for the first time with Bel: bottles of hard cider and watching the sorts of horror movies my parents and her mom never let us see. I was going to go to prom. I was going to spend a Friday night dancing at The Bend. I was going to spray-paint my initials on the big rock outside of the high school's football stadium.

Nothing blank about it.

What happened to this girl? I think, tracing my fingers over the lines.

I could blame it all on Nadia, I suppose—the pace she kept and the way she worked ensured that the only real plans I could ever make, the only futures I could ever imagine, involved how to make her life work better. Every assistant I knew in LA worked hard, some of them to the point of total burnout or worse—dangerous habits that would keep them wired all day and into the night. But I also know that a lot of them absorbed the routines of whomever they worked for—up at the same time, familiar with favorite mealtimes and favorite meal spots, drop-offs and pickups with the same set of service providers each week, preferred modes of travel, whatever. Nadia, though, was a hurricane—her creativity huge and borderless, seeping into every decision she made. Sometimes she wanted me to book flights for early in the morning, sometimes for the middle of the day. She liked trying new places to eat, went through early-morning yoga and Vitamix phases and phases where she'd sleep until eleven and refuse food until after four in the afternoon. With Nadia, I never bothered to think much about what the next day or even the next hour would bring. What future I saw for myself was my phone in my hand for my waking hours, ready to execute whatever she asked of me.

A willing puppet.

The problem with this, though, is that I know I can't blame Nadia. I got hired by her *because* I was suited to withstanding hurricanes of her type, had built a reputation for my total unflappability in the face of chaos. I'd learned it first in the trenches of restaurant work, had honed it on those early sets I worked on, had perfected it in my first gig as a full-time personal assistant, a six-month temporary gig for a French director who was in LA for meetings. I spoke no French and he spoke hardly any English, and yet I showed up every day and made it happen. I'd get his Google-translated texts and then I'd get to work. Meal delivery, dry cleaning pickup. Scheduling massages. Replacing cell phones dropped in the tub. Sending thoughtful gifts to his girlfriend. When he went back to Paris, he cried when he said goodbye to me. Every once in a while, I get a random email from him, asking how I am.

And before all that? Before all that, there was this house, with its gutters that'll get fixed someday, with its maybe-we'll-clean-before-our-trip and maybe-we-won't vibe. Before that, there was Harris County High School, where I got teachers off my back by saying things like, *Maybe I could be a flight attendant,* or *Maybe I'll be a nurse.* I said those things the same way I've said to casual acquaintances that I'd like to *backpack around the world*, or the way I've said, to my two long-term boyfriends over the years, that I *maybe want to have kids someday*. Placating, offhand. Conversation pieces at best, conversation stoppers at worst. No real intention behind any of it. For as long as I can remember, my own future has been blurry and indistinct to me.

But I'd forgotten about the fic.

I flip a few pages, end up at the entry I wrote about the Buzzard's Neck dock, a secluded spot between Darentville and Blue Stone that had a sort of mystical reputation among teenagers in town. I read over it again, excited anew by this other me—this me who saw things with clarity. I've written with such detail—everything from clothes Bel and I are wearing to the sensation of hitting the warm, brackish water off the dock.

It's such a small idea.

But it represents something big.

Years ago, when I lived here in this house, when I rattled around this town with Bel on the cusp of what was then a big transition, when I had time to dream of these tiny imagined futures, I was a person who made plans for *me*. It sounds strange, contradictory to say it, but I hadn't calcified my way into the kind of flexibility that became my most defining feature to the people I worked for. I hadn't yet become a person who never thought about the next day, the next week, the next month for myself at all.

I don't know how long I read, but it's long enough that the sun is nearly set, the rustle of crickets and cicadas rising outside. I didn't even finish my toast, but it doesn't matter. I am *absorbed*. At one point, I almost get derailed by a painful realization: For all the work I put into these scenarios, I didn't end up actually doing most of them, or at least not in the way I envisioned them. Probably it was too expensive to get clothes in Sott's Mill, and The Bend ended up closing for three years because of a fire. I don't know why we never made it to Buzzard's Neck, but I do know I never wrote a wish in Sharpie and jumped off the dock there. I went to prom, but of course not with Evan Fanning; in fact, not with a date at all—instead with a group of girls who weren't coupled up at the time. The first time I tried alcohol, it was a beer that Chad Pulhacki gave me at his parents' annual fall bonfire, and it tasted like socks and anxiety. Bel's mom never relented in her ban on horror movies, and I never wanted to get her in trouble.

But I don't let that trip me up. In fact, I let it light me up—I'm half on fire with the fact that so much of this is unfulfilled.

It's given me an idea.

The first idea that doesn't have something to do with someone I work for in *ages*.

I stand from the couch with the notebook in my hands, flipping back to the first page, excitement buzzing in my fingertips. *How We Conquer High School*, it reads, which is funny and sweet and silly, the most low-stakes strategic plan in history. But when Nadia had told me this was the time for me to do all things *I* want to do; when Mrs. Michaels had looked at me with knowing pity; when Bel had offered me *time to think*, I'd felt the leaden weight of my blankness every time, and I still feel it now. I don't know yet what I want for my life, don't know whether I want to simply take on another PA gig, or figure out whether I could do a different sort of job altogether. I don't know if I want a family someday or to travel the world on my own; I don't even know if I want some combination of all of these things. I need time to figure it out, to fulfill the promise I made to myself in Nickel's, and I need the confidence to believe I can.

This friend fic? It feels like that confidence. Once upon a time, I told a story about myself. And maybe if I can make some of that story come true—Buzzard's Neck, The Bend, whatever—I'll be closer to writing a new one. Maybe spending the next two months in the same town as my favorite person, the first and only person who ever *read* these plans, the person who sometimes wrote smiley faces and exclamations and *OMG*s above my prose . . . well.

Well, maybe then I can finally make a version of them come true. Follow through with these plans while I figure out my next ones.

I pace across the worn, faded carpet, mostly avoiding the piles of hastily unpacked stuff from my duffel, flipping through the pages with a quickness now. I count ideas off as I go, and what's funny is that even though a young me wrote these, a lot of them still appeal to me now. They're manageable and fun and relaxing; they'll loosen me up for the bigger stuff. I'll have to do some tiptoeing to avoid the extreme amount of context that involves Evan Fanning, but that seems easy enough, since I haven't thought about him in probably a decade. I'll focus on the parts of this that are about me, and me and Bel. I'll start by making a list—

I'm interrupted by a noise at the back door, a *thunk* that I first think might be a raccoon. Good thing I locked it behind me, because those furry, hateful garbagemen have gotten into this house more than once owing to my parents' door-locking neglect. But when I hear the distinct sound of a key in the lock, hear the door creak and stick and creak again, I'm headed back toward the kitchen, forgetful of my half-dressed state. There's no way it's my parents; last night they were somewhere in Colorado doing a hypnosis retreat. It could be Ricki, my dad's sometimes employee who's checked on the house before during their travels, but it's a weird time for her to come by.

I see a shadow—a big shadow—moving behind the sheer curtain that covers the windowpanes of the back door, and I feel my first pang of alarm. One shove and the door is coming open, and I do the first thing I can think of, which is to grab the peanut-butter-coated knife I left on the counter and brace for confrontation.

I put it together in pieces first—the olive-green ballcap, the jeans, the stained T-shirt. That beard and, when he raises his head, that look of utter consternation with everything in his line of sight, especially the woman he had to bail out for milkshakes this afternoon. I get that whisper of familiarity again, but this time, I've got a peanut butter knife in one hand and many, many pages of my teenage dreams in the other, and suddenly it becomes shockingly, absurdly clear.

I can only think of one thing to say.

"Evan?"

Chapter 4

Levi

Of all the damned things.

Of all the damned things to be called.

Today of all damned days.

I'm standing in the doorway of the house I'm supposed to be sleeping in for the next two weeks and staring at a half-dressed woman who's just called me by my brother's name. She's got a butter knife in one hand and an old notebook in the other, and the look on her face is somewhere between bewildered shock and delighted surprise.

"No," I say flatly, and her forehead crinkles, and then she seems to realize two things.

First, that I am not, in fact, my brother.

And second, that she isn't wearing any pants.

"Oh my *God*," she yelps, shoving the notebook in front of her lap and lifting the butter knife into the air, and because I'm not any less shocked by this scene than she is, I do something equally as ridiculous.

I turn my back on her, and then, for good measure, I lift

my hands into the air in a surrendering posture that's still, all these years later, shamefully familiar.

"I didn't see anything," I say, which is mostly true. I saw enough to know that she's the woman from Nickel's this morning, that she's got legs for days, and that she has real questionable taste in loungewear, if that robe is any indication.

"Oh my God," I hear her repeat, more quietly this time, and I open my mouth to say something—something that'll keep this woman I've clearly intruded on from throwing a blunt butter knife at my back—but before I get even half a word out, I hear the fast, rhythmic clink of my dog's collar, the panting, unrestrained joy that accompanies it. I shoot an arm out to stop the next phase of this disaster, but my reflexes are slow from the surprise, or I'm bracing for that little knife's impact, and Hank zooms right past me, knocking me off balance a little, leaping through the back door and into the kitchen, where this pants-less, probably terrified woman is surely still standing.

"He's friendly," I say, too loud and too sharp, a thud of fear landing in my gut at the thought of something happening to Hank—brawny, barrel-chested, often misunderstood Hank, who even after three years with me still has a bit of hand and foot shock from previous hits he must've taken wherever he was before the shelter found him—in the middle of this mess. I slap a hand over my eyes in deference to the woman's unclothed state and turn back to the doorway. "Please don't—"

I'm interrupted by the sound of her soft "Awww," Hank's paws pattering in excitement on the tile floors, and I know that, at least in terms of my dog, all is well. Maybe that'd be more of a relief were I not still standing in the doorway with a hand over my eyes, wondering what the hell had happened since I last spoke to Paul Mulcahy, who promised me an empty house.

I clear my throat, but I doubt the woman can hear me over Hank's snuffling delight.

"Pants!" she blurts after a second, as if she's newly struck by the absence of them and the presence of me, so I say, "I'm a friend of Paul's," before she can also remember the knife-throwing option.

"Back up," she snaps, and yeah—whatever blend of mistaken identity and shock and Hank-charm is wearing off, I can tell. I keep my hand exactly where it is, squeezing my eyes shut tight for good measure, but I've got the sense she's still wielding the butter knife. However patchy my past is, I never made a habit of home invasions, and I definitely never scared someone like this. I do exactly what she's asked and take a step back.

And feel the whoosh of air as the door slams shut in my face, the lock clicking firmly behind it.

I'm not locked out—the key that I used to get in is still in the door—but I can see how, in all this chaos, she'd forgotten that. And I'm sure not going to use it again, not after—

Hell.

"Wait," I call through the door. "You've got my—"

Hank barks happily from inside the house, as if this is some new fun game, and the woman yells back, "I'm getting *pants!*"

All of a sudden, the full weight of my day settles over me. The extra-early morning I'd needed in order to pack up the last of my shit for the next couple of weeks, the hustle and nerves of getting Hank to the one daycare place within thirty miles that'd take his breed. The messy morning hours I'd spent in waders over at Barbara Hubbard's place, her reminding me every twenty minutes, with narrow-eyed skepticism, that I did things "real different" from Carlos. The rushed stop at Nickel's for groceries that I'd only had time to drop off here before heading out again to deal with a permit snafu that's probably going to stall payment on a job for the next month. The long drive back to pick up Hank, and the petty but brutal annoyance of getting stuck behind a tractor on a two-lane road for six miles of a commute I don't usually have to make.

I scrape the hand that was covering my eyes down my face, over my beard. At this point, all I want is for the woman to crack the door and let Hank back out. I need to sleep off the remaining hours of this day, and if I have to do it outside of my own house but inside of my own truck, fine. It wouldn't be the worst place I've ever spent a night.

Except . . . shit. Paul isn't just doing me a favor by giving me a place to stay for a couple of weeks; I'm meant to be reciprocating by keeping an eye on things while he and Shyla are tooling around the country in an old RV that is, as near as I can figure, held together with zip ties and duct tape. Even before I had to vacate my house this morning, I'd been coming here every couple of days, picking up mail and checking on the plants and tidying up some of what Paul and Shyla seemed to have forgotten to put away before they'd gone. I can't leave off now without finding out who this woman is and what she's doing here, and whether she's got their permission to be in the house.

Fuck.

I raise my eyes back to the door as she comes back into view, pulling back the faded sheer curtain to peer out of the glass. Her face is framed in one of the panes, and I get my first clear look at her—the riot of reddish-brown waves that falls past her shoulders, the dark brows over her narrowed brown eyes, the spray of freckles across her nose and flushed cheeks. She's got her lips pursed and pulled slightly to one side, the expression so determinedly suspicious that I know for sure she's let go of any illusions that I'm Evan, who I doubt has ever been on the receiving end of this sort of look in his life.

"I'm Levi," I say through the glass, hoping she can hear me well enough. "Evan's my younger brother."

I've seen it before, what happens next. The recognition, then the slight recoil that tells me she's from around here. She's probably got a dozen memories of the Harris County rumor mill running through her mind as she looks at me. Mostly I stopped being bothered by it a long time ago.

Seeing it on her face, though, after I'd bailed her out earlier today? For some reason, it has me shifting on my feet in embarrassment.

"I just need my dog," I say. And even though, so far as I can tell, she's the intruder here, I add a placating, "I'll call Paul from my truck, let him know what's happened."

She waits a few seconds, making some kind of calculation in her head. Probably weighing my gallant gesture from this morning against all the shit she's heard about Levi Fanning, local troublemaker.

Then she unlocks and opens the door.

"I'm Georgie," she says, still cautious. Hank stays inside, wagging his whole body beside her, as though he's the one facilitating this introduction.

Oh Christ. Paul and Shyla's daughter; I should've realized. I probably *would* have realized, back at Nickel's, if I hadn't had AirPods shoved in my ears and a podcast playing right up until I'd gone to check out. I've never met her, though I know she's a few years younger than me, which would've kept us from crossing paths much, but I'd say about fifty percent of what Paul talks about is related to her.

Our girl lives out in California, sees the ocean right outside the window of her house every day!

Quite a success story, my Georgie. Working in a restaurant one day and rubbing elbows with the beautiful people the next!

Georgie got herself an Oscar last night! Well, she didn't get one, but I gotta tell ya, my Georgie makes things happen in that town!

I don't suppose I ever thought too much about the stuff Paul said about his daughter, since he's got a real penchant for exaggeration. Once he told me that he met the ghost of Woody Guthrie in a fire circle after taking mushrooms he bought from Don Talbott, which could be true, but it seems awful unlikely. But now that Georgie's actually in front of me, it's clear how Paul's stories had formed an inaccurate picture in my head about her—I would've guessed blond and tan, what with the bit about her living by the ocean, though that doesn't make any more sense than meeting Ghost Woody Guthrie in a fire circle. And with all Paul's talk of her Hollywood job, I would've figured a bit more polish about her—makeup on her face, fancy clothes, whatever.

But this girl. She looks like a country girl. Earlier today, when I stepped up to the counter at Nickel's, I was mostly trying to keep my head down and that harpy music teacher from my high school out of her business, the only kind of public service I'm qualified for, since most people give me a wide berth unless I'm doing work for them. But I'd noticed that she'd had on a pair of wrinkled overalls that'd seen better days, and I'd noticed that cloud of wavy hair, her wide and embarrassed eyes. She didn't have any kind of polish about her then, patting those pockets and pleading with Ernie, and she's got even less now. She's kept on whatever that robe is, bright as a peacock tail, and pulled the sides of it closed over her top, even though she's got pants on now—soft and slouchy ones, and also bright pink, which truly look bonkers with the robe. I'm pretty sure she's got food on her face, too. Peanut butter, if I had to guess. Dang, she looks a mess.

But she's awful pretty, too.

"Mulcahy," she adds, because I probably look like I'm trying to put things together here.

"Right, I figured. I've heard a lot about you."

She narrows her eyes again, and I get it. No one ever means anything good when they say that to me.

"From your dad, I mean."

Her expression softens, but she looks embarrassed. He's probably told her about the fire circle, too. She knows the deal with the stories he tells.

"How do you know my dad?" Her eyes wander to my keys, still swinging in the outer lock. "Like how do you know him well enough to be coming into our house with a key at nine o'clock on a Monday night?"

I lift my cap from my head, rubbing my fingers through my scalp. It's a relief to do it; it was hot as sin out all day, and the chaser is going to be the headache that's already starting. But before I can sigh into the relief, I shove the hat back down, knowing the hair beneath it is probably a sweaty, sticking-up mess.

"I own Chesapeake Dock Service. Your dad and I run in the same circles."

That's true, but not really the whole story. Paul Mulcahy could've ignored me in the same way a lot of the local craftsmen around here did at first, but he didn't. He's not the type, and he's always recommending me to people who have problems with their docks, or who want something new built on the scale that we do.

Her eyebrows raise. "What happened to Carlos?"

She doesn't say it the same way Mrs. Hubbard does. But she says it in the way that'd make me know she's a Darentville townie even if she didn't have that country-girl look about her. She says it in the way of someone who grew up knowing Carlos as the institution he is.

"He retired. I took over officially last year."

It's still hard to believe, frankly. I keep waiting for someone to show up and tell me it was all a mistake. Not Carlos, who isn't the type to worry over mistakes, and who's always had a heap of faith in me, even when I didn't deserve it. My dad, maybe, who used to be real accustomed to telling me about my mistakes.

"Oh," she says, her gaze curious. At first I figure she's doing some kind of reassessment, knowing that I'm gainfully employed or something, but then I realize she's waiting for me to answer the other part of her question.

"I'm having some work done at Car—" I catch myself, clearing my throat. I guess it's another thing I still find hard to believe, that Carlos sold me more than the business—he also sold me his old place. "My house for the next couple of weeks, and it's the kind of work Hank and I can't be there for. Your mom and dad said I'd be helping them out if I watched the house while they were gone, so—"

She closes her eyes, takes a deep breath.

"Yeah," she says, but it's more . . . *Yeeeeaaaahhhhhhhh*. A *this is awkward* yeah. Hank loves it; he yips and hops on his front paws.

"Come on, bud," I say, patting my thigh, because there's sure no point in making this any more uncomfortable. I know enough about Paul Mulcahy to know it's well within the realm of possibility that he promised me a place to stay and forgot that his daughter was coming to town, too. I'm sleeping in the truck tonight. Maybe tomorrow I'll see if there's a hotel nearby where I'll be taking Hank for the next couple of weeks. I dread thinking about what kind of shitty food I'll have to cobble together, living in a hotel room, but whatever.

Hank turns and runs farther into the house.

I put my hands on my hips to stop the slumping of my shoulders from being obvious.

"Sorry about this," I mutter. "Hank!" I call, but no way he's paying attention. I can hear the familiar sound of him snarfling in pure, unrestrained joy at the experience of rubbing the sides of his face and his flanks against uncharted pieces of furniture. If I was in there, I could stop him, but I don't want to go in without permission. He's sure taking advantage, though. I hear him make an almost human-sounding groan of pleasure. The back of my neck heats in embarrassment.

"Why don't you come in," Georgie says, surprising me, and I raise my eyes up to hers. She's smiling, but it's not any kind of self-satisfied smirk or anything. It's more quiet acknowledgment of the way we both might find this funny later, once we're not in each other's presence anymore. It doesn't make the situation better, but it doesn't make it any worse, either, and that's about the only time that's happened today.

So instead of doing the thing that seems most natural—which is to say no, snap at my dog again, and get the hell out of here, I say, "You sure?"

She nods. "Yeah, we'll give my dad a call, figure out what happened here."

I nod, more curtly than she did, and it's annoying, but I can't help thinking of my brother. I know it's only because she got us confused there for a second, but it's a gut check all the same. I may not know him anymore, but I still know for sure that Evan wouldn't do a curt nod; he wouldn't do any of the grumpy shit I've done since I opened this door and found a beautiful mess of a woman behind it. He probably would've charmed the hell out of her, polite and smiling, because that's how all the Fannings—except for me—are.

"Just so you know, though, I have this." From behind her back she holds up a can of Raid. "This is wasp spray and I will absolutely unleash it on your face if you do anything . . . un*toward*. It'll hurt and you'll probably go blind."

I almost—*almost* smile. Except then I figure that she wouldn't have threatened Evan with a can of wasp spray. My annoying jealousy over my brother is what drives me to take a step inside.

"Don't *tell* me you've got the wasp spray," I say.

Her brow furrows and she looks down at the can and then at me. She nods thoughtfully. "That's a good point. The element of surprise, and all that."

This time, I have to bite my cheek to keep from smiling.

Strange, that.

Hank's still in there rooting around, having the best night of his life, and I shake my head, moving into the living room with Georgie following behind me. It's worse than I thought, because the dog seems to have—oh, *Jesus*—unpacked her bag all over the living room floor, and he isn't rubbing himself on the furniture after all. No, he's flat on his back, legs in the air, rubbing himself all over a pile of her clothes. I think he might've knocked over a candle somewhere in the process, though at least it wasn't lit. Worse is how he's somehow got his tail stuck through the leg hole of a pair of her underwear; it kind of waves back and forth like a flag as he wiggles himself around.

"Hank," I say, sharp in a way I held back before, sharp in a way I rarely use with him, and it works. He rolls onto his feet, that big, wide, tongue-lolling mouth of his stretched into the kind of great big grin that makes me think it's crazy for anyone to be afraid of him. I'm glad he's up on his feet, but in some ways this is worse, because the underwear-as-flag situation is much more noticeable now.

"Oh my God," Georgie says, which is getting to be her catchphrase during this encounter. I can't say as I blame her.

"I'm sorry," I say, but she says the same thing at the same time, and I know I'm giving her another grumpy look. "What do you have to be sorry for?"

She looks back over the mess on the living room floor, clothes scattered all over, and winces. "Uh," she says. "Yeah, I don't know."

I make a move toward Hank because I have to solve this flag situation, but then I realize I can't touch this woman's panties without her permission, even if they're not attached to her. I freeze with my hand out, and I know it looks ridiculous. This is *ridiculous*.

"Oh, I'll—" She moves past me and with her non-wasp-spray-wielding hand, she snatches her underwear from around Hank's tail. He is thrilled; he believes this is the start to keep away, the game we play with the stuffed duck I've got out in my truck, along with his other things. He leaps up and her eyes widen in surprise; then she shoves the panties into the pocket of her robe. For the first time since this shit show started, Hank takes the hint and sits down. Onto more of her clothes, but still. This is an improvement.

"Stay," I say firmly. I look over at her and she is either red in the face from embarrassment or from the effort it's taking her not to laugh. Maybe both. For a second we stare at each other, and I've got this feeling I'm not all together sure about. Curiosity, but with some kind of edge to it. Some kind of thing I don't want to acknowledge.

Georgie breaks the spell by grabbing her phone off the arm of the couch, and—oh *man*, there's a bra there; it's underwear all over the place in this house. I drop my eyes again while she shoves it behind a pillow. Then she makes her way back to the kitchen, the robe trailing behind her. I've never seen a robe like that in my life; it reminds me of water, the way it moves. It's growing on me, the look of it on her, which is not the kind of thing I should be thinking about, especially in regard to a woman who, however toothlessly, has recently threatened to blind me.

I summon Hank to follow me, toss him a treat from my pocket when he obeys my command to lie down on the rug by the back door. I look over to see if Georgie has noticed that my dog does in fact listen to me when circumstances are more settled, but she's setting her phone on top of that notebook she was holding when I came in. She cringes slightly when she swipes her fingers across the screen, but it passes quickly. I stand on the other side of the counter and she puts it on speaker, the sound of ringing cutting through the awkward silence. She keeps the wasp spray within reach.

"My parents are lousy with phones," she says, after the third ring. "He might not answ—"

"Is that my Little Red Georgette calling me?" Paul Mulcahy's voice booms from the other end, and Georgie winces. I clear my throat. That's a pretty funny nickname.

"Dad, you're on speaker."

"We're in a place called Durango!" he says, as though that's the natural response to being on speakerphone.

"Okay, but—"

"Your mom met a woman who teaches pottery here." There's rustling. "Shyla!" he calls, loud enough that Georgie and I both take an instinctive step back from the phone. "It's the Midnight Train on the phone!"

The Midnight Train?

I smile as I realize it, "The Midnight Train to Georgia." I bet Paul's got a million of these. When Georgie rolls her eyes I can tell she hates them all, but sort of in the same way I used to hate it when Carlos would make fun of me for being "named after pants."

"Dad," she groans. "I'm here with—"

"Oh, *Georgie*," comes Shyla's voice. "Wait, where is she? Why can't I see her?"

"It's a voice call, Mom."

"Let's put you on video!"

Georgie sets her elbows on the small island countertop and presses her fingertips against her forehead. Maybe she's got a headache coming on, too.

"Listen," I say quietly, and she raises her head. I'm almost mouthing it. "I'll get out of here. It's no big deal."

"No," she says, to me and to her mom.

Shyla's forgotten about the video call, though; she's plowing right ahead. "Did your dad tell you about Kizzy? She teaches pottery! And she's taught a lot of folks who've got hands like mine. I'm taking a class tomorrow!"

Georgie's face softens, and my stomach flips. I can't remember the last time I ate, so I'm sure that's the problem.

"That's great, Mom," she says, and I can tell she means it. Pretty much everyone around here knows that Shyla has rheumatoid arthritis, a condition that's gotten bad enough in recent years that her hands don't always work all that well anymore, not to mention some of the difficulty she has getting around sometimes.

"This Kizzy, she makes all sorts of things," Paul says. "Yesterday we happened to get a pipe—"

"Dad," Georgie says sharply, and I guess she doesn't want him talking about smoking in front of me, though that's no secret, Paul and Shyla's fondness for a little herbal remedy, and I'd never judge. "I'm at the *house*," she says, trying to lead him, I know, but he doesn't get it.

"Been a while, right? How's it look to ya? You see the new yellow on the door?"

"Yellow was always your favorite, Georgie," Shyla chimes in.

"I'm not . . . *alone* at the house?"

I'm not real sure why Georgie's playing a guessing game here.

I like Paul and Shyla a lot, but they're pretty scatterbrained, and it's clear what's happened here—one way or another, they forgot they double-booked the place, and I don't think Georgie's leading statements are going to get them anywhere.

"Paul," I say, to keep it moving. "It's Levi Fanning."

There's a long stretch of silence, and I can imagine Paul and Shyla looking at each other inside that busted RV.

Then Paul says, "Well, shit!"

He doesn't say it like he's mad at himself about it; he says it with a laugh behind it, and I'm pretty sure that noise I hear is him slapping his leg once in that way he's got, like when Carlos told him he could get lumber for fifteen percent cheaper if he'd be willing to drive all the way out to Greenport, or when I showed him he can deposit checks from his phone.

"Right," Georgie says.

"Huh!" Shyla says, a *how did this happen?* huh.

"Didn't y'all go to school together?"

Georgie's given up on the fingers against her forehead; at this point, she's got her palms pressed into her eyeballs.

I decide to field this one for her. "I'm a few years older than Georgie."

"Right, right," says Paul. "Oh! You went to school with Ev—"

"*Dad,*" she says again, harsher this time, like me talking to Hank back there in the living room. I guess she doesn't want him to bring up my brother, either. I wonder if she dated him; I know Evan got around in school. "Can you . . . explain?"

"Well, the thing is, On My Mind"—"Georgia on My Mind," and even I hate that one—"you only mentioned you were coming a few days ago, see?"

Georgie shakes her head in disagreement, maybe joining her mom in forgetting that this isn't a video call. But she doesn't argue. Instead she says, "Yeah," but with her hands over her face her voice sounds muffled and nasal.

"And last time Levi and I talked about him staying was . . . when was that, Levi?"

"Last week," I say. Paul and Shyla stopped by with a key on their way out of town.

"Ages ago! Guess my wires got crossed in the meantime! You know how planning for a trip can be! Heck, how was your drive, Peach?"

"Long," she says, deadpan, as if she means more than the drive. I'm pretty sure she means this call.

"Paul, I'm gonna find a hotel," I say.

"Oh, you can't do *that!*" says Shyla. "What about the *plants?*"

I kind of want to press my palms into my eyes now, too. "Well, your daughter is here now, so . . ." I trail off, waiting for her to pick up the thread.

Shyla laughs. "Oh, right. Where's my head! Georgie, can you keep an eye on the plants?"

She sighs. "Sure, Mom."

"I'm sure sorry for the confusion here," says Paul. "I put you both in an awkward situation, didn't I?"

He doesn't know the half of it. I've seen his daughter in a state of undress, and my dog's worn a pair of her underpants.

"It's no problem. I'll get that hotel," I repeat.

"Georgie," Paul says, no nickname, which maybe means he's got a hold of the gravity of the situation, "take me off speaker for a second, would ya?"

I stiffen on instinct, and I don't know why. I've got a good relationship with Paul; we talk business and obviously he trusts me enough to stay in his house and watch over things while he's away. But it's old wounds, imagining he's in a mind to give her some kind of private warning. He'd do it nice: *Levi Fanning's an all right guy, but I don't know if you ought to be spending time with him.*

It makes me want to walk right out that door.

But before I can do anything, Georgie's tapped the screen of her phone and held it up to her ear, sending me another apologetic glance before turning her back and moving back into the living room, the robe rippling behind her again. Hypnotizing, that thing. Anyway, it'd be weird to leave while she's in there, disorienting probably, so I lean back on the counter and cross my arms to wait. Hank raises his head from the rug and gives me a look that says, *I like this rug and I ain't leaving.* I don't know if I can find a hotel that'll take him, so I'll have to ask if that daycare place can board him overnight. I hate the thought of it. Maybe I'm fussy about my dog, but me and Hank, we're a team, have been since the day I brought him home with me.

I'm still working it out in my head, what I'm going to do with him and myself for the next couple of weeks while Carlos's— dang, *my* house—is getting torn up, when Georgie comes back in. She's smiling again, but it's different this time, and I can only assume it's fake.

"Guess we're roommates for a bit," she says, shrugging.

"Naw," I say, shaking my head, tugging on the brim of my cap. "I'll leave you to it. I know this must be uncomfortable for you." I gesture to the wasp spray.

"I trust my dad," she says, shrugging again. "It'll be fine."

I shake my head again. That's nice, whatever her dad said, but this is crazy, staying in a house with this woman I don't know.

"But if you want, I can try to go stay with my friend for the next couple of weeks. Maybe not tonight, because . . ." she trails off, then presses her lips together. "It doesn't matter, the be- cause. But I could probably go there tomorrow."

"This is your place," I say.

"No more than it is yours," she answers, which is a pretty strange thing to say about the house where you grew up, but who am I to say. I haven't been back to my childhood home in over a decade. "Anyway, I owe you for the milkshakes."

It's the first time she's brought up that we met—such as it was—earlier today. Frankly I wasn't even sure she remem- bered. She'd seemed pretty flustered in Nickel's, which I get. Mrs. Michaels still makes me feel like I ought to be standing up straighter, even if I never listened to her back then.

I make a noise, probably close to a grunt. I don't want her to owe me for the milkshakes.

She blows out a breath.

"Look," she says. "I have had a long day. Series of days, really. I know this is weird, but there's two bedrooms here and locks on both the doors, plus, I've got the wasp spray." She nods toward it and blows a wayward strand of hair out of her face. "You had a plan for yourself and your dog and it'll be a hassle to try to change it right now, even if you're wanting to. So let's be roommates for the night and we can figure out things tomorrow."

Hank farts.

"Sorry," I mutter, sending him a scolding look. He's got no fucking idea why; he's a dog.

"What're *you* sorry for?" she echoes me, that genuine, knowing smile on her lips again.

"He probably has some stomach upset today. Out of his routine and all." Hank never does all that good at daycare places; he gets too nervous with all the other dogs barking. He's a people dog, mostly a me dog.

"Sure, totally," she says, which is a kindness. The fact is, she's taking this whole situation more in stride than me. I prefer things settled, solid and planned out, which is probably why I shouldn't have counted on Paul Mulcahy to set me up for a couple of weeks.

"I'll take my parents' room," she says, as if she's done talking it over. "I haven't looked in there yet, but I know my old room still has a full-size bed. You may have to move some of my mom's craft stuff around."

I don't want to tell her that I already moved a fair bit of craft stuff around. When I first came over here there were twenty-five tissue paper flowers on the dining room table. Shyla does crafts to keep her hands limber, I know, and even if I'm not much one for flowers, I thought they looked nice. I moved them, one by one, real careful-like, onto the top of the dresser in the room where I guess I'll still be sleeping tonight.

Georgie goes on, obviously having fully accepted this thing. "I'll pick up my stuff from the floor and get a quick shower." She pauses and eyes the notebook, then grabs it up and holds it close to her chest. "I've got some . . . uh . . . plans to make, so I'll go to my room after that. Then it'll be all yours. Do you get up early?"

I snort. "Yeah," I say, because my kind of early is an understatement for most people. I always have so much to do, keeping the business going, especially when we're in the warmer months. Plus, Hank has his routine.

"Okay, so you'll probably be gone before I get up. I'm still adjusting from West Coast time."

I nod. Even though she looks even more of a mess than she did this afternoon, this doesn't seem like the woman in Nickel's who couldn't pay for her shakes. This seems like a woman who has her shit together, and that eases my mind somehow, makes this situation more controllable. It's been a hard day and I don't want to sleep in my truck or drive all around trying to find a place to stay. Hank'd probably get diarrhea if I did that, and honestly I don't think I could take another thing going wrong.

She moves the notebook away from her chest, flipping through it. I'm not trying to look, but what I see even from a quick glance is more like that bright bathrobe than it is like her telling me her schedule and asking about mine. That thing looks like a teenager wrote in it, pink and purple ink everywhere.

She comes to a blank page and pauses, tearing off a crooked strip before moving past me toward a drawer and yanking it open. Oh man, talk about mess. That's more than a junk drawer; that's a landfill drawer. Georgie doesn't seem to notice, though; she takes out a pen and makes an attempt to scribble onto the scrap paper. Pens one and two are both out of ink, and instead of tossing them she puts them back in the drawer, which I'm pretty sure makes my right eye twitch. Finally she lands on one and scrawls her phone number on it. Before she passes it to me she frowns and adds her name above it.

As if I could forget who this number belongs to, after all this.

She hands it over. "Text me tomorrow and we'll figure it out. I'll talk to my friend about staying at her place."

I nod down at it, then look back up at her. She's got the notebook clutched to her chest again, as if it's real precious. I'm trying to think if Paul ever told me she was a writer or something, but then I shake my head free of that thought. What am I trying to do, make conversation with this woman? I don't make conversation. I keep my head down. Anyway, I've got to feed Hank and get him settled, and then say good night to this day, exactly as planned.

For a second, I think she might be waiting for me to ask about it, but the moment passes and I can't quite decide if I'm relieved.

"I'll go pick up my things," she says, gesturing over her shoulder toward the living room.

"Sure. I'll get some stuff from the truck. Feed Hank."

She smiles down at my dog, whose tail thumps against the floor in excited reciprocation. I get that stomach flip again. I guess I'll cook up some of those eggs I bought before I turn in, try to be quiet about it.

"Okay. Well, good night then, Levi."

I don't know why that makes me react the way it does. A simple, "Well, good night then, Levi," as though I'm just a nice guy and there's no problem at all here. It's more than the hungry stomach flip; it's a flush all through me. I don't recognize it, don't know what it's about. I'm almost scared by it, the boyish thrill I get from her easy, generous acceptance of me.

So when she turns to go, I stop her by clearing my throat. She turns around, and I hold out the can of wasp spray to her.

I nod as she takes it, and head back out the door.

Chapter 5

Georgie

"You slept in the *same house* as him? As *Levi Fanning*?"

Bel levers herself up from the position she's only just gotten comfortable in, atop a person-size, U-shaped pillow that she has on her side of her and Harry's king-size bed, and that she has informed me is her soul mate, damn the wedding vows. I showed up an hour ago, right at the tail end of Bel's half day of meetings, and she was rubbing at her hip and grimacing, complaining that Herman Miller is no match for pregnancy-induced sciatica. I'd forced her into her bedroom and dragged in two boxes from the junk room, positioning myself on the floor so she could see me hold up items for inspection. So far, what I have learned is that Harry's junk boxes contain a lot of old T-shirts, and I hope he's not sentimental about them, because Bel has told me to donate almost every single one. Then again, since I've never seen Harry wear a T-shirt, probably she's right.

I'm ashamed to say it, but the sciatica and the surplus of T-shirts have been a worthy distraction, since I showed up ready to stall. I knew telling Bel about my current living situation would prompt exactly this reaction, and I know what's coming is a renewed argument about me moving over here for a while. I may have promised Levi that I'd look into it, but now I'm not sure I want to. Even aside from the awkwardness of sharing a space with him—the way I *bolted* from the bathroom to my parents' bedroom last night, not wanting him to see me with a towel wrapped around my head!—I still think I'd be more comfortable there than I would here. Sure, there's the junk room, but the otherwise pristine sorted-ness of this house continues to mock me. Plus, Bel has a pretty sizable hickey on her collarbone, evidence that Herman Miller might not be the only man to blame for the sciatica. I'm happy for her, but jeez.

"Why do you keep saying his name that way?" I say, holding up another T-shirt.

She ignores it. "Why don't *you*?"

I sigh and lower my hands, accordioning the T-shirt into my lap. I know, basically, what she means. I realized it as soon as he'd said his name, through the panes of glass that separated us, that he was Evan's older brother—a light switch flipped on in my head, and I remembered every low-spoken story I'd ever heard about him. Levi Fanning was the black sheep of a family that otherwise never put a collective foot wrong. By the time I'd started high school, he was long gone, but rumors about him persisted. Kids said he'd shoplifted, stolen cars; they said he'd punched the teeth out of Sammy Hayward's mouth over a sideways look. They said he'd dropped out of high school after being stoned for the whole of his junior year. They said he sold drugs in Richmond, that he ran with a crowd that was into even worse.

Last night, lying on my parents' bed, I tried to call to mind any time I'd seen Levi Fanning around town when I was a teenager, but I couldn't think of a single one, and that's saying something, given how interested I was in anything having to do with Evan. It's a sign of how fully off the grid Levi was by the time I'd gotten deep in the weeds of my crush.

So it's pretty strange, how *back* he seems to be now.

"He seemed all right," I say, smoothing out the T-shirt. It's another marathon souvenir, which is approximately fifty percent of the shirts. "My dad said I should let him stay."

Bel rolls her eyes. "Your dad would."

Bel's the only one I'd let get away with this snark, and that's because I know she loves my dad as much as I do. He's responsible, after all, for Bel and I being best friends, since I first met her when my dad was repainting her mom's house the summer I turned nine. They'd been new to town, had moved to Darentville after Bel's mom divorced her Grade A jerk of a husband. It'd been one of the first times I'd gone with my dad on a job, right around the time my mom's arthritis symptoms started in earnest. I'd been disappointed, sullen—I'd wanted to go to my regular day camp at the pool, but it'd been shut down for cleaning because Jenny Westfeld swam in it with impetigo the day before. My dad had promised I could paint my name and whatever else I wanted on the side of the house while he worked on the trim, though, as long as I knew he'd cover it up by day's end, and that seemed sort of fun. There I'd been, swiping big, uneven stars all over the parts of the old siding I could reach, smudges of paint all over my arms and face, and then I'd heard the crunch of dry pine needles behind me. When I'd turned around, there had been Annabel Reston, big eyes blinking at the mess I'd made of her house.

I'd never thought of myself as a shy kid; my parents were the kind of people who'd talk to literally anyone, and they definitely weren't the "children should be seen, not heard" type of parents. At mealtimes, we always talked a lot—about our days, about music, about plants and projects my mom was doing, about people my dad met on the job. And I talked at school a lot, to my detriment. But that first day I'd met Bel, I'd *felt* shy, either because she was more reserved or because I had the instinctive sense that I wanted to be her friend.

So it was my dad who'd had to break the ice for both of us. He came down from his ladder and talked a blue streak to Bel, boring stuff about the type of siding on her house, as if a nine-year-old cares, but it was a tactic. After a while she was desperate enough not to listen to him anymore that she asked if I wanted a popsicle, and then we were off to the races. I went on that job with my dad for six whole days, even after the pool reopened. I only ever got Bel to paint something on the siding once, but when she did, it was the word *shit* in small letters, and we'd laughed and laughed and become best friends forever.

Still, it's not fair for Bel to lay this at the feet of my dad, because even though he *did* tell me Levi was a good guy—"a real standup fella, who's in a mess with the pipes beneath his house"—the truth was, I'd already decided I wasn't going to toss Levi out, and it wasn't because he was as attractive as I'd remembered from my brief staring problem in Nickel's. No, it was because he'd looked . . . he'd looked how I felt. Tired and out of sorts at the end of the longest day. He also looked like I'd punched him in the stomach when I'd called him Evan.

The thought of sending him back out to find somewhere else to stay felt like leaving someone in the checkout line without money for their milkshakes.

Plus, he had that nice dog, no matter that the goofy, brawny pit bull had gotten into my underwear. He'd still been a convenient scapegoat for the stuff I'd left all over the floor, and the sound of his toenails on the kitchen floor this morning was weirdly comforting as I'd dozed in bed, time-zone rattled and vaguely confused about my whereabouts.

"I didn't mind having him there. I think he's going to get a hotel for the rest of the time, anyway."

I get another guilty pang for not raising the suggestion of my decampment with Bel, but then again, I'm pretty sure the hotel option is what he'd prefer. He didn't look that comfortable with the thought of taking my dad's help if it would mean putting me out. If he's booked one, though, he hasn't yet texted me about it, and I hadn't asked for his number back last night.

"Guess The Shoreline isn't an option, huh?" Bel says.

The Shoreline is the name of the Fannings' inn, and it's been in their family for at least a couple of generations now. It's on a prime piece of real estate in Iverley, a jutting peninsula on a particularly wide part of the river. Around the county, it used to be known for serving out-of-towners only; most people around here never even went to its fancy restaurant unless they had a job there. I know from my parents that it's expanded since I moved away, but they've never gone into detail about it. Then again, they also never told me they knew Levi Fanning, let alone that they knew him well enough to have him as a houseguest, so who knows. Maybe The Shoreline is a behemoth now.

"I guess not," I say, unsettled. If he didn't go there, or if he didn't go to his own parents' house, the black sheep situation is surely still on. I think again of that look on his face when I called him Evan, and wince. I should've known better than to mix them up; if Evan Fanning had grown up to look like that—all haunted eyes and tense, cautious bearing—I would have been shocked. But he *had* been on the forefront of my mind, what with the fic . . .

Right, the fic. That reminds me.

I hold up the shirt again, shaking it out and raising an eyebrow at Bel, who makes a gesture with her thumb to indicate it gets donated, too. I am definitely going to check with Harry before I carry out these orders. Maybe she's holding a grudge about the sciatica. And the hickey.

Once I've tossed it on the pile, I take a deep breath and focus. I can't let myself be distracted by the Fanning I used to know and the one I only just met. I want Bel to know what I found in the fic, want her to know what I'm thinking, and not only because she's my best friend. I want her to know because that notebook was as much hers as it was mine, even if there is more of me in it. I'm not looking for permission, but I'm definitely looking for . . . a blessing, maybe? A *that's a great idea.* I'm desperate for validation, a withdrawal I'm going through from my job. Nadia was demanding, but she was also grateful. She always acknowledged everything I did; she always made sure I knew how necessary I was to her life.

I open my mouth to speak, but before I can, Bel sits up again, propping herself on an elbow. *"Wait,"* she says excitedly, the same light in her eyes as when she wrote the word *shit* on the side of a building. "Did you ask him what Evan is doing these days?"

"No!" I say, as if I'm affronted. As if I didn't, for a split second, collapse the two of them in my fic-addled brain.

"Obviously I haven't been back long enough to know the gossip around here, but I'd bet good money he's still in Iverley," Bel says. "He had hometown hero written all over him! Before the brother packs up, ask him. Imagine! You could have a hot little affair with your big-time teenage crush! It's practically a Hallmark movie!"

I snicker, but Bel cannot know how much this idea does not appeal. First of all, the last thing I need is some sort of romance when I'm supposed to be focusing on myself and figuring out what I want. Second of all, in a Hallmark movie, no one ever has a hot affair. They open up a bakery and then get married six months later, and to me that sounds like the worst.

But the ribbing she's given me is the opening I need, and I stand and crawl onto the bed beside her, shoving thoughts of the sciatica and the hickey out of my brain as I lie flat on my back. This way, we're both staring up at the ceiling fan that's circling lazily above us, and it's familiar in a way that makes us both go quiet. When we were young, we'd lie this way during sleepovers, lights off, talking about all kinds of stuff—Bel's strained monthly weekends at her dad's, especially after he got remarried, my mom's ups and downs with her arthritis, Bel's schoolwork, and, of course, my crush on Evan Fanning. Probably this is how we came up with the idea for the fic in the first place, though I can't quite remember its specific origins.

"Okay, so," I finally say, which everyone knows is the agreed-upon code for best friends when one of them is about to drop some kind of bomb. "The notebook from yesterday."

She laughs. "Oh, now see. You *do* want to have a summertime fling with the one that got away!"

"No, I'm serious." I can tell she turns her head to look at me, but I keep my eyes up. "I read it last night, cover to cover."

I don't tell her that I read some parts of it twice, or that I dog-eared some of the pages. I don't tell her that I went to that empty page, the one I tore in half so I could give Levi Fanning my number, to make a list of what I thought were the best ideas from the fic. I don't tell her that the list is the first thing I looked at when I finally came fully awake this morning, sometime after ten.

"Yeah?"

"I know we were just kids screwing around."

"'Just kids' isn't a thing. Important stuff happens to kids. Kids do important stuff." She nudges my foot with her own. Bel is going to be such a good mom.

I nod. "I noticed that I . . . well, I put a lot of effort into that notebook."

When I glance over at her, I see her expression has turned serious. "So what?" she says, immediately defensive. "There's nothing wrong with that."

It's not Bel being sharp with me—it's Bel being sharp on behalf of me. In school, whenever I'd get even in the neighborhood of beating myself up about my grades, she'd always remind me—no matter that her own were off the charts—that grades weren't everything, that I was the smartest person she knew, that algebra was probably a scam anyway.

"I know there's not. I actually . . ." I trail off, trying to find some way of explaining to her everything I thought about last night. "I actually think it could help me."

She turns partway onto her side, rearranging her soul mate to support her bump. "Tell me," she says, her voice soft and serious.

I clear my throat. "Remember how I told you what Nadia said to me, the day she announced her . . . retirement, or whatever?"

"Ah, yes." I don't even have to look over to know she's got a full face of annoyance on. "Her *intentional isolation*," she adds, using the phrase Nadia had repeated with an almost pathological frequency in the weeks leading up to her move. A ranch she and her husband owned, in New Mexico. Hours from the closest airport. "An opportunity to escape all this," she'd said. "To be my own person again, to be self-reliant."

"Right."

"I remember she told you that you shouldn't take another job right away," Bel says, her voice laced with disdain. She's certain Nadia only said that because she wants me free as a bird for when she remembers she doesn't know how to make a doctor's appointment by herself and has to beg for me to come back. But I know Nadia better than that. She's different from the other principals I'd worked for; she didn't make it in the business until she was in her early forties. Before that, she was a public school teacher in Bakersfield, writing short stories and screenplays at night after her two kids from her first marriage went to bed. She knows how to run her own life—she *wants* to run her own life again—and she'll do fine now that her time is her own. The fact that my phone has stayed silent is proof.

"I mean the part about me. The part where she said working as a PA for as long as I did meant I never had to think about myself, or . . . what I truly wanted for myself. That I never really got to do things I wanted to do."

Bel's got algebra-is-a-scam face again. "Well, maybe she

shouldn't have texted you fifty times an hour. Then you could have had time to think about it!"

I laugh. "It wasn't fifty times an hour," I say, though I silently add a qualifying *mostly* to that. Then I prepare to say the hard part. I take a breath, and Bel waits.

"She wasn't wrong about that," I finally add. "I don't even think she knows how right she was. I've never . . . I don't like thinking about what I want for my own life, because I don't think I've ever known. My job was always a good distraction from that problem."

"Georgie," she says softly.

"In the fic, I *thought* about it, you know? I was making plans to do things I wanted to do. Plans for *myself.* And when did you ever know me to do that?"

"Of course you make plans for yourself!" I swear, this woman would defend me for literally anything. *Of course you didn't* mean *to murder him!* I can practically hear her saying.

I raise an eyebrow at her; it says, *give me an example.* And in the silent communication I can see that she can't. She can play a reel of my life for the last decade and a half and see the same stuff I do. I'm going from one thing to another, half lucky breaks and half pure grit. I'm living in hotels close to sets or, eventually, in a guest cottage I never even had to decorate. I'm flying by the seat of my pants, available whenever, to do whatever. I'm making a life for myself by making other people's lives for them.

"You're very successful." *You murdered him cleanly,* she's saying.

"I'm not saying I haven't been."

Given my background, it's fair to say I'm more than successful. Unlike a lot of people who work as PAs, I didn't grow up anywhere near the business, and I don't have a college degree. I also didn't have any of my own ambitions in the industry—wasn't interested in acting, wasn't interested in screenwriting, none of it. While that sometimes meant a steep learning curve for some tasks, Nadia always said my disinterest in these things was an asset for the kind of work I did, not a liability. I have a reputation for my commitment to the job, and *only* the job. And Nadia paid me well, because her wins were, in small ways, facilitated by me and the work I did—the way I made it possible for her to keep her eyes on the big picture.

"My job let me . . . stay distracted," I continue. "It made it so the only future I focused on was the one that mattered for the people I was working for. And right now, I have this slice of time where I don't have to do that."

I don't mention that I was fully prepared to wholly sublimate myself to the project of helping her get her house ready.

"So maybe this is my chance, too. To figure out who I am, and what I want."

To not be such a blank, I add silently.

It's not easy, explaining this to Bel, who's always known exactly who she was. In school, she was a rare kind of popular— president of the student body, homecoming court, whatever. But it wasn't because she played by anyone else's rules, or because she did the kind of tribute-paying to other popular kids that would ensure she'd always get invited to the right parties. It was because she was fully herself, and completely immune to bullshit. She didn't keep her head down, but she didn't stick her chin up in the air, either. She looked straight ahead.

"Who you are is wonderful," she says, and of course I love her for it. But I don't want a murder defense at this moment. Sometimes, someone loves you so much that they can't quite see you clearly. Right now, Mrs. Michaels might be more right about me than Bel is, and that's a bummer, since Mrs. Michaels truly sucks.

I blink up at the ceiling fan, and after a second, she pokes me in the shoulder with her finger.

"The fic," she says, and I can tell she knows she put a foot wrong, can tell she's trying to get back to where I want to be. "What do you want to do with it?"

"I want to do it. Some of it, at least."

I turn on my side, too, so we're facing each other.

"*Not* Evan Fanning?" she says.

"Correct," I say, but the mention of him has set off a ping in my brain, and I take my phone from my back pocket, for once not thinking of Nadia at all.

Nothing from Levi yet.

"He's a supporting character in there anyway," I say, which is true even if the heart *a*'s make it hard to see at first. I tuck the phone away again. "Easy to cut out. It's the other stuff that matters."

I tell her about the ideas I pulled from the fic for the list. Buzzard's Neck, Sott's Mill. The Bend. The hard cider/horror movie lineup. The rock outside the high school. The stuff that I could tell, from the detailed way I wrote about them, had represented a rite of passage for me. Had represented some kind of *feeling* to me.

"It's a bucket list," she says. "Except you're doing it to start something, not to end it. What's the opposite of a bucket?"

I have no idea what the opposite of a bucket is. The only thing I can think of is the metal thing you strain pasta in, and a *colander list* doesn't sound super engaging.

"Never mind, I'll think of something," she says, in project manager mode. "When do we start?"

"*We?*" I try not to give a pointed look at her hip. There's no way Bel is jumping off Buzzard's Neck in her condition.

"Yeah, *we*. Evan may have been a supporting character, but I wasn't, right? I should do this stuff with you." She gives me a narrow-eyed look. "If you say *one word* about me being pregnant. . . ."

"I didn't! But also, you do have a job. And a husband."

"I work from home now. Isn't the point of all this that I can be more flexible?"

I have doubts. As much as I'm flexible, Bel is . . . not. Schedules are her lifeline.

"As for Harry, I'm his wife, not his babysitter. I don't see what he has to do with it."

"I'm not trying to rope you into my mess, Bel."

"Georgie Mulcahy," she says, poking me again, harder this time. "We've been inside the same rope since we were nine years old. I *want* to do this with you."

The way she says it . . . it's almost vehement, and I know she won't accept me turning her down. If she wants to do this with me, then it's like she said: We're in the same rope, and have been for ages. And it's too rare to have this opportunity, where we actually can stand right next to each other inside it, where the rope isn't having to stretch across the whole country.

A new excitement sparks inside of me, and I smile at her.

"Okay, Belly Button," I say. "Let's, you know, Conquer High School."

WHEN I LEAVE Bel's this time, no one's waving concernedly from the porch at me, and that feels pretty good. In fact, lots of things feel good. It's a gorgeous day, sunny and low-humidity hot, a rarity around here, and the air is so clean that the river smells salty and fresh.

Better than that, though, is the sense that I'm on to something. A plan for how to keep my promise to myself, a plan for being done with the blankness.

With this in my head, other plans take shape easily: I should get groceries, should actually unpack, especially since the garbage bags are still, shamefully, in the back seat. I decide to go back to Nickel's, even though I dread who I might run into this time. I don't think Levi Fanning is expecting that eight bucks for the milkshakes, but Ernie is, and I don't want him to think I flaked, nor do I want to explain that I slept one room away from Levi last night and could've left money for him on the kitchen counter.

When I pull into the lot, there's more cars—sleek SUVs, a few with out-of-state license plates, a couple of minivans with car-top carriers on. Tourists, which suits me fine. I'm checking my purse to make sure I've got my wallet this time when my phone chimes with a new message.

MAYBE: LEVI FANNING, the screen reads, and my stomach swoops with anticipation. This does not seem much healthier than hoping my old boss will text, but whatever. One victory at a time, and all that.

I swipe my finger across to read the message.

Any chance you were able to talk to your friend?

I frown down at the screen. That's a little short. Or maybe I'm still wrestling with my guilt about not even raising the issue with Bel. I stall, either because of his curtness or my misgivings, adding Levi to my Contacts before I type back.

I'm guessing you struck out on the hotel front?

Cowardly, answering a question with a question.

There's no point to me sitting here in this car waiting for him to type back; I can read and reply inside of Nickel's as easily as I can inside of here. But something keeps the phone in my hand, my head down as I watch the typing bubble appear, then disappear.

Several times.

Finally: **No problem. Thanks for last night.**

Then, right after: **Letting me crash I mean.**

I furrow my brow. He didn't really answer, and also, what was all that typing and deleting about? I truly do not know why I care, since it's not as if I want another hugely awkward evening during which a dog might end up wearing my panties. Plus, I've got enough on my plate now, what with my plan and all.

But I *do* care.

Did you find a place to stay or not?

There's no typing bubble this time, nothing at all for a long minute. I look out my windshield and see a family come out of Nickel's—two men in swim trunks and T-shirts weighed down with reusable totes and two kids, faces pink from the sun, mouths bright blue from the popsicles they're holding. They go to one of the vans and I smile on Ernie's behalf. Tourists, indeed.

My phone finally chimes again, but it's not an answer. Or if it is, it's in some kind of code. Two *o*'s and a capital *I*.

Without thinking, I press the button for an audio call at the top of this newborn, nonsensical text chain. As soon as I do it I realize it's not a good idea; these days actual phone calls are for intimates and robocallers, and there's no in between. But it's already ringing and it'd be weird to hang up, and anyway he answers even before the second ring has begun.

"That was an accident," he says, by way of greeting. His voice is . . . extremely irritated. *Ernie, I'm in a hurry* irritated, which means now I'm irritated, too.

"Look, did you find a—" I break off when I hear a low, long, mournful whimper. "What was that?"

I hear Levi sigh. "Listen, I've got my hands full at the moment."

"Was that your dog?"

Another one of those awful whimpers. I'm suddenly intensely worried over this dog who passed gas in my parents' kitchen last night.

Levi makes a noise of assent. "He's all right," he says, but it's almost as if he's saying it more to Hank, more to himself, than to me.

"What happened?" I know that at this point I'm pelting this man I hardly know with questions he clearly doesn't want to answer, at least when it's me who's asking. But even over the phone, there's still that tug inside me about him.

I can't turn him away.

There's a long pause on the other end, probably while Levi weighs the relative convenience of simply hanging up on me and blocking my number.

Then he says, "Hank got attacked at daycare today."

"Oh *no*." I think of that big goofball's humongous smile. His toenails tapping on the floor while I dozed in the predawn hours.

"He's all right," he says again. "Ten staples in his right ear."

"Oh no," I repeat.

"It wasn't his fault."

I furrow my brow. "I didn't think it was."

It seems long pauses are a real feature of conversation with Levi Fanning, so I wait him out. The door to Nickel's opens again, and an older couple comes out, big visors and sunglasses. Retirees.

"Hank's timid around other dogs, always has been," Levi finally says. "A little terrier got after him. She jumped up and hung on, tugged a bit. Hank just . . . stood there until one of the supervisors came over."

This might be the most Levi has ever said to me all at once, and his voice is different, raw in a way that gets me right in the chest. I'm strangely affected, strangely desperate to see him.

"I shouldn't have taken him there." The regret in his voice is so forceful that I almost ask where he is.

Instead I say, "I don't think it's your fault."

He says nothing.

"You can't take him back there, though." I've made it sound like a statement, not a question, and I hope he notices.

"No." There's noise on the other end of the phone, a door creaking open. "Look, the vet's coming back in. I need to go."

I frown. Go where, though? As in, where's he going to go tonight? I can't imagine it'll be all that easy to find a hotel around here that'll let Levi have his dog, at least not one that'll be comfortable.

Before he can hang up, I say, "Levi?"

"Yeah?" He's being short again, but I ignore it.

"You and Hank stay out at the house, okay? I'll be there, too, but . . . we'll figure it out. It'll be fine."

It's what my dad would want, I know. More than a few times

when I was growing up, Mom and Dad had a friend staying on our couch, the old "getting back on their feet" houseguest. It used to be annoying, sometimes awkward, but this time, it's what I want, too. And what I want . . . well, that's all part of the new plan, isn't it? Get groceries, prepare for one human and one canine houseguest, wade through whatever awkwardness it brings, get going on conquering high school.

"Are you su—"

But I don't let him finish.

I say, "See you there," and hang up, and then I head into Nickel's, no longer all that worried about who I'll see inside.

Chapter 6

Levi

For the second time in as many days, I'm driving up to the Mulcahy house, feeling beat all to hell. This time, though, it's still light out, and I actually notice the Prius beneath the carport, which should have been my first hint yesterday that I'd be walking into something unexpected.

But the prospect of another night with Georgie doesn't have me near as rattled now, not after all the other shit I've dealt with today. After I'd dropped Hank off this morning, I'd found a motel over in Blue Stone that'd take me, at least, and I figured I could board Hank overnight while I figured something else out. But then I'd gotten the call, right there in the lumber aisle of the Home Depot, and everything after had been awful.

First, there was the way my stomach dropped into my feet when the lady from the daycare place had said Hank was hurt. Maybe some people would say I'm too attached to Hank, but also, I bet those people never had a dog as good as him. Second, there was the sight of him once I'd arrived—a bloody temporary bandage wrapped around his head, his big body trembling all over in waves of panic so strong he couldn't even walk out to the truck with me. I'd had to pick him up—no mean feat, given the bulk of him—like he was a baby. He'd gone limp in my arms, and I'd felt my own wave of panic crest, but it turned out he was just relieved, I think. I didn't even bother strapping him into his special seat belt; I let him huddle close to me on the bench seat of my truck the whole way to the vet's office, where—and this is the third shitty part—he whimpered and fussed as if he'd had the worst day of his whole life, and that's saying something, given where I know he came from. I'm being ridden by about ten thousand pounds of guilt, putting Hank in a situation where he got hurt.

I made all the right plans, but somehow they've all gone wrong.

The truth is, the guilt's the main thing that's gotten me to come back here tonight. The hotel I'd booked gave me a flat no about bringing my dog, no matter that it was only for one night. Maybe if Hank hadn't had his ear half torn off by a Yorkie with an attitude problem, I would've gone back to our place, pulled out my old tent from the shed, and made it a campout for a while. But I can't force Hank to sleep outside after what he went through, and the house is way too much of a mess to even attempt sleeping inside—I called to check. The contractor laughed and said I didn't have floors in half the house or running water, and wouldn't have the latter for a couple more days at least.

So it's night two at the Mulcahy motel, and I can only hope the proprietor is fully dressed this time. Last night I had a dream about those legs, which made me feel like a real fucking pervert, seeing as how I'm a guest of her parents. If I would've had that can of Raid nearby, I might've sprayed myself. Frankly the dream is half of what had me so insistent about looking for that hotel first thing this morning, after I'd crept around the house quiet as a mouse trying not to wake her, cringing with embarrassment every time Hank made a sound. That's to say nothing of how it'd felt to hear the shower running while she was in there last night, how I could smell her soap and shampoo on the steam that wafted into the house after she'd gotten out. Or how the walls are thin enough that I could hear she was still awake when I finally got in bed, turning the pages of something.

But tonight, I don't need to notice any of that. I need to take care of Hank.

He's pushed himself up from where he had his head lying on my lap, recognizing that we're back where we were last night. When I let him out then, he'd run all over this bonkers yard, sniffing at that big rooster and nudging all the wind chimes he could reach with his snout before tearing two circles in the weedy grass and then, obviously, bolting through the open door, carefree and excited. Now, though, he looks balefully at me when I get out, as though it's all four of his legs and not his ear that have been torn up.

"Come on, pal," I say, patting my thigh, but he only looks at me. *I can't be expected to move after what I've endured*, that look says.

A real drama queen, my Hank.

Still, I do what he wants, ducking back into the cab of the truck and getting my arms around him, avoiding his injury as I lift him gingerly, backing my way out of the cab once I've got a hold. It's gangly, Hank's toenails scrabbling against my shirt, me trying to avoid hitting my head on the doorframe. When I straighten, I turn toward the house, and damn if Georgie Mulcahy isn't standing there in the back door, watching me awkwardly hold my dog as if he's an unruly toddler.

Hell.

I crouch, setting Hank down. He clings a bit at first, but once he sees someone else around he forgets all about me, and about his ear, because that big old tail gets wagging again and he starts going toward her, already panting happily.

"I see how it is," I mutter to myself, but inside I'm relieved. Probably he'll never see a Yorkie without shitting himself again, but at least he still seems all right with people. Georgie's already on her haunches, arms out, like Hank's her long-lost friend, and I have to avert my eyes. She's dressed, thank Christ, but she's got on cutoff jean shorts and bare feet. I'm still seeing an awful lot of those legs I had the dream about, and I'm rattled all over again.

Wasp spray, I think, as if it's some kind of talisman.

I busy myself with getting things out of my truck—Hank's bed and kit, my bag, the same stuff I brought out here this morning, assuming I'd be finding another place to stay. Probably I'll be doing the same thing tomorrow morning, but I'll think about that then. Tonight I'll get Hank fed and settled, give him one of those pain pills the doctor prescribed, and I don't know what else. I guess hide out in the guest room until Georgie goes to bed, so I don't make her uncomfortable with my typical grouchy silence. Maybe I'll turn on a podcast real loud, avoid the shower sounds.

Something tells me, though, that she's got other plans.

When I reach her, she's still crouched down, talking to Hank as if he's giving her answers back. "And then what happened?" she says, eyes big, and honestly it's as if he's trying to talk to her, the way he makes these snorting, gasping noises in reply.

"Ugh, *so* unfair," says Georgie, gently patting his flank, listening intently again. "Truly, what a *bitch*," she says, and dang, Hank almost seems to laugh. This is dog whisperer shit. I almost cried when I first saw Hank, and Georgie's fixed him up simply by acting like he had a schoolyard scuffle. It works so well that Hank bolts out into the yard to take care of his business, and Georgie unfolds herself easily, as if she's been welcoming neurotic dogs home from school every day of her life. She's tall like her dad is; in her bare feet the top of her head comes almost to my nose. Her hair's damp, which means I'm going to be spared shower sounds, but probably not shower smells. I think her shampoo has rosemary in it.

"See what I did there?" she says, jolting me out of my thoughts. About *rosemary*, for God's sake.

I clear my throat, nod. "Yeah, thanks. You made him feel better."

She wrinkles her brow at me. "Oh. I meant . . . *see what I did there*"—here, she waggles the wrinkled brow—"calling the dog a bitch? Because you said it was a fem—"

"Oh. Yeah, I see."

There's a long stretch of silence, probably while Georgie thinks about how I don't have any sense of humor. She's not wrong. I can tell she's funny; I'm just not easy to laugh. Man, I need about fifteen hours of total silence to get over the last two days. Maybe I should go straight to my room once I feed Hank. I've got a few energy bars in my bag.

"Well, anyway," she says, "I made dinner!"

I don't even manage an "Oh" this time. I don't suppose I could start my fifteen hours of silence during a dinner this woman's cooked, but the truth is I'll probably try.

"It's something simple," she adds, and I still can't think of a thing to say. "And I mean, I was making it for myself, because obviously I eat. I wasn't, you know, making *you* dinner. But I made *enough* dinner. If that makes sense."

It's not a quadratic equation, so yeah, it makes sense. But also, it sort of doesn't, because we've had all of two conversations, and both of them have mostly been about how we could successfully avoid each other in a pretty small house. Now she's made *enough* dinner? I don't even want to think about what I'll say if she's made something I don't eat. Probably better if I turn her down now. I don't want to accidentally insult her cooking on account of being a vegetarian.

I clear my throat again, getting ready to say . . . something, *anything*, but she cuts me off.

"It's veggie pasta, super easy. I got everything from Ernie. Also, I left him eight dollars for those milkshakes, if you ever want to collect on that debt."

I swear she's using the same shit on me as she used on Hank, pretending my standing here staring is the same kind of panting answers Hank gave her. She turns and goes back through the open door of the house, but she's still talking, and because I'm no better than a dog, I follow her, Hank now on my heels.

"Ernie has this whole farmer's market section in the back of the store; I can't believe that! I mean, you know that already, living here and all. He used to keep Lunchables and jarred pickles in that spot! The opposite of fresh, you know what I mean? I don't know, I may have gone overboard in there. Also, to be honest, I was maybe trying to show him I could pay for my food, after what happened yesterday . . ."

I set down my stuff and I can't say if she went overboard at Nickel's, but damn if she didn't go overboard in here. The kitchen is a mess. I mean, a *mess*. There's three cutting boards on the island, all of them with some kind of food waste left behind, as though she needed a whole new surface for every vegetable she chopped. Also a new knife. I don't even own as many knives as are out on this island. Pretty good thing I didn't walk in unexpected when this was going on, because these ones could do some damage.

She's got three pots on the stovetop, too, spoons on the counter, a colander in the sink, spices out. This is not a clean-as-you-go type person. I take a second to breathe through the stress. It doesn't take a whole lot of self-awareness to know I spend a lot of time alone; I'm not used to other people's habits. Except somebody who'd destroy a kitchen for veggie pasta doesn't seem too interested in habits. This is a chaos-only situation.

". . . in the end I didn't even spend a lot of time thinking about it! So this recipe is not even a recipe. I made it up, which I hope is fine?"

Chaos.

"Fine," I say, which sounds harsher than I intend. I clear my throat. "I'll go wash up."

"Sure! I'll finish this and talk to my friend here about the revenge we're going to exact on the prom queen."

I stare.

"The dog who bit him," she clarifies.

I cannot imagine this woman wants any more than this one night of having to explain her jokes to me. I better renew my search for a different place to stay tomorrow.

When I duck into the bathroom to wash my hands and splash some water on my face, I can hear her in the kitchen, soft tones as she keeps on talking to Hank, his toenails tapping around as he follows her. I hope she's not tossing him any of those tomatoes I saw on the counter, or else I'm in for a long night. Hank can't do seeds. Still, I take more time than I have to, because it's strangely nice to hear them in there. It shouldn't feel normal; what would be normal is me and Hank at my place, him not having a bunch of metal holding his ear together. But this is kind of calming, somehow. Maybe it's the rosemary smell, or maybe it's sinking in that Hank's all right, and at least we've got a place to stay tonight.

When I come out, Georgie's setting two steaming, shallow bowls on the round table off the living room. Hank's watching every move she makes, a line of drool coming from one side of his mouth. I gesture toward the kitchen. "I'll get him some food first, then I'll join you. Don't wait."

Hank finally remembers who I am once he hears his kibble rattling around, and he comes tapping into the kitchen, sitting down the way I always make him do before I put his bowl on the floor. Back when I first got him, I paid a truckload of money to a trainer to help me get him settled into house life, and this was one of the things we practiced a lot, mealtime manners, to make sure Hank'd never get food aggressive. When I give him the go, he tucks in, but in the way he does—real slow, almost one piece of kibble at a time. Sometimes he takes a few pieces out and puts them on the floor before he eats them, like he's got to leave some time for anticipation, or like he's delighting in the fact that no one's going to take it from him. It's strange, but it's a habit, at least.

I don't have any reason to stand in here and watch him, so I resign myself to the fact that I'm about to share a meal with someone I barely know. I guess one habit she's got is taking suggestions, because she's already tucked into her food, and that makes me more comfortable with taking the seat across from her. I put the paper towel she's set next to my bowl on my lap and take a closer look.

It's vegetables, which pretty much means it's all things I eat, but yeah, it's chaotic in here, too; I don't suppose I or anyone else would put green beans in a pasta dish. Well, it's fine. It's food, and the sooner I put it in my face the less likely it is I'll have to keep any conversation going.

"The thing is," she says, as soon as I've taken a bite, "it'd be a lot easier for me to be able to stay here. My friend has only recently moved into her house, and she's pregnant, so . . ."

I nod curtly, swallowing before I speak. "It's all right. We'll be out of your hair tomorrow."

I can feel her looking at me. It's hot like the outside in here; I don't see what the Mulcahys have against a few well-placed fans.

"But . . . how? I mean, you said you can't stay at your house. Is that still right?"

I push the pasta around my plate. The green beans make it weird; I can't deny it. I nod again. "Yeah, it's—" I gust out a breath, thinking of the mess I know is over there. "There's clay pipes beneath part of the house that need replacing. It's a big job."

"And it's probably not easy to find a dog-friendly hotel, right?"

I shrug. "Gotta go further afield. Certainly nowhere in the county."

That's not true, and I wonder if she knows it. My family's

place has a wing that allows dogs, but it might as well be on a different continent for all it's accessible to me. I haven't set foot on that property in years. I'm not even sure what'd happen if I tried.

"I think you have to stay here," she says, matter-of-fact. She picks up her fork and starts eating again, as though it's settled. She's still chewing when she hovers a hand over her mouth and says, "It's only for a couple weeks."

"I don't want to put you out." *Or think about you in the shower.*

"You're not. We can make a plan for, you know, our schedules, or whatever. So we're not in each other's way."

I spear a green bean, skeptical. About the bean and also this plan. "I work a lot. Early mornings, long days."

"See? It'll be easy then. Plus, I'll be busy, too. I'm doing this—" She cuts herself off, waves her fork. "It'll be easy."

I nod, trying to believe it. I'm running through the jobs I have scheduled for the next two weeks, thinking through what I can tell her about where I'll be for how long and on which days. I've got it all in my phone, but it seems rude to take it out at the table. We eat in silence, except for the sounds of Hank's slow progress in the other room. It's so familiar that I almost forget about what happened today.

"Shit," I mutter, once I remember.

"What?"

"It's nothing. I'll figure it out."

Georgie Mulcahy may not be one for making up recipes, but she sure is perceptive about people, because she says, "I can watch him. If that's the issue."

"That's a lot of trouble. Not sure if he'll be aggravating those staples." I got one of those cones for him at the vet, but when the vet tech and I tried putting it on him he stood paralyzed, couldn't figure out how to take a single step with it on.

"It's no trouble. He's a nice dog. Besides, once I had a job where I had to put sweaters on a French bulldog every morning. He had epilepsy, and also when he got overexcited he'd breathe so hard that he'd faint dead away. I'm used to complicated stuff."

I'm staring again. "I thought you were a . . . uh. I thought you worked for actors or something. Hollywood people."

"I do," she says, then clears her throat. "I did, I mean. But my duties were"—she widens her arms, fork in hand, and a tomato hits the ground—"expansive. Hollywood people have dogs sometimes."

I'm going to have to get that tomato when she stands up; I don't think she noticed it. I'm also sort of wondering what the dog sweaters are all about, because I thought it was hot in southern California all the time. But that is definitely not the point of this conversation.

"What about your stuff?" I say. "Your . . . you said you had stuff to do, right?"

She shrugs. "It's flexible. Anyway, does he travel well? I could take him some places with me, probably."

Maybe she thinks that'd be easy, but Hank's no French bulldog in a sweater. Some people are afraid of him, which is why I rarely take him on job sites with me. That and one of my regular guys, Laz, is allergic, so if we're working on the same job, it's a no go. Mostly I try to leave Hank at home during the day, stopping by to let him out when I take a break. He's comfortable there, has his routine.

"I don't want to trouble you," I say, but even as it comes out, I realize I'm not even thinking about my response. It's automatic, to say no to her help, as if I can't trust her with Hank. That's not really fair, since she's letting me stay in this house, and I haven't even seen that wasp spray today. I can't afford to be dismissive, not with the bind I'm in. I hate being stuck this way, but I don't have many options.

Hank chooses that moment to come in, and he nudges his snout against my thigh the way he always does after he eats, which I take to be a thanks.

"He's a good dog," she says.

"He is." I scratch his head, the uninjured side. "Settle in, pal," I tell him, and he moves into the living room, turning twice before lying down. He seems comfortable here, comfortable with Georgie, and maybe I should take a lesson. Paul and Shyla are good people; there's no reason to think Georgie's not, too. Carlos used to tell me I have trouble trusting people, which is an understatement. I don't think he meant it as a judgment, just a reality, and he knew I had my reasons. Still, that reality is really fucking with my ability to solve a problem, so I better get over it.

I clear my throat, spearing another bite of her pasta. "I'd appreciate it," I say, and it sounds as if it's being wrung from my throat. "If you don't mind."

"Nope," she says, ignoring my tepid response, and tucks right back into her food, a green bean bending into her half-smiling mouth.

That's how Georgie Mulcahy becomes, for now at least, both my roommate and my dog sitter.

AFTER DINNER I insist on helping clean up, though Georgie resists, and I think it's because it's the first time she's registered how big of a mess she made. She tries to shoo me out of the kitchen, telling me to keep an eye on Hank, but he's out there snoring, the first good rest he's had all day. I mutter something about letting sleeping dogs lie and start collecting all the food scraps into a bowl. Paul's got a composter outside, similar to the one I have at home, so at least it won't go to waste.

The kitchen's small, too much brushing against each other for my comfort, but Georgie's quieter now, and the job of cleaning up calms me. I'm sure we'll work out a routine, for however long this lasts. And we'll probably barely see each other, which means I won't be as tempted to look at those legs every time she walks by me.

It'll be fine.

Then she says, "So, docks?"

It takes me a second to realize she's not doing some kind

of random vocabulary exercise; she's actually asking about my job. Too bad Hank's sleeping. He's a better conversationalist than me.

I nod, and move to take the towel she's holding out to me.

"What's that like?" she asks.

The only word I can think of for long seconds is *wet*.

I pretend to be very committed to drying off the pot she hands me.

"Busy this time of year," I finally say. "We're a small operation. Repairs to existing structures and small residential builds."

There, that was pretty good. A normal answer. I look out the corner of my eye at her, see her nod as she rubs a sponge across one of the knives. After a few seconds, she passes it to me and speaks again.

"I guess I meant, you know. Do you like it?"

"Oh." So, not a normal answer then? Well, whatever. I did my best. "It's all right. Get to be outside, mostly. Get to be on the water, or close to it."

In spite of the fact that I was more comfortable with the quiet cleanup, I get that it's my turn, that I should ask her about her own job, the one with all that expansiveness she mentioned. I think about how she stretched her arms out. Might be nice to hear about it from her, rather than from Paul.

But before I can say anything, she speaks again. "How'd you get into it?"

I swallow uncomfortably. I don't much want to get into the how of it. How Carlos pulled me out of the gutter on the worst night of my life. Gave me a chance when everyone I knew here had written me off.

I keep my answer simple.

"I'm good with my hands. Steady-legged on a boat." I almost say, *fast learner*, too, but I don't want to sound arrogant.

She passes me another dish. "Well, it's more than that, right? Since you run the whole business now?"

I shift on my feet, clear my throat. "I apprenticed with Carlos for about seven years. I knew the business well. It only made sense."

It's more complicated than that, but I don't know if I want to get into the details of why it made sense, of all the extra work I did and classes I took to make sure I could handle some of the things Carlos tended to have inefficient systems for. Recordkeeping, payroll, billing protocols. By the time he retired officially, I knew the business better than he did.

Once again, I'm on the verge of shifting the subject, or at least of shifting the focus to her. I've always known I'm uncomfortable talking about myself, but with Georgie, I see clearer than ever how truly strained I am at it. She seems easy and open, comfortable in this small space. To me, even a conversation about something as neutral as my job is full of tiny trap doors, spots in the story of it that'd lead to places I don't want to go.

But then, impossibly, she makes things worse.

"I'm sorry I confused you with your brother," she says, sudden and quick. "Yesterday, I mean."

I clench my teeth together, the muscles in my jaw tightening. I have no idea what led her from asking questions about my job to bringing up the mistake from yesterday, but I don't care what prompted it. I care that she's opened up one of those trap doors to a mistake of my own, one I work hard not to think about, at least outside of my therapist's office. And I haven't been there in a while.

"It's because I went to school with him," she says, either because she doesn't notice the tension wafting off of me or maybe because she does. "And I, uh, remember him."

I clear my throat. "Sure," I manage, but I'm folding the towel in half, draping it over the sink. "I'll finish drying later, if that's all right."

She goes on as if she hasn't heard me. "And for a second you sort of looked—"

"Georgie," I snap, and I realize it's the first time I've said her name out loud. For some reason I don't want to think too much about, I hate that it was like this. Harsh, hard.

She's looking at me, her eyes wide, her hands covered in suds from the sink. I've finally got her to see that talking more isn't the best way forward here, but it's not a relief. I can only imagine what her next set of questions would've been. Probably she wants to know how he's doing. Maybe she even wants to know how to get in touch with him.

I wouldn't be surprised.

But more important, I wouldn't know what to tell her either way.

"I don't see him," I say, preempting her, and it's an effort to make my voice come out softer. I know this isn't her fault; it's mine. "Or anyone in my family. I prefer not to talk about that."

"Oh," she says quietly. "Oh, of course."

It's the *of course* that gets me, even though it shouldn't. Didn't I see it on her face last night, the recognition? Didn't I know already she probably has a host of stories about me at her disposal?

Still, it stings, makes this room closer and less comfortable than it was even before, though this is for a different reason. She's broken our fragile peace, reminding me that we're not strangers, not in the way that'd make this whole roommate/dog sitter situation easier. Instead we're the kind of strangers who grew up in adjacent tiny towns in the same small county, where your business isn't ever your own. Where one of you has the kind of reputation that sticks around, no matter what you've done since.

I grab for the bowl of food scraps, slap a hand against my thigh, and call for Hank.

"I'm gonna take him out. You can leave the rest for me to clean up."

"No, that's okay. I'm s—"

I don't let her finish what I know is going to be an apology. I don't deserve one, and I know it.

"I appreciate what you're doing. Letting me stay, and with Hank."

Hank's collar clinks as he comes into the room, his bearing sleepy. He shakes his head, ears flapping, forgetting his injury. I should've left him alone to rest more, but I'm desperate. I need to get out of this kitchen.

"I told you, it's no prob—"

"But let's keep this simple," I say, cutting her off again.

No conversation, I mean. *No trap doors.*

She nods, her face flushed in what I'd guess is embarrassment, and it's as if I've fallen through another one anyway. I'm far beneath her, down in the musty dark of my past, and all I want is to climb up and out.

So I don't apologize, don't try to explain. I open the door and go, knowing her eyes are on me as I walk away.

Chapter 7

Georgie

So far, I wouldn't say it's going great.

Bel and I are only a few hours into our first fic-inspired effort, and I'm tense and distracted, half of me frustrated that it's not how I imagined and half of me embarrassed at having done this at all. When I got to Bel's house early this afternoon, she was pacing back and forth along her porch, holding her phone in front of her face and talking animatedly to whomever was on the other end. I'd sat in the car and attempted to scroll through my social media feed, but since the signal here sucks, it wasn't so much scrolling as it was waiting for things to load. By the time Bel had opened the door, I was staring at an ad for a two-hundred-dollar necklace that looked like it was made of paper-clips, and desperately trying not to think any more about Levi Fanning and the disastrous ending to our dinner two nights ago.

"What's with your face?" Bel had said, which I took to mean that my efforts had been in vain. I'd told her I was thinking about the current composition of the Supreme Court and then changed the subject and asked her about her phone call. For the rest of our drive, Bel had gone into great detail about a refurbished laptop program she's trying to organize for five different school districts across the DMV area, and while that had stopped me thinking about Levi, it'd also kicked up another unpleasant train of thought. By the time she was done, I was thinking, *A notebook from eighth-grade, Georgie? Really?*

Still, I'd pulled into a spot along Sott's Mill's main street and tried to gather up all my scattered enthusiasm before we got started. When I'd been getting ready for the day, Sott's Mill had seemed like the perfect starting point, and not only because I haven't figured out a way for Bel to be an active participant in jumping off an old dock or getting drunk on hard cider. It'd seemed like the perfect starting point because it was low-key, familiar. After all, lunch and shopping are things I did fairly regularly with my rare off days back in LA, meeting up with another PA whose principal had worked on Nadia's wildly successful Netflix series a couple of years ago. Pretty much the only thing Jade and I had in common was our jobs, but she was friendly and well-adjusted and loved fashion, and wandering in and out of boutiques with her had always given me a pang of longing for Bel.

Plus, the Sott's Mill entry is one of the few that has absolutely nothing to do with Evan Fanning, which is a good choice under the circumstances, and those circumstances are that his brother, who I can't stop thinking about, has avoided me for two straight days.

But still . . . it's not going great.

"This place is so different," Bel says, as we exit our third store, which looked decent from the outside but turned out to have a lot of painted signs that said things like, ALWAYS KISS ME GOOD NIGHT and I'D RATHER BE AT DISNEY WORLD. No offense to kissing good night or Disney World, but I remember Sott's Mill having more stuff that I actually wanted.

"I'm so glad you said it," I say, blowing out a breath. "Weren't there . . . a *lot* more shops?"

Bel nods, squinting down the street, which used to be two blocks of occupied, well-maintained storefronts. In the fic, I'd described this street as "fancy," and it was, at least compared with Darentville's main shopping street at the time. Now, though, it's faded, a little sad. It's as if everything's been sent through the most depressing Instagram filter, especially if that filter also turned a shop that used to sell a popular brand of brightly colored, busily patterned luggage and purses into an "ammo depot."

"At least we had good fries?" she says, referring to the lunch we had at a restaurant two blocks back.

Bel's taking this all in more stride than I am, and I'm guessing that's because the decline of Sott's Mill is another harbinger of Darentville's ascent. Since she's a new homeowner there, I'm sure it's affirming. I bet she thinks we would've been better off going to the revamped shopping district there, but if she does, she's not saying, and I'm grateful. Who knows who we would have run in to? Probably another teacher who sent me to the principal's office.

And also, the fic said *here.*

I'm trying to stick with the plan, even if, at the moment, I can't seem to find any trace of the fullness I apparently felt back when I made it.

Instead, it's blankness again: that sense that I don't know at all what I want, even if I know I'd rather not be at Disney World.

"What if we try the antiques shop we passed?" Bel says cheerfully, probably because I look like I'm thinking about the Supreme Court again. "Obviously antiques were not our thing when we were thirteen, but who cares, right?"

"Right," I say, wrangling my sense of purpose. In the fic, the appeal of Sott's Mill had been the choices it offered us—it had seemed thrilling, grown-up, *independent* to go someplace and decide for ourselves about things we wanted to buy. Back then, we'd fixated on clothes, both of us having grown up with parents who hadn't put much stock in keeping up with trends. One whole page of the fic about Sott's Mill is about the polo-style shirt dress I imagined buying, which now makes me cringe with secondhand embarrassment for my younger self.

But maybe I'm into antiques now? Talk about choices! Choices between old things, but what's more grown-up than an antique? Not much, I'd bet. Maybe what I want is an apartment decorated with a candlestick from the nineteenth century. I do need to start thinking about my living situation after all this.

I link arms with Bel and we head toward it, Bel chattering happily about those fries we ate.

The unexpectedly cavernous store is lined with long aisles, all packed with furniture and lamps and odds and ends in various states of repair. There's a fair number of customers wandering through the inventory, and the proprietor greets us cheerfully. She clearly has not received any memo about never mentioning a pregnant person's body, because she calls Bel "sweetheart" and tells her she looks "ready to pop!" before insisting on ushering her over to an aisle with old cribs and trunks and changing tables. Bel doesn't seem to mind, and she also doesn't seem inclined to tell this lady that her nursery is already done.

Been there, Antiques Lady, I think.

I stop in front of a table of old clocks, running my fingers over the curved, tarnished top of one. This would look ugly in any apartment, probably.

I wander down another aisle, my eyes passing over old, dusty picture frames that would probably do a pretty good job at holding a cursed painting of your decaying self. Before long, my mind is back to wandering away from all these things I definitely do not want, and in the relative privacy of the haunted frames aisle, I do exactly the thing I should not be doing, and check my phone.

Surprise: still no word from Levi.

Stop, Georgie, I immediately scold myself, but it's too late. I'm slipping easily into the same nagging set of thoughts I've had in nearly all my moments of solitude over the last two days. It's a bruise I can't stop pressing, that conversation with Levi, and the strained quiet of its aftermath. *Why* had I brought up Evan? *Why* had I felt, right at the moment we'd finally been having a normal conversation, that I'd needed to apologize for something Levi had probably already forgotten about?

Also, why had I put green beans in that pasta dish?

Strangely, it feels connected: the blurted apology and the beans in a pasta dish. Left to my own devices—when I'm picking up my own puppet strings—I'm like this: impulsive, unthinking. I'd seen those beans and thought, *these look good,* and I'd wanted to use them, no matter whether they fit with anything else I'd picked up. I'd gotten a few pieces of information about Levi's professional life and then suddenly brought up something painful from his personal one.

I shake my head, opening the text thread I now have with him, his last message sent at six o'clock this morning, when I was still asleep. **I'll be taking Hank with me today**, it reads. **Thanks again for watching him yesterday.**

I'd winced when I'd first read it, feeling like I'd lost another job somehow. Levi probably had no choice yesterday, letting Hank stay home with me, but I expect he's working hard not to need me again. I've been checking my phone so much because at any moment I'm expecting a text telling me there was a hotel available, after all.

Let's keep this simple, I can hear him saying, in that quiet but impatient voice, and my face heats in embarrassment. I shove my phone back into my purse, determined to leave it there for the rest of the afternoon.

This day is *not* about Levi. It's about ghost frames!

"Georgie!" calls Bel, from somewhere deeper in the store. "Georgie, come here!"

Grateful for the distraction, I make my way toward the sound of her voice, expecting she's found something incredibly disturbing to show me. Maybe an old doll in a sailor suit with all its hair plucked out, or a vintage speculum. I peek down a couple of aisles before I find her, her and the proprietor's backs toward me, and as I get closer, I can see they've got a beautifully polished, cherrywood trunk on the floor in front of them. I don't have any idea where Bel's going to put it, but I suppose that's not my business.

"This is nice," I say, my eyes on it as I come to stand beside her, but then she pinches the back of my arm.

"Ow," I say, immediately lifting my hand to rub at it. I aim an appalled look her way, but that's when I realize she and the proprietor are not standing around this trunk alone.

"Oh," I correct, and wouldn't you know it.

This time, I actually *am* staring right into the face of Evan Fanning.

"Look who I ran in to!" Bel says, sounding as delighted as an antiques dealer commenting on the stage of a new customer's pregnancy.

"Oh," I repeat, but this time, it's less shock and more revelation: I know immediately, bone-deep, why I blurted that apology to Levi two nights ago. It's because, even after knowing him for only a few hours—gruff, rough-around-the-edges Levi, who's tenderhearted about his dog and shy to talk about his success—it seems absurd that I could have had a moment's confusion between him and the glossy, confident, ultra-popular teenage boy I'd once had a crush on.

Today, Evan Fanning looks very nearly the same as that teenage boy. Older, sure, but somehow, still the same. Thick brown hair combed back from his brow, clean-shaven face. Straight nose, strong jaw. Sun-bronzed and smiling. Hands tucked easily into the pockets of pants, his posture casual, comfortable.

"You remember Evan Fanning," Bel says, and I'll give it to her, she does not say it like I've written half an amateur novel in this person's honor. She says it like, *Oh, hey, here's this guy from our high school!*

"Of course," I say, trying to match her casual tone. "Hi."

"Georgie, right?"

I scan my body for the instinct to swoon in adolescent *he knows my name!* glee.

There's nothing except a vague relief that I'm not wearing wrinkled overalls. Bel, however, is all excitement beside me. As soon as we get in the car, I'm going to pinch her right back. Lightly, on account of the pregnancy, but still. It's too much pleasure she's taking in this.

"That's me," I say, and turn to his companion, a young woman with long hair the same color as Evan's—and Levi's—and an excited glance that bounces between me, Evan, and Bel. "Hi," I greet her, holding out my hand.

She takes it, shaking it enthusiastically. "I'm Olivia, Evan's sister! Probably y'all don't remember me, though; I was way behind you in school!"

I don't have the chance to tell her whether I do or don't (I do, vaguely, and mostly on account of the Evan obsession), because she goes right on talking. "Basically you are a *legend* to me. Working for Nadia Haisman? I *love* her films."

I also don't have the chance to tell her that this isn't true anymore; apparently she hasn't run in to Mrs. Michaels anywhere in the last few days. It's a nice change, though, to have a reputation for something other than getting detention or sleeping through my PSATs.

"Liv is a big movie buff," says Evan. He does this small, warm, teasing chuckle that probably would have given me a cardiac event a dozen years ago and nudges her. "Believe me, I'd know."

Olivia rolls her eyes dramatically and nudges him back. "Ev and I are roommates the past few months. Last night I made him watch *Legally Blonde.*"

"Classic film," Bel says, obviously absolutely *thrilled.*

"With commentary," Evan adds, groaning for effect, and Bel and Olivia both laugh lightly. But all I can think about is Levi, saying he doesn't see his brother, or any of his family. Evan and Olivia seem close, comfortable with each other, and I'm inexplicably resentful on Levi's behalf. How can they watch *Legally Blonde* (with commentary!) without their brother? Levi would be perfectly nice to watch a movie with, I guess, as long as you don't . . . bring up the exact people I am irrationally annoyed at for excluding him.

Bel notices my uncharacteristic silence and clears her throat. "Georgie's in town helping me get ready for this little one," she says, smoothing a hand over her stomach. "My husband and I recently moved back. Well, he's from Connecticut originally. But you know what I mean."

"I've been showing her some hope chests!" the proprietor chimes in, and Olivia *oohs* and *aahs* at the one on the floor that I'd forgotten all about.

"Another great find, Pam," Evan says, and approximately sixty-year-old-Pam has the approximate vibe of thirteen-year-old me at the moment. "We've picked out a few things, too, when you're ready for us."

Pam clasps her hands together. "The Fannings are my best customers," she says to Bel and me. "How many of your guest rooms have pieces from here, Evan?" I'm pretty sure she bats her eyelashes.

"Oh, about every one," Evan says easily, and her cheeks flush. He's still got it, I guess. For a second, his eyes meet mine, and I don't know how he does it, but it's as if he's winking at me without actually winking. Like he's telling me he noticed that I noticed his charm, like we're in on a secret together. Somehow, he manages to do this without seeming smug, and I admit it: the body scan turns up something this time. Not a full-on stomach flutter, but . . . a stomach *something*.

"Y'all still work at The Shoreline?" Bel asks, and I narrow my eyes at her a little. I haven't heard Bel say y'all since sophomore year, right about the time she joined the debate and forensics team.

Olivia beams. "Evan's the general manager now. I run the spa."

Bel's eyebrows raise up. "I didn't know there was a spa! Georgie, there's a spa! We'll have to come out sometime."

"Oh, I'd *love* that," says Olivia. "We have a pregnancy massage that people rave about." She looks to me. "And obviously tons of other services! Probably not as fancy as what you're used to, coming from California!"

"I'm sure it's wonderful," I say with a smile. Olivia seems nice, even if this meeting overall is extremely confusing for me personally. I'm standing on a cliffside and the water below is comprised entirely of the question: *Why don't you two talk to your older brother?* I'm itching to jump in.

Instead I say, "I didn't usually have time for spa visits, anyway."

"Oh, I mean. You wouldn't, right? You're probably so *booked!*"

Not anymore! my brain chirps. *It's just me and my old notebook full of silly ideas for now!*

"Speaking of booked," says Evan, looking down at the smart watch he's wearing. "Pam, maybe we'll give you a call about the pieces. Unfortunately we both have to do fill-in shifts in the restaurant tonight."

Pam clucks her tongue. "Still having trouble, huh?"

It's Olivia's turn to groan. "You would not believe it. Tons of competition for servers right now! We've got a couple of new people onboard, but it's still tricky staffing shifts."

"Last week I tripped up the steps from the patio and dropped a half-full bottle of Moët," Evan says, shaking his head, all easy comfort with his own clumsiness. "I wonder what disasters await me tonight."

"I'm sure you're *wonderful*," says Pam.

"You know," Bel says, and it's the way she stretches out the *know. You kno-oh.* It's the way her elbow presses into my side. I know what she's going to say even before it's out of her mouth, and I'm powerless to stop her.

"Georgie has *tons* of restaurant experience," she finishes.

Olivia puts her hands up, spreading her fingers wide, her mouth in an O that she transforms into a dramatic, *"Ohmygod."* I have never seen anyone be this impressed by my past work as a waitress, but it makes more sense when Olivia adds, "Isn't that how you got *discovered?*"

At this description—as if I'm a model or an actress or something!—I actually do laugh. "Sort of. I was working as a waitress in Richmond when I got my first on-set job."

A fluke, really—at the time, there was a prestige cable drama about the Civil War filming in and around the city, and four nights a week, the director came in to the restaurant where I worked to have dinner. He wanted the same table every night, was usually alone, and always had his laptop. When it crashed halfway through his entrée one Wednesday evening, I helped him out by texting Justin, the guy who lived in the apartment two floors below and ran a side gig doing tech support. Justin got a thousand bucks in cash and two pieces of chocolate torte that was going to get thrown out at the end of the night, the director got his laptop up and running better than it was before, and I got an offer to come by the set as a thank-you for helping save the next day's shoot. Soon enough, I had a new temp gig during my days—delivering coffees, picking up dry cleaning, reporting to the AD about how long the lead actor had been arguing with his boyfriend on FaceTime.

"You must be a real talent," says Evan, and there's Bel's elbow again. Jeez, she's gotten strong. I wonder absently whether I should renew my subscription to the fitness app I only used six times last year.

I take a half step away from her and wave a hand in embarrassed dismissal of the compliment, although I'm not sure why. Maybe I've gotten used to the word *talent* as describing a certain sector of the workforce I was involved in, a sector that didn't include me.

"I mean," I say, a teasing note in my voice, "I never dropped a bottle of champagne."

Evan laughs and Olivia claps once, bouncing on her toes. Pam seems a bit miffed over there, because she thinks I'm trying to steal her boyfriend.

I catch Evan's eyes on me, and he reaches into his back pocket, pulling out his wallet and sliding out a slim white card.

"It's a long shot, I know," he says, "but if you'd have time to lend us some of your talent for a spell while you're here, we'd sure appreciate it."

Olivia whispers *"Ohmygod"* again, and Bel closes the space I put between us.

He holds out the card, and for a second, all I can think about is Levi. His stern face in contrast to this smiling one. How hard it was for him to ask for help, and how easy it seems for Evan.

But this time, Bel doesn't even have to nudge me, because my own sense of self-preservation does. Why am I thinking about Levi, who's probably packed up and gone by now? Why am I not focused on the stir of anticipation at the prospect of having something else, something useful, to fill my time?

Why am I not thinking about the fact that this prospect—a job at the Fannings' inn, however temporary—is also, conveniently, *magically*, even, a ready-made opportunity from the fic, one I hadn't even considered including in my new plan? Never mind that I don't have a stomach flutter over Evan anymore, shouldn't I be taking this as some sort of sign to keep going?

Shouldn't this, like everything else on my list, be an opportunity for me to think about what I want?

I reach out my hand, ignoring the way Bel makes a quiet *peep* of excitement beside me, and also ignoring my lingering Levi-related misgivings. I send a bright smile to his younger brother, add a nonchalant shrug that belies all the swirling emotions of the last several minutes, and say, "Sure. Why not?"

* * *

MY SELF-ASSURANCE lasts right up until I pull into my parents' drive and see Levi's truck parked beside the carport. I'd so thoroughly convinced myself that he wouldn't be here that I'd been looking forward to getting home to an empty house after dropping Bel off, eager for some time to process the day in general and the fact that I've accepted an invitation to The Shoreline tomorrow in specific. But there's Hank, lying at Rodney the metal rooster's feet, and as soon as he sees me, he barks and heads in my direction. I look immediately toward the back door and see Levi on the porch, standing with his arms crossed over his chest.

Great, I think, taking in that closed-off posture, feeling a frustrating pang of guilt. The card from Evan might as well be burning a hole in my back pocket.

I take the distraction Hank offers when I get out of the car, patting his flanks and talking nonsense to him about his day. Eventually, though, my stalling is pointed, and I make my way to Levi, Hank hopping at my heels excitedly. I half expect the man to simply turn his back and go inside without greeting me, now that his dog is headed in, but he simply stands waiting.

He's freshly showered, the ends of his short hair still damp, his beard newly trimmed. He smells great, like the blue bar of soap he's got in the shower, and like the light salt tang of the water when you're close to the shore. Without his ball cap on, I can see his eyes, and that's trouble. They're a deeper blue than Evan's, hooded with thicker brows and framed with longer, darker lashes.

"Hey," he says, arms still crossed forbiddingly. Maybe he can somehow sense I've seen his brother and sister. Maybe he's got a secret love of antiquing and he saw the whole thing.

"Hi," I say, desperate to shake off this unnecessary guilt. "You're home early."

As soon as it's out of my mouth, I realize how weird it sounds. *Home?* He doesn't live here. *Early?* I don't know his regular schedule. I might as well be the one-dimensional wife in a bad TV pilot.

If he hears the strangeness in it, he doesn't let on. He only says, "Finished up early today. I had some trouble keeping track of Hank on the job."

"Oh. You should've texted. I could've—"

"You're not on call for me," he says before I can finish, and then he blows out a breath, uncrossing his arms. He lifts one and rubs a hand roughly through his hair. "Sorry."

I shrug and bend to scratch at Hank's uninjured ear.

Levi clears his throat. "I wanted to say, I'm sorry about the way I acted the other night."

My hand stills on Hank's ear, and I rise up again, meeting Levi's eyes. He looks earnest and nervous and determined, and for a second, I can't say anything at all.

"You caught me off guard," he adds. "I'm not the best conversationalist."

I'm still staring. The problem is, I'm having a humongous stomach flutter.

"And I'm not used to—" he breaks off, clears his throat once more. "I'm not used to talking about my family."

No more stomach flutter. Is my back pocket ticking?

"No, I'm sorr—" I begin, but he cuts me off again.

"This is a one-way sorry. I didn't act right. Especially after all you've done for me, letting me stay. Watching Hank, and that nice dinner you made."

"It's no problem. And I know the dinner was . . . I know those beans didn't really go in that pasta."

"It was real good."

Oh, jeez. I can tell he's lying, but it's the loveliest lie I've ever been told. My lips curve into a smile.

"I thought I'd return the favor," he says. "Not that you got a dog for me to watch. Or need a place to stay."

My smile gets bigger, and that stomach flutter? It comes back, and it gets more . . . fluttery. With him looking at me this way, half hope and half embarrassment, I forget all about the disappointments of the day, and I definitely forget about the way that business card offered a potential escape from them. Frankly, I forget all about Evan Fanning entirely. I forget about everything except the man standing right in front of me, and the invitation he offers up next.

"What I'm saying is, would you have dinner with me?"

Chapter 8

Levi

For the next half hour, I split my mental energy between prepping ingredients and doubting myself. The look on Georgie's face when I asked her to have dinner was a mix of surprise and hesitation, and I almost backed off, told her I could simply leave her some leftovers. Why would she want to try a meal with me again, after last time?

But after today's realizations, I'm trying to stay determined. All morning, I worked out at the Quentin property with Micah, one of my seasonal guys who does good work on floating docks, and that's the only real option for the Quentins, who've got a pretty fragile setup on their property for a structure—a fluctuating water level and soft bottom conditions. Micah's a good guy, a good worker, but he likes two things I don't on the job: music and chat. The music bit has to do with the work itself, which I think goes better when you can hear everything you're doing—when you're paying attention to the water, to the wood, to the wind, to whatever else is going to affect how your final product functions. The chat, obviously, is a weakness of mine, but Micah loves it, can't stop it. One thing is, if he has a playlist going, he won't talk as much. Instead, he'll sing.

But the Quentin property is a dead zone for cell and wireless service, so Micah couldn't get his playlist cued up, and that meant it was chat straight through. At first, it was pretty innocuous. Micah and his wife, Natalie, live over on Varina Creek with their three kids, and they have a family project going this summer, something involving an expanded coop for these guinea fowl they've been raising for the last year or so. In the first hour I learned more about guinea fowl than I ever wanted to know, including what sound they make when they're agitated, since Micah performed it for me. I was getting lulled in, figuring he'd keep on about the coop or the birds or the fact that one of his daughters tried to have a tea party out there with them, which got Natalie mad enough she made Micah sleep on the couch for two nights.

But then out of the blue he said, "You still staying over there at the Mulcahy place?" and he said it as if he *knew.*

I'd accidentally knocked over the box of fasteners I'd been sorting through and looked over at him, but he was working away, seeming not to care about my answer.

"Yeah," I said, suspicious.

"Heard Georgie's back in town, is why I'm asking."

"How'd you hear that?"

"Natalie ran in to Deanna Michaels at the Food Lion. Said she saw Georgie at Nickel's, and you, too."

I'd rolled my eyes and thought, *This fucking town.*

"Georgie and I graduated in the same class," Micah continued. "Nice girl. Kinda flaky."

I'd looked over at him again, annoyed. What's a guy who lets his kid have a tea party with wild birds doing calling anyone flaky? I'd been working up a defense of her—which probably would've been a simple grunt of disapproval—when Micah had said, "So you staying in the house with her?"

I focused on the fasteners that were scattered all over the grass and said, "For now."

I'd hoped that'd be the end of it, but with Micah, it's not the end of anything until you're not in the same room with him anymore, or until he's got something playing he can sing to. For the next ten minutes he told me every story he could remember about Georgie Mulcahy, including the time she and her dad spent a Sunday afternoon power-washing Micah's grandmother's deck, free of charge, to help out after Micah's grandpa passed on. "Those Mulcahys," he'd said. "Friendly, aren't they?"

It'd been that word, for some reason, that'd stuck with me, and my face had heated in shame as I'd sorted those fasteners back into their spots. The other night, I'd gotten awful fragile about that friendliness, hadn't I? In the first place, Georgie hadn't been anything but nice to me, and I'd rebuffed her on account of something she's got no reason to know I'm uncomfortable about, other than rumors she's probably heard. In the second, I shouldn't care if she did want to call up my younger brother and say hello; that's no skin off my back. That's something a normal, friendly person who's back in their hometown might do, and I don't have any reason to be sensitive about it.

Or at least any reason that's fair to her.

For the rest of the workday, I'd steered Micah back toward talk of fowl so I could think on my predicament. I knew I needed to apologize for the way I acted and for the way I'd been avoiding her. I knew that Paul and Shyla wouldn't have liked the way I'd treated Georgie, but more important, I knew *I* didn't like it, either. If I meant what I said to Georgie, that I wanted to keep things simple, then that meant I needed to do what was obviously simple to her, too.

And that meant being friendly.

Not fluctuating-water-level, soft-bottom conditions fragile.

By the time Micah and I had gotten spanner boards into our second frame, I'd decided on a plan: Apologize to Georgie and even things out with a dinner of my own. I'd told Micah we were stopping early, then I'd rounded up Hank—who'd been off and on trying to dig holes all day, even though he knows he's not allowed—and gone to Nickel's for groceries, attempting to act normal when Ernie took eight bucks off my bill.

So now I'm in it, the first part of my plan done, and that had gone all right after a bit of a rocky start. Part two is riskier. I'm a good cook, so that's not the problem, but the citronella candle I lit on the outdoor table is giving me fits. I can't take eating another meal in the warm closeness of that dining room, but the problem with outside is, the bug control we need makes the situation look more romantic than I intended. Plus, I can *make* the dinner, but then *having* it means more conversation, and obviously that's where things went wrong last time.

Friendly, I tell myself. *Not fragile.*

While Georgie's washing up, I make a couple of trips from the kitchen out to the back, laying out ingredients and getting Paul's grill going. Back in the kitchen, I finish rolling out the dough I've made, shaping it the way I want. Georgie's got good timing, coming back into the kitchen when I'm ready to transfer it outside, and I'm grateful to have cooking to focus on, because I still don't feel all that friendly once I get a good look at her. She's put her hair up high, but the pieces that are too short to stay up trail along her neck, which is circled with three thin gold necklaces of varying lengths, delicate overlays to the decoration already provided by her freckles. I was too nervous to notice what she was wearing when she got home, but I know it wasn't this: a pair of faded, cropped jeans with holes in the knees and a thin, loose-fitting tank top that almost makes me swallow my own tongue. There's nothing fancy about any of it, but that's the problem. Around here, Georgie's in her family home, comfortable and casual and soft, and it makes me hungry and desperate, a dog left out in a thunderstorm.

"Whatcha making?" she says, looking down at the trays I'm holding.

"Uh," I say, dropping my eyes to remind myself, since my

brain got wiped clean by her reappearance. "Pizza. On the grill."

"Pizza on the grill!" It's as though this is the most exciting thing she's ever heard. I picture her out there in Los Angeles, surrounded by movie people, eating at the sorts of trendy restaurants I've never seen.

"Can I help with anything?"

I shake my head. "I'm all set, I think. You could get the door?"

She leads the way back out, Hank beside her, and when she settles into one of the chairs, she makes a groaning noise of relief that reminds me of my own at the end of a workday, at least when I'm alone.

"Tough day?" I ask, checking the temperature of the grill.

It takes her a beat longer than I expect to answer, and my nerves kick at me. But I shouldn't expect that she'd go right back to the way she was before because I've made a minor effort.

"Unplanned antiquing," she finally says. "My friend found a hope chest that she wanted, and I had to do some heavy lifting."

"She didn't help?"

Georgie smiles. "Pregnant, remember?" She makes a gesture with her hand, a big, round belly gesture.

Now why am I thinking about Georgie pregnant? That's not right. I turn back toward the grill.

"You might know her," Georgie says, sparing me from having to think of a follow-up. "Annabel Reston? Well, Annabel Reston-Yoon, now. She grew up here, too."

"I don't think so."

"Oh. Well, she and her husband bought a house over along Little Bay."

I may not know the person, but I probably know the house. Little Bay's a recent development in Darentville, a small number of large builds that made a big mess along the shore, hemmed in by a long retaining wall that's got no kind of care for the plant and wildlife around here. I get calls every once in a while to come out for estimates on dock builds, but I've turned them all away, same as Carlos would have.

"I know the area," is all I say.

"Honestly, I'm still pretty surprised by it," she continues, as I set the dough on the grill, moving quickly to close the cover. "She and her husband both worked on the Hill for years; they had *super*-intense jobs. But, you know . . ." She stops, blows out a big, gusty sigh. "Reinvention! It's the thing to do nowadays."

I should say something, but I am suddenly acutely aware of the two minutes and thirty seconds I have before I need to flip the dough over. My dinner plan should have included opportunities for constant activity, to avoid this sort of thing. Suddenly Georgie's mess-making seems more strategy than chaos.

"That what you're doing?" I finally say.

She looks up at me, blinking those big brown eyes, and for a fleeting few seconds there's a look on her face unlike anything I've ever seen, and that's including the time I walked in on her in her underwear. She looks confused and lost and maybe a little afraid. I'd like to stick my head inside that grill at the sight of it.

"Moving back here, I mean," I add, because I'm trying to make it smaller, more specific. I'm trying to get that look off her face.

"Oh, *God* no," she says, sharp and decisive. "I'm not moving back."

It has the desired effect in terms of her face, but not in terms of the way it makes me feel. She sure was forceful about not moving back here, though I don't know why I should care.

Friendly, I remind myself. *Not fragile.*

I nod and busy myself rearranging the ingredients I laid out, an unnecessary task that helps me pass the time before I turn back toward the grill, flipping the dough over and setting about loading the cooked side with toppings. I should've asked after her preferences, but then again, I've got that pasta as a precedent. She's not a real particular eater, if I'm going off that.

I ask if she'll get Hank's food for him, and she seems grateful for the opportunity to leave the table. I use the time to finish off the food prep and also to debate myself on whether I should blow out the candle. In the end, I leave it, because I might as well not risk adding the West Nile virus to this situation, and when Georgie comes out again, I'm shifting the finished pizzas onto the wooden cutting board I brought out with me.

"Holy shit!" she exclaims when I set it down. "This looks like a professional made it!"

The compliment warms me. Cooking's one of the few things I consider a hobby, and I've gotten pretty good since I've taken over Carlos's house.

I murmur a thanks as I get to slicing, but I doubt she hears me.

"I didn't even know you could make pizza on a grill!"

She seems so excited. I like that about her, how easy she shows her pleasure. I better not let that train of thought get too far, wondering how it works in scenarios not related to dinner.

I split the pieces between us, and she takes a bite right away, moaning her enjoyment even as she fans a hand back and forth across her slightly open mouth, steam puffing out.

"This is so good!" she says, with her mouth still half-full, and I don't know why it's sexy, but it is. Big, unrestrained, uninhibited. I think about the way she held out her arms the other night when she told me about her job.

I shift in my seat, try to focus, bring things back around to that simple, friendly place I'm determined to stay in.

"So you're helping your friend move in to her place?"

She shrugs, swallows. "Not really. I'm . . ." She cocks her head slightly and stares at her pizza for a beat. "I got laid off from my job. Back in LA."

Jesus, I hope the pizza didn't somehow bring that up for her. "Sorry to hear it."

"My boss there, she decided to take her life in a different direction. A more . . . she wants more simplicity." She doesn't do the gesture, but I can tell there's air quotes in the mix around that last word. "So she didn't need me anymore. An assistant, I mean."

"You in money trouble?"

She shakes her head, takes another huge bite of pizza, but doesn't wait until she's all the way done chewing to answer. "I didn't have many expenses when I worked for her, so I have savings. And she gave me a nice severance. I've got time. Options for other work like I was doing before, if I want it."

I furrow my brow, chewing slowly. I don't mind admitting it's hard to understand what she means, *if I want it.* What's work got to do with wanting?

"I know I'm lucky to have that. I'm trying to take this opportunity . . . well, it's hard to explain."

"Try," I say, surprising me and I'm sure her—going by the way she blinks up at me—with the demand. But I'm curious now, and a second later I confront an uncomfortable thought: Is this how it felt for Georgie, the other night, trying to talk to me?

She seems to think for a while, and I wonder if she might shut me out the way I did her. I'd deserve it, I guess.

"When I was a kid," she says, and dang, I might've been holding my breath. "I made this . . . it was sort of a list of things I thought I would do as a teenager. Once I got to high school. You know how it was, switching to that big school. It felt so important, back then."

I doubt it felt the same to me as it did to her. I was already in a lot of trouble by that time; I'd had three school suspensions and one night in a holding cell by the time I started at Harris County High School. The only important thing to me back then was wrecking shit, including myself.

But I say, "Yeah," because I want her to keep talking.

"So I had the list, but as it turned out, I didn't follow through with much of it. I got distracted or derailed, or I don't know what. And then I graduated, and I hadn't done any thinking about what I wanted for my future. After that, I kind of fell into this career where my job was about making sure other people had what they wanted."

Honestly I figure that's what most jobs are. Barbara Hubbard wants a dock bench even though her original structure is too narrow, and now she's going to spend a bunch of extra money to get it to work, and she'll probably only sit out there twice a year because she's always worrying after ticks dropping down from the trees hanging over her shoreline. Last year Dale Hennessy wanted me to install four big cleats on the dock we built him, even though he's got no intention of having any sort of watercraft, ever. "For authenticity," he'd said.

We'd put in the cleats.

"Anyway," she continues, "I found the list, then figured I'd do the list, or at least some of it, you know? Sort of an exercise. I wanted these things once, and maybe they'll help me understand something about myself now."

I think about the notebook I've seen her with the last couple of days. It didn't look much like a list to me, but maybe Georgie's lists are similar to her meal preparation.

"Is it working?"

She huffs—a messy, inelegant sound, and all I can think is: I want to have that sound up close. I'd get her to laugh, somehow, and she'd do it, a noisy puff of her breath against me.

It'd feel so good, I think.

"Not yet," she says, her face falling. "Today was my first one. I went to Sott's Mill, which was always a big deal when I was a teenager."

I get up to Sott's Mill sometimes for jobs, but I know what she means, about what it was like when we were younger. Kind of a destination spot. My mom and dad used to take us there every couple of months for shopping, at least back when it didn't embarrass them to take me places.

"It wasn't what you expected?"

She frowns, shifts again in her seat. "Well, there were more antiques."

Then she looks down at her plate, her expression thoughtful, a little sad. I've got a mind to wrap my hand around the arm of that rickety old chair and yank it up against mine. I know I've entirely lost sight of friendly, and it's all on account of how fragile she looks right now.

"It was maybe a silly idea," she adds. "I'm not sure if I should keep going with it."

I think of Micah calling her flaky. But the thing is, she doesn't seem flaky to me. She seems . . . she seems *expansive*, to use her word. Full to bursting. The kind of person who'd have a hard time with any sort of list, but somehow, in the best possible way.

"Doesn't seem silly to me," I say.

"It doesn't?"

I shake my head. "Sounds like a nice opportunity to . . . to go back, in a way. See if that sets you on a different path."

"Yes!" she says, straightening in her chair, her eyes wide. "That's exactly it!"

I thought her excitement about my pizza was nice, but this is better. I don't want to lose that feeling yet.

"What's on the list?"

The excitement in her eyes turns to trepidation.

"Oh. Well, silly stuff mostly. The kind of thing I did today. Probably I should've put *study for my SATs* on there."

"That wouldn't do you much good now, though. Don't think they let anyone as old as you take it."

She laughs, and I think of that breath I wanted on my skin. I'm so restless with the wanting of it—*you did it, you got her to laugh*—that I stand, moving toward the door to let Hank back out now that he's done eating. He nudges at my leg in speedy gratitude and then bolts out into the yard to see that rusted-out rooster he's gotten fond of, and I sit back down. For a few minutes, Georgie and I eat quietly, until I remember the last thing I said is something about her being old.

"If it makes you feel better," I say, "I never would've thought to make a list like that when I was that age."

She eyes me cautiously, and I get it. It's close to where things went wrong the other night, but it's different now—there's fresh air, the sound of Shyla's wind chimes tinkling, fireflies starting to light out in the tree line. No trap doors, or if there are, I'm opening them myself.

"Yeah?"

I nod, and I can see her swallow, see the wariness in her gaze. I can sense what she wants to ask.

What would have been on it, if you had?

But she doesn't ask, and I should be relieved, because I don't have an answer. I should let it go, change the subject. I could probably get into something about guinea fowl. Not the noise they make, but the other stuff.

Instead, I clear my throat, stack some of the dirty plates, and say, "Seemed I only ever could think about the day I was on. Everything else was pretty much a blank."

At first I think she must not have heard me, that my plate stacking drowned out the low, guarded way I spoke. But when I steal a glance up at her, I see that she's watching me closely, intensely, all caution in her gaze gone.

"How do you mean?" she says quietly. "How do you mean, a blank?"

I resist the urge to slam the trap door shut again. I'm the one who started this, and anyway, I don't think I could look away from her now. I can see the flicker-flame of the not-meant-to-be-romantic candle in the bright pools of her eyes, and they look full of the kind of hope I'm not used to having directed at me unless it's about repairing pilings.

"Couldn't see where I fit. Couldn't see what everyone else seemed to see for themselves, that's for sure. College, or a career." *The family business. The family at all.*

She blinks, but it doesn't clear any of that hopefulness. She looks strung tight like a bow; for once, the opposite of expansive.

"But now you do? See where you fit?"

I swallow, blink down, and resume my plate stacking. "I see some things," I say, which isn't a lie. I see the jobs I have lined up; I see the plans I have for my house. I see the things I have to do to take care of Hank every day. I see more than I ever did when I was young, and that's a good thing. Healthy and stable and better than anyone ever expected of me.

But none of that's about fitting, and I've got the sense that saying so would disappoint her. I don't want to end the meal that way. I want to keep that light in her eyes, the one I've put there just by understanding something about her.

"I think you should keep going with it," I say. "It's a real good idea."

She's about to say something back, I can tell, but then Hank barks and we both look over at him. He's sitting right in front of the rooster, looking up, as though they're having a conversation. I'll be honest, that rooster makes me uncomfortable. I don't think of myself as superstitious, but there's only so many times your dog can try to communicate with a lawn ornament before you start to wonder if the thing is sentient.

My eyes track back to Georgie as soon as hers track back to mine, and for a long second, we look at each other in shared *isn't that just like Hank* amusement—her smile soft and easy again, surely mine smaller and more strained. But it's so jarringly, unexpectedly intimate that I push back my chair and stand, gathering the plates to take inside.

"I'll be right back," I say, remembering how I'm not being fragile tonight. I only need a second to breathe without her right there, pushing against all the glued-together pieces of me with her nearness. I'll tell her about the guinea fowl when I get back, maybe.

But before I can go, Georgie stands, too, and if I thought she was *right there* before, well.

Well, my thinking was all wrong.

She's close enough that I can see her chest lift when she takes a breath. She's close enough that I hold my own so I don't miss the feeling of her releasing it.

"Levi," she says, setting her hand on my forearm to still me. It works, because I turn into a statue beneath her touch, if statues had big, beating hearts and also blood flow directly to their dicks. I've never felt this fragile and firm at the same time in my whole life.

"Yeah," I say, or think I say. Could be I only make a noise. I catch myself looking at her mouth, her lips soft and pink. She's got a smudge of pizza sauce on the left corner of the lower one, and it feels like a crime, how much I love the look of it there. How much I want to touch my thumb to that spot.

"Thanks," she says. "For the dinner, and for . . ."

She lowers her eyes, looking at her hand on my arm, as though she's surprised to find herself touching me. She moves one of her fingers the slightest bit—the slowest, smallest stroke over my statue-stillness, which I'm holding on to with every ounce of my strength.

"And for . . ." she repeats, trailing off again, and it's me who's strung tight now, all anticipation for how she's going to finish her sentence. I'm waiting for her to say something about how I talked to her, offered something of myself to her. Encouraged her about her list.

Was *friendly* to her.

But that's only because I never expected the alternative.

And the alternative turns out to be Georgie—with a gentle squeeze of the arm she'd stroked so softly—lifting onto her tiptoes and pressing her mouth to mine.

Chapter 9

Georgie

He isn't kissing you back.

I don't know how long it takes me to realize it—I can only hope it's one bare, humiliating second, maybe even a matter of *milli*seconds, but the truth is, I suspect it's longer. I suspect that the things I felt when my mouth first touched Levi's—the warmth of his lips, the teasing scrape of his beard, the hard, flexing tension in that forearm beneath my hand—stunned me into some kind of stupor, where my only thoughts had been about all the perfect textures of him, and all the ways I wanted to explore each and every one.

But once I *do* realize it?

Once I do realize it—total stillness standing there before me—the only texture I can think of is that of the ground beneath my feet, since it would be great if it could open up and swallow me whole.

I jerk back so quickly that Levi's hand—the one not holding a stack of dishes—reaches out to steady me at my elbow, and of course . . . of *course* the texture of his hand is delicious, too—

soft heat and the rough ridges of a calloused palm, the strong curve of his gentle fingers shaped to my arm.

"Wh—" he begins, and I cannot *bear* it. I cannot bear him asking, *What was that?* or *Why did you do that?* or *Where is the shovel so I can help you dig your humiliation hole?*

"I'm sorry!" I say, stepping back again, losing the heat of Levi's hand on my skin. The backs of my calves bump against my chair, the metal legs of it making an unholy clatter on the brick patio. Hank barks, the clink of his collar telling me he's coming over to see what all the noise is for, and I realize that eye contact with this man's dog is also too embarrassing a prospect at the moment.

"Georgie," Levi says, his voice low and quiet in a way I recognize, and it's definitely not the kind of muted impatience that's about discreetly buying your milkshakes for you, but it's also got a note of something familiar, something I've heard from all sorts of people in this town who've seen me screw up.

It might be something slightly . . . pitying.

I actually do know where the shovel is; it's in my dad's stuffed-full garden shed. I'll wait until Levi goes inside, then I'll get it out and dig the hole myself.

He *pities* me.

"I didn't mean to do that," I blurt, which is so inane that I have to squeeze my eyes shut for a second. "I wasn't thinking."

That doesn't sound much better, but it's certainly more true. If I'd been thinking, I would've remembered that Levi had asked for simple, and kissing's not it. I would've remembered that only hours ago, I'd resolved to put him out of my mind and focus on myself. I would've remembered that I've still got his brother's business card in the back pocket of a pair of pants I left in a heap on my parents' bedroom floor.

I hadn't been thinking.

I'd been *feeling*. Feeling like someone finally understood me, and feeling strangely thrilled it was him. Feeling like he was strong and sensitive and sweeter than I expected. I'd been feeling, for once, like I was full of wanting.

But that doesn't mean I should've *kissed* him.

I see his throat bob in a thick swallow, see the fingers on his right hand flex. In his left, he's holding that stack of plates steady and still. I can tell he has no idea what to say, and honestly, fair enough.

"Did you need me to watch Hank tomorrow?" I ask, because it's the least I can do—bring it back to what was supposed to be simple about this. Roommates. Dog sitting. Occasional meal sharing, though I'm pretty sure that won't be happening again after tonight, which is too bad, because that pizza was fucking *great*.

He blinks, and for a second his eyes drop to my mouth. My brain scrambles in the same way it did in the seconds before I kissed him—in the seconds before I apparently misread everything about the moment. I won't be making that mistake again; I *can't* make that mistake again.

"I can keep him with me tomorrow," Levi says.

I nod quickly, stepping to the side—*away* from the chair this time—and back again. "Great. That's great."

"Geor—" he begins, and not to sound too Los Angeles about this whole thing, but I *literally* cannot. I have to get away from this, immediately.

"You can text me if you end up needing me," I say quickly, even as I'm taking another step back. "It'd be no problem."

"Sure, but—"

"I need to run inside to use the restroom." I jerk a thumb over my shoulder, heedless of how unconvincing an exit strategy this is, even if it's effective. No decent person—and Levi Fanning *is* decent; I know it down deep—is going to ask you if you're lying about that.

It's not until I'm in the house, in my parents' bedroom, the door closed behind me, that I realize I've left him to clean up everything from dinner, without any real intention of ever going back out there. At least Levi's efforts in the kitchen didn't produce anything close to the mess I made two nights ago.

The mess you made just now, I chide myself, groaning quietly and covering my face with my hands. I'm contemplating my strategy for staying inside this room until the rapture, or at least until I hear Levi and Hank turn in for the night, when I hear a familiar, bubbling trill from my phone—the first time I've heard that particular tone in days and days. It's Nadia's text notification, and I'm ashamed at the gust of relieved anticipation that blows through me.

Please ask me for something, I'm thinking, as I move toward the nightstand. *Please give me a reason to think about something I can do for you, instead of all the things I apparently can't do for myself.*

When I unlock the screen, I see that she's texted multiple times, and that, too, is familiar—she often had a flurry of requests or ideas, as if the thought of one task for me to do would trip her into the thought of a dozen others. But the ten total messages here aren't requests at all. There are two texts, each a bookend to the eight photographs in between.

Came into town today and have a good signal, so sending you some pictures! We are living the dream out here! I've never been happier or more relaxed.

Then: three nearly identical photographs of rose-gold sunsets over a cactus-dotted landscape. One picture of Nadia's husband, Bill, standing beside a donkey, its back draped in a colorful blanket. Two photographs of white plates filled with delicious-looking food—brightly colored vegetables, thick cuts of meat, a swirl of creamy potatoes. One snapshot of a crystal-blue swimming pool surrounded by lounge chairs and potted succulents. Two selfies of Nadia, tanned and smiling, and one of Nadia and Bill, another rose-gold sunset as the backdrop, their hands holding half-empty wineglasses, toasting the camera.

Hope you are doing well, too! xo

I stare down at the phone, embarrassingly disappointed. I

imagine what I'd type back if I was being totally honest. *Due to recent events involving my hot, uninterested roommate, I'll probably get started on digging a hole later!* I might say. Or, *Limped my way through living a teenage dream at an antiques store earlier; here's a photo of an old weathervane that Satan himself might've made!*

Still haven't worked out what I want!

But Nadia doesn't want to hear any of that, and anyway, I don't want to tell her. She's found happiness where she is, and she encouraged me to do the same. Before I got derailed—*again*—by Levi Fanning, I was getting somewhere. Sure, it'd been a rough start in Sott's Mill, but things had turned around, hadn't they?

I reply with a quick heart-eyes emoji, adding that I'm doing well and will update her soon. Then I toss the phone onto the bed and move toward the discarded pants on the floor, pulling out the card from The Shoreline Evan gave me. I walk to the dresser, where I left the fic this morning, and page through it, searching for the first mention I can find of the inn. Once I see it, I slide the card in and close the notebook again, resting my palm on top of its cool, flat, worn surface. I close my eyes, trying not to think about the contrast to the way Levi's skin had felt beneath my hand. When that doesn't work, I force myself to think about the stiff way—the *blank* way—he responded to my kiss, and the notebook seems to get more solid and comforting beneath my hand.

I think you should keep going with it, I hear in my head, and I try to pretend it's my own voice, and not Levi's, leading me on.

DURING HER VERY busiest times—seasons that were jam-packed with long days on set, with press interviews and business meetings shoved into inadequate fifteen-minute slots, with late-night writing sessions fueled by espresso and sheer determination—Nadia used to have this saying. I'd be following her around, ushering her to her next *very necessary* thing or trying desperately to shuffle something she'd been running late for, and she'd be doing this autopilot listening thing she used to do, where she'd be typing on her phone or turning over an idea in her mind, totally confident in my ability to handle the details I was running through about the rest of her day. I'd say something like, *Okay, now you're going to talk to* Variety *for ten minutes about the exclusive streaming deal, and then you have a meeting with Tony about location scouting, and then at 2:15 we'll need to leave for your dermatologist appointment,* and Nadia would look at me, seemingly unbothered, and reply, *Out of the frying pan, into the fire, right?*

I may not have had to talk to anyone about a streaming deal or location scouting or forehead wrinkles, but by the time Friday afternoon rolls around, I'm pretty well reacquainted with both the frying pan and the fire.

The frying pan, it has to be said, is the lingering embarrassment over what happened with Levi last night: the restless night of partial sleep, most of which I spent tossing and turning while jumbotron-size memories of my planting my face against his played on a loop, followed by the fact that I'd woken up to him still in the house, moving around quietly and murmuring soft words to Hank. In the few days Levi and I have been staying together, he's never still been home when I woke up, and I had the terrible frying-pan sense that he was waiting on me, probably to finish off the pitying *Don't worry about it* I'd known he was working up to last night. I'd stayed in bed, cooking in the oil of my own cowardice, until I heard the rumble of his old truck start up and drive away.

The fire, though?

Well, the fire is my new job.

My *very sudden* new job.

"The guy at fourteen wants another order of calamari," Remy says quickly as they pass by me, rolling their eyes. Seeing as how I have only worked at The Shoreline's restaurant for about two and a half hours, I do not know its floor layout well enough to be able to tag table fourteen by sight; however, I can discern from Remy's eye roll alone that I am getting an order of calamari for the guy in the Hawaiian shirt who has slammed three gin and tonics over the last hour while steadily increasing the volume of his voice as he talks to his golf companions about interest rates. They all look sunburned and heat exhausted, and I keep dropping off fresh water at their table, fearing imminent man-fainting.

"Right," I say, whirling back toward the kitchen and calling out the order to a woman running the line whose name I have, embarrassingly, already forgotten in the chaos.

When I arrived at The Shoreline earlier this afternoon—determined to get back to the business of the fic, or at least the business of it that had dropped into my lap at the antiques store—I expected a pitch. A tour of what I could tell was a newly renovated and expanded space, probably accompanied by some light pleading for my temporary help. I'd figured I'd get an hour's worth of distraction from the frying pan followed by a chance to figure out whether I wanted to take on waitress work at my teenage dream spot as part of my project.

Instead, what I'd gotten was a panicked Olivia Fanning, pulled away from her day spa duties in order to accommodate a very unexpected gathering of mortgage brokers from across central Virginia, all of whom wanted to eat lunch at the restaurant after a round of golf during an extremely short-staffed shift.

"Evan's stuck dealing with an irrigation problem on the ninth hole," Olivia had said when I'd made my way to the dining room, a tremor in her voice, her brow sheened with sweat. "And my mom is who knows where, and my dad is doing a sailing tour, and I'm—"

"Put me in, coach," I'd said, smiling brightly. And honestly?

Honestly, Olivia Fanning's face full of relief had made me feel as purposeful as I'd felt in weeks, notebook goals or not.

Of course, my bright smile had belied everything I'd forgotten about waitressing in the years since my last gig, and I've spent the last couple of hours scrambling—trying to figure out the flow of an unfamiliar kitchen, stumbling my way through reading off the lunch specials, shaking out my hands and arms every time I turn away from setting down the unfamiliar weight of multiple dishes and drinks.

I grab a few plates now from an order coming out of the kitchen, recognizing the accompanying ticket as one of mine. Loaded up, I make my way back into the packed dining room, and my body—clad in an ill-fitting spare uniform of branded polo shirt with dark pants—transforms in the way it used to when I did this job full-time: my brow smooths, my lips shape into a placid smile, my shoulders straighten, my stride balances at that perfect point between quickness and calmness.

"Here y'all are," I say when I arrive at the table, because unlike Bel I never did debate and forensics, and also because this kind of confident folksiness always got me big tips at the end of a shift. I'm not even sure how I'm getting paid for this, come to think of it, since there was no time for paperwork, but it doesn't matter at the moment. I go through all the motions: ask if everything looks all right, laugh when one of the mortgage brokers pats his belly and asks whether his eyes were bigger than his stomach, promise to come back and check on them in a few. When I turn to scan my other tables, I catch sight of Olivia across the room, scribbling an order down and looking stressed, her ponytail sagging and her forehead still sweating.

Remy passes behind her, cringing slightly at whatever they must hear. I can tell they're not new to this work, and also can tell they've been carrying a pretty heavy load here.

It's hectic for another hour and a half; we cycle the brokers through meals and desserts and coffee that doesn't much seem to sober them up, though they can still slur their way through a truly impressive amount of conversation involving acronyms like PMI and FHA and APR. Predictably, Hawaiian shirt guy and his table companions are the last to leave; he sways when he stands and I brace for fainting, but in the end he steadies himself and says, "Thanks, honey," to me on his way out. Once I blink through the contact buzz I'm pretty sure I get from his gin-soaked breath, I turn to find Remy closing the doors to the dining room, sealing all of us lunch shift survivors into blessed, long-awaited quiet.

"What the *hell*?" Remy says, sagging back against the door.

Olivia's already on a barstool, her head down on her folded arms, and the bartender—I think his name is Luke—tosses a wet white rag into a bussing tray and slams his way through to the kitchen, clearly fed up.

"Well!" I say. "We did it?"

Olivia groans.

"Two hours until these doors need to be open again for dinner," says Remy, gesturing toward the mess that still needs to be reset. "We didn't do it yet."

"Five minutes," Olivia says, her voice muffled and miserable. Remy does another eye roll, and I start clearing plates. "Five minutes to let me replay the moment I dropped hot buttered rolls on a man's lap."

Could've been worse, I think automatically, before I can remember I'm replaying the moment I kissed her brother. I desperately shove the memory away, annoyed that my thoughts have so readily returned to the frying pan, right when I've finally stepped out of the fire.

"This is all my brother's fault," moans Olivia, and the answering tremble in my hand sends a knife and fork sliding noisily off the plate I've picked up. I contemplate asking whether Olivia's day spa offers memory-erasing hypnosis. I know she can't be talking about Levi, and yet—

"It's not his fault," says Remy. "It's his wife's."

Thank goodness I keep hold of the cutlery.

Olivia raises her head and narrows her eyes at Remy. "His *ex*-wife," she says.

I must be staring, because Olivia turns on her stool to face me and clarifies. "Evan's *ex-wife* ran the restaurant for three years.

Until she *abandoned* everything six months ago for her dirtbag high school boyfriend who she'd been DMing for a *year*."

"Oh no," I say, and mean it, even though I hate the knot of irrational tension that loosens knowing for sure that we are not talking about Levi being married. If Bel were here, I know she'd be pinching me big time, Hallmark movie thoughts in her head. *Friend fic* thoughts in her head. But I don't seem to feel much of anything beyond vague surprise and sympathy at the news that Evan's newly single.

"He should never have married her," Olivia says, sliding off the stool again and joining Remy and I in the cleanup. "She was awful."

Remy snorts. "You liked her!"

"I was blinded by her extremely white teeth and her skill with a curling iron. I haven't had truly great beachy waves since she left."

"She thought unicorns were a real animal," Remy says to me. "Like a certain kind of horse. Rare and expensive."

In spite of myself, I laugh. "Really?"

Remy nods, smirking, but then shrugs as they consolidate a table's leftover drinks into an empty glass, stacking as they go. "But she was great at this job. She kept this place running pretty smooth."

"Which is why Evan needs to hurry up and *hire her replacement*," Olivia says, clearly disgusted by the state of a napkin she's picked up off the floor.

"You have any experience in management?" Remy says, giving me a half-hopeful, half-joking look. "I can't do it; I'm starting vet school in the fall."

"Oh, that's nea—" I begin, but Olivia cuts me off.

"*Ohmygod*, Rem!" she exclaims. "I didn't even have time to tell you about Georgie; she works for Nadia Haisman!"

I don't get the opportunity to correct the tense on this, but it doesn't much matter, because for the next half hour, the conversation slips easily into the kind of coworkers-getting-to-know-each-other banter that reminds me of my early waitressing days. Some of it's about me—the jobs I've had, the famous people I've met and not met, whether my parents are the ones who leave free plant cuttings on sidewalk corners all over the county—but a lot of it, owing to my expert deflection, is about Remy and Olivia. I find out they're cousins; Remy's mom is the sister of Olivia's mom. Luke's a cousin, too, on the Fanning side, and he and the chef (not a cousin on either side, thankfully) are in what Olivia calls a "not very secret situationship." Remy tells me about wanting to be a large-animal vet, Olivia tells me about the spa, and both of them tell me about how Evan's ex-wife transformed the restaurant's décor into its current modern farmhouse meets seaside cottage aesthetic, which I suspect must be being kept a secret from that lady who runs the antiques store.

And even though there's still the sizzle of that frying pan—especially anytime we veer close to family dynamics that obviously have nothing to do with Levi—I realize, sometime in the middle of stacking chairs, that I'm . . . *enjoying* myself.

I can't quite say that I'm enjoying the actual work I'm doing, since my feet hurt and I smell like seafood and I am definitely going to need to change this mop water, but the time I've spent at The Shoreline has been more connected in spirit to the fic than anything I did in Sott's Mill with Bel. Maybe I mostly wrote about wanting to be close to Evan, but I also clearly saw The Shoreline as a way to be *part* of something, part of a world I didn't have access to when I was younger. And sure, Remy and Olivia and Luke and I have been stretched thin out here all afternoon, but I *have* felt like I was part of a group, more than I often did in the time I spent working for Nadia. In the last couple of years especially, I'd taken on more, had worked mostly alone or only with Nadia herself, and today it's been nice to be on a team, to trade knowing looks as we served and to talk as we've cleaned up. Maybe I need to keep this in mind for what I want, after I go back to—

A throat clears behind me.

It sounds so familiar.

But also, somehow, not.

"Hi, Dad!" Olivia calls from the bar, where she's wrapping silverware.

Levi's dad.

My internal stove burner is turned all the way up.

I turn to face him slowly, getting my serving-plates smile back in place, since this man is technically my boss for the job I have not agreed to do yet. It isn't the first time I've ever seen him, obviously—I used to see him pretty regularly, in fact, in the stands at the Harris County High football games, cheering Evan on enthusiastically. But it is the first time I've seen him since I've met Levi, and it's strange how different he looks to me as a result, how I measure everything about him against the son I hardly knew a thing about less than a week ago. His eyes are the same color as Levi's, and he's almost exactly as tall, though not as broad. He doesn't have a beard, but somehow, the set of his jaw reminds me of Levi, too.

"Cal Fanning," he says, extending a hand to me, and it's strange—it's Levi in the eyes, focused and a little suspicious, and Evan in the smile, easy and charming. "And you are?"

"Dad!" Olivia says, all excitement as she comes to stand by me. "This is Georgie Mulcahy! We told you she might come by today? Well, she did, and she saved our a—"

Okay, maybe *not* Levi in the eyes, since I've never seen him be the language police toward an adult woman before.

"Behinds," Olivia corrects.

"Ah, yes, Georgia," Cal says, which is extremely annoying. Georgie's not short for anything except for my dad's weird nicknames. I shake his hand anyway.

"Hi, Mr. Fanning."

He doesn't ask me to call him Cal, which obviously means

I will only ever privately think of him as *Calvin* or *Calthorpe* or whatever name I decide Cal is short for.

"Your father used to do some work for me," he says.

"Yes!" I say, enthusiastic, as though I'm talking to a drunk mortgage broker. *Calorie. Callous. Calcium.*

"And have my son and daughter managed to convince you to come onboard for a while? As you can see"—he says, gesturing to the room we've been busting our *behinds* to clean for the last hour—"we are very short-staffed."

I can almost hear Remy's eye roll, but I'm too preoccupied, too stuck on the other part of ol' Callow's sentence, to be bothered by the commentary on the dining room.

My son and daughter.

Maybe it shouldn't rankle me the way it does, the exclusivity of it; after all, Evan and Olivia are the only two of Cal's offspring who actually work here. But it's a bell ringing in my brain, that tidy pairing of Evan and Olivia, and all I can think about is Levi—the quiet, gruff way he'd said that he couldn't ever see where he fit. For the first time all day, I let go of the embarrassment over last night and focus instead on the way I'd felt walking up to Levi with Evan's card in my back pocket—like I'd done something wrong by agreeing to come here. Like I'd betrayed him somehow. I swallow, shifting on my aching feet.

I realize I've gone weirdly silent when Cal speaks again. "We could be flexible about your hours. Olivia and Evan mentioned you're in town helping a friend."

"I'm not sure we made the best impression today," Olivia says, looking sheepish.

"You did," I say quickly, because whatever guilt I experience from being around Cal *(Calisthenics, Caliper, Calculate)* Fanning, Olivia has been nothing but kind and hardworking. And anyway, maybe I'm being too harsh, too judgmental. Families are complicated, after all, and I don't know the full story.

I'm only trying to know *my* full story. The one I'm working on telling myself these days. I'm at The Shoreline; it's gone well;

it's taught me something about what I want. It has not, to speak metaphorically, stood still while I tried to kiss it. Probably if I stick around I won't see Calamity Cal that often anyway.

"I had fun," I say, not lying, and Olivia looks thrilled. Mr. Fanning—fine! I'll use the appropriate name!—smiles, Evan-style, and starts talking about paperwork.

And I listen, pretending that part of me isn't still in that frying pan. Pretending I'm not still thinking of Levi out on that back patio, making me pizza and telling me to keep going. Pretending I'm not wondering about him waiting for me to wake up this morning.

And most of all—worst of all—pretending I'm not wondering whether he's been thinking of me, too.

Chapter 10

Levi

"Levi!"

I jerk on my stool, nearly dropping the flask I'd been distract-edly holding up to the light while I waited for Hedi to sort and file the samples I've brought her. By the way she's said my name, she's done with the sorting and filing part, or at least she's been trying to talk to me while she's doing it. Well, she can get in line. I haven't paid close attention to anything anyone's said to me in hours and hours, not since I felt Georgie Mulcahy's body against mine.

Not since I froze in shock. In desperate, confused longing.

Not since I chased her away with my indecision.

I set the flask down gently, because I know better than to fidget with equipment in Hedi's lab. If I'd broken that, she would've had my ass.

I clear my throat. "Sorry, I missed that."

She huffs a sigh, shutting the fridge and turning to face me. "I *said* you brought more than I expected."

"Right. I wasn't building today, just checking on some sites my guys have in progress. Thought I'd take up some extra samples while I was out."

She nods, moving to scribble notes on a clipboard she has on the table where I've been sitting. I've been working with Hedi for a while, collecting water and plant samples from the river, all of them from close to or beneath the docks I've built or repaired. Hedi's research area is underwater grasses in the bay and how they're being affected by algal blooms, which crop up a lot in areas of high development, or wherever there's big recreational marinas. The bay, shallow as it is, can handle this shit even less than the deeper ocean waters that also get more polluted every year, and Hedi's on a mission to get those grasses back in shape. At first I thought it was a pretty specific area, but I've learned over time that most academic shit is real specific. Hedi's got a guy in the office next to her that works on one specific kind of oyster, which he thinks can save the whole bay if there were only enough of them.

I know her eyes are on me, sharp and incisive. She doesn't miss a thing.

"What's the situation with your house?"

"Still a mess," I say, eyeing that flask again. Dang, I want to fidget. I regret leaving Hank in Hedi's office with one of her grad students; he's always a formidable distraction. But no dogs in the lab, that's the rule. "Contractor says a few more days, at least."

Maybe Thursday next week, he'd said this morning when I'd called him from my truck, defeated by Georgie's clear avoidance of me. I'd tried not to groan audibly, thinking about the next six days of staying in the house with her, wanting her the way I do and knowing it'd probably do her no good to know it.

"But you *are* staying at your friend's house, right?"

I pick up the flask again.

"Levi," she scolds, and I set it down. "If you and Hank are sleeping in a truck or a tent, I swear, I'll—"

"We're not."

"Are you staying in a *house?*" she asks, pointedly, because she's like this. Bossy. Unrelenting. Attentive to every detail. I look up at her and she's got her eyes narrowed at me. The back of my neck heats up, remembering the time Hedi caught me sleeping in my truck right here on this campus, because I was too tired to drive the hour back to Darentville after a night class that'd followed a full day of dock surveying work in the rain. I never got yelled at like that in my life, and that's saying something. I'd been twenty-seven years old at the time, well out of the range where I thought I'd ever get another earful from a teacher.

"Yeah, I promise."

Her gaze softens, and she pulls out a stool, sitting across from me at the lab table. It's been five years since that time she caught me out in my truck, and since then Hedi—Professor Farzad to me at the time—and I have become something like friends, or at least something that's more than teacher–student. Once I finished up her class, Hedi asked if I'd be willing to keep working with her sometimes, collaborating on how dock builds can best accommodate those grasses she's trying to save. I'm one of a few watermen in the region she works with on collecting samples, though I get the sense that my having been her student, even if it was for only one class, means she's always treated me different than she does them. In the years I've known her, I've seen how she is with students, and it's not like any kind of thing I ever saw from the teachers I had as a kid. She's always on about "intersections," about how your life outside the classroom or the lab has an impact on what happens in it. That's how she got me seeing that building docks had a lot more to do with marine science than I would've thought initially.

That's also how I can tell she knows something's wrong with me.

"I'm not alone there, though," I say, because I might as well get ahead of it. And Hedi isn't the same as Carlos or Laz or Micah, or anyone I know from town. Hedi is separate from all that, and it's always made it easier to talk to her.

"Oh?"

"The couple whose house it is—their daughter came to town unexpectedly. She lives out in California. Los Angeles."

"What's she like?" Hedi says, pretending to look at her clipboard. I know what she's really doing is making it easier for me to talk.

Funny. Alive. Messy. Impulsive. So pretty I can still see her when I close my eyes at night.

"She's all right."

Okay, it's not *that* easy to talk to her. I'm still me, after all.

"LA, huh? Must be a pretty big change of scenery for her."

I make a noise of assent, and Hedi gives me an annoyed look that I recognize. A couple years back she asked if I'd take a few of her summer interns out with me on my boat to do collection work. I'd done it, no problem, but the next time I'd come to see her she'd made this exact face at me and told me that if I was going to keep taking interns out I had to make at least five minutes of pleasant conversation with them so the kids wouldn't think I was bringing them out on the water to do a murder. I've gotten better, but every one of those kids still makes me feel like I'm a thousand years old.

"She grew up here," I say, "so she's familiar. But yeah, real different from California, I suspect."

Hedi's flipping pages on the clipboard, making a show of being busy.

"What're you testing for this time?" I ask her.

"The usual." She flips another page. "So, are you making a new friend, then?"

I sigh. Talk about the usual. She's always had a real bug up her ass about me being antisocial, and that was even before we became friends. When I took Intro Bio with her, she always said I'd do better if I was more collaborative and communicative, because that's how scientists achieve great things. I'd told her I didn't have any intention of being a scientist, but she said as long as I was in her class, I was one, and I better do the work.

Once I was no longer getting graded by her, she'd ask me what I did other than build docks and bring her water and plant clippings, and I've never had an answer for that. Hedi knows I don't see my family, but she doesn't concern herself with that; once she told me her elderly parents and all three of her siblings are involved in some kind of religious cult out west, and she hasn't talked to any of them in over thirty years.

No, what Hedi concerns herself with is how I haven't done what she's done, which is to make a family of her own, one where blood doesn't matter. Hedi's married to an English professor who lives in Maine, but they're both also in a long-term relationship with a woman named Laura who lives with Hedi full time. During the holidays and over the summers, the three of them live and travel together. Laura's got two kids from her previous marriage, and they're around, too; they call Hedi "Mom" and sometimes Laura's ex-husband comes to Christmas at their house, along with a host of the various friends and neighbors and former students Hedi always invites. Plus, she's got animals out the wazoo over at her place, a motley crew of rescues. I got Hank because of Hedi, though that hasn't quite satisfied her in terms of improving my social life. Or, as she puts it sometimes, "having more meaningful relationships."

"No," I say, more firmly than I intend, because what's one hundred percent clear about last night is that I don't see Georgie Mulcahy as a friend, and I guess she doesn't see me as one, either.

But I don't know the right thing to do about it.

"Oh, I see," she says.

"No, you don't," I mutter, but probably she does. I swear she sees everything. Eyes in the back of her head, same as all teachers, except these ones see the stuff that matters. Not you carving an anarchy symbol into your desk, but you frustrated and heartsore because something you want might not be a good idea for you.

"I'm not sure what you're bothered about, young Levi," she

says, teasing me the way she used to when I was the oldest person on her roster. "Temporary roommate, temporarily in town? That's your sort of thing exactly. No fuss there."

Here's what Hedi doesn't, *can't* see: Georgie Mulcahy is all fuss. I've fussed about her for fucking *days*, and that's to say nothing about the hours I've spent since I didn't kiss her back, miserably replaying that split second where I lost the opportunity to keep her lips against mine. I fuss about her sleeping in the room right beside me. I fuss about the way her laugh sounds. I still fuss about her legs, sure, but now I also fuss about those big eyes and that bright smile, and how she aimed all of them at me on a quiet summer night over a danged citronella candle. I fuss over the way I seem to understand her, fuss over the way it feels like I fit with her, fuss over how I know it can't go anywhere between us.

All right, it's me who's all fuss.

"Levi," she says sternly, obviously frustrated by my silence.

"You know me, Hed. I keep things steady in my life. Simple."

And she's not simple, is the silent implication. *Not for me.*

She gives up with the clipboard, clasping her hands on top of it. "Listen, I've given up on lecturing you about the life you've decided to lead. You build your docks, work on your house, hang out with Hank, do work for me when you can. That's a good life."

"It is a good life," I say, and I mean it. It isn't only that it suits me, that it's quiet and clean and calm and stable. It's that I'm determined to keep it that way. Every year that goes by, I'm doing something: I'm being the Levi Fanning no one in four counties ever thought I could be. The Levi Fanning my father never thought I could be.

"I *said*," she insists, rolling her eyes. "But you know, life is long, if you're lucky. When I finished my postdoc, I applied for jobs all over the country. And you know what? I could see myself at every place I got an interview."

I nudge absently at the flask. This is how she was in class;

she'd start off with some anecdote or quote before winding around—a long way around, if I'm being honest—to the important bit. It was fucking stressful taking notes in her lectures.

"As it turned out, I only got the one offer, and that was lucky, given the state of things. When I first started, I was still always thinking of those other places that didn't pick me. I never thought I'd settle in Virginia, of all places."

I frown across the table at her. I don't see what's so "of all places" about Virginia. Not to be biased, but she could've ended up somewhere worse.

"And now look at me!" She spreads her arms, gesturing to the lab all around her. *Expansive*, I think, because Georgie's moved into my psyche. "I've been here twenty-two years!"

"You wish you weren't?" I'm still in the metaphorical frantic note-taking stage of this whole situation; I've got no idea where she's going with this.

"No, I'm thrilled! What a good job I have. What nice people I've met. But also, it's a job. I like to travel, too, and to try new things. On my last sabbatical I took a trapeze class in New York City! It was wonderful. And then it was wonderful to come back to work, too, you know?"

Not really. Which means she wants me to think about it.

"She's not a trapeze," I say after a few seconds, annoyed.

She snorts. "Yes, I *know* that, Levi. But I'm only saying, having a nice woman in town for a few weeks isn't going to mess up your life. Have some fun. Do something different."

I swallow, pretending like those phrases—*Have some fun. Do something different.*—aren't a little terrifying to me. I don't have a good track record picking fun, or different. I've got a good track record at picking trouble when fun and different are in the mix, and that's why I keep it simple. My dog, my work, my house. No trouble there.

But Georgie's not trouble. Not a trapeze, not trouble, and also, not fuss, either. She's a person. A nice person who I'm attracted to, a person I pushed away all because I got overwhelmed by how strong I feel for her already, and how those feelings don't seem suited to steady and simple.

Hedi and I are quiet, though I suspect her quiet is the kind where she's waiting for someone in the class to raise their hand. She stands and goes to the fridge, rearranging the samples she's got in there. Back when I took Hedi's class—it'd been a whim, an uncharacteristic break from the accounting and management courses Carlos had recommended I take—she'd sometimes ask me whether I'd want to keep going, whether I'd want to work in a lab someday. I'd brush her off, always telling her the same thing. I'd enjoyed what I'd learned, but more school wasn't for me: It was too inside, too far off the water. Maybe it doesn't make a lot of sense, but I think about Georgie again, and the part of me she appeals to. It's the outside part of me, I think. The part that wants to breathe fresh air. The part that wants the movement and noise of nature. When I think of it that way, all I want is to go back to last night, that moment when she stepped into me and gave me a taste of her soft, full lips.

All I want is to hold all her fresh, noisy movement against me. All I want is to taste it, even if it's not simple.

"I better head out," I say, and Hedi smiles at me as if I've put up my hand to participate in the discussion. "Thanks," I add, sheepishly.

She shrugs, as though she doesn't know what I'm thanking her for. "See you in a couple weeks," she says, and I know her well enough to know she means I better have sorted myself by then.

THE DRIVE BACK to Darentville is beautiful—pinks and purples streaking the sky, the air taking a rare break from brutal humidity. Hank's alternating between sticking his snout into the narrow strip of open window on the passenger side and giving me an impatient look for not opening it more, but I can't be letting his ear flap out there in the wind. I get a sense of how he feels, though—excited and frustrated, equal measure.

I give him another inch.

I tap my thumb against the steering wheel, wondering whether Georgie'll be home when I get there. Would it be too repetitive to make dinner again, to light that candle and invite her to sit with me on the back porch? Would it be too much to hope that I could redo the whole night, get another chance to do the end of it differently?

By the time I pull up to the Mulcahys', I've done a fair bit of this kind of thinking—thirty percent about what I ought to cook for her and probably seventy percent about what might happen after. I've even done a good deal of thinking about how I might get her to wear that robe again.

Her car's not in its usual spot, but I don't worry too much over it; I might even see it as an advantage. Time for a shower, time to get something prepped. Hell, I'll set up two candles this time, get more of that glowing light that played over her skin while she ate, more of that flame dancing in her eyes while she looked at me.

At the back door, I fumble with my keys, caught off guard by this nervous anticipation. Part of me thinks it's Hedi's influence—she's a one-woman idea generator, always coming up with some new hypothesis, some new experiment to test it out.

But this anticipation, this excitement . . . I doubt it's the same as coming up with a new idea. I search for a memory of the last time I felt this way, and can't come up with one easily. When Carlos offered me a job? When I signed the papers for the business, or for my house?

No, it's not like any of that, either.

This is something fiercer, more absorbing. Maybe something I've never experienced at all.

Georgie's been here; I see her dishes in the sink and one of her hair ties on the counter. In front of the couch, a pair of her shoes lie haphazardly on the floor, as if she toed them off right there. I picture her bare feet and bare legs, curled up while she maybe took a nap there.

Come home, I think, with all that fierce anticipation stirring in me.

I'm headed toward the shower when my phone chirps in my pocket, and automatically, instinctively, anticipation shrinks into disappointment. I slide it from my back pocket, and Hank sniffs at my hand, as though he's got that sense about things, too.

I'm going to stay at my friend Bel's tonight. I can be back early tomorrow, though, if you need me to watch Hank! Hope you had a good day.

I stare down at the phone, feeling like my hands have slipped off a trapeze bar, but I shake it off quick, reach down to pat Hank's flank, make my body physically unbothered even as I wrestle down the disappointment.

No need, I type, once I've got myself under control again. **Thanks for checking.**

I put my phone on silent and toss it onto the couch.

And when I head to the shower, I try to tell myself that this isn't disappointment, after all.

I try to tell myself it's relief.

Chapter 11

Georgie

"Now that I'm thinking about this . . ."

"Harry," I say, trying to keep the irritation out of my voice, "Do *not* say it."

He goes quiet for a half second, then clears his throat. I don't look over at him.

"It's only that—"

"Honey," Bel interrupts him. "Why don't you go wait in the car?"

He doesn't answer, but actually maybe he does; he and Bel are probably doing the kind of silent married-people communication that makes this moment all the worse. It's pretty much the same kind of communication they did when I showed up unexpectedly after my shift at The Shoreline, desperate not to go home yet. Desperate enough to have dealt with these sorts of looks all evening, especially when—after insisting on working on the junk room—I asked if I could stay over.

Because I am a coward. An embarrassed, still-guilt-ridden coward.

When I finally glance their way, I can see Harry's still wrestling with himself. It's eight o'clock on a Saturday morning and he is wearing an unwrinkled blue linen button-up, which is why I am definitely going to pull the trigger on donating all those old T-shirts. I guess except for the one I'm wearing, which I borrowed this morning. I enjoy the way it makes me appear as a person who runs long distances for pleasure.

"Agree," I say gently. "Wait in the car."

He sighs, giving one more long, suspicious look at the water surrounding the Buzzard's Neck dock, but I ignore him. I may have been a coward last night, but I am not going to be one this morning.

At least not about the fic.

"Fine, but I'm going to be watching." He turns to Bel. "You're not going in, right?"

"Definitely not!" she says, patting her belly. When he walks away she makes an annoyed face but also a dreamy, in-love face. "He's so protective."

With Harry gone, I breathe easier. I love the guy, but I don't think he understands the notebook, which is fair enough but also a little lowering, especially since he's tried, ever since Bel and I told him about it last night, to be supportive. When I'd announced that next on my list was Buzzard's Neck, he'd said, "I'll drive you two." I hadn't wanted to turn him down, especially since I'd known already that for Bel, Buzzard's Neck would be a spectator event. At least this way, she wouldn't be left totally behind.

I slip off my old Birkenstocks.

"The thing is," Bel says, "Harry *might* have a point."

"Not you too," I groan.

"I mean! Now that we're here, I'm kind of wondering! Maybe this is one of those things that would *only* be fun for a teenager?"

I gust out a sigh and rub at my tired eyes, taking in my surroundings. Buzzard's Neck looks a lot worse for wear than when we were kids, unless my memory is faulty. Back then, it had an air of mystery about it, a plot of land where there was nothing much besides an abandoned farmhouse and this dock. What made it appealing was that it had a pretty much perfect cove of water, clear and protected, a wishing well for your body. The farmhouse might not be all that different looking— still dilapidated—but the water's lost its crystalline quality. I wouldn't say it's murky, exactly, but I wouldn't say it'd make your dreams come true, either.

"I'm doing it," I tell her, because last night, lying in the probably three million thread count sheets of Bel's guest room bed, my lower back aching from my unexpected shift, staying on top of the list had felt . . . *insistent.* I had a win at The Shoreline, whatever my lingering misgivings about Levi had been, and I needed to stay focused, stay confident. I'd do Buzzard's Neck, and then I'd be ready to go back to my parents' place. Fully set back on my new path of no-more-blankness, with absolutely no distractions.

Bel's quiet beside me, and I think she's given up on trying to talk me out of it. But then she says, "Teenagers probably don't think about brain-eating amoebas."

"*What?*"

"You know, the . . . amoebas. That get into people's brains, from water."

"From this water?"

Bel shrugs. "I don't see why not this water."

"You built a *house* on this water!"

She chews her lip. "*This* water is different, though."

I roll my eyes. "I'm not going to be in there long. Hand me the Sharpie."

She hesitates. "I think amoebas move fast."

"Oh my God, Bel."

"I'm only *saying.*"

I breathe through an unexpectedly sharp pulse of annoyance, vague memories nudging at the edge of my brain. Why was it that we never got around to doing Buzzard's Neck back then? Was it stuff like this, worries over microscopic brain eaters? Was it Bel having too much homework, or Bel not wanting to lie to her mom?

I hold out my hand, palm up, making a curt *give it over* gesture. She sighs and takes the Sharpie out of her purse.

"Okay," she says, her voice softer as she passes it to me, and I can tell she's chastened. "What was this one all about, then?"

I take a breath, hoping that gunky smell isn't amoebas. "Magic, maybe?" I know I'm not quite capturing it. "Taking a risk for something I wanted, maybe, even if it was something silly."

Bel nods. "Okay. So, wish on your arm, and then you jump in, yeah?"

"Yep." I tap the Sharpie against my wrist. I'm thinking about what I'll write when she speaks again.

"Don't be mad."

I look over at her. She's shifting her weight back and forth between her feet, and I know what's coming.

"I'm not going to be mad," I say, resigned.

"I have to pee."

I groan.

"I'm sorry! It's the sound! All this water, you know?"

I heave another sigh, tucking the marker into the pocket of my shorts. "All right. We'll go back home."

She looks affronted. "Are you kidding? I won't make it back home." She gestures back toward the copse of trees, near where Harry's parked. "I'll go over there."

"Bel, you cannot pee in the woods! How are you going to lecture me about brain-eating amoebas and then drop trou in the woods?"

She shrugs. "My bladder doesn't listen to arguments; it has no fear! My bladder is a teenager."

"Fine, go pee." I take out the marker again, uncap it. "I'll think of what to write."

"Do not jump in there before I get back. Georgie, I swear, do *not*."

"I won't." I'm a strong swimmer, and none of the water around here is all that deep, but now I'm also nervous about amoebas, not that Bel's going to be able to do anything about those.

Soon enough, she's gone the way of Harry, and I wonder if on her way to pee she'll stop and give him a married-people look through the windshield. I move farther down the dock, toward the edge of where I'll eventually jump, and hook my left arm, turning it so the pale, lightly freckled expanse of my forearm faces up. I hold the Sharpie poised over the surface, but I'm stumped. For kids, the point of this tradition wasn't to wish for the big, important things; no one came to Buzzard's Neck to write "WORLD PEACE" on their arm before plunging in. People wrote things like "Making cheer team" or "New F-150 for my 16th." It's not difficult to think of what I would've written back then—it definitely would've had to do with Evan, who I'll probably be serving food alongside sometime this week, and who I have no wishes for other than a new hiring strategy for his family's restaurant.

I consider doing a wish for Bel's baby, something about climate change or universal health care, but that's world peace adjacent, and anyway, it's not a wish about me. I need the grown-up equivalent of wishing for a specific date to prom.

Annoyingly, I think of Levi. That dark beard and that quirk in his cheek when he smiles. The way he looks at me, at least when I haven't just kissed him. The fic I could write about that look alone . . .

I close my eyes, trying to shut out the thought.

"Hey!"

At first I think I might be having some kind of auditory hallucination brought on by thoughts of him, or maybe by a brain-eating amoeba that got to me through the air. But then I hear it again, a sharp, urgent, *"Hey!"* and I know I'm not hallucinating that.

"Levi?" I say, opening my eyes and seeing him in the near distance—him *and* Hank—in a small johnboat that's the same olive-green color as Levi's ball cap. I'm surprised enough that I forget for a second all about my embarrassment. I smile and raise my hand to wave enthusiastically, wholly delighted by the coincidence of finding them here.

"Get off of there!" he yells, and I look around, as though he could be talking to someone else, but it's still definitely only me here. Okay, I don't own this dock, but neither does he. I know I've heard rumors about Levi Fanning trespassing once upon a time, to say nothing of the time he barged into my house while I was in my soap opera robe. I cock a hip against the nearest piling, crooking my arm again. Maybe I'll make my wish something about this man not intruding on my moments of personal discovery anymore.

"Georgie!" he calls again, and I can see he's redirected his boat my way. Hank barks happily, and I can't ignore that, especially because he's wearing a bright yellow doggie life jacket. That's about the most darling thing I've ever seen.

"Hi, buddy!" I call to him, waving again, too enthusiastic, and—huh. This piling is kind of unstab—

"I told you to *wait*," calls Bel from behind me, at the same time Levi yells my name, and also at the same time Hank barks again, and it's all a bit chaotic, overwhelming. I turn to face Bel, the boards beneath my feet rocking a little.

"Wait!" I call to her, holding up a hand, aware that I've either disrupted something on this dock or didn't notice that it was already disrupted. "Don't come out. I'm coming back, okay?"

She stops where she is. "Oh yikes, is it bad?" She looks past me. "Hey, who is—"

I'm not quite sure I could say for sure what happens next—if my turning to face Bel got me closer to the edge than I thought, if that board rocking threw me off balance—but in a split second I'm falling back, the Sharpie in my hand, and before I hit the colder-than-expected water I hear Bel's yelp of surprise, Hank's bark, and the low rumble of Levi's boat engine.

And it *is* murky under here—murky and . . . planty, slick tangles beneath my feet and along my calves. The me who grew up swimming in this river should be ashamed, but I kick frantically, disoriented by how dark it seems under here. Something sharp drags across my shin, and that only makes me jerk and kick harder toward the surface. Ridiculously, I remember the Sharpie, and I twist my body clumsily as though I'm trying to reach for it. When I finally emerge, my hair is in my eyes and I'm coughing, one arm raised awkwardly in the air, and oh man. That has to be the worst entry into the water off Buzzard's Neck in history, nowhere near the joyful, triumphant, running-start cannonball I'd written about in the fic.

I swipe the hair from my eyes and the first person I see is Bel, still in her spot right at the start of the dock, Harry coming to join her, and for some reason, it's so funny all of a sudden—me treading water here and her standing there, her mouth in a perfect O of shock that transforms into a smile, and then we're both laughing, at least for a few seconds, until Bel's face grows serious again. I don't have much time to wonder why, because before I know it I'm being picked up—firm, rough hands beneath my armpits, lifting me in a straight shot out of the water, and oh my goodness, Levi is *strong*, and within a second I'm in his *boat*, and Hank is barking and full-body wagging in his delightful jacket, licking at my face, and I can't help it—I'm laughing again.

"Oh my God," I say, breathless. "This is *ridiculous*."

"You're goddamn right it is!" Levi shouts.

I push myself up, craning my neck to get out of the line of Hank's lapping excitement and into the line of my roommate's inappropriate anger.

"Hey," I say, annoyed now. "I *can* swim, you know! You didn't have to come get me!"

"What were you doing on that dock?" His voice is still raised, rough.

"Georgie?" Bel calls from the shore. She takes a step forward, and Harry halts her with a hand on her arm.

"Georgie?" he echoes. I don't see how his technique is any more effective than Bel's, but whatever.

I point at my angry rescuer. "This is Levi."

I look over at him, waiting for him to acknowledge Bel and Harry, but he doesn't. He's looking at me, madder than milk-shake face, his jaw set and his eyes alight. For the first time it truly hits me that I am soaking wet, and that Harry's marathon T-shirt is mostly white, and also, I am . . . chilly.

I cross my arms over my chest.

"Oh!" calls Bel. "Well, it's nice to meet you, Levi! I've heard a lot about you!"

I silently thank past Georgie for being too embarrassed to tell Bel about the kiss. The not-kiss, whatever.

Levi makes a face, as though he cannot possibly imagine how this happened to him this morning.

"What. Were. You. Doing," he repeats.

"Early-morning swim," I scoff, because I am *not* bringing up the notebook again, not after the other night. No! Levi Fanning gets no more of my secrets, not after he passed on the . . . the secret of my mouth, I guess.

"This is one of your journal things." It's not a question.

Annoying. I cross my arms tighter against me, a determined nonanswer, and he sighs. He reaches beneath the seat he's on and pulls out a thin windbreaker, handing it over.

"Was it?" he asks again, once I take it from him.

"I'm fine swimming back to shore on my own," I say, zipping into it. It stings my pride, but then again, so do my erect nipples. The windbreaker is the lesser of two pride-destroying evils.

"You ought to have asked around. No kids have jumped off this dock in years. Because it's in shitty condition, which you apparently didn't notice. You could've done your damn wish somewhere safer."

"Hey!" I say, the only comeback I can think of for his scolding rudeness. I remember the way Calculus Fanning gave that silent reprimand to Olivia yesterday at The Shoreline; it's clear that Levi and his estranged father have something in common. But before I can dwell too much on the comparison, my interest is piqued in another direction. "You know about the Buzzard's Neck wishes?"

"I grew up here, too, remember?"

"Georgie?" Bel calls again, and when I look over at her and Harry, I can tell they've been watching us with interest.

"Are you all right?" Harry says.

"I'm f—"

"I can take her back to my truck, give her a ride back home," Levi says, for the first time acknowledging that there are other people here. "If you don't want a swamp thing in your car."

I open my mouth to object, but Bel smiles and says, "Really? That would be great, actually."

"Hey!" I repeat. I give Bel a narrow-eyed look of censure, but she only shrugs, looking apologetic. She *is* particular about that car.

"Plus she's bleeding," Levi adds, annoyed, and for the first time I look down to see a thin line of dark red blood running down my shin.

"You probably caught a nail." He mutters something I don't catch about "half-done repairs," and then says, "Hope you've got a tetanus shot."

"I do," I snap, but I will definitely have to check on that later.

He reaches forward, his arm brushing against my bare leg as he grabs for something beneath my seat. His skin, even from that fleeting touch, is deliciously warm. I scoot closer to where Hank stands beside me.

Levi hands me a small kit. "First aid in here. Hank, sit."

"Georgie, you're really all right?" Bel calls again, and this time, I know she's looking for me to confirm it—that her shrugging, leave-me-with-Levi nonchalance needs my permission to truly go forward. I look over there, and it's Bel in a pretty cream-colored maxi dress and Harry in his blue linen button-up, and I do not want to swim over there to them, river-ragged and bleeding, only to get driven in a spotless BMW to the same place Levi is going. I don't even want to imagine the married-people, *poor Georgie* looks they'll give each other the whole way home.

"I'm fine," I call back, and she promises to drop off my phone and purse later. When she and Harry turn to go, Levi maneuvers his boat toward the dock and stands, giving me a view of those steady legs he mentioned back on that first night we had dinner. When he gets close enough, he leans forward and swipes my Birks off the dock, tossing them back into the boat before pivoting to steer us expertly back out into the cove.

All in all, that was a very impressive display, and my backward, probably-pinwheeling fall into the water now seems all the more clumsy.

I concentrate on cleaning my cut—it's narrow and shallow, probably not even worth a bandage—and eventually all I can focus on is the heavy silence, the way that we have nothing to say to each other now that I'm not in perceived danger of drowning. He's probably over there hoping I won't kiss him again.

Still, I can't stand it, this quiet.

"So, what did you wish for?" I ask, filling the space between us.

"What?"

"When you did this. When you jumped off Buzzard's Neck."

"I didn't say I did it."

Right. Too cool for this tradition, probably. Troublemaking, couldn't-see-where-he-fit Levi, not the type to do what the other kids did.

He shifts on his seat. "I probably would've wished for a boat," he says, voice low. "A canoe or something. I really wanted a boat of my own back then."

I look up at him, even though he keeps his eyes on the water. "Nice," I say, my stubborn heart tripping over itself.

"What about you?" It's a peace offering. His color was high when he first got me into his boat and got to shouting, but it's evened out now, along with his breath.

"I didn't get to it," I say, lifting my arms and miming my clumsy splash. But then I look back down at my shin, concentrating on not showing the disappointment that I'm sure has crept into my expression. All things considered, it's a lousy omen, failing at Buzzard's Neck. I couldn't even think of anything I wanted for the arm-writing exercise.

"I'm sorry," Levi says.

"About manhandling me into your boat?"

His cheek quirks. "No, about you not getting to do your wish."

I shrug. "It's all right. It probably wasn't a good choice anyway. Bel couldn't participate."

He nods and steers us back toward a straightaway. The sun's brighter out here, the water sparkling and fresh-smelling now. I used to love this about living around here, the way the river had these temperamental facets, the matter of a few feet making a big difference in the water you'd be meeting.

"What brought you out here this early?" I ask him.

His color picks up again.

"Just needed to get out on the water for a bit. Didn't sleep well."

"With the house all to yourself?"

I say it in a joking way, but when he looks at me, it doesn't feel like a joke. It feels like he's answering me, like he's saying, *Because it was all to myself.* Obviously, I'm not trying to get caught misreading this man's face again, but it's hard not to. It's hard not to notice the way he looks at my mouth again before his gaze travels back up to my eyes.

If I had the Sharpie, I know what I'd write now. No hesitation.

"Georgie," he says, and this time, I don't think it's pity. It sounds like heat and want, like a delicious shudder up my spine.

He's leaned so close to me.

I'm the barest inch from him before I remember it—before I remember that the reason I didn't go home last night wasn't only my embarrassment over kissing him. It was something else, too, and all of a sudden I'm cold and wet and messy again, and I speak before I can think better of it.

"Your father offered me a job."

AT FIRST, I THINK seriously about diving back into the river.

It's the better alternative to the look on Levi's face, which transforms from hot to cold in a split second. Back in LA, I used to lament the hipster trend of facial hair on local guys, hating the way it seemed to obscure their expressions. But with Levi, there's no such problem. His beard *communicates*.

Right now, it is communicating that I have, in fact, betrayed him.

"It's part of why I didn't come home last night," I say, which, *ugh*. I've always had this penchant for disclosure when I'm pressed. Probably every detention or bad grade I had in school was the result of this sort of thing. *That's my note, Mr. Zerelli. I honestly forgot all about the project, Ms. Harrison. Yes, I did cut holes in my gym uniform, Coach Wymouth, but in fairness it is because I don't want to do gym today, or ever.*

But I'm in it now, and Levi's beard is maybe saying, *You're dead to me.*

"I mean, that and the kiss!" I add, fully rambling. "Which I needed some distance from, obviously. Not as much as you, I'm sure! But the thing with the job, I knew it might make you uncomfortable, and I already felt guilty because I hadn't even told you that I ran in to your brother and sister . . ."

Something in Levi's eyes shifts, and the beard gets less angry looking.

"At the antiques place?" I continue, holes in my gym uniform everywhere. "They were looking for stuff for the—"

He clears his throat. He doesn't want to hear about what they were looking for.

"Anyway, they're having staffing issues in the restaurant at The Shoreline, especially with servers, and, you know, I used to be a waitress, so . . ."

I trail off, because *wow*, it is *quiet* out here. It's just me and Levi and this awful, transformed tension, and Hank's panting, and I have no idea how to finish my sentence. *So I said yes, because as it turns out your family's inn was part of that notebook project I told you about? I said yes because it was your brother who asked me first, and he's all over that notebook, too? I said yes because I'm a mess, always a mess, and I still don't know what I'm* doing *here?*

Finally, he breaks the silence and, honestly, breaks my heart a little while he's at it.

"They doing all right?" I almost don't hear him. His voice is like the river—barely a ripple. "My brother and sister?"

I look at him for a long time. He seems braced against whatever answer I'm about to give him.

"They seem fine." It's the most neutral answer I can think of. I don't want to say all the things that pinged around in my head about their closeness. I don't want to say that they're roommates who watch movies together. I don't want to say, *Did you know your brother's been through a divorce?* or *Did you know your sister runs the day spa?* What if I said any of those things and ended up breaking Levi's heart a little, too?

He doesn't do anything other than nod. Hank stands from his spot next to me and takes a few unsteady steps before settling in a lopsided sit between Levi's spread legs. Levi drops a hand and strokes absently at Hank's good ear, and goodness. Maybe it's a brain amoeba, but I think I might cry. It's such a familiar, automatic gesture between this man and his dog. Sweetly codependent.

"I don't have to do it. The job."

As soon as I say it, I'm annoyed with myself. Why should it

matter how Levi feels about me taking a waitressing job? I'm one for three on my fic efforts after today's bungled outing; I'd be ridiculous to give up the only thing that has a semblance of working out so far.

"You should do it," he says, before I can take back my offer. "If you want, I mean. I'm sure it's a good gig."

Obviously, I don't need his permission, but I don't think he meant it that way. I think he meant it the same way he meant what he said the other night, that I should *keep going with it.* We lapse into strained silence again. The chill from the river is down to my bones now, and I know I smell like the stagnant Buzzard's Neck water. It's probably a good thing I blurted my confession to him at a critical moment; now he can have a reason other than my river stink for not kissing me.

"Georgie," Levi says, that low ripple again, and I look toward him, hating the way the sound of it warms me automatically, hating the way it fills me up.

"Yeah?"

I'm the one bracing now. What if he tells me that it's going to be a hotel for him after all? What if he tells me that I *did* betray him, but he can't even explain why, since he won't tell me anything about the family he never speaks to, and that seems to never speak of him?

"I could do some of your list with you," he says.

I could not be more shocked.

"What?"

"The stuff your friend can't do. I could do some of it with you. If you wanted."

"Really?"

He lifts one shoulder. "It's like I said. Might be all right, to go back on some things."

I'm blinking through my surprise, watching him watch the water. I don't know for sure why Levi's offering—if he's worried I'll fall off a hundred more docks before this thing is over, or if he's got a secret store of whimsy that he's showing only to me.

But I realize it doesn't much matter. What matters is how *I* want to experience the fic, and for some reason, I really, *really* like the idea of experiencing some of it with Levi.

"Okay," I say.

He nods, but he doesn't look at me when he adds, "I'd go back to the other night, for example. When you kissed me."

"You would?" I say, which he might not even hear, because I'm pretty sure I basically . . . breathe it. I've never wished for a time machine to a Thursday night more in my life. I'm flushed all over, practically vibrating against this uncomfortable seat.

He looks at me now—mouth, eyes, mouth again, his gaze warm and focused.

"I would," he says, his voice gruff. "We're on a boat with my dog between us and you're cold and soaked through, and I've got overtime work at two build sites today. But maybe sometime after that, you'd let me go back."

"Uh," I say, because this man sure knows how to make a sexy time machine type of offer. "I would."

His lips curve up, and I'm pretty sure that's because I must be beaming at him, waterlogged and stinking and smiling.

I may not have gotten to make my wish, but I have the sense one came true anyway.

"Pick something from your list for us," he says. "And then we'll go back together."

Chapter 12

Levi

It's days before we get to go back.

By Wednesday night, I'm starting to wonder whether my Saturday morning sighting of Georgie was a mirage, same as I thought it was when I first spotted her out on the rickety edge of Buzzard's Neck dock—wearing those ragged cut-off shorts and an old T-shirt, bathed in perfect morning light. After all, I'd gone out on the water to try to clear my head, having spent the whole night before thinking about her—tossing and turning with the knowledge that she wasn't asleep in the next room, that I might've missed my chance.

I've been tossing and turning pretty much every night since, waiting for that chance to come around again.

Worrying over it coming around again.

When I dropped Georgie off at home on Saturday and headed out to my first job site of the day, I figured I'd be seeing her again soon—that night even—and I think she'd figured the same. It'd been why we'd both seemed to silently agree to not start anything until we could do it right—when one of us didn't have to get to work and another one of us didn't have a fair bit of soggy plant life tangled in her hair.

But neither of us counted on the call Georgie got later that day—her friend from the dock was having contractions, too-soon type of contractions, and Georgie had spent the night at the regional medical center about forty-five minutes outside of town. By Sunday morning, things were settled enough for Annabel to be discharged, the problem mostly being Braxton-Hicks, but also an elevated blood pressure that needed to be watched. Georgie had come home only long enough to do some quick, frantic packing. The plan was for her to stay at her friend's place for the next few nights, since the husband was headed out of town on business, and Annabel had insisted he not cancel his trip.

Since I'm not an asshole, I'm not resenting anyone for a medical problem, or for being the kind of friend Georgie is, stepping in where she's needed. And Georgie's been texting me every day, checking on how I'm doing with Hank, whose staples will be coming out any day now. Sometimes she texts me with other things, too—funny updates about setting up her bedridden friend's videoconferences; pictures of high school memorabilia findings from some storage room she's sorting through; a long, multi-text story about trying to get Ernie Nickel's strawberry milkshake recipe over the phone. It's more text messages from one person than I've ever gotten in my life, and I can't say as I mind them, even if half the time I've got no idea how to respond.

But they're not the same as seeing her, as hearing her. They're not the same as having her close.

And the time on my own hasn't done me any favors.

"Come on, pal," I call to Hank, who's been working on chewing at an antler in the living room while I've been cleaning up the kitchen. Every night we've been here alone, Hank and I have taken to going back out into the yard after dinner, where he gets some face time with that rooster and I get to work on

154 • *Kate Clayborn*

distracting myself with stuff Paul Mulcahy's not been tend-
ing to. Tonight I've got a mind to get after one of those rotted
planter boxes, and once Hank settles in front of his gigantic
bird friend, I start in on pulling rusty nails, wishing my mind
was as simple as my dog's.

It isn't that I'm regretting the offer I made to Georgie as she
sat across from me in my boat, sopping wet and struggling hard
against her own vulnerability. The truth is, I'd make that same
offer ten thousand times over if I could see her smile at me that
way again. It's more that without getting started on it—without
making that offer to do her list, *to go back*, into a solid reality—
I've instead been thinking about the reason I made it.

It'd started simple, or at least as simple as anything gets when
it comes to the way I feel about Georgie Mulcahy. There I'd
been in my boat, only Hank for company, thinking for a second I was seeing the sort of mirage that made my chest ache
with longing. Then the mirage—Georgie, real-life Georgie—
stumbled and fell into the water, and fuck the ache.

I'd thought my whole entire heart had stopped.

Maybe I'd done too much, pulling her out of the water as if
she were a rag doll, as if she couldn't swim herself, but I panicked at the thought of her under there, too close to that old
dock, and all I could think about was getting her out. As soon
as I had her across from me, as soon as I'd had a good look at
her—eyelashes all tangled together, drops of water magnifying
the freckles on her cheeks, her soaked hair so dark it almost
looked burgundy—my heart had gotten going again, and it
started beating out one word to me.

Mine, mine, mine.

I yank at a board I've loosened, grunting with the effort.
Hank looks over at me like I've lost the plot, and that's fair
enough.

See, I maybe could've handled that *mine* if it'd stayed that
simple—me wanting her, me giving in to wanting her. But then

Georgie mentioned my father offering her a job at The Shoreline, and I thought I might grab on to the gunwales and tear apart my own boat with my bare hands. If I'd thought that *mine* was the beat of my heart before, it suddenly became my whole entire brain.

Don't take her from me, I'd thought, a fire kicking up in my belly, which is pretty much how I feel when anything about my family comes up.

It's fucked up, and I know it is.

But I sure didn't stop it.

Instead I'd asked her if I could do her list with her. If I could do *more* than the list with her.

I pull off the rotted board and toss it on the pile I've been making the last couple of nights. Eventually I'll add it to the stack of scrap Paul's got behind his shed, which is in real desperate need of sorting.

I've been kicking around this pebble of guilt ever since I knew Georgie wasn't coming home on Saturday, but it's transformed into something heavier, and I know that's because she's not over at Annabel's anymore. In fact, she's at The Shoreline, working her first official dinner shift, and then—since Annabel's husband got back this afternoon—she's coming here. I should be focusing on that second part, the she's-coming-here part, but instead I'm thinking about her at the inn, probably making friends with Ev and Liv, probably charming the hell out of my parents. Moving around in spaces where I never fit.

So, yeah, I've lost the plot. Bad enough I'm halfway to boat-destroying over a woman I barely knew existed before last week. I don't want to add to the mess by getting Georgie near the old wounds I've got from my family, and more than once I've thought about packing up my shit and leaving to spare her from it. It'd be all right to do now; the contractor called me today to say I had running water at my place again, that his team would be wrapping up work tomorrow.

But if I think about the way she smiled at me? If I think about how happy she looked when I asked to do the list with her, as if I was the missing piece to this whole thing? I know her first couple of efforts at it haven't worked out, know they've both been as rickety and uneven as that dock, and I—well, that's what I *do* these days. I make things sturdy; I make them stable.

So maybe I *am* the missing piece; maybe I fit right in. And don't I want that chance with her again, for as long as she's here?

I'm arguing with myself about this shit, about to hack away at this terrible box again, when Hank stirs from his rooster watching, first raising his head from his paws and then standing and shaking himself out, his tail starting to go. Even after not seeing her for a few days, it's clear he has a real thing for Georgie, and I guess that's another way me and this dog are two peas in a pod.

I keep my head down as her car pulls in and shuts off, still struggling with myself. Maybe when she gets out of the car, I'll know the right thing to do. She'll probably have a uniform from The Shoreline on, and that'll as good as destroy me.

But of course it doesn't go that way; it goes the same as having her across from me all wet inside my boat. She gets out of her car and I don't notice if she's got a uniform on or not. I notice how Hank runs to her, and I notice how she says "Hi, buddy!" while she bends to pet him as he huffs and preens under her attention. I notice how it feels to be out here waiting for her, because that's what I was doing, fussing with the planter boxes. I notice how it's natural, the kind of homecoming I never pictured for myself.

I want to take it for every single second I can.

I straighten and make my way over to her, brushing my hands off on my jeans as I step beneath the carport. Good thing I wasn't sweating too much yet, but I probably smell like bug spray, which sucks. I try not to think about it.

"Hey."

"Hi," she says, tentative, and I wonder if in spite of all those freewheeling texts she's been sending me, she's been wondering about all this, too. She looks past me toward the planter boxes. "Doing a project?"

"Yeah. They're rotted all to hell."

She shrugs, as if it's expected, and I guess it is. Even in the days we spent around each other last week I got the sense that Georgie's kind of an improviser when it comes to her living situation. Before I fixed it last night, the toaster in the kitchen wouldn't work unless you held the lever down for the whole time your bread was in there, and she never seemed to mind at all. She'd stand there with her finger on the tab and talk to Hank. She's used to her mom and dad's way of doing things; she's like them herself. Flexible, welcoming. Fun.

Of course that's when I notice the uniform, though, which is pretty much the opposite of fun. She's got The Shoreline shirt tucked into slim-cut, cropped black pants, and since Georgie Mulcahy doesn't strike me as the tucked-in type, I hate the way it looks. I don't realize the way my eyes are roaming over her until I get to her bare feet, and she wiggles her toes self-consciously.

"I took them off in the car," she says. "I forgot what it felt like, to be on my feet for that long."

She looks at me cautiously, as if she's testing me. Seeing whether she's stepped on a mine by bringing up where she's been.

But those bare feet have sunk into me. Maybe she couldn't step on anything with those.

"How was it?" I ask, as if this job is the one she goes to every day. As if I'm the one who welcomes her home from it.

She shrugs. "Busy. Kind of fun, in that way restaurants can be. Tiring."

I nod again, looking down at where Hank's sat on one of her feet. "You must want to sleep."

She doesn't say anything, not until I raise my eyes to hers again.

"I don't," she finally says, giving me boat-eyes, and my heart's saying *Mine*, same as it did then. She turns back to her car, bending down to fish something out of the passenger seat. I try not to look at her ass, but it's right there. That uniform isn't so bad.

When she comes up, she's holding a brown paper bag, weighted down, and she's blowing a wayward strand of hair out of her eyes. If that's takeout from The Shoreline, she's got to know I don't want it.

I must have a look on my face, because her own transforms, her eyes taking on a wary cast.

"I thought you wanted to do this," she says, a note of disappointment in her voice. "My list?"

I realize then that I don't ever want to disappoint this woman. I'll eat that food even if my father himself cooked it.

"I do." Probably it sounds too heavy for the occasion, like I'm making a different sort of vow to her. "I didn't figure—with all the time since Saturday—"

"I still want to," she blurts. "The list, and . . . to, you know, go back."

"All right." I'm not sure if it's the heart part of me that's saying *Mine* right now, but I didn't miss the way she mentioned her list first. I can wait to go back, if she wants. I've waited since Saturday, after all. "What're we doing tonight then?"

She gives me that smile again, and I'm helpless against it.

"Well, Levi," she says, hoisting the bag. "It's got to do with this here hard cider."

IT TAKES some negotiating.

In the first place, when she tells me this list item requires a horror film, I've got to tell her that zombies cannot be on the agenda, because I'm afraid of zombie shit and I'm man enough to admit it. She laughs and agrees to no zombies but says in exchange I can't ever close my eyes during the movie she does end up picking, no matter what, and that's because the point is to experience the whole thing.

After that we negotiate over the snacks, because Georgie tells me she hasn't eaten since lunch, and that's why she picked up a gigantic box of Junior Mints when she bought the hard cider. No matter what Georgie says, I can't agree that a box of candy counts as a meal, so while she gets a quick shower to wash off her shift, I heat up the leftovers from my dinner, then I sit with her while she eats them, her mouth half-full most of the time as she tells me about how much better Annabel is, about how they did three craft projects for the nursery and cleaned out the photo library in Annabel's phone. I pretty much pay attention to all of it, but also, she came out of the bathroom with that robe on again, loosely tied over a pair of sweat shorts and another one of those tank tops that's been sent to murder me. I probably miss a few things.

And I'm sure I miss more than a few things once the movie gets started, including a good number of people getting murdered by things other than tank tops. After all my fussing over the last few days about this, I'm surprised by how easy it is—how I'm comfortable on this too-small couch, even if I've got to prop a leg up on the coffee table; how I don't mind the taste of this overly sweet hard cider I've managed only a half bottle of; how I like to hear Georgie's periodic squeaks and gasps of surprise when something on-screen scares her. She's got herself smooshed all the way on the other side of the couch, her knees pulled tight to her chest, and every once in a while I'll catch her breaking the rule she set for me—squeezing her eyes closed up tight before opening them again, sending me a guilty, exasperated look. I ask her twice if she wants to quit, but she only shakes her head and takes another sip of her cider.

It's real fucking cute.

There's something sweet about watching this movie with her, and that's because I never had this kind of night—sitting in the dark at a girl's parents' house, pretending to watch a movie while I think about how much I want to kiss her. By the time I was old enough to be interested in girls, I was the kind of kid parents didn't want in their houses, no matter my pedigree. I feel like I'm fifteen years old, so I'm starting to think there's some kind of magic about Georgie's list and how well it works at going back.

"Oh no, oh no," Georgie says, squeaky again, and this time she doesn't slam her eyes shut. Instead she scrambles for the remote, spilling cider on her top and the robe in the process, but I don't think she notices. When she's got it in her hand, she's pressing buttons hard and haphazard, not having much success at stopping the movie at all. I reach out and take it from her, ignoring the brush of her soft hand on mine.

I turn the remote the right way around and press pause.

"That what you wanted?" I say, trying to keep the laugh out of my voice.

"Oh my God," she says, dropping her head back and placing a hand over her chest. I can see it rising and falling quickly, and suddenly this is no longer easy. Her head thrown back, her breathing hard . . .

It puts me in the mind of things other than movie watching.

"This is *stressful*," she adds, laughing at herself and rubbing that hand on her chest back and forth, as though trying to soothe her heartbeat.

Mine, mine, mine, I think, like an animal.

I sit forward and set my hard cider on the coffee table, concentrating on the sound of Hank in the other room. He went to bed a half hour ago, huffing in annoyance at me, and Georgie teased me about how I was staying up past my bedtime. Hearing his gusty dog-snore at least brings me back to my own humanity.

"You think you could've handled this in high school?" I ask her, gesturing at the screen, now that I've got a semblance of control again.

She laughs again. "Probably not. I would've pretended for Bel and then I wouldn't have slept for three weeks."

I lean back again, but things have changed in the couch environment—now that the movie's paused, Georgie's un-wound herself, stretching her legs out so that the tips of her bare toes graze along the outside of my thigh when I settle in. This would absolutely count as an erotic experience for a fifteen-year-old.

I clear my throat, desperate for a distraction. "Somehow I figured you'd be pretty immune to movie magic."

She furrows her brow in confusion.

"Because you worked in movies, I mean."

She nods, wiggling those bare toes. "I didn't, not really. I mean, aside from the fact that I didn't work for anyone who made this kind of movie"—she looks toward the screen, winces, and wiggles her toes again—"my job was more about . . . not-movie things."

She falls silent for a minute, looking down at where her toes have set to rest against the outer seam of my jeans. The me who is very nearly in my midthirties can't feel anything through the denim, but the me who is still a little bit fifteen definitely can.

"Honestly, sometimes I wonder if the work was wasted on me," she says, and I turn my head toward her. "I mean, so many people in that town, they live and breathe movies. So many people *outside* of that town, even! Like, tonight, Oliv—"

She breaks off, closing her lips tightly, her face flushing in embarrassment, and it doesn't take me but a second to realize why, to realize whose name she was about to say.

My sister's.

I flush a little, too.

"I'm sorry," she says, and I give her credit for not trying to pretend she was going to mention someone other than my sis-ter. I may not have seen or talked to Olivia in a lot of years, but I've got no trouble believing she's as interested in movies as she was when she was a kid. It used to drive my dad crazy, the way she'd rattle off film trivia at meals. For her ninth birthday Evan and I pooled our allowances and got her a VCR off eBay so she could watch a box of ancient tapes she found in our grandma Sue's house. Olivia barely left her bedroom for a week. When she finally came out she spoke in quotes from some old movie called *Moonstruck* for days. "Snap out of it!" I remember her shouting periodically for months afterward.

I clear my throat again, but this time it's to swallow the ache in my throat. It isn't as if I don't ever hear about my brother and sister, but mostly what I hear is the big stuff—Liv running the spa at the inn, Evan splitting with the wife I never even met. Somehow it hurts worse to hear something small, that my sister still loves something she loved back when I knew her.

"It's all right," I say gruffly, and wait to get angry the way I did that first night. But I don't, not now. Maybe it's because I know Georgie better now, or because it's been so easy here with her tonight. Maybe it's because of her magic list and how it lets me go back, lets me be a version of myself who wouldn't have minded a mention of my sister.

"I didn't tell her I know you," she says softly. "I didn't tell any of them."

My family, she means, and to anyone else, that probably wouldn't be much of a compliment. It might even be an insult, me a dirty secret that she can't speak of to her new employers. Instead, I get that flare of possessiveness again, an unearned glory. It's a feeling I don't get that often—like there's something that's only mine around here, something that's not about my reputation or the way I've had to rebuild it.

"Why not?" I ask her, my voice low and quiet to match hers. I don't know if I'm wanting her to disabuse me of those possessive notions, if I'm wanting her to say that she was being practical, avoiding something dicey. Avoiding something I told her I don't ever talk about anyway.

She lifts her eyes to mine. "Because I like how this is, only the two of us. I didn't even tell Bel. I was . . . I couldn't wait to come back. To go back, with you."

I should say something here, and my mind is spinning with possibilities, simple and complicated. *I like it, too. I like this messy house and your hair still wet; I like that robe and the color of your mouth from the cider you've been drinking. I like that you're a hometown girl from far away, that you know me and I know you, but not in the way everyone else around here does.*

I like the way we fit.

But I can't get any of them out. Instead all I can do is wrap my hand gently around her bare ankle. She's warm and soft and smooth when I rub my thumb along her skin. I can hardly believe I've done it.

But Georgie?

Georgie can believe it; Georgie has been waiting for it. Before I can process what's happening, she's pulled her ankle from my hand only so she can tuck her legs beneath her and lean forward, lean into me, and then—then, I'm enveloped. It's her damp hair and her silky robe and her hard cider mouth on mine, and it's a *mess*, this kiss; her bottle pressed between us and cool droplets from it on my shirt, but I can't care, not when I'm trying hard to keep it, to clean it up so she doesn't realize the clumsy start and decide to stop. I don't want to see her flush from embarrassment again; I want to see her flush from *this*, from our mouths pressed together and our hands all over each other.

I shift, tucking a hand between us and taking the bottle from her hand, keeping my lips on hers while I set it on the small table next to the couch. Then I get my hands on her hips, over the fabric of her flimsy robe, and she gets it—she comes right over, settling herself on my lap, straddling my thighs and leaning forward, deeper into our kiss. It's better this way—stable and so good, her mouth opening against mine and her tongue dragging across my bottom lip in a way that draws a hoarse noise from my throat. I clutch at her tighter, holding her to me. I'm caught up in her, everything about my senses dialed way up, but not so much that I can't think of how *Georgie* this kiss is, how right away she put her whole self into it. *Sure you can stay here, sure I'll watch your dog, sure I'll tell you about my strange list* Georgie. *Expansive* Georgie. I've never met anyone like her in my life, and getting this close to her is perfect, dizzying, overwhelming.

"Just this," I murmur between kisses, trying to cling to some sense even though I'm pretty sure I have no blood left in my upper extremities. "You've been drinking."

She laughs against my mouth, and that's my favorite way I've ever experienced a laugh. I want to *eat* it, that laugh, and I kiss her harder, tighten my grip on her waist.

"So have you." She rocks her hips against the hardest part of me. Every day I waited and worried over whether this was worth it for that one hot, perfect pulse of her lap against mine.

We make out as if we're back in time, as if we're teenagers— so long that the screensaver on the TV comes on, a bouncing white logo that eventually gives over to a black screen. My hands are in the damp mass of her hair, and Georgie's got hers on my neck. If I kiss her a certain way she squeezes her fingers gently, right on the tightest, tensest muscles I've got on my body, and every time, I make a grunt of helpless pleasure. It sounds like sex; it *feels* like sex, even though neither of us has taken a stitch of clothing off.

When she starts rocking her hips again, rhythmic and desperate, all I want is to give her what she needs, even if I'm dangerously close to desperation myself. I get my hands beneath that robe, set my thumbs at the bottom edge of her tank top, rubbing at the line of warm, perfect exposed skin there, trying to ask for permission in a way that keeps me kissing her.

She nods, pulls away only long enough to whisper a panting yes, her hips moving faster now, and that's it: my hands are up and under her thin tank top, no bra—*Jesus Christ, no bra*—my fingers are teasing the part of her that's sensitive, the part that tightens and peaks beneath my touch. I match her pace, meeting her movements and listening for the moments where her breath hitches in pleasure. Half of me hates that I said we'd only do this, but half of me loves it, too—this is going back, this is having something I was too stupid and scared to take for myself the other night when she first kissed me, and I can see how it could become its own perfect, magic list:

Tomorrow we can go back to tonight, and we can take more.

The next night we can go back to tomorrow, take more.

The night after that, and after . . .

Georgie gasps and pulls her mouth from mine, pressing her forehead against my shoulder. I know she's close, and I'm aching for her to have it—this wild and soft and expansive part of her coming apart against my firm, stable control. I clench my teeth and concentrate on everything about her and nothing about me—her scent, her speed, her sawing breaths that eventually give way to her soft, satisfied collapse against me.

I'm holding her close, tight, because it's how I'm holding myself together. But I'm wound up, too close to the edge of a coming-in-my-pants cliff, and that is the sort of back in time moment I absolutely do not want to revisit in my thirties. I gently move her off my lap and to my side, keeping her pressed against me as best I can, relishing the soft murmur of protest she offers up in answer.

"Give me a minute," I say quietly, and when she laughs softly again, her warm breath on the side of my neck, I wonder if *that's* my new favorite way to experience a laugh. She cuddles down, her head against my chest and her hand resting on my stomach. I watch both rise and fall as I try to even out my breathing, try to get to a place where we can go back again.

We stay that way for long, perfect minutes—Georgie melting into my side, the wild mass of her hair tickling my neck and beard, me keeping every one of my senses focused on her as I calm myself down. I suppose that's why those senses are dead to everything else: the sound of a large vehicle lumbering up the drive, the light from the back porch flicking on and filtering through the back door that eventually must get shoved open. The faint smell of incense, mixed with a hint of weed.

If there's any comfort, it's that Georgie misses it all, too.

That is, of course, until we're both surprised by the sound of Paul Mulcahy's booming laugh.

Chapter 13

Georgie

I'm pretty sure we've broken Levi.

In the fifteen minutes since my parents made their surprise appearance—"What were we doing, driving all around God's creation while our baby girl was home!" my mom had said—Levi has barely uttered five words, and that's grading on a curve, because he said "Hello" twice, one right after the other, when we'd both scrambled up from our tangled-together position on the couch. My parents looked at him with fleeting concern, and I get the sense that, in normal times, such as when Levi is not looking at their faces five minutes after making me come, he has a much more casual relationship with them both.

As for me? Well, sure, I'm embarrassed, but not overly so. Levi and I were spared the worst sort of walk-in, and even if my parents had seen more than Levi and me fully clothed and cuddling, they've never been precious about sex. Other kids seemed to get the "talk," whereas my parents had more of an "ongoing conversation" philosophy, the sort where I'd get regular and extremely frank insights into everything from "what to

expect during your moon cycle!" to "why you don't need a part-
ner to find your pleasure!" When I was sixteen and trying to get
over my fruitless crush on Evan Fanning—very uncomfortable,
thinking about that right this second—I went out with a kid
from my English class for two months, and after the second
time we hung out my mom sat me down to discuss whether I
might want some privacy with him.

I could go for some privacy right now, even though I'm of
course happy to see both of my parents. But holy *smokes*, Levi
Fanning kisses like it's his calling. He's got strong hands and
he knows right where to put them, and he smells like wood and
sweat and citronella, plus, that bulge in his jeans might as well
have been my best battery-powered partner-less pleasure machine. If Mom and Dad had only waited until the morning to
show up here, maybe I could've asked Levi to reconsider his
gorgeous, growling *just this* directive. Or maybe I could've simply kissed him all night, making a study of that mouth, imagining what it could do to me next time.

"We thought about stopping overnight again, but I'm in
great shape this week, barely any pain at all, so we figured,
why not forge ahead?" my mom says. She's on the couch with
Hank, who's obviously fallen in love: He's staring dreamily at
her face while she rubs his good ear. Over by the dining room
table where we ate our first meal together, Levi looks as if he'll
never go near that couch again. Like it's the scene of a crime.

I try to catch his eye, hoping we can share an embarrassed
smile, or maybe even an indulgent one at the picture my mom
and Hank make, but I get nothing.

My dad comes back in from the kitchen, carrying a tray of
mugs. "This is the tea I was telling you about!" he says, but I
honestly don't remember what tea. They've talked about approximately three hundred things since they walked in—the
length of my hair, the new signs on 64, Levi's work on the yard,
the status of every single indoor plant in the house, Hank's in-

jury, and even the "sweet moment!" they walked in on, which they seem to have accepted without any surprise at all.

"Oh, this *tea*," says Mom, leaning forward on the couch. Hank looks bereft. "This tea might be the secret. What herbs did he say, Paulie?"

I try to catch Levi's eye again while my dad hands him a mug. If he had any concerns over that hard cider altering his decision making, he should not have this tea. You never know, when it comes to my parents.

But he still won't look at me, and if there's any comfort it's that he won't meet my dad's eyes, either. He takes the mug, but I can tell he has no intention of taking a sip; he only stares down at it like it's a green bean in a pasta dish.

I take a mug just so I can get a break from seeing that look on his face.

My parents settle in, both of them on the couch now, neither of them in any way mindful of the time—one o'clock in the morning, which means Levi and I were making out and more for over an hour. Once that's in my head, I see Levi's point in avoiding eye contact with the couch, though to me it's not the scene of anything other than the best I've felt in ages.

But as the minutes pass and Levi's determined silence persists—contrasted with my parents' borderless, wholly unbothered chatter—I get restless and uncomfortable. From where I'm sitting, in an old wicker chair near the TV that's still playing the screensaver, the tableau of this living room starts to look embarrassing. The couch is sagging in the middle, and my partially drunk hard cider sits perilously on the edge of the side table. My parents, bless them, fit right in, both of them a little wrecked, too—my mom's hair a wild tangle, her beaded bracelets clacking together every time she pets Hank; my dad's socks halfway up his shins, his old cargo shorts ragged at the hems. It's not as though I can judge, since I'm in a soap opera robe and have stains on my top, plus I'm pretty sure my chest and neck are still splotchy from the flushing, perfect heat of my orgasm. Levi being a few steps away might as well put him in another county—he's in his dark, no-stains-showing T-shirt; he's standing stiff and tall as though his posture is about to be inspected. Maybe I should take comfort in the fact that his hair is mussed, too, but it's not enough to take the sting out of the words he says next.

"I better hit the road."

My parents look up in surprise, interrupted in the middle of their sporadic two-person game of Remember-the-Herb.

"What about your tea?" Dad says.

"I'll pass on the tea, sir," Levi responds, and it's . . . it's absolutely bizarre, is what it is. No one calls Paul Mulcahy "sir." It doesn't seem respectful; it seems stilted, strained, embarrassed. My stomach flips over, queasy. Dad blinks and furrows his brow.

"I've got an early day tomorrow," Levi adds.

"But, Levi!" my mom exclaims. "All your things are here! We never wanted to put you out."

"Oh no, ma'am," he says, and I roll my eyes. "I can gather up my things quickly. I believe they finished work on my house today."

I jerk my head toward him, and for the first time since this whole farce started, he spares me a look. A fleeting, slightly guilty one.

There's no way they finished work on his house today; he would have told me already.

But he's back to not meeting my eyes again, and something inside me curls in on itself, tender and bruised and so, so disappointed. I'd meant what I'd said to Levi before we'd kissed—about liking the privacy of us, liking *the two of us* here—but I hadn't explained to him how *much* I'd meant it. I hadn't explained how, over the days I'd spent with Bel, truly helping her this time, I'd loved every small, secret break I'd taken to text him, loved getting each of his short but sincere replies. I hadn't explained how it'd felt at The Shoreline tonight, moving through my shift with buzzing, relieved anticipation thrumming through me, all because I knew I'd be coming home to him tonight. I hadn't explained the way it had been a revelation, to have a real sense of the boundary between being at work and being at home. To realize that the boundary is something I haven't had in a long time, and something I want to have in the future.

Now, though? Now, with Levi not looking at me—with him moving around the house and gathering his things, Hank following at his heels and panting nervously—everything about that *how much* feels reckless, messy, too soon and too intense. All Levi had said that morning on the river was that he'd do some of my list with me, that he'd like to have some fun going back. And I've spent the last five days flinging myself forward, making up a new fic in my head, imagining that Levi was in it with me.

"Want me to put some of this in a to-go mug for you, Levi?" my dad says, holding up Levi's untouched tea, and that's when I realize Levi has spent the last few minutes making himself a pack mule, his and Hank's stuff arranged on various parts of his upper body—a bag over each shoulder, Hank's bed rolled up and tucked beneath one arm, a cloth tote gripped in each hand. This is the kind of *I only want to make one trip* desperation usually reserved for bringing grocery bags into your house.

"That's all right, s—" he breaks off and clears his throat, which means he's wised up to not calling a man in a Phish T-shirt sir. "Paul," he corrects.

My mom stands and moves toward him, heedless of all he's carrying as she wraps him in a clumsy hug. "What would we have done without you!" she exclaims, and over her shoulder, he finally looks at me.

"Georgie would've handled it," he says, and this time, it's me who can't keep eye contact. Maybe he's being polite, but right now, it lands like a blow. It's as if the man I spent the last few hours having a great night with is all of a sudden wishing he could go back to a time when he wasn't staying here, caught up in my mess.

Somehow, I manage a cheerful, smiling goodbye to Hank, and I've never been more grateful for how bad my parents are at reading a room, for how willing they are to fill up spaces with conversation. They talk Levi all the way into the kitchen, and if they notice that I hang back, they don't say. I stay in the living room, listening to Hank's nails tap across the floor and to my parents' voices growing more distant as they walk Levi outside and to his truck. I shut off the TV, straighten and fluff the sagging cushions, pick up our bottles. Step back and take it in.

There's too much in this house for it ever to be truly tidy. But right now, it seems pretty painfully blank to me all the same.

FOR THE SECOND day in a row, breakfast feels like a punishment.

Yesterday's had the advantage of starting late, but that's only because it had the vibe of a half bottle of hard cider hangover, which in truth was actually a stayed-up-most-of-the-night-thinking-about-a-man hangover. I'd shuffled out of my old bedroom—*Levi's* room—at around noon, bleary-eyed and grouchy, and struggled to muster up a cheerful good morning for my parents, who were sipping more tea and giving me the same sorts of meaningful but undemanding looks they'd offered up after Levi had left. I'd distracted them by pretending I'd considered Miracle-Gro for their houseplants, then suffered through the gentle outrage that followed.

It should have been comforting, of course, to have my parents there, both of them slotting easily into the home that, not even two weeks ago, had welcomed me back into all its untidy, easygoing respite. But instead all I could think about was the way Levi had left traces of himself behind—his food still in the pantry, his milk in the fridge. I didn't even have to hold down the toaster lever while I made my favorite comfort food, a fact that had filled me with ridiculous frustration.

My lips had still been tingling from the bristles of his beard.

This morning, the tingling has worn off at least, but my mind is no less preoccupied, and since it's my first breakfast shift at The Shoreline, the distraction is a liability. For the first hour, things had been quiet—only a few early risers, probably guests who were getting ready to check out before the weekend. But then things picked up, and since there's only three of us serving, I've been scrambling. Twice I've taken orders to the wrong table, and once I nearly poured fresh coffee into a water glass. Each time I've made an error, I've apologized profusely but then also thought about how Levi Fanning hasn't apologized at all.

If all that wasn't bad enough, I've also got an audience.

"Georgie!" Bel calls from a table by one of the massive picture windows, waving me over enthusiastically. She looks good, her color fully back and some of the worry eased from her face now that Harry's home. They've both taken the day off so they can go to Bel's doctor for another follow-up later, but what Bel doesn't know is that Harry's also planned for her to have one of those relaxing pregnancy massages here at the spa before they go. Since he is a person who actually puts his phone to meaningful use—unlike *some* other men I know—he texted me yesterday to get help setting up an appointment.

"Hey," I say to them both, hoping I don't sound breathless with all the effort I've been putting into not messing up any more orders. "Everything good over here?"

Bel points at the tiny jar of artisanal jam that came with her scone. "Georgie," she repeats, lowering her voice into an excited whisper. "Everything here is so *fancy!*"

Since I know Bel, I know exactly what she means with this excitement over a tiny fancy jam jar. It isn't as though she's never seen anything like this, what with the circles she's moved in for the last decade, but it's definitely that she hasn't ever seen it around here. For all that The Shoreline was an upscale Iverley institution when we were growing up, it's even more so now, and Bel's taking it with the same kind of Darentville-kid surprise that I'd felt when I'd first seen Ernie Nickel's new front window.

"I know, right?" I say, topping up Harry's coffee in his actual coffee mug.

"Harry," she says, nudging his hand. "This reminds me of . . . what was that place we went to for our anniversary two years ago?"

He quirks a brow, tilts his head to the side.

"You know, the place with the"—she waves a hand at her scone—"with the pastries? I can't think of it, you know how my brain is with this pregnancy."

Harry nods and looks around, and I'm pretty sure he either does not remember the place with the pastries or he does not think The Shoreline is similar. Still, he says, "I can see it," because he is wonderful. He sends text messages and also pretends to remember anniversary dates from two years ago, and I bet he would never leave you alone with your chaos agent parents ten minutes after absolutely rocking your world.

"We should have come here sooner, babe," she says. "It's so nice!"

"It's good for dinner, too," I say, because I am pretty much auto-in with anything Bel is trying to get excited about; I had a lot of practice at this during the days I stayed with her. After Harry left on Monday morning, I could tell she was still rattled, even though she was doing her level best to hide it by going down various Pinterest rabbit holes. That afternoon we spent three hours looking for first birthday party ideas, and I made a very strong case for serving something called "baby Bundts" even though I don't even know if one-year-olds are allowed to have cake.

"You can put it in the date night rotation once you're comfortable leaving the baby with a sitter. Good food, close to home," I add, in the same way I argued for the improved hygiene prospects of individual Bundt cakes at a birthday party that will not take place for another thirteen and a half months.

"Yes!" She clasps her hands in front of her chest, looking thrilled. "Date nights!"

I look around the dining room, making sure I'm not slacking on the job. The crowd's thinned out considerably, my remaining tables almost all wrapped up.

"Plus," Bel says to Harry, "this will be a way for us to meet new people. You said more locals come here now, right, Georgie?"

"Yeah, pretty much an even mix, according to Olivia."

"Oh, is she around today?" Bel says.

"I don't think so." That's a lie, but I don't want to mess up the massage surprise. "I don't think she comes in this early—"

"Well, *someone* does," Bel not-really whispers, something teasing and significant in her voice, and I don't even have to turn around to know who she means. If I'd done the smart thing and actually told Bel about the situation with Levi, there's no way she'd still be banging this drum about Evan. But since I have not done the smart thing, here I am about to be face-to-face with my sort-off boss while my best friend probably plans a Pinterest board for our wedding.

"Annabel," Evan says, coming to stand beside me, easy as can be, his perfect smile perfectly in place. He would look better with a beard, not that it's any of my business. "I'm glad you made it in."

"I was just telling Georgie how wonderful it is here!" She gestures again at the jam jar, but definitely Evan doesn't get that in the same way I do. His whole life has probably been full of tiny fancy jam jars, and I'm newly annoyed at Levi. He's a tiny fancy jam jar person, too, even if he doesn't seem like it now.

"More wonderful now that we have her on our team," Evan

says, and Bel probably decides on what sort of bouquet I should carry down the aisle. "She's a real pro at this."

Good thing you didn't see me almost put coffee in a water glass, I think, but also, my face flushes from the compliment. Or maybe it's not so much from the compliment as it is from the way Evan's giving it—as if he's offering it up to parents who are desperate to be proud of their newly employed kid.

"Evan, this is my husband, Henry Yoon. Harry, Evan's family has owned this inn for . . . oh, decades!"

Evan and Harry shake and nod at each other in that specific way businessmen seem to have with each other—more of a sizing-up than a greeting. It's strangely funny, seeing them meet. They're both handsome by almost any standards, but honestly Evan—love of my teenaged life—suffers next to Harry. Evan is high school football team handsome; Harry is black-and-white watch ad handsome.

I'm thinking about what kind of handsome Levi is (*carpenter handsome, loves his dog handsome, leaves you wanting handsome*) while Bel makes one of those professional-people extended introductions, explaining to Evan that Harry is in finance and explaining to Harry that Evan manages this place. They slip easily into chat about their respective jobs, and even though I could keep standing here quietly, contemplating whether *toaster-fixing* counts as a kind of handsome, I also start to feel strangely out of place. Should I ask someone whether they need any more miniature jam or a fresh glass of orange juice? Sure, Evan works here, too, but it's not as if he's serving this morning. He's beside me in flat-front gray pants and a crisply pressed button-up, the sleeves rolled neatly up to his elbows, and I am wearing a uniform and one of those half aprons where I can tuck everything from my server books and extra pens to the cheat sheet I made for myself about the breakfast menu.

It gets worse when Evan puts a hand on the back of one of

the chairs around the four-top and Bel immediately invites him to join her and Harry. When he smiles and sits right down, I'm frozen for long seconds, because I don't know if I should—

"Can I get you a coffee?" I blurt. My brain went right on ahead and decided that the proper thing to do here was to wait on him.

Evan looks up at me, his smile crooking charmingly. It's such a bland smile, easily given. I pray that he sends me to get him a scone or something, but instead he looks at his watch and says, "Aren't you about off the clock?"

I clear my throat. "Almost, but—"

"Join us," he says, gesturing to the seat beside him, then pulling it out.

"Oh yes! Please, Georgie, sit down with us for a few minutes," Bel says, a teasing twinkle in her eye.

I would try to give her a meaningful look meant to convey that I made out with this man's brother two nights ago, but since he's watching, waiting for my answer, I instead try to make my excuses, gesturing vaguely over my shoulder. "I should start helping with cleanup."

"I insist," says Evan, still holding out that chair. "One coffee."

Bel pins an updo idea to the "Georgie and Evan Wedding" board that now lives in her brain. I can tell it from the look on her face.

I hide my sigh and smooth my apron, taking a seat. "For a minute," I mutter, though I don't think anyone hears me. Evan catches Remy's eye and waves them over, and if I could rocket ship myself directly into the sun, I probably would. Remy and I are equals, colleagues, and now I'm slacking *and* getting some kind of weird special treatment.

"Rem," he says, "do you mind getting me and Georgie each a coffee?"

I nearly groan in embarrassment, mouthing an apology to

Remy before they go. They at least look understanding, as if they've once or twice been roped into one of Evan's thoughtless whims, but I'll still apologize later. I will change the water in every mop bucket in this place.

"Did you want anything to eat?" Evan asks. "I can tell Rem to—"

"No!" I say, overloud, and then try to correct it. "Thanks, but no. I ate before I came in."

This is also a lie, because I couldn't face the fixed toaster again, but obviously I don't want to explain that to anyone. Including myself.

"Want the rest of my scone?" says Bel, and all of a sudden, everything about this situation strikes me as grimly, ironically funny. I have a very detailed fic entry in my notebook where Bel and I were on a double date with our perfect boyfriends. Hers was Joe Jonas, and mine was the guy sitting right next to me. I wrote about Joe and Evan becoming best friends. I do not know what I imagined Joe Jonas and Evan Fanning would have in common, but it could not possibly be more boring than golf, which is what Evan and Harry start talking about as soon as I've passed on the scone.

Levi would never talk about golf, I think grudgingly, which is so off the rails that I seriously contemplate dumping the coffee Remy brings me onto my own lap. It'd give me a valid reason for excusing myself.

When talk turns to Bel and Harry's house, I at least have some familiarity with the topic of conversation. Evan admits to Harry that he's been staying with his sister since his divorce, a touch of charming, disarming embarrassment in his eyes, but says that he's a fan of the area where Bel and Harry live now, and he'd consider it for himself someday, too.

"Oh, you *should,*" says Bel. "Our house is wonderful! Isn't it wonderful, Georgie?"

"It is," I say, even though it's the sort of question that already has an answer.

"It was move-in ready," Bel adds. "The biggest project we have left to do is build a dock."

I choke a little on my coffee, clear my throat indelicately. *Please, don't talk about docks*, I'm thinking, but that train has left the station. We're off the rails now, and I have no one to blame but myself. *Why* didn't I tell Bel about me and Levi, warn her that any topic adjacent to him is off-limits?

"You ought to call Hammersmith Marine," Evan says. "They do all our work here."

"That's a good tip," says Bel. "But your docks here are a lot bigger than what we'd need. We want something small."

Evan nods. "Well," he says, pausing to take a sip of his coffee, and in those few seconds of quiet a puddle of dread settles in my stomach. "I'd tell you to call my brother, but he won't take on your build."

To her credit, Bel blinks in surprise at this mention of Levi and darts her eyes to mine. *Should I spill the coffee now?* I'm wondering, but before I can attempt it Harry—who is obviously hugely uninformed about years-old gossip around here—says, "Why not?"

Evan takes another sip of his coffee, shrugs. It's the first time since I've been back that I've seen him look anything less than perfectly comfortable. "He doesn't take any jobs along that part of the river. Something about compromising the shoreline." He clears his throat. "That's what I hear, at least."

Harry frowns across the table at Evan. "What does that mean, 'compromising the shoreline'?"

"The Realtor said we could put in a dock," Bel adds, her brow wrinkling in concern. Both of them, obviously, are missing the major point here, which is that Evan has acknowledged Levi's existence.

"You can," Evan says. "But not one built by my brother."

I can tell Bel and Harry don't like this answer. If there's someone out there who thinks they shouldn't build a dock on their property, they'll want to know why.

"Not much of a business plan, if you ask me," Evan grumbles, and I'm not even sure he intended to say it out loud. I don't think Bel and Harry heard him, but I did, and when I look over at him, I don't see an expression on his face that matches the casual insult. If anything, he looks kind of sad.

"I think his business does well," I say, and as soon as it's out of my mouth I realize what I've walked into.

Evan turns his head toward me. "You know Levi?"

"Oh, I—um. Not really," I say, which I decide is not actually untrue. I thought I knew Levi, thought I was *getting* to know Levi. But the Levi I thought I knew wouldn't have left me hanging. "He runs in the same circles as my dad."

Even though Evan nods, I know I haven't made this totally convincing. I just hope I haven't made it so unconvincing that everyone at this table catches on to the fact that I was halfway to sleeping with Levi the night before last.

"My goodness, I better stretch these legs!" Bel says suddenly, pushing back in her chair and standing more quickly than I thought she was capable of at this point. Harry looks startled, and I don't blame him. She practically vaulted her way upright.

"I hate to cut this short," she says, smoothing her tunic and sending me a conspiratorial look that tells me I was not, in fact, very convincing about *not really knowing* Levi. "But I *am* supposed to keep my circulation going!"

Harry stands, too, probably worrying over how this sudden departure affects the massage timing. When Evan rises I follow, signaling the end to the weirdest double date I never could have dreamed up. He insists on paying for their meal, "a manager's prerogative," and points them toward the manicured path off the patio that'll make for an easy walk for Bel. She leans in to hug me goodbye and then whispers intensely in my ear that I *have* to call her later.

When they're finally gone, I do what strikes me as the most natural thing and start clearing plates. Evan reaches for one, too, but I wave him away. "I've got this," I tell him, desperate for him not to ask me anything else about Levi. "Thank you for the coffee."

"My pleasure," he says, but he doesn't make a move to go. "You do a great job here, you know? Remy says you're terrific."

Probably they won't say that anymore, I think, *since they had to serve me coffee while I'm still on the clock.*

"Well, I'm an old hand at it."

He smiles, and I almost wish I felt something, because this scenario—getting Evan Fanning's attention by working at his family's inn—is so like the fic it's almost fated. But there's nothing, only a dull ache that his face isn't the one I wish I was seeing right now.

"I saw my sister on my way in. She mentioned your parents are back in town?"

I nod, gathering more plates. "Yeah, it's been a while since we've all been together. Nice to be in the same house again."

"I feel that way, too, staying with Liv." I catch sight of his hand curling around one of the chair backs again. "Most of the time. Some days, I think I'm going backwards. After everything with . . . well, you know."

I pause in my plate gathering, look up at him. He looks young, or maybe it's that he looks, for the first time in my memory, a little lost. I realize that he's trying to commiserate. Him, divorced and living with his sister, me back from LA and living, however temporarily, with my parents. He aims another of those charming smiles at me, this one self-deprecating.

But I can see that it's masking something honest, something sad. Even though I don't harbor any bit of that old crush I had on him, I still don't want to leave him hanging.

"I'm sure it's only for a little while," I say, thinking of him all those years ago, larger than life and self-assured, and still always so *nice* to everyone. There's a reason Bel called him a hometown hero.

"I watched you play football, Evan Fanning. You never stayed down all that long."

He looks at me like I've healed something in him. His face softens and his eyes brighten, his smile transforming into something more authentic.

"That's true," he says quietly. Gratefully.

I catch Remy looking flustered over by the bar. "I'd better get back to it. Thanks again."

"Anytime." I've been single long enough to catch the tone in it, to know it's not a neutral, obligatory *anytime*.

It's a suggestion.

But I pretend I don't hear it that way. I nod my head as though I'm saying goodbye to my boss, my boss and that's it, and then I hustle over to Remy and hide out in end-of-shift tasks for another hour. The whole time, I'm jittery and unsettled. It somehow feels like a failure, to have lived through a moment—two moments, if I count that weird double date—that my younger self wanted with an almost pathological desperation, and to experience nothing but longing for something—*someone*—else entirely.

When I finally clock out, it's habit to check my phone, not necessity. But there's probably at least a few things there—that sweating, concerned-face emoji from Bel, maybe, or one of my mom's accidental voice notes. At this point I wouldn't turn my nose up at more donkey pictures from Nadia. At least I'd know someone was thinking of me.

But if there is any of that, I don't notice, because the only message I seem to be able to see at the moment is one from Levi.

An address followed by a blunt invitation, as clumsy as Evan's was smooth.

Come over, it reads.

Chapter 14

I'm guessing she won't come.

I'm out on my dock, Hank snoring softly at my side, trying to calm my mind by taking in the view. I missed it, this specific spot, even though the Mulcahy property is pretty—big and heavily treed, with sunlight that plays all day through the leaves. It doesn't have the river, though, and that's what I like best: the quiet lapping, the briny breeze, the occasional splash from a fish or a diving bird.

When Carlos first told me he wanted to sell me this place, I could hardly believe I'd gotten so lucky—getting to take over a property that had been, at the lowest time of my life, a refuge. In the last year, it's sometimes felt less stroke of luck and more neverending project, but when I get to come out here on the dock I rebuilt myself last fall, I know it's all been worth it. It's taken a lot of work, making this slice of land my own, but it's meant I get to live the way I've always wanted.

Quietly, privately, and on my own terms.

Growing up, I didn't get much of that—first in my parents'

house, where almost every rule was one I didn't understand or didn't want to follow. After that, at the school my dad sent me to, where I had no privacy and not a second of peace at any point in all the miserable days and nights I spent there. When I finally left that place, I could only swing a shitty two-bedroom apartment in Richmond that I shared with three other guys. Even when I eventually moved back here, living at first in the trailer Carlos used to keep on the property, I couldn't shake the sense that I was never truly alone.

It's no real surprise, then, that I can count on one hand the number of people who aren't contractors who've come out here since I've owned the place. Carlos, of course, who visited six months ago and heaped praise on me for the improvements I'd already made. Laz and Micah, who'd helped me reshingle the small roof in exchange for beer and pizza. Hedi, but only one time, and only to see the river and take some samples from the bank.

So part of me can't believe I did it, sending Georgie my address, telling her to come over. I know it was clunky, doing it in a text message. But I also know that after the way I left her two nights ago, I owe her an explanation, a *real* explanation, and I've spent all this time preparing to give it. I took a half day yesterday and all day today, and I've spent the time cleaning and carefully putting my house back together, keeping busy while I'd practiced what I'd say to her. Hank's heard it enough times that I'm pretty sure I gave him depression, or else he was more attached to that metal rooster than I thought.

Beside me, he stirs and huffs out a heavy, bored sigh, and I suppose I ought to go in. It's been over two hours since I sent Georgie that text, and it's fair enough that she's ignoring it. My plan isn't going to pan out, and I don't deserve it to after the way I acted. It's time I start thinking about other alternatives for how to explain what happened to me when Paul and Shyla had walked in on us the other night.

I'm standing from my chair when I hear her car coming

down my drive, close already owing to that quiet engine she's got. Hank abandons me, of course, because by now he's well and truly sick of my shit, and by the time Georgie's parked beside my truck, he's barking out a greeting and turning in excited circles.

I swallow my nerves, turning my back and pretending I'm checking on a piling, as if a dock I built would ever have that sort of flaw. It occurs to me that I'd only been considering the disappointment I'd feel if she didn't show; now I'm wondering if I'll be worse off if I see her here and can't convince her to stay.

"Levi Fanning," she calls out, irritation in her voice, and soon enough I hear her feet stomping onto the wood of my dock, and dang, I love that sound. There's nothing like it, the sound of steps on wood that's built over water, even if they're angry ones.

When I turn to face her, at first I think she's come here in that robe I had my hands all over the other night, but as it turns out, it's a dress—soft cotton, no sleeves, brightly patterned, long enough that it grazes along the boards. Her hair is a puffy, perfect red-orange halo around her face.

"You are something else," she says, setting her hands on her hips. Beneath the bottom curve of her big sunglasses, her cheeks are flushed.

She's pissed.

I open my mouth to speak, but she cuts me off. "After all that, you sent me a *you up* text?! At eleven a.m. on a Friday?"

"What's a *you up* text?"

She shakes her head, mutters something that has the word *backwoods* or *backward* in it. Either way, it's not real flattering to me.

"It's a text you send when you want to see if someone's up for . . . you know."

"No," I say, but I have a pretty good idea, what with the way she said "you know."

"Levi," she says, gusting a sigh that's more irritated than

Hank's. I shouldn't like it, but I do. Her saying my name that way—it's the kind of annoyance that's somehow knowing. As if she's saying, *Of course this is what Levi would say.*

"It wasn't a *you up* text. I don't think."

She raises her chin. "Well, forget it, either way. You *bolted* the other night."

"I know I did. And I'm sorry."

She drops her hands from where they were resting on her hips, her bare shoulders slumping, and part of me wants to tell her not to give me even this much, because I remember how she looked the other night, how I got quiet and her parents got loud, and how she seemed somehow to do both—smiling and talking with them but shrinking in on herself all the same.

But the other part of me is so disarmed by her softening posture that I lose sight of all the careful things I planned to say.

"I was embarrassed."

"Yeah, well," she scoffs, firming up again and crossing her arms over her chest, closing herself off. "Me too."

I clear my throat, and immediately make it worse.

"I like to keep my nose clean around here."

It is such a colossally wrong thing to say that Georgie uncrosses her arms, shoving her sunglasses on top of her head. She levels me with a glare.

"Are you *kidding* me?"

I know exactly what she means. I've made what we did together sound dirty, when it was pretty much the sweetest night I've ever had. That's part of what I planned to tell her during all the practice talking I did with Hank, who's probably glaring at me in disappointment.

"Let me try to explain. Please."

She recrosses her arms, taps her foot beneath her. The posture might not be welcoming, but the sound grounds me enough to get started.

"You know I've got a reputation. You know I was trouble,

back when I was younger. You haven't wanted to say, but I know you know."

She lets go of the glare.

"That was a long time ago," she says, her voice softening. I remember that word again, *expansive*. Even when she's trying to be closed, Georgie stays open, and it makes me want to protect her from anyone who'd take advantage, including myself.

"This place is full of people with long memories."

She snorts, one side of her mouth quirking. "Tell me about it."

"Sometimes," I say, finally getting to the stuff I practiced, "Sometimes I think there's not one person in the whole county I didn't give some kind of hassle to. Vandalizing their property. Stealing out of their sheds. Starting a fight with their kids. Once, I broke into Bob Vesper's house and stole all of the liquor he kept in his kitchen."

"Bob Vesper was the sheriff."

"I said I was trouble, not that I was smart."

"You're smart," she snaps. Then she looks down and kicks off her sandals, her bare, wiggling toes peeking out from beneath the hem of her dress. This seems to satisfy her, and I like that, because it's one of my favorite sensations, too—the bottoms of my feet on sun-warmed wood. Every once in a while, when I finish a job, I take off my boots and socks and walk the dock, doing the final test of its mettle.

"Why'd you do all that?" she asks. It's the most incisive question possible, slipped right into the silence I left open too long.

I clear my throat again, all off track. I don't much want to tell her about the why.

But what questions she asks, I'll try to answer. I owe her that.

"Pretty likely story, I'd say. Every prominent family needs a square peg, a black sheep. I'm that, for the Fannings."

She narrows her eyes, but not in a suspicious way. In a waiting way. I don't want to tell her all of it—the parts I'm ashamed of, and the parts the man she's now working for should be ashamed of. But I can tell her some.

"My dad," I begin, ignoring the way my teeth seem to want to clench together at the thought of talking about him. "He's a guy who cares a lot about reputation. His own, and the whole family's. He's successful, and my grandfather was successful, and so was my great-grandfather. He had a lot of ideas about how his kids should behave."

How *I* should behave. He was harder on me than he was on Evan, certainly harder on me than he was on Olivia. He seemed to have a deep-down sense that I'd come out wrong, that I needed a firmer hand. More rules, more discipline. Whatever passive impatience he showed to my mom or my siblings, he turned to active cruelty when it came to me.

Georgie's watching me close, and I can see her mind working. I wonder if, with Paul and Shyla for parents, this is almost impossible for her to understand. But I keep going anyway.

"I hated his rules." I hope she hears the way I mean that *hated*. I was so angry, all the time, like there was a wild animal inside me. "I hated how all he cared about was the way things looked. Going to the same church service every week, getting a family photo taken at the same time every year, being at the inn for events. Always dressed a certain way, always smiling, no matter what he and I had said to each other in the car on the way over."

"You fought?"

I shake my head, dropping my eyes and shoving my hands in my pockets. Fighting isn't the right word for it. We were a powder keg, me and him; it was more complicated than simple fighting. I can't think of anything kind we ever said to each other.

"All I cared about back then was messing up what he cared about. He wanted things in our family to look a certain way, then I pretty much wanted them to look the opposite. That's why I did all that shit. To be petty. To hurt him. To make him look bad around here."

"Levi," she says, and that way of saying my name is nice, too. "I'm sure you didn't mean—"

"I did," I interrupt her. "I own it."

She presses her lips together, obviously stopping herself from arguing. Instead, she asks another one of those incisive questions.

"Is that why you dropped out of school?"

I swallow. "I didn't drop out of school. My dad sent me to a different school, out in western Virginia."

"Oh."

Every part of me is begging her not to ask another question, because I don't want to try to answer anything about this. It wasn't so much a school, after all, as it was a "facility," a place where families—and sometimes judges—sent kids who kept causing trouble. The learning part was secondary to everything else, and everything else was basically a bunch of troubled teen-aged boys whaling on each other while the people in charge of teaching us "discipline" pretended not to notice. If I was fucked up before I went there, it had nothing on how I was when I finally got out.

"Your mom was okay with that?"

Well, at least she didn't ask about the school.

I shrug. "My mom left the running of things to my dad. She's not the most involved of parents. I doubt she noticed I was gone."

She furrows her brow, looking down at her feet.

"But then you came back." There's a thread of hope in her voice, as though we're coming to the part where I turned it all around. But it was a lot of mess before I got to that point, including the one I made the first time I finally got up the courage to see my family again after I'd left that place. The worst mess, made all in one night, and the reason I don't see any of them anymore.

Even though I try hard not to, I can still see my dad that night in my mind's eye. His face blazing red with anger, his fists balled. I'd thought, *I'm killing him, just from all the effort he's mak-*

ing not to hit me, and for a terrible split second, I couldn't decide what I wanted more. Him gone, or him finally giving in and getting me gone.

You are a poison to this family, he'd said to me. *Leave this town and don't come back, ever, not even on the day they put me in the ground.*

"My dad was right about some things," I say, forcing that night out of my mind, focusing on everything I learned after it. "A man's reputation does matter, and I'd pretty much ruined mine over the years. I spent a long time getting people to see me different so I could make a living around here. I run a business now, one I'm lucky to have. I've got a house that I probably don't deserve but that I take good care of. I keep to myself, and I try to be responsible. To make sure people see me a certain way."

She furrows her brow. "My parents don't—"

"I know. But I didn't know, not when they walked in on us. Or I couldn't get to the knowing, if that makes sense. I—" I break off, shaking my head. "It was old wounds, opening up. I panicked. Your dad, he's one of the only people who passed on good words about my work around here when no one else but Carlos would. I owe him."

Everything about her has softened now—her posture, her eyes, her lips. But when she speaks it's with a grudging, tentative sort of softness. "Okay, but you don't owe him, you know . . . my chastity."

It's the first time I've felt like smiling. I can tell she's forgiven me, or at least she's on the way to, but I haven't given her enough, not yet. I practiced another part of this, and I'm going to say it.

"The other night was the best night I've had in a long time. Maybe the best night I've ever had. I'd give anything to go back and not leave it the way I did, and you'd have every right to never do any part of that list with me again after I messed up my first shot at it."

"The best night, huh?"

"Yeah."

I take a step toward her and put my hand in my pocket, taking out what I put in there this morning, after I texted her. She might say no, might think it's too presumptuous of me. But if she does, I'll understand. At least I'll have tried.

I hold out the Sharpie to her.

"This is a better dock than Buzzard's Neck," I tell her. "Sturdier. Good water quality around here."

She takes a tentative step forward, and then she takes the marker from me, turning it over a few times in her fingers, lowering her eyes. "I couldn't even think of a wish when I was at Buzzard's Neck. Not even something small."

"You can try again. Maybe you're out of practice."

When she looks up at me, there's something grateful in her expression. "Maybe I am."

But she doesn't make a move to uncap that marker.

"I could leave you to it, if you want. You could call out if you needed me. Hank and I'll stay close by."

She turns the marker again, thinking about it.

But then she says, "I thought you wanted to do some of these with me." Her lips curve into a gentle, teasing smile. A peace offering.

"I do," I say, recognizing that I've made this vow to her before. This time, I won't break it.

She nods and uncaps the marker, holds her forearm in front of herself. She doesn't hesitate, and I don't watch for what she's writing, in case she wants to keep it private. When she's done, she makes a point of transferring the marker to her other hand, so that when she holds it out for me to take, she's also making it clear: She's showing me her wish.

Another kiss from Levi Fanning, she's written, and when I look at her, she's flushed, tentative, and so, so pretty. I'd make her wish come true right now, but I know she wants me to play along, to write a wish of my own. I take the marker, and what I want to write is, I know, all wrong. Too big for the moment.

Georgie, I want my skin to say.

Georgie here forever.

But she's waiting, and I want to give her what she wants from her list—the spirit of Buzzard's Neck, simple and small scale. I turn my arm and write a wish that's a complement to hers, because we're doing this thing together.

No interruptions this time, I write, and show it to her.

She smiles big—maybe the biggest smile she's ever given me—and I swear my heart might stop for a minute. But it gets going again when she turns, giving me her profile and in one fell swoop pulling her dress over her head—fast, un-self-conscious, joyful. She's wearing a white bra and panties, and oh *man*. When she gets in that water . . .

"Well?" she says, keeping her gaze on the river.

I don't have to be asked twice. I pull off my T-shirt and toe off my shoes, then unbutton and push down my jeans, getting my socks off as I go. As soon as I'm in that water, Hank'll make a bed out of my pile of clothes, but I don't care. Being honest, I hope I'm headed to where I don't need clothes for the rest of the day.

We stand beside each other, quiet and excited, and then she grabs my hand in hers, swinging it back and forth. Once, then twice, and I get it; she's counting.

On three, we jump.

In the water, I don't wait. When Georgie comes up, it's with more delicacy than she did that morning out on Buzzard's Neck—her head tilted back, her hair smoothed away from her face, her smile close-lipped. I want to make every wish she's ever had come true, but I start with the one she made on her arm, and I reach for her, my hand finding her hip beneath the surface of the water unerringly. It's the smoothest dance—her weightless legs wrapping around my hips, her arms around my neck, and my God, the way she looks out here. Sun and salty water, trees all around. A dream I didn't know I had, coming true.

We kiss like we've been doing it forever, like we never stopped the other night, but it's different now, too—no boundaries, no *just this*. Georgie is pressing against me, rubbing the center of herself along my abdomen while I hold her tight.

"Levi," she whispers against my mouth, "now I want more."

"I'll get the Sharpie."

She tips her head back and laughs, but it lowers the warm center of her farther down my body, right against the part of me that's hard and aching for her.

"Come inside," I say, gruff now, and she kisses me again and nods.

It's messy how we clamber up, me helping Georgie onto the dock with my palm on her ass, an act that gets my brain going with all sorts of new wishes, the kind that make it a dangerous situation for me to hoist myself up without getting a splinter in the dick. In the end I must look a real sight, trying to delicately get myself up on dry land again, but Georgie doesn't seem to notice. Hank's jumping in excitement all over our discarded clothes, and once I'm on my feet Georgie and I both look down at them and shrug, and then I'm taking her hand and we're running back toward my house, laughing as we slip on the grass, Hank barking in confused glee beside us.

When we get to the back door, I slide it open and let Hank go before us both. I point to the fancy bed he's got and toss him his favorite antler, telling him to settle in. I'm newly grateful for the time I took to get things straightened in here—my furniture back in place, everything tidy. But I don't think Georgie notices, because she doesn't look around.

She looks only at me.

And it feels so good, that look—nothing tentative, no suspicion or judgment or misplaced curiosity. She looks at me like I'm exactly what she wants.

My hands are back on her hips, my mouth back against her skin, and I walk her toward the bedroom, a short distance given the small size of this place. Our skin is damp, our remaining clothes soaking wet, and Georgie reaches around long enough to unsnap her bra, letting it fall to the ground between us as she presses her bare breasts against me. My brain is still short-circuiting from that when she gets her hands on my wet waist-band, rolling my boxer briefs down over my rock-hard dick, and it's so fast, getting naked with her. The other night, I was fully dressed with her for hours in the dark of night, and now here we are, stripped totally bare in the broad light of day. It's so hard to believe that I have to stop and ask her, stop and make sure of her.

"You want this?"

"Yes," she says, then repeats it after she kisses me again, *"Yes,"* breathy and insistent. I love the way she says that *yes*. I decide I ought to find out everything in life she wants to say yes to, so I can hear it over and over again. Ice cream, a vacation, a piece of jewelry, a night out, a new house, whatever.

You want this?

Yes, yes.

Once we're on the bed I'm wild with it—her naked body and the wanting written all over it in the flush along her perfect, dappled neck, the peaked tips of her pink-brown nipples, the wetness between her legs against my thigh. I'm so overwhelmed by it all I hardly know where to start. I duck my head, licking a path down her neck.

"Levi," she breathes, writhing against me. "Everything is so good. I want everything."

"You can have it," I say against the skin of her stomach. "Anything you want."

She gazes down at me, and then she smiles again, setting her hand on the top of my head and gently pushing down.

Thank God.

She tastes perfect between her legs, like the clean salt tang of the river, like Georgie—fuss and chaos and fun, and holy shit, if I thought she was expansive before, sitting across from me at a table or grinding herself to orgasm on my lap or forgiving me for a fuck-up, I had no idea what I was in for when I got her like this. She opens her thighs and keeps her hand on my hair, guiding me right where she wants me; she moves against my face and sounds out her pleasure to me; she *soaks* me. I take everything, starving for her—I lick at her and inside her; I suck softly at the place where she's most sensitive, the place that makes her fist her hand in my hair and gasp my name as if it's the only one she's ever heard or said or thought of.

When she comes it's different from before; it's not the kind of rolling, sweet orgasm where I can stay steady and stable for her. It's a wave, the kind I imagine comes from that ocean she spent all those years near—big and pulsing and loud, nothing like the mostly quiet placidity of the river outside. I've got to concentrate to keep from getting swept away with it, from pulling away from her too soon and levering my body up to anchor myself inside her. She hasn't asked for that yet, and I can stay under here in the pounding aftermath of her pleasure until she asks me for something different.

I rest my forehead on her stomach, breathing hard. Her hands push through my still-wet hair, and I expect she'll need a minute. Or longer, given the way she's panting, too.

But after what only must be a few seconds, she speaks again, her voice rough and reedy, but I can tell, somehow, *ready*. Still ready or ready all over again, it doesn't matter.

There's a smile in her voice, an invitation.

"You said I could have everything."

Chapter 15

Georgie

When I tell Levi I want everything, I know what he thinks I mean. He thinks I mean sex, and I definitely, definitely do, especially now that I've felt his bare, hard erection against my skin. And when he pushes himself up from where he'd been between my legs, and I get my first good look at what's between his, I admit—that *everything* does narrow down, pretty much, to things having to do with him inside of me.

But I meant something more, too, and when he leans down to kiss me, my taste still on his lips and tongue, it comes back to me—the *everything* meant the last hour I've spent with Levi made infinite somehow, that apology he made to me on the dock giving way to all the stories he hasn't yet told me about himself; that wild and unrestrained jump off the dock unspooling into days and days of laughter together; that kiss in the water becoming the kiss between my legs, the kiss he's giving me now, the kiss he'll give me tom—

"Georgie," he whispers against my lips. "Wait."

I freeze beneath him, hoping I didn't say any of that stuff

about infinity out loud. But as it turns out I've gotten so lost in the thought of it that I've wrapped my legs around his hips, pulling him bare against me. Almost *inside* me.

"Let me get something," he says.

"Oh God!" I exclaim, loosening my grip on him and tipping my hips back. "I'm sorry."

He laughs against my neck, tickling my skin there with his beard. "That's not the sort of thing I ever want you to be sorry for. I'll be right back."

When he goes, I push myself farther onto his bed, and it's soft, clean perfection, with sheets that smell like Levi's skin. I want to roll around in them while I wait for him, want to press my face into his pillow, want to see a strand of my hair on the bright white of his pillowcase.

It's *amazing* how many things I want.

He comes back with a box of condoms, un-self-conscious in his nudity, and I know I haven't been in this house with him for very long, but I can already see the way he's different here— looser and less restrained, not the kind of man who keeps to himself or worries over his reputation. I decide right then on another thing I want.

I want to see him let go completely.

I want him to feel the freest he's ever felt.

I sit up and take the box from him, grabbing his wrist and pulling him onto the bed, pushing him onto his back and straddling his thighs. I take him in my hand, stroke once, and his breath hitches. "Georgie," he says, his voice low and desperate, so I keep going.

"Is this okay?"

He half laughs, half groans. "It's not gonna be okay for long."

He closes his eyes and inhales. Steadying himself. *Controlling* himself.

I firm my grip and slide my other hand down to cup the soft weight of his sac, rubbing him gently, and his hips thrust, quick and probably involuntary. He breathes out a curse.

I bend to his mouth, still stroking, and run my tongue across his lip—a reward for what he's shown me, and when I pull back he thrusts again, letting himself give in to it. In this position, I can look my fill at all the things I felt move against me—the network of cording muscle from his shoulders to his wrists; the dark hair across his strong, broad chest; the narrow, shallow trench that shows off all the definition along either side of his long, tanned torso.

"Open your eyes," I tell him, because I want to see those, too—that dark blue gaze, hungry and desperate.

"I won't last that way," he says, keeping them closed, and I decide I have to scold him for that disobedience.

I lean down and lick along his shaft.

"*Jesus,*" he breathes, and *then* he lets go—jackknifing upright, gripping my arms and pulling me off him so he can roll me beneath his tense, trembling body. He hooks one of his legs to the side, spreading me wide beneath him, and reaches for the box of condoms. His face isn't soft and satisfied anymore, the way he looked after he licked me; instead it's all the hard, impatient lines I first saw on his face in line at Nickel's, or standing in the doorway of my parents' house that first night. In those contexts, it was off-putting, rude; it made me feel messy and inconvenient.

In this one, it's the hottest thing I've ever seen.

It makes me think I'm the hottest thing *he's* ever seen.

I watch him smooth the condom over himself, trying to hide all my own impatience, but when he touches the broad head of his cock to the place where I'm wet, I'm pretty sure I whimper.

"All right?" he asks, which obviously isn't impatient, but it's perfect—the sentiment makes me feel safe, but the strain in his voice makes me feel so *wanted.* I nod and lift my hips, and oh . . .

Oh *God*, it's good.

One hard thrust to put him deep inside me, one of his palms pressed into the mattress beside my head. Both of his eyes on mine as he rolls his hips and grunts, using his other hand to grip my hip and lift me toward him, exactly where he wants me. He's so hard inside me, the pressure of him insistent and perfect and I don't know how I've never felt sex like this—rough and gentle, filthy and sweet, selfish and still giving. It's everything all at once and I decide that must be Levi, who's been everything all at once ever since I first met him. Mad at me while he buys me my milkshakes; sharp with me but only because he's so soft.

I don't expect to come again—I never have before, not so soon after one orgasm, but when Levi's thrusts get even harder, something tentative builds inside me. When he leans down and takes my nipple into his mouth, sucking hard, I gasp and jolt beneath him, nothing tentative about it now. He lifts his chin and scrapes his beard across my breast, a perfect, electric sensation that I know I'll ask him for again later. For now, I relish the way he tucks his face against my neck and murmurs my name, that vulnerability the perfect contrast to the way he somehow shoves deeper, hitting a place inside me that shocks me into another orgasm. It's fast and clenching, my nails digging into his back as I inhale a sharp gasp of surprise, a rush of perfect, wrecking release between my legs. For a split second, I'm almost angry about it—I didn't keep my control, couldn't wait for him.

But then there's Levi's rumbling grunt again, his hips pounding against mine in a rough, uneven rhythm. He shoves an arm under me, banding it around my lower back, holding me close to him for when his body turns stiff and unmoving all over, for when he lets out the most gorgeous, ragged sound I've ever heard a man make.

I hold tight, wrapping my legs around him again, keeping him against me while he breathes heavily, his forehead pressed into the mattress, and I can't help it—I think about it again.

Everything. Infinite.

The very opposite of a blank page.

* * *

FOR A WHILE, we both sleep.

At first Levi says he doesn't ever sleep during the day; in one of those infinite storytelling moments I was hoping for, he confesses a months-long bout with insomnia a few years ago that made him vigilant about sleep hygiene. But in the end, he dozed off even before I did, his lids growing heavy as he stroked his fingers up and down my back. When I wake up an hour later, he's still out—breathing like it's a *sleep*, not a nap, and after years of having to catch the tiniest slices of rest in the rare empty spaces of Nadia's relentless schedule, I know the difference.

I won't let him sleep for long, not after he told me about the insomnia, but I'm grateful for this moment of privacy, because I can't believe how I feel. The first thing is my body, which is summertime tired, sunshine and being in the water tired, warm and well used. The second thing, the more noticeable thing, is my mind. It's clear but not blank, excited but not restless.

Hank taps his way into the bedroom, looking curious, and then he comes to my side of the bed, resting his chin on the mattress and giving me his big dog-breath smile. It's a little gross, but it's also adorable, and I wonder if he wakes Levi up this way every morning. I slowly raise my hand and press a finger against my lips, as though Hank understands the human gesture for *Shh*, then I gently disentangle myself from beneath Levi's arm. Hank wags but stops panting, as though he's understood me, and when I stand, I remember that my dress is in a heap on Levi's dock and my bra and underwear are still pretty wet. I grab a hoodie that's hanging from a hook on Levi's closet door, pulling it on and cursing my height as I zip it up. I wish it fell a bit farther down my thighs.

Hank follows me into the hall, and I quietly close the door behind me. I know it's near his usual dinnertime, and he doesn't make me work to figure it out—he muscles me with his flank toward the bin beside the fridge that holds his kibble. I do my best to follow the routine I've seen Levi do before: wait until

Hank sits, get his food in the bowl, tell him, "Go ahead, pal," in the same way Levi does. I know it'll take a while for him to eat, so I get myself a glass of water and start taking in every detail of this house I can see without doing any real snooping.

Of course, it's clean in a way that makes me think Levi probably found my parents' house overwhelming, but it's not sterile, either. In fact, it's cozy—vacation-cabin cozy, in a way that's got my brow furrowing in confusion. I don't see how this could be the same house that didn't even have running water a few days ago, unless Levi's been lax about that sleep hygiene thing since the night he left me. In the galley kitchen, there's open shelving, ivory dinnerware stacked tidily, occasionally separated by a few colorful hardback cookbooks, everything vegetarian. In the small living room, on the other side of the main kitchen counter, there's a plush, deep couch that actually has throw pillows. Opposite that, there's a TV on the wall, flanked by bookcases, and I wander over, tugging the hoodie down as best I can as I go.

It's not only books on these shelves; it's decoration, too—a few framed landscape shots of the river, a small wooden carving of a canoe, a glass paperweight in the shape of a bird in flight. I hate to generalize, but every guy's house I ever went to in LA that was even halfway curated either had a decorator or a girlfriend, and I'm surprised by how much I hate the thought of Levi having recently had the latter.

"Hey," comes his voice from behind me. The way I startle and shove down the hem of his hoodie absolutely makes it look like I was snooping.

"Sorry!" I say, turning to face him. "I was waiting for Hank to finish eating."

"That's okay." His hair looks bonkers, his beard flatter on one side than the other. He's wearing a pair of soft, loose pants and a gray T-shirt. He crooks a small smile and says, "It's not like I chained you up in there."

I raise a teasing eyebrow, making a big show of taking a step back when he starts to come toward me. "Is that something you're into?"

He backs me against the bookcase, leaning down and pressing a kiss to the bare skin on my neck left exposed by the not-all-the-way-zipped hoodie.

"I'm more of a rope guy," he mutters, nipping my skin softly, and I'm pretty sure he's teasing me back, but my nipples tighten anyway.

He keeps his head bent, inhaling me, humming in the back of his throat.

"Thanks for feeding Hank."

I raise a hand, rubbing it through the mess of his hair. "You were out."

He nods and lifts his head, looks down at me. "Don't think I've slept all that well since I met you."

"You're great at compliments."

"I had to think of the most boring shit to keep from going into your parents' room at night and waking you up. Old church sermons. Golf. Building permits. Anything."

I laugh, and he kisses me. Swallowing my laugh all up.

"I like your place," I whisper, when he lifts his head again.

"Yeah?"

"It's cozy."

"I was putting it back together for you. Before I asked you to come over, I mean. Hoping you'd come over."

"I like it," I repeat, but I don't mean the house this time. I mean that I like what he said, that he made all this effort. Levi Fanning abandoning his sleep hygiene all for me.

He looks so pleased as he turns me around, backs me toward the couch. But when he gets close his brow furrows, a frown at the corners of his mouth.

"What's wrong?"

"I still don't know about those pillows. I got them right before I had the repairs started. Wrong color, maybe."

My mouth drops open, and Levi looks down at me again.

"What's that face?"

I close my mouth. "What face?"

"You're looking surprised. Men can pick throw pillows. I got one of those sites, where I get ideas."

"Oh my God, Levi! Do you mean a Pinterest?"

He picks me up and dumps me on the couch. "So what if I do?"

His eyes widen when he sees I've got nothing on under this hoodie, and I tug it down again, giving him a scolding look. I'm not done with the Pinterest. I probably won't be done until I see it, and also until I make sure Bel knows about it. Maybe until I write a letter about it to the local newspaper.

"Cookbooks *and* home decorating! You're a domestic god. *I've* never picked out a throw pillow for myself."

He drops next to me, pulling my bare legs across his lap, smoothing his wood-roughened palms over my shins. "Is that right?"

"I lived in Nadia's guest house for the last few years. It was all furnished, with really nice stuff."

"What'd you do with all your things?"

"What things?"

Levi frowns. "Your furniture. Your . . ." He waves a hand toward the shelves, where the landscapes and tiny canoes and nature paperweights sit.

"Oh," I shrug. "I didn't really have any. Before I got hired by Nadia I'd been working on a set for three months, so I was living in a hotel. Before that I rented a room in an apartment with two other assistants, but it was just a way station. We all traveled all the time with location shoots."

"Huh."

"Nomadic, I know."

I'm suddenly shy, no doubt intimidated by Levi's grown-up decorating prowess when I've never even owned a set of plates. I swing my legs off of him, standing again to continue my shelves inspection. Behind me, he makes a strangled noise and I tug at the hoodie again.

"Behave," I say, but I put a gentle sway in my step.

The thing about Levi's books is, they're pretty lovingly arranged—some standing upright, some stacked on their sides to serve as tidy bookends. It's almost all nonfiction, almost all about the bay or about climate change: *Chesapeake Bay Explorer's Guide, Chesapeake Requiem, The Weathermakers, All We Can Save.* On his lower shelves the books are thicker, heavier, and I cock my head to read their spines.

Principles of Management. Introduction to Accounting. Basics of Computing. Fundamentals of Biology.

"Textbooks?"

"Mm?"

I'm pretty sure he is very distracted by my legs in this hoodie, which is nice. But I want the story behind these. "What are these from?"

He clears his throat. "I got an associates' degree a few years back."

I spin to face him. "Really?"

He nods.

I walk back toward him, intending to sit beside him again. But he pulls me over him so I'm straddling his thighs, and I have to hold the hoodie down over my lap.

He makes a noise of disapproval, and I give him a quelling look.

"Tell me about it," I say.

He looks down at where I'm covering myself, his eyes half-glazed. "Now?"

"Yes, now." I wriggle against him. "I want to know."

I'm desperate to know. Levi going back to school seems *important* for me to know. Isn't that one of the things I'm supposed to be considering, after all? One of the things I might want?

He stills me with firm hands on my hips. "You're gonna have to stop moving if you want me to be able to talk."

I freeze dramatically. "Tell me," I say again, barely moving my lips.

He smiles. Levi has kind of a silly streak. I wonder if anyone else knows about it.

I hope it's only me.

"After I worked for Carlos for a couple years, he suggested I take some classes at a community college so I could help out with the books." He shrugs. "I did, and then I took a few more. They were pretty easy."

"Biology was easy?" That's hard for me to imagine. I barely passed biology in tenth grade. Plus, my parents wrote a letter of protest to my teacher about the required animal dissection.

He lowers his eyes, rubs his palms up my legs. "Biology was something separate."

"Separate how?"

He shrugs again. "Those classes I took for Carlos, they were fine, but they were boring as fuck. Or at least they were for me."

"Accounting," I say, squinting my eyes and nodding, as though I'm committing this information to memory. "Not riveting, got it."

He smiles. "So one semester I was in a class with this guy who was getting a transfer credit taken care of for his minor; the rest of the time he was doing a Bio major over at William & Mary. He was almost always studying for those classes, and sometimes I'd look over his shoulder and read. Or look, it's more fair to say. His books always had tons of pictures."

"Cuuuuuuuuute," I say, wriggling again, and he sets his palms on my thighs.

"Anyway, one time I asked him about it, and he knew about this adult degree program W&M had. So I took a biology class there one semester."

"Oh, I see. 'So I took a biology class,'" I mimic, playing up the *no big deal* way he's told me about it. But it must've been a big deal. It probably took a lot for Levi—quiet, contained Levi—to ask some guy in his accounting class about biology courses. "Probably you got an A, huh?"

His lips quirk. "I got an A plus."

"You're disgusting!" I swat at his arm, and he gently digs his fingers into my sides, tickling me. When I drop onto his chest, yelping, he nibbles at my neck again.

"Quit teasing," he grumbles, but I think he likes my teasing.

I shift, moving off his lap and tucking myself close against his side, looking up at the line of his jaw, his still-mussed beard.

"An A plus!" I repeat, but I'm not teasing anymore. I'm genuinely impressed.

"I had a good teacher. I still collect samples for her sometimes. She's a friend."

"What kind of samples?"

"River and creek water, but sometimes plant cuttings, too. She mostly studies algal blooms and what they're doing to the bay. She taught me a lot about sustainability, climate change stuff. It's been useful to know for doing my work in the right way."

I stifle a cringe, thinking of my conversation with Evan and Bel and Harry this morning, Evan's insistence that Levi wouldn't build them a dock. I don't know if I should mention to Levi that I've already caught wind of the way he cares about sustainability.

I decide not to risk it, not now. "That's really cool," I say instead.

He brushes off the compliment, redirects it. "She's brilliant. She lobbied the state legislature last year about regulation. She walks the walk."

"Is she pretty?" I blurt.

He looks down at me. "What?"

I can't pretend I said something else; I don't know any biology terms that rhyme with "pretty." Actually, I don't know if I know any biology terms. Either way, it doesn't matter. I'm still mostly naked on this man's couch and among the infinite things I'm interested in knowing about him is everyone he's ever dated, including if one of them is a brilliant professor who's now become a friend.

"You know. Hot for teacher pretty."

He makes a face, laughs. "I don't know. I've never thought of it. I know she's not pretty like you," he says, and I flush.

"What's pretty like me?"

He lifts a hand, runs his index finger gently down my forehead, over my nose and the rise and fall of my lips, along the curve of my chin. "Like this. Everything I'm looking at."

He leans in, captures my lips, kisses me long and languid before pulling away again, sliding a hand up my thigh, finally getting beneath the hem of his hoodie.

I shift, trying to get his fingers closer to where I want them. "You're pretty, too," I whisper.

"Yeah?"

I nod and kiss him how he kissed me, slow and deep, and this time, we get caught up in it. Before long I'm beneath him, his hand tugging down my zipper.

Then there's a tongue on my ankle, and I nearly knee Levi right in his sensitive parts.

"Hank's done eating," he says, deadpan, and then groans in frustration. "He needs a walk."

"Ah." I scoot back, disappointed. It's a break in the glowy aftermath, and what we do next is undetermined. It's early evening now, and it's got the feel of a shift change—one thing ending, the next one beginning.

But I find I want this shift to keep going and going.

"Walk with us?" he asks, keeping hold of me.

"You don't think he'd mind?" I'm not really asking about Hank.

"Nah," he says, and I know he's not answering for Hank, either. "He likes you as part of his routine."

"Okay." I try not to crack my face open with my smile. "I can stay for a walk."

"And then for dinner," Levi says, his tone more demanding than requesting.

"And then for dinner."

He leans down for another kiss, pressing the hardness in between his legs against the space between mine. "And then after," he adds.

I nod and agree again, counting each one of his *after*s. I make sure to remind myself that they're not infinite.

Chapter 16

Levi

"Don't move."

Beside me, Georgie stops the restless fidgeting she's been doing for the last five minutes—bouncing on her toes, shaking out her hands, lowering the bill of her ball cap only to adjust it higher on her head after a few seconds.

"Did you hear something?" she whispers, sounding more excited than is probably right for the potential of what she's asking about. I'm pretty sure it wouldn't be good for either one of us if a cop caught us under the bleachers of the Harris County High School football stadium at two o'clock in the morning on a Thursday night.

Still, I can't help smiling, even as I keep my eyes out and my ears open.

Georgie lasts about thirty seconds before she fidgets again, this time poking me in the side. "Did you?" she whispers, louder this time.

I look down at her, the half of her face I can see cast in the slatted shadows made by the football field's lone emergency light, filtering through the aluminum stands above us. I've been seeing Georgie Mulcahy's face every single day or night since she showed up on my dock nearly two weeks ago, and I don't mind saying that I've made a study of it. In the early morning, in my bed, she has pillow creases on her pale skin, and her freckles are less prominent, as if they've been sleeping, too. In the late afternoon, if I come home from work and find her sitting with Hank on the dock, her cheeks are flushed pink, her forehead and nose cast in the faint powdery white of the sunscreen she never rubs all the way in. In the evenings, her features are more alive than at any other time—her eyes big when she tells me something she did with Bel or her parents that day, her brows furrowed low with concentration when I tell her something about a job I'm working on, her lips soft and shiny when she wants me to kiss her. Tonight, when I can't see her all that well, I'm grateful for all the looking I've been doing at other times.

"Leviiiiiiiii," she says, poking me again.

"No," I finally answer. "I was only testing you."

She clucks her tongue and rolls her eyes, lifting her hands to tug at the straps of the old backpack I'm wearing.

"I don't need a test," she mutters, then gestures down at herself. "Look at me! Between the two of us, there's only one who knows how to dress for criminal activity, and it's not you, Levi Fanning."

I'm not going to spoil Georgie's fun and tell her that dressing in black boots, black leggings, a tight black turtleneck, and a black ball cap is actually not the way to dress when you're about to do a criminal activity; my inconspicuous jeans and long-sleeved navy T-shirt are the better bet. Selfishly, I'm also not going to spoil the view I get when she wrestles the pack off my back and drops it to the ground, its contents clinking together as she bends over to unzip it.

"Now," she says, flipping on her phone's flashlight and aiming it down while she shoves a hand inside. "Bel wants hers done in the gold, so I'm going to start with that. Although, I didn't ask if I should do the hyphenate as part of her initials. How do you think that would work, would I do *A-R-Y* for Annabel Reston-Yoon, and leave out her middle name? Oh, except her middle name is Iris, which means I need to include it! *A-I-R-Y!* That'll be *great*. Why am I just now thinking of that? It's so cute!"

I don't say anything, because I don't need to, not when Georgie is in this kind of mood. Back when I was staying with her at her parents' place, I'd thought she was friendly, quick to talk, chaotic. Now that I've been with her, though—now that I've given in to all the ways I want her—I see all that plus more. I see how Georgie is always at her most expansive in moments like this: when she's thinking about someone else, or learning about someone else, or doing something for someone else. At home with her mom, she's been making dozens more of those tissue paper flowers while Shyla deals with a flare; they're watching a Netflix series that Nadia directed, and Georgie says Shyla insists on stopping it regularly for Georgie's "behind the scenes" scoops. Over at Bel's, she's helping with a baby memory book and she's almost done with that junk room, plus, she's gotten so good at making strawberry milkshakes that three days ago she brought one over to Ernie Nickel, insisting that he do a blindfolded taste test to see if he could tell the difference between hers and his. I get the sense there's more—that she's probably involved in all kinds of things over at The Shoreline, even though she doesn't say a word to me about it. I don't press her, but sometimes—like when she came over last night, cheerfully exhausted and wearing a different shirt than she usually wears for serving—I almost want to ask.

"Okay, what color do you want yours? I could do black, but green is more *you*, except green might be too school-spirit-y under the circumstances? Then again—"

"Georgie," I say, and she looks up at me, lifting her chin extra high so she can see me over the brim of her hat. "Come here."

"Nuh-uh." She clutches the bag of spray paint and awkwardly scoots back. "I know that tone of voice."

"What tone of voice?"

"You know what tone of voice," she says, scolding. "The same one that got us here at two a.m. instead of midnight. You're trouble, Levi."

I grin, thinking about the moment Georgie came out of my bedroom dressed like a cat burglar. The only thing I don't enjoy about those pants is how hard they were to peel off of her.

It should bother me, maybe, Georgie calling me trouble, should get me in the same place that'd sent me bolting out of her parents' living room that night I almost lost my chance with her. But I like the kind of trouble I am with Georgie—I like keeping her up late and making her gasp in surprise; I like going to the hardware store and buying five cans of spray paint so she'll have options for knocking another thing off her list.

She points a can at me now, and though I can't see much of her eyes, I'll bet they're narrowed. "Don't smile at me that way!"

I hold up my hands in surrender, but I'm not sure I all the way wrestle the smile.

"Okay, you have to pick," she says. "Black, green, yellow, gold, or"—she squints down at another can—"pink?"

I shrug. "It was on clearance. Hand me the yellow."

She looks up sharply, clutches three of the cans close to her chest. "No," she says, her voice firm.

I made Georgie a promise when I offered to come along with her tonight. Spray-painting the rock outside our old high school was, apparently, something she and Annabel had planned to do together—first, back when they were dreaming of their time as teenagers, and then later, when Georgie found her list again and decided to do it. Georgie says she can't quite remember why they didn't do it back when they actually went to this school, but figures it had something to do with Annabel's mom, who was pretty strict. Apparently, this time, Annabel was more than game, but the baby she's got coming wasn't—mostly she's got to keep her outings low-key, and for the last week her hip's been bothering her enough that she's been on bed rest.

So tonight, I'm a stand-in, and Georgie said the only way she'd let me come was if I didn't do anything that could get me into trouble. I know that's because of everything I told her that day a couple weeks ago. Tonight, she made me park my truck four streets over, and she says I'm to stay under these stands and aim her phone flashlight at the rock while she's painting. Also, I'm supposed to run if anyone shows up.

"Come on," I tell her, gesturing again for the can, because the truth is, I never intended to keep that promise. I'm not letting her go out there alone, and I sure as shit wouldn't run from anyone who found us. My luck and it'll probably be the same dickhead who used to work security at the football games here on Friday night. I know he knows I'm the one who slashed the back tires of his Firebird when I was sixteen.

"Levi, you promised."

"I lied," I say, and it's strange to admit it so baldly. Once upon a time, I used to lie a lot—about where I was, what I was doing, what I was thinking. When I cleaned up, I told myself lying was something the old Levi did, that there'd be no cause to do it on the straight and narrow. But that was before I knew about Georgie Mulcahy, and I'd do all sorts of lying to keep her out of trouble. It doesn't make me feel like the old Levi.

It makes me feel brand-new.

"No," she says again, shaking her head. "You said you like to keep your nose clean."

I reach down and snatch one of the cans she's not holding. "I won't get it on my nose."

She blows out a heavy, frustrated sigh. "This isn't worth the risk."

"Georgie, there's probably twenty-five years of spray paint on that rock, some of it real fresh. People aren't getting arrested over this. Don't worry about the risk."

But she is worrying about it, I can tell. She's going to need more convincing to let me go out there with her.

I step toward her and hold out a hand, hauling her upward when she takes it, the cans knocking together between us. She smiles.

"Good thing this isn't that wasp spray," she says. "I could spray your face and leave you here, incapacitated. Go about my business alone, like I meant to do."

She softens the threat with a fast, hard kiss that lands crookedly against my lips, but I'm not going to let her distract me.

"I'm doing this with you. Let's go."

She shakes her head. "It's such a silly thing; it doesn't even matter. I don't know why I wanted to do it, except that everyone else did."

It's Georgie who's lying now, and that's another thing I know from spending the last couple weeks with her. She doesn't show me the journal, but she talks about it a lot—about everything she's trying to learn from it, about how what she's picked from it is stuff she thinks will help her in some way. If she picked spray painting this rock, then there's a reason, and it's not because everyone else did it.

I don't say anything. That works pretty well on Georgie, I've learned. If I leave it quiet, then she won't leave the thoughts inside her head.

She fidgets against me.

"I was thinking," she says, talking pretty much to my chest at this point. "When people did this back in high school, it was kind of . . . you were saying, *I was here*, you know?"

"Sure," I say, though I can't say I understand the *I was here* impulse. For me, I was here until I wasn't. It was bad here and then it was bad somewhere else, and I'd rather no one remember it at all.

"And when I wrote about it the journal, I imagined Bel and I . . . I don't know. We'd get to high school and we'd make our mark. With our initials on the rock, but in other ways, too."

She pauses and steps back from me, enough to shake one of her cans of spray paint. *Clack clack clack.*

"Bel, she definitely made a mark. I bet if I went inside that building right now, I could find her name on a debate trophy, or her picture hanging on the wall somewhere for all her academic achievements."

I swallow, an uncomfortable pang of recognition inside me. If I walked inside that building right now, I could find something similar about my brother, and probably my sister, too. Evan's football trophies, the all-American recognition he got in his junior year, his name listed as salutatorian for his class. I don't know much about Olivia's high school years, but it's not hard to imagine she had successes. She was smart, athletic, had taken dance classes since she was little more than a toddler.

"But I didn't make any mark. Below-average student. No clubs or sports. Didn't go to college. If I made a mark, it's the kind that Mrs. Michaels remembers, you know?"

I don't think I have to say that I do, in fact, know. If I made a mark, it's worse than the sort Georgie did. But also, I saw the way Mrs. Michaels looked at her that day in Nickel's, and I know why it hurts, why it made her feel small. Reduced to the moments where she was trouble for someone else. Me and Georgie, we fit in this way.

"I made a mark at my jobs over the years, but they were invisible marks. That was the point of me. Fade into the background so that my bosses could make the marks."

She shakes the can again. *Clack clack, clack clack.*

"So you want to get your initials on there. See what it's like to make a mark?"

She lifts her head, and it's too dark to see her eyes, but I can tell she's looking at me. "Yeah," she says, her voice quiet but intense.

This is so important to her, this experiment, and I know in my gut she'll need me—someone who understands her the way I do—out there with her. If I don't want to stand under these bleachers all night arguing about my promise, I know that I have to be *in* it with her—that I have to give her a reason of my own for wanting to try this out.

Surprisingly, it's not difficult to come up with one.

"I want to do it because everyone else did," I say.

"What?"

"I mostly didn't do anything anyone else did; I pretty much did the exact opposite, on purpose. I'll see how it feels to do this."

I don't add that it's not about *anyone* else. It's that I'm sure my brother and sister both did this, the kind of good, clean fun that's not "allowed," but that everyone in charge gives a knowing wink to, that my dad would've thought was okay. Spray-painting my initials on a rock is the closest thing to a shared experience I'll have had with my siblings in years.

Clack clack clack.

"Okay," she finally says. "But you have to promise you'll run if someone comes."

"I promise," I tell her.

But this time, we both know I'm lying.

ALMOST AS SOON as we get up close to the rock, Georgie gets distracted from making her mark.

She's contemplating where Annabel's initials should go, weighs the pros and cons of all the options—vertically, along the side; horizontally, in the center; diagonally going up or diagonally going down. She's given up any pretense of whispering and is mostly running through these thoughts at regular volume, as if it's broad daylight and she's somewhere totally innocuous. I'd warn her, but then she tells me she has the *best* idea, and that's getting onto my shoulders so she can do Annabel's initials way at the top.

"That's what she'd want." She's already moving into position behind me, pushing on my shoulders.

"Be quick," I tell her, as I bend down. "I'm old, you know."

She laughs as she settles her weight over me, one leg draping over my shoulder and then the other. Getting into the position for a chicken fight isn't inherently arousing, but Georgie's thighs anywhere close to my face is, and I have to breathe slowly through my nose to keep myself from getting worked up enough that standing is a problem. When I finally do, my hands firm on Georgie's shins, she whoops and clutches at my hair and then whispers "Sorry!" but I'm pretty sure she's talking to the quiet night air and not to my scalp.

She clacks the gold paint can, makes a contemplative *hmmm* noise.

"Anytime, Mulcahy." I squeeze her shins.

"That's fun, you calling me Mulcahy. That's teen-movie crush fun. You're really leaning into this going back in time thing."

"If you don't hurry up, I'm going to be leaning into a chiropractor's office come Monday. I don't have a teenager's spinal column."

She snorts a laugh. "Get closer. Should I do all caps? Or all lowercase? Cursive?"

I pretend to lose my balance and she whoops again, but then the cap of the spray paint can lands on the grass beside me. "Okay, I'm ready."

I lift one hand off her shin, grab my phone from my pocket, and flip on the light, pointing it up. Georgie gets quiet—concentrating quiet, and I don't want to rush her, even if it means I herniate something. But after a few seconds, I hear the familiar aerosol sound as Georgie makes her way through her best friend's initials.

When she's done she taps gently at my forehead, and I lower to my knees, holding on to her hands as she moves herself off my shoulders, leaving all her warm heat behind.

"That looks good, right?" Her voice sounds a little funny, but maybe she's winded.

I look up, and sure, it looks good, as good as I imagine is possible when you're up on someone's shoulders and you've never graffitied anything before. The *Y* looks like a V. But that funny note in Georgie's voice—it's the same as the one that told me I needed to come out here with her. I know my answer matters.

"Real good."

"I messed up the *Y.*"

"No, you didn't. Come on, let's do yours."

But beside me, I can tell Georgie's lost her nerve. She tugs at her ball cap, looks down toward her boots.

I hear the smallest, saddest sniffle.

"Hey," I say, reaching out and catching her elbow, pulling her against my side and getting my arm around her. The first thing I think is that I don't know what to be mad at: the spray paint can or the rock or maybe Annabel. But when Georgie leans her weight against me, I don't want to be mad. I don't want to be anything but focused on her.

"What's this about?" I ask her, keeping my voice low.

"This is weird, right? It's weird that I'm crying right now?" She reaches up and swipes a hand across her cheeks. "God, I'm a mess."

"You're not a mess. The *Y* looks good."

She snorts another laugh, but it's a wet, sorry-sounding thing.

"I'm not jealous of Bel. I haven't ever been. What I said before, about her making her mark . . . I don't want you to think I resented that, or anything."

"I wouldn't think that."

"It's only that—being here, seeing her initials up there—it sort of reminds me of those last few years I spent here."

"Yeah?"

She nods against me, then takes a breath through her nose and blows it out noisily.

"Remember that night you made me pizza on the grill?" she says, after a few seconds of silence.

"Sure. You kissed me."

She groans. "Don't remind me."

I duck my head and steal a quick kiss from her now, because I do want to remind her. I want to remind myself how many times I've managed to kiss her since.

"That night, you said something about . . . you said you could only see the day you were on. Everything else was a blank, you said."

Sounds pretty bad when she says it, but there's no point in denying it. It is what I said, and it's how it was.

"That's how it was for me, too. But obviously not always, right? The journal is proof of that. But then we got to high school, and the more Bel filled her life up—the more *everyone* filled their lives up—the more mine seemed to empty out. I didn't want to join any clubs, or play a sport. I didn't want to research colleges, not that I'd done enough to get into any. I didn't want to talk about what job I should do some-day. I wouldn't have known how to make a mark, even if I'd wanted to."

I shift, moving Georgie in front of me, holding her back close to my front while we both look at this big rock that I can tell—even in spite of the way its covered in years of paint, the excited scribbles of other kids making their marks over the years—is another big blank to her.

"Knowing what you don't want isn't a blank," I say. "Maybe the problem is, everyone makes it seem like one. Because mostly they only know a few things you can fill up your life with. Sports or clubs or college or jobs. Whatever. There's other things in life."

She's quiet in front of me, her body unmoving. It's rare for Georgie to be this still, and I can tell she's thinking. It gives me time to think, too. Back then, I didn't know what to fill up my life with, either, and I ended up picking trouble. I wonder what it would've been like if I could've picked something else.

If I could've somehow picked Georgie. If I could have had her in my life all along.

"I never thought of it that way." She tips her head down and presses her lips to where my forearm wraps around her chest, and the gesture is so soft and grateful that I can't help wanting to give her more.

"I think you probably made all sorts of marks. Probably most of the people around here couldn't see them, is all. Maybe you couldn't see them, either."

She turns in my arms, lifting the brim of her hat and showing me her eyes—everything I felt in that kiss on my arm right there for me to see. I think maybe she's about to thank me, which isn't necessary, but instead she presses onto her tiptoes, kisses me hard, and says something that nearly knocks the wind right out of me.

"You're not trouble, Levi Fanning," she whispers. "Maybe nobody here could see *that*."

Before I can tighten my arms around her, hold everything about what she said close to me, she spins away and marches right up to the rock with the same can of paint in her hand she used for Annabel's initials.

This time, she doesn't hesitate. As soon as I get my head together enough to point my phone's light her way, she lifts her arm and in big, bold, gold letters, she writes her initials: *GMM*.

Smack in the center of that rock.

She stands back and looks at her handiwork for long seconds, then turns back to me and smiles sheepishly, shrugging. "All done," she says.

I can tell she's still thinking about it—figuring out how she feels about this thing she's attached so much weight to. Not just in the journal, but in her life.

"What's the *M* for?" I ask her, and that sheepish smile transforms into something teasing, something playful.

"None of your business, mister," she says, which means I've got to know now.

I bend to snatch a can off the grass, marching right up to that rock myself. I put my initials below hers, smaller, so I don't mess up the big effect she's got going here, the way she tried out this way of making her mark. When I step back, I do what I suspect she did. I search for some kind of feeling—the sense of connection I thought I'd experience if I did this thing that my siblings probably did.

But there's nothing there, and I'm not all that surprised, not after all this time.

It doesn't feel good or bad. Hollow, maybe.

"*LPF*," she reads, interrupting my thoughts. "What's the *P* for?"

"I'll tell you mine if you tell me yours."

"No deal. What is it, Peter or something? That's nothing compared to mine."

I shake my head. "No. It's Pascal."

She blinks at me. "Pascal?"

"Yup."

"What is that, French?"

I shrug. "I don't know. It's my dad's name."

She blinks again, and then she hoots a laugh, loud enough that she's got to slap a hand over her mouth.

"Your dad's name is *Pas*-cal?" she says after she quiets herself, emphasizing the syllables all wrong. Sure, it's not that common a name, but I never saw anything particularly funny about it. Maybe I'm missing something, though; it's not like I've got any sense of humor when it comes to my dad.

"Pas! Cal!" she repeats, bending to laugh again. It's so funny watching her laugh that I eventually join in, too. I think again of what I said to her before we came out here. *I want to do it because everyone else did.*

That's how I feel when Georgie laughs: the purest sort of peer pressure.

She wipes her eyes as she straightens herself, shaking her head and catching her breath. "Okay, okay!" she says, a relenting note in her voice. "For that, I'll tell you mine."

I make my face mock serious, cross my arms. "Let's have it."

"I realize this is a lot to ask after *Passsssss*-cal"—she giggles again—"but please, try not to laugh."

"I won't."

She sighs. "It's . . . Moonbeam."

I clear my throat. My promise not to laugh might as well be the one I made about running if anyone found us out here.

"Don't you dare," she warns, but I can't say anything; I'm too busy biting down on the inside of my cheek.

"Obviously it's not a family name. Unless you count that my family is extremely chaotic. Anyway, I was born on a night of a full moon. My mom said the sky was so clear that her hospital room was all lit up with silver light while she held me. She said it was something she'd always want to remember."

Any urge I had to laugh fades. That's about the nicest reason I ever heard to give someone an embarrassing name. It's so much nicer than me getting Pascal, a shoved-in reminder of a man I never understood and who never understood me, probably not even on the day I was born.

"It suits you," I say.

She scoffs. "I'm sure it does. My teachers used to give me tons of shit about it. Not the sort of name that gets people to take you seriously."

"That isn't what I mean. Anyhow the teachers here weren't any good." I know that's painting with too broad a brush, but that's all right, as long as it makes Georgie feel better. "It suits you because you're like that. Bright and rare. A little mysterious. That's you, Mulcahy."

She does pretty much what that name of hers says she was meant to do. She *beams* at me.

Then she comes back to our pile of spray paint cans, picking each one up until she finds the one I got on clearance. She doesn't wait for me to ask her what's next. She goes right back up to that rock and—as though it's the most natural thing in the world—she sprays a big pink heart around our initials.

"There," she says, as if she's finally fixed it, finally figured it out.

Georgie Mulcahy, making her mark on me.

Chapter 17

Georgie

"Are y'all gonna get *married*?"

I nearly slice the tip of my finger off at the last word of Bel's blurted question, my face immediately flushing.

I press my lips into an annoyed, flat line and blink meaningfully across the marble island at Bel. Who brings up marriage when someone's slicing an onion!

Rude, if you ask me.

"*Are* you?" she repeats.

I point the knife at her. "Why aren't you grating?"

She sighs heavily from her perch on one of the stylish breakfast bar stools that were delivered to her house yesterday and picks up the triangle of parmesan I've assigned her to. Even this small interruption has my concentration all discombobulated, because, as the green beans in the pasta dish once proved, I'm no chef. My eyeballs superglue themselves back to the cookbook I borrowed from Levi's kitchen this morning, because I'm so concerned about staying on the proper step for this vegetarian lasagna. *Freezes well*, it says, which is why I picked it.

Dice the onion into quarter-inch pieces, I read, and weakly reassure myself that I'm capable of this.

It's a mistake, maybe, to have picked meal prep for today's very important distraction activity for Bel, who, as of today, is two weeks from her due date and also on her first official day of maternity leave. For the last few days, I've sensed her anxiety ratcheting up—every time we texted or were together, she'd talked almost fanatically about work, about meetings that had gotten off track or projects she couldn't trust to anyone else, and I'm certain she's regretting not working right up until she goes into labor. I can tell, too, that Harry's noticed her intensity about it; two nights ago, when I was over here labeling the last few newly organized boxes in the junk room—thanks to me, it's a storage room now, with plenty of available space for the Peloton Annabel ordered at three a.m. two nights ago—I'd seen, for the first time, them snap at each other. Harry had curtly asked how long it'd been since Bel had gotten up from her chair to stretch, and Bel had rolled her eyes and told him—in a tone I'd never heard her use with him—to mind his own business.

So maybe I should've picked something that would've kept me calmer, more confident, less concerned about potential failures. That way, I could've kept focused on Bel entirely, could've probably laughed off her question about marriage, the same way I've laughed off every other question she's asked over the last few weeks, ever since I first told her—in a text I'm not ashamed I sent from his bed the morning after we first slept together—about me and Levi. At first it was *Does he go down* (God, yes) and *Is his bathroom clean* (extremely), but then it became *How nice is he being to your parents* (very; he rebuilt all their outdoor planter boxes) and *Does he have a pet name for you* (not yet, unless you count my last name, and I do). The other night she asked if Levi had given me a key to his house (yes, after the very first night I stayed over), and so maybe to her marriage is the natural next inquiry in this series of pelting but well-meaning questions.

But it's the first one that's made me—for some reason—restless and hand-shaky.

"I'm *grating*," she says, but what she's really saying is, *I'm* waiting.

"We're having a good time" is all I'll say, pushing my diced-onion pile to the corner of a cutting board, bending my head again to the cookbook. I'm only on step two.

Of, like, ten million.

I suppress a groan, trying to shake off this strange mood.

It isn't, of course, that I'm lying to Bel with my answer. Levi and I *are* having a good time—the best time, really, better than anything I've ever had with someone I've been in a relationship with. The sex is incredible; the conversation is easy and interesting and meaningful; the jokes are funny and increasingly personal to the two of us, a private language we're building in all the moments we're alone together.

But being with Levi—*really* being with Levi—it isn't *just* a good time. It's . . . it's a big time, a full time, an *infinite* time. A time where something inside of me is trying desperately to click into place. The first time outside of the bedroom that I truly stopped to let myself feel it was that night a couple of weeks ago at the high school, when I drew that big pink heart around our initials. I'd chalked it up to the fic, to the way the night had been so different from what I pictured for my high school self.

So much *better.*

It's only that the feeling has kept chasing me in moments that have nothing to do with the fic. Being in Levi's boat while he collected samples for his former professor, him quietly explaining to me what he could see about the water quality from looking at a half-inch of plant stem. Lying alone on Levi's bed with Hank snoring beside me, flipping idly through one of those old textbooks. Sitting on my parents' back porch, watching Levi listen patiently to my mom tell him all about his star sign, his face betraying none of his natural suspicion. Letting myself into

Levi's house after work, the smell of something cooking in the air, the sound of Johnny Cash playing from the speaker Levi keeps in the living room. Hank greeting me with his wagging tail; Levi greeting me with his low voice.

But whatever that trying-to-click sensation is—it won't turn over, it won't slide fully into place, and over the last couple of days, while I've been keeping pace with Bel's changed energy, it's gotten harder to ignore. Between Levi and me, there's this ocean of unsaid things, big blanks that hover uncomfortably between us. I don't tell him that I've started working two days a week at The Shoreline's day spa, too; I don't tell him that last Thursday I met his mother, a polite but distant woman named Corrine who Olivia told me spends half the year in Florida and the other half treating her family as little more than acquaintances. He doesn't tell me what that look on his face meant when, as part of his star sign reading, my mom had asked him about his siblings' birthdays, or why, when I needed to take the Prius into the shop yesterday for a new back tire, he didn't offer to drive me over himself to my dinner shift at The Shoreline. My dad had taken me instead.

This morning, when I'd woken up alone in Levi's bed and checked my phone, Bel's 7:30 a.m. **I'M ALREADY BORED** text had greeted me like a judgment, and I'd suddenly felt overwhelmingly under pressure: two weeks to Bel's due date, two weeks to the big event that had been my reason for coming back here, and had I gotten any closer to fulfilling that promise I'd made to myself that afternoon in Nickel's? If I were to stop in there again, if I were to run into a curious, judgmental Mrs. Michaels while waiting in line, what would I have to say for myself? That I took a job waiting tables and scheduling massages and beauty treatments, but it's not permanent? That I've got half my scarce belongings at my parents' house and the other half at Levi Fanning's, and he and I don't talk about his past or our future?

That I'm almost through with my old friend fic, but still not sure if I'm any closer to getting what I wanted out of it?

"That's it?" Bel says, breaking into my thoughts. "A good time?"

I clear my throat, hating the way my own words sound repeated back: superficial and small, when the way I feel about Levi is anything but. I think again about that night out at the rock, and how he'd seemed to understand me automatically, completely. I cling to what he said—that knowing what I *don't* want isn't a blank, after all.

But it'd still be nice if I could know what I do.

I concentrate on slicing a zucchini, wishing I'd picked a freezer meal that would've required less chopping.

And less self-doubt.

She shakes out the cheese grater, sighing heavily as she transfers the pile of parmesan to a bowl. "Fine," she grumbles, grudgingly accepting that I want to change the subject. "Have you heard from Nadia again?"

Oddly enough, that particular question does remind me of my progress—a few weeks ago, the mention of Nadia's name would've either had me at best twitching to check my phone or at worst slipping into the sense of emptiness I used to feel without her telling me what to do. Now, though, I'm simply pleasantly surprised that she's still into donkeys and cacti, and the desert in general.

I nod. "We texted a bit last week. She sent me pictures of a blanket she's crocheting."

I'd sent her back some pictures of my own: the spray-painted rock, no explanation. Hank asleep on the dock, a tiny blep of pink tongue peeking out. A view from the restaurant's patio on an impossibly clear day, the water and sky arguing over who was the more beautiful blue. The mobile for Bel and Harry's baby that I assembled, hanging above the waiting crib. The pile of tissue paper flowers my mom and I finally finished, which she says she might turn into a wall art installation.

Nadia had replied with so many red hearts that I'd had to scroll to reach the end of her text bubble.

"Crocheting!" Bel says. "She *is* done working, huh?"

"I think so." I've finished with the zucchini, and according to Levi's fancy book, there are still approximately one hundred more vegetables to chop. Following recipes is terrible.

"And you? It's . . . you're still liking your work, at the inn?"

"Sure," I say, noncommittal. Across the island, that tight, insistent energy is coming off of Bel, and I recognize it as the same fixation she'd had on work, only now it's redirected. She's taking the first day of this maternity leave hard, so I'll handle the questions if that's what she needs from me.

"I've never minded waitressing, and adding in the spa shifts has been nice—Olivia's got a good thing going there, though she's understaffed, too."

"Maybe you can take over! Be the manager or something?"

I huff a laugh, amused by Bel's stalwart commitment to giving this situation a Hallmark-movie ending: The Shoreline as the proverbial cupcake shop, my professional future tidily settled.

Across from me, she's quiet for a few seconds, and my shoulders relax slightly—my strained mood matched with my efforts at recipe-following are enough stress without the interrogation. But then she says, "Can we go out tonight?"

I blink up at her. "Out?"

She shifts awkwardly on her stool. "You haven't done The Bend yet, right? From the fic?"

"No, but—"

"I can do that one with you. My hip is good, honestly, and my doctor says moving around regularly is the best thing for it. My blood pressure is fine, too."

"Bel," I say, and as soon as I do, I hear it: that subtle note of caution that I've heard in Harry's voice a dozen times since the night we spent at the hospital. I know I've made a mistake.

Bel's eyes flash in frustration.

"I want to go," she says, her voice firm in the same way she uses during her work calls. "This is one I can actually do with you, and I want to."

"I *want* you to. It's only—"

She holds up a parmesan-dusted hand, stopping me. "It's only nothing, Georgie. You've been so good to me, doing everything around here and"—she waves a hand at all my accumulated chopping—"finding all these ways to help me, but now without work I . . ."

She closes her eyes and takes a shaky breath, and I set down my knife and reach for her hand, not caring that we're probably going to melt a glaze of parmesan between our warm palms.

"Babe," I say.

"I know I'm not useless, because . . . *hello*, I'm growing a baby? But also, I feel useless. I feel . . . not like myself. I want to go somewhere that's not this house or the doctor's office, and I want to be the me I was before I got pregnant."

"I get it." Obviously I've never grown a baby, but still, I relate at least on some level. I know all about feeling useless, about wanting to go back, and if that's what I need to do to help Bel now, I will, even if I'm about to get a howler from Harry. It'll probably be like, *Georgie, I don't think this is a good idea*, but that's the same as Harry being mad.

"Also, I want to meet Levi. *Actually* meet him. I'll text Harry; you text Levi, and we'll *all* go out."

I drop her hand and set my own on my hip, narrowing my eyes at her. I like this plan because it doesn't cut out Harry, but I don't like that Bel is probably still going to be in the sort of mood that makes her ask Levi whether we're getting married.

She reads my mind. "I promise, I won't ask after his *intentions*," she says, accentuating that drawl I hear more in her voice lately.

"He might not want to go. He . . ." I trail off, never having explained to Bel about Levi liking to keep his head down, his nose clean. "The Bend probably isn't his scene."

She laughs lightly, waving off that excuse as she slides awkwardly off her stool and stretches her arms above her head, as if she's already getting herself limber for tonight.

"Georgie Mulcahy," she says, "from what I've been seeing the last few weeks, wherever *you* are is that man's scene."

THE BEND IS probably no place for a pregnant person.

There's no smoking allowed in here anymore, thank goodness, and the place overall—big, U-shaped bar and a dining area that gives way to a dance floor—is cleaner, more spacious, and better lit than the way I pictured it back when I was young. Still, the music is loud and so are the people, and drinks get served in big portions and with the kind of quickness that suggests no one except the night's designated drivers stay sober all that long. When the three of us first walked in a half hour ago—Levi's set to meet us after he finishes up work—Harry took one look around and I was pretty sure he was going to grab Bel's hand and walk right back out.

But he must have gotten a version of the same speech she gave me earlier today, because he only clenched his jaw and continued to seem suspicious of everything. Bel told me he called the doctor three times to ask whether coming here was okay, and also there's a blood pressure cuff in the back seat of the car they picked me up in.

Now that we're here, though, both of us can see it: Bel is having the best time.

Harry and I are newly installed at a table that's just come available, ignoring our menus and watching Bel finish up her conversation over at the bar, where we'd been waiting. She's talking animatedly to Melanie Froggart, who used to be Melanie Dinardo when we were in high school. Melanie was nice enough back then, though my opinion of her suffered because of her attachment to Mrs. Michaels, who rightly thought Melanie had the best singing voice in our class and gave her any solo there was to be had. Melanie never learned my alternative lyrics to "The Circle of Life," and I know I can't hold it against her.

She looked about as happy as a clam to see Bel was expecting, because she's got one toddler at home and another baby on the way in about five months' time.

So, I guess The Bend *is* a place for pregnant people.

"She shouldn't be on her feet," says Harry. I look over at him, catch his brow furrowed in an expression I've gotten used to ever since that night at the hospital. When Bel's around, he keeps the brow furrowing in the I-am-sensible-and-in-control range; right this second, though, it has a sort of I-am-in-a-constant-state-of-mortal-terror vibe to it, and my heart clutches for him.

"She's okay, Harry."

He adjusts his cuffs—because he is wearing a very nice dress shirt in a not-all-that-nice bar—and leans back in his chair, though he keeps his eyes on Bel. She's wearing a short, floral-print maternity dress with a denim jacket over top, and she's got on a pair of old cowboy boots that we found a couple of weeks ago in a box of her mom's stuff. In her left hand she's holding a bottle of root beer. She fits right in.

"Now," I say, picking up my menu, determined to distract Harry until Bel comes over. "This place used to be famous for its fried rockfish, but I don't think any of us should get that, since Bel's off seafood. Do you like hot dogs? There's ten different ways they serve a hot dog here. Can she have hot dogs?"

He finally looks over at me, giving me a grateful, embarrassed smile. "Ten different ways?"

I nod enthusiastically, immediately launching into a summary. I'm on the Philly cheese hot dog when Bel comes over, waving her phone back and forth.

"We exchanged numbers!" she announces, lowering herself into the chair beside Harry, leaning over to smack a kiss on his cheek. "She said we can do play dates, isn't that great?" Then she looks over at me. "She also said you're even more adorable than you were in high school."

"Ha," I say, batting my lashes dramatically and pretending

to smooth my hair. The truth is, I took extra time with my appearance tonight, too—I'm wearing my favorite pair of vintage jeans with a drapey, marigold-colored cotton tank that I've always thought looked nice with my coloring. I've even got makeup on, because in the fic, makeup was a feature—the key, I'd thought, to getting in without having our IDs checked.

While Harry and Bel bend their heads together over his menu, I take a few seconds to take it all in, to remind myself of other parts of the fic that involved The Bend. The dance floor isn't too crowded, but there are a few small groups of people shuffling distractedly to the twanging sounds of country music, leaning in to talk to each other over the noise, leaning back to laugh. At the bar, there's a group of guys clustered at one end, all of them staring up in rapt attention at something on the TV I can't see, until they all let out a collective groan, nudging each other and shaking their heads. Two tables away from us, a woman holds up her phone to her three companions, who all lean in and gasp. Then they dissolve into cackles, one of them slapping her palm down on the table with barely contained glee, rattling the rickety table.

I'm not sure preteen me got the full import of what this place offered, but nearly thirty-year-old me does: The Bend is about blowing off steam, and I'm suddenly so grateful Bel insisted we come. While I never made it to this bar back when I lived here, my life after Darentville had, for a while, involved this kind of night—in Richmond, when I was waitressing, my fellow servers and I would often go out after shifts, and my early gigs on sets sometimes involved similar after-work bonding and bitching sessions. Working with Nadia, I'd definitely gotten out of the habit. And while I like my coworkers at The Shoreline, there's no denying the way I keep a measure of distance, the not-quite but not-quite-not secret of Levi always at the front of my mind.

Now that I'm here, though, I can see the way I want this—this noise, this unique buzz of separate-but-togetherness with other people who are out for the night, this collective offload of whatever stress accumulated during the day. I'm light, excited; I'm shuffling off that strange, pressured mood from earlier. And I'm all anticipation for Levi to arrive—for him to see me in my cute top and fancy eyeshadow, for him to sit here with my best friend and her husband, for him to have me cajole him out onto that dance floor later. In this place, it's as though the outside world doesn't exist. This is where everyone goes to get away from their outside worlds, and tonight, I'm ready to play along.

For the next few minutes, I divide my attention between Bel and Harry and the front door. When Levi arrives, my heart flutters in anticipation—he looks so good walking into this room, his best pair of still beat-up jeans, a long-sleeved T-shirt that's pushed partway up his forearms, his expression stoic and remote until he spots me. Once he does, his eyes turn warm and his mouth quirks beneath his beard.

God, I hope he'll dance with me. A slow song, I think. The scruff of his beard tangling with my hair, that soft shirt against my cheek, those strong arms holding my body to his.

I stand as he gets close, and Harry does, too—both of us shoot a warning look at Bel, who rolls her eyes but then seems to agree it's not worth it. Instead, she smiles brightly from her seat, offering up a single, small clap of approval when Levi bends to kiss my cheek in greeting.

"Hi," he says quietly, before turning toward Bel and Harry. "Hello," he says, which I now recognize as Levi's word of greeting when he's nervous, and my heart pulses with affection for all the soft vulnerability in him that only I see.

I set a hand low on his back and make introductions, keeping it simple, nothing like the careful, business-y introductions Bel once made between Harry and Evan. When we're all finally seated again, I've picked up some of Levi's nerves for myself; I'm suddenly worried that there won't be anything on this menu for him to eat, or that the conversation will be strained, or that Levi will wonder about why Harry is wearing a dress shirt at a place with peanut shells on the floor.

But almost immediately, Harry turns to Levi and asks him about building a dock on their property, and everything in me loosens again. I know Levi enough now to know that he can talk about this for hours—everything about what's wrong with bulkheads, with seawalls; everything that's right about living shorelines, about docks built with the right materials. He tells Harry all about why a dock at their house is a bad idea, but he does it in a way that makes Harry nod along in agreement and rapt attention. At one point, I catch Bel's eye and know she's thinking the same thing I am—it's *this* that we pictured when I wrote the fic, no Joe Jonas or Evan Fanning necessary. Harry and Levi hardly stop talking long enough for us to order food, and while I know Bel cares about plans for her house, I can also tell that right now, she cares more about the fact that she's not the center of Harry's nervous attention, that he's finally relaxed enough to enjoy himself.

We smile at each other across the table, and then something even *better* happens: a song by The Chicks starts playing, one of Bel's and my old favorites from back when we were still in elementary school, and both of us whoop in surprised excitement. Bel pushes herself up from her seat, slower now than that day at The Shoreline, but with the same urgency in her expression.

"Georgie, we have got to get out there!"

The dance floor is filling up, the women with the shocking cell phone content already out there, singing along and shaking their hips all out of sync with the music. Harry looks up at Bel, frowning, but I'm on her side—she looks as happy and as excited as I've seen her in weeks, and a little dancing won't hurt. I'm on my feet, too, sparing a glance at Levi, who's looking up at me with that quiet pleasure he does so well.

"Wanna dance?" I ask him, winking.

"I think I'll do just fine here," he says, a teasing note in his voice suggesting that he fully intends to watch.

"Your loss," I say, linking arms with Bel and shimmying out to the dance floor, the chorus kicking up to greet us. The women singing along welcome us as though we're somehow a forgotten part of their party, one of them shouting at Bel to "Get on out here, mama!" Bel laughs and keeps hold of my hand, both of us joining the singalong, both of us laughingly adjusting our moves to accommodate Bel's protruding stomach.

Both of us, frankly, having the *best* time.

I twirl back to face the dining room, catching Levi's gaze. I'm too far away to read his expression, but I can tell he's watching, can tell he's looking at me like I'm the moonbeam he once said I was: bright and rare and mysterious. Out here, I lean into that trying-to-click feeling: on this dance floor, with his eyes on me, it's so close, so good, exactly the right sort of pressure. I'm not worrying about those big, blank spaces between me and Levi; I'm not worrying about two weeks from now, or about what Mrs. Michaels would say, or even about what I want or what I don't.

Bel's left me to get spun around by a woman who's holding a gigantic margarita; she's got a streak of pink in her white hair and the biggest pair of earrings I've ever seen, and she says something to Bel that has her cackling, too. When a small hand settles on my shoulder, I think I'm about to meet another member of this reckless, hilarious party of women, and I turn around with a big smile on my face, ready for the adventure. I'm so caught up in the moment that it takes me a second to register who I'm looking at and how her presence here is about to change everything.

It's Olivia Fanning.

And her brother Evan is standing right behind her.

Chapter 18

Of course I've seen them since that night.

I remember every time it's happened, more frequently in those early days, when all of us were still learning the new normal. Two weeks after, still raw and rattled and barely aware of what I was doing most days, I'd seen Evan from a distance when I was waiting for Carlos's truck to get serviced—his arm in the sling I was responsible for, his head tilted down as he walked across the parking lot of a squat strip mall across the way. Two months after, I'd seen Olivia and my mother inside of a CVS, where I'd gone to pick up the prescription for antidepressants my then-new-to-me therapist had written for me. Olivia hadn't seen me, but my mother had, and one look at her—the flinty, barely interested gaze she'd slid over me—had told me that of all my family, she'd probably miss me least of all. My dad at least felt something toward me, even if it was mostly anger, or maybe something worse.

There'd been other times, too, unavoidable around the county, but most of them had been the sort where everyone tried to pretend they didn't notice each other. Once, almost a year to the day after that night at my parents' house, I'd been hauling wood scrap for placement into Carlos's off-site storage unit over the winter, and I'd looked up from the bed of my truck to see Evan standing there, his hands in his pockets and his jaw set with nervous tension. "Hey, Lee," he'd said, and I'd been about as mean as I ever had, hardly letting him get more than those two words out. "Get gone," I'd said to him, barely moving my mouth, every muscle in my body tight with shame and frustration and a sadness I couldn't admit to back then. "We got nothing to say to each other."

I didn't bother looking at his face to see whether I'd hurt him, but that spring, when I'd been out in Carlos's boat, I'd passed him and my father on theirs, and the way he'd looked right through me suggested I'd succeeded in making sure he wouldn't try to reach out again. I'd told myself I'd done the right thing. I'd protected him.

But as soon as I see my brother and sister show up on that dance floor with Georgie, I know down deep that tonight isn't going to be like those other times.

Maybe I've known it for a few weeks now—not that it'd be here at The Bend, which is the first place where I ever got into a real fistfight, and also the place where I once threw a full plastic pitcher of beer at Barnett Gandry's face for calling me a "stupid rich prick"—but that it'd be somewhere, and that it'd be soon.

It's Georgie who's put the idea in my mind, though she's never said a word about it. In all this going back we do together—horror movies and dock jumping, spray painting at the school, a second trip we took together out to Sott's Mill—Georgie stays well away from the stuff with my family, even though she spends a few days a week around at least some of them. It's the one place she won't go back to, the one place I *told* her never to go back to, and maybe if she meant less to me, I'd say that was just fine.

I'd say that's the way I wanted it to stay.

But she doesn't mean less to me.

And I want her to stay.

I don't suppose I have any illusions about the likelihood of it—of Georgie settling down here with me. I know she's seen a lot out there in the world; I still hear her sometimes, in the quiet of my mind, say that scoffing *Oh, God no* to my question about whether she was moving back here for good.

But I hear other things, too—her funny chatter with Hank when she thinks I'm not listening, her sleepy sighs when I pull her close to me in bed, her bright laughter when she talks to her parents. I hear her big, expansive brain whirring with the ideas she says out loud—what she's going to do over at Bel's, whether I should get one of those robot vacuums, why it's roundabout time for her dad to think about putting some additional accessibility features in their house. Sometimes I think I hear the ones she doesn't say, too, and all of them have to do with the two people who right now look thrilled to see her out on that dance floor.

I know that if I want to have any hope at all of her staying, I can't go on asking her to keep two parts of the life she does have here separate. I know I've got to make them fit, if I want her to fit with me.

"Are you all right?" says a voice next to me, and I realize that I caught sight of my siblings right at the moment Harry was asking me a question about sediment runoff. Who knows how long I've been sitting here like a block of stone.

I clear my throat, nod toward the dance floor. "Georgie's run into some of her colleagues there."

I sound deranged, referring to my brother and sister this way.

Even from here, I can see she's not comfortable—before, she was laughing and dancing, more ray of sunshine than mysterious moonbeam. But now she's neither, all her light switched off. She's gone still; when Olivia gives her a quick hug she seems surprised and stiff, momentarily relieved when Olivia turns her delighted attention to Bel, but only until my brother leans in for a hug, too.

Right when the music changes to something slow.

He keeps a hand on her hip, as if he's making a suggestion. As if he's about to hold her close.

I stand from my chair.

Harry stands, too. He's a pretty good guy, and I'm not just saying that because he obviously cares about climate change.

"Oh, wait, that's—"

Whatever the rest of his sentence is—maybe he recognizes Evan from The Shoreline, maybe he recognizes the resemblance we have to each other—I don't hear it. I'm too focused on the way Georgie steps back from my brother, her smile wobbly and her eyes darting to mine, something miserable and anxious in them.

I'm moving toward her before I have time to second-guess it.

Before I have time to think about what I'll say.

"Levi," she says, the first time I've ever heard her say my name in that tone—cautious, tight, small. I can feel my brother's eyes on me, but I can't look at him yet.

"This is . . ." she begins, then trails off, obviously realizing the awkwardness of making an introduction between two brothers. Out of the corner of my eye, I see Harry guide Bel away into a slow dance, though I'm guessing they're both still watching this trainwreck, too.

"Evan," I say, finally meeting his eyes, right at the moment Olivia returns to Georgie's side. "Liv," I add, my voice barely audible even to me.

We're an unmoving, unsmiling foursome at the edge of this dance floor, and I know I ought to have something else to say. But I might as well have taken a plastic pitcher to the face, and for long seconds all I can do is take in the changes to theirs— Evan sporting light stubble, Liv wearing a full face of makeup; both of their cheekbones more defined and grown-up looking than what I remember. I know how my own face must look: tense and set.

Olivia breaks the silence first. "Well, it's . . . it's really something that we'd all run into each other here."

There's the lilt of a question at the end of her sentence, and I realize that it's not clear to her—or, obviously, to Evan—that I didn't come over to say hello, despite all my years of doing determinedly the opposite. Despite all my years of not being seen anywhere other than on the job or out doing errands.

They don't know I'm here with Georgie, and I've got no one to blame for that but myself.

All of a sudden, there's a trap door beneath me again. I know in the rational part of my brain that I'm staring an opportunity right in the face—right in three faces—and all I need to do is say something polite, something normal, something that'd get Georgie to see it'd be okay if she stayed working at The Shoreline for as long as she wanted to, that we'd all be okay in this town together, if she'd stay.

Something that'd get my siblings to see that she and I fit.

But I'm not listening to that part of my brain. I'm listening to the part of my brain that sees Evan shift closer to Georgie, as if he has to protect her from me; I'm listening to the part of my brain that sees Liv looking at me with wide, disbelieving eyes. I'm listening to the part of me that says—no matter that it makes no kind of sense, no matter that Ev and Liv never punished me the way my dad did—*Don't take her from me.*

"Georgie," I say, my voice rough, clipped. "I'm ready to go."

She stares at me, blinking once in surprise, her mouth opening and then closing again, her face paling, and I know I've fucked up. This was more than an opportunity to act polite and normal, to show her I could handle her job here, her life here. This was an opportunity to name this thing between us, and not in a way that makes me seem like an impatient asshole.

"We just ordered our food," she finally says, clinging to practicality in the face of this absolute mess I'm making.

Evan looks back and forth between us.

"You're together?" he says, a note of suspicious surprise in his voice, and I hate the way it sounds. It's the same one I got used to hearing in those first years I worked for Carlos, when he'd introduce me to clients as part of his team. "Levi Fanning?" they'd say back to him, with the same tone.

"That a problem?" I say, sharp and challenging and automatic, and I hate the way that sounds, too. As if I'm a few harsh words from getting into another fistfight in here, when I'd never lay a hand on my brother, not ever. When I'd do everything I could—when I *have* done everything I could—to never hurt either of my siblings again.

But there's an old war inside me now, and the Levi I want to be is losing. My body is braced, tense, everything about me forbidding. From the outside, I know how I must look.

Like trouble.

If Georgie walks out of here and never speaks to me again, I'd deserve it.

Instead, with her eyes steady on mine and her voice flat with disappointment, she says three words that should reassure me, but somehow don't.

"Yeah, we're together."

"I'M NOT getting out."

Over on her side of the bench seat, sitting about as close to the passenger side door as she can get, Georgie's got her arms folded across her chest and her lips set in a firm line. Her eyes are on the dark river ahead, my dock barely visible from the spot where I've parked in front of my house.

It's the most I've heard her say since we left The Bend, since she'd followed her declaration to my brother and sister with another one: She was, in fact, ready to go. She'd said, "Excuse us," and then she'd taken my hand and yanked me toward where Bel and Harry were dancing, both of them hardly concealing the way they'd seen everything.

"Levi and I have to leave," she'd said sharply. "Harry, I'll Venmo you our half of the check."

"No, I'll—" I'd tried to interject, but Georgie had given me a look that was like to slash my insides to ribbons. She'd stomped right past my siblings and back out the door I'd pushed my way through less than an hour before.

Then, she sat pressed over against that door in stony silence the whole way home.

I pause in the act of unhooking my seat belt, confused. I expected that we'd get here and she'd get out, go back to her parents' place. Her Prius is parked only a few feet away, after all, and I don't think she even had time for a drink at the bar.

"You're not?" My voice sounds like I haven't used it in ages. It wasn't even that long of a car ride back here, but every second was an eternity.

For the first time, she turns enough to look at me, her eyes flashing. "*No*, Levi, I'm not. I want to talk about whatever *that* was back there."

I swallow, part of me relieved and part of me still awful afraid of that trap door. I go ahead and unhook the seat belt. "Out here?"

"Yes, out here!" she snaps, then huffs, facing the windshield again. "I don't want to argue in front of Hank."

I face the windshield, too, mostly because I don't want her to see that she's given me a scrap of hope, saying that. I don't want Hank to see me and her arguing, either.

"Tonight was important to Bel," she says. "And you know what? It was important to *me*. I was so close to—"

She breaks off, shakes her head, looks down at her lap.

"To what?"

"It doesn't matter." She sighs heavily and starts over. "You treated me like I was something you'd called dibs on."

I wince, rubbing a hand over my face, down my beard. "I'm sorry."

"And you treated Evan like he was some random guy you were

about to scrap with. You barely even *looked* at Olivia, and listen, I know you don't want to talk about your family, but these are people I work with, and to me, they've been nothing but kind. If they've done something to you, and that's why you acted that way, then you need—"

"Georgie," I say softly. "I know I have to tell you."

She quiets, and I spare a look at her. She's still got her head tipped down, her arms crossed tight.

"I've been thinking about telling you."

She says nothing, but I can hear her anyway. *Well, you didn't.* I take a breath, steeling myself.

"They haven't done anything to me," I admit, finally. "My brother and sister, I mean. I don't talk to them because my dad asked me not to. Told me not to."

She lifts her head and meets my eyes.

"There cannot possibly be a good reason for that."

There is, I want to say, but also if I say that, I'll be making the same sort of mistake I made out on that dance floor, not letting her decide for herself. I face the windshield again.

"That school my dad sent me to," I say, a sick roiling in my gut, "it wasn't a nice place. I thought I was pretty tough going in there, but I basically got my ass beat for the first few weeks, and that wasn't even the worst of it. It was the kind of place where someone would take a shit on your mattress to teach you a lesson."

"God, Levi," she says, but if she's about to offer up more pity, I don't want it. I press ahead, not giving her the chance.

"You learn how it works, after a while, and then you get on with it. But by the time I got out, I wasn't right in the head. I moved to Richmond with this guy I bunked with at school, Danny. Got a job, but also mostly—" I shake my head, grip the steering wheel. "I don't know. Smoked a lot of weed to help me sleep, took a lot of Adderall I wasn't prescribed to help me get awake enough to work. I wasn't ever myself."

I clench my back teeth, letting a wave of old, familiar embarrassment pass over me. I thought I'd let go of the shame about this part of my life, the way I was basically medicating myself twenty-four hours a day. It's no different from what millions of people do, good people who are in pain or unsure of where to turn; good people who need a break from everything in this world that's hard and sad and unforgiving.

But telling Georgie, that's a different story.

She hasn't moved over there.

"When I was twenty-two, I got it in my mind I'd come home for Thanksgiving. Danny and I had both been working construction for a few months, and I felt like some sort of big man, making decent money. I hadn't been back here since my dad sent me away, and I figured I'd be showing him something. Evan was in his first semester of college, and Liv had just started high school. I thought I'd be showing them something, too, that I wasn't the brother they remembered."

I was worse, I know now. But I didn't know that then.

"For all I thought I was being tough, coming back here, I was too chickenshit to come alone. So I brought Danny. I thought—"

I stop myself from saying that I thought he was a good guy. He was my friend; we had some laughs, and he helped me out when I came up short on utilities a few times. But that doesn't make for a good guy, and I knew it. I knew Danny did harder stuff than me. I knew he treated the women he brought home like they were garbage that needed to be taken out the next morning. I knew he could cover my utilities because he wasn't only working construction. I knew he had pain of his own, problems of his own, but I also knew he was more trouble than me.

I knew, and I brought him with me anyway.

Later, I realized, it maybe was its own vengeance of a sort. I wanted to show my dad more than me with a steady job, living on my own, out from under his thumb. I wanted to show him what crowd he'd gotten me into, sending me to that place. I wanted to show him how far outside of his circles I'd gotten.

I didn't think about anything else. Anyone else.

I roll down my window, let the cool night air and the breeze off the river calm me. I want to get the next part over with, and quick.

"I didn't call ahead or anything. I showed up with this guy, and I could tell my dad didn't like it, and that meant I did. I drank too much, because I could, because I was legal and he couldn't stop me, and because I knew it'd make him mad."

I pause, a short, humorless laugh caught in my throat. "Our pastor was there. I thought that was a real opportunity, embarrassing him in front of a church person."

"Levi," she says, sympathy in her voice, and I shake my head again.

"I told you before. I own it."

And I own this next part, too.

"I was in the bathroom, digging a pill out of my pocket, because I was drowsy from all the wine I'd had. And then—" I swallow again. "I heard this awful racket, glass breaking and my sister screaming, my dad shouting. A good few seconds, I froze. Too fucked up to move quick."

For all the chaos that happened after, I remember that moment in the bathroom the clearest, for some reason. The glass soap dispenser, the hand towels that had pumpkins and fall leaves embroidered on them, the mirror free of chips and streaks. I'd never noticed any of that before. *This is such a nice bathroom*, I was thinking, trying to get a hold of that pill.

"Evan found Danny on the back deck," I say, wishing I could make my voice harsh enough for this, the worst thing I ever did to my family. "He had a handgun. He was showing it to Olivia."

"Oh, Levi," Georgie whispers.

"Evan went after him, eventually shoved him through the back window. Broke his own collarbone while he was at it, which is why he didn't play the second half of his first college football season. Pretty sure he never played again. Danny got all cut up from the glass, so there was blood everywhere in the house. Olivia got sick when she saw it."

She'd looked so young. She'd looked terrified. And Evan—all that anger on his face, and Danny's blood on his shirt.

He'd looked like me.

You are a poison to this family.

"That night, my dad told me he didn't want me around anymore. Not around the house, around the inn, around him or my mother. But especially not around Ev and Liv."

If they contact you, ignore them, he'd said. *Or I will cut them out, too.*

"He can't still feel that way," she says.

"Georgie. I could've gotten my sister killed. I could've gotten my brother killed. That gun was loaded."

"But—"

"No," I say, firm and hard, because there's no excusing it. "No."

She goes quiet again.

"I wasn't sober enough to drive home, obviously. I don't know if Danny was, but he did anyway. I walked for hours that night, and then I passed out in what I thought was the middle of nowhere." I nod out the windshield. "But it was roundabout there, where my dock is. Carlos found me the next morning."

Everything after that, I'll tell her about, too, if she wants to know it. The way Carlos took me in and cleaned me up, the way he gave me work that kept my hands busy and my body near the water, the way he got me going to therapy, eventually.

But I'm running out of energy—the comedown after a rush of something intense and unexpected. I'm grateful that she doesn't ask me anything else about that time where I was getting straightened out, even if it means she's over there thinking this isn't enough of an explanation for the way I acted tonight.

"If I'd done everything my father wanted, I would've left here and not come back. But I built my life back here, and I'm sure he hates that enough. The least I can do is keep away from Ev and Liv. Not because he told me to, but because it's the right thing to do for both of them. I know that makes things hard for you, Georgie, with your job—"

"Seriously?" she yells.

I look over at her, surprised. This doesn't strike me as a yelling kind of story, but maybe I'm too close to it.

"I don't care about my *job*, Levi!" She blinks when she says it, as if she's surprised herself, but it's only a split second before she moves on. "Your dad is . . . he is *terrible*."

I'm not going to argue with her. He *is* terrible, or at least he always was to me, and I don't have to forgive him for the things he did that made my life harder. But also, I know who I was back then, and he was trying to pro—

"I'd like to tell him what I think about his parenting!" she says, because I guess she's decided I'm good and done talking for a while. "What an awful thing to do to a person—*your son!*—who was in *trouble*! And also!" She sort of . . . points at the air. "Your brother and sister should *know* it was an awful thing to do!"

"It isn't their fault."

"Well, it isn't *yours*, either!"

She gets out of the truck.

For a second, I'm not sure whether she wants me to follow her. I've had a lot of experience with people being mad at me, but I'm not real sure I've ever experienced someone being mad on behalf of me, and I think that's what Georgie is.

It's got to be one of the best things I ever felt.

She's stomping across the yard, past her Prius and out toward the dock, and maybe she wants a minute to herself or something—I can kind of see she's still gesturing at the air, keeping on with her yelling even if no one's hearing her—but she's got to know I won't let her go out there on her own when it's dark. Probably she doesn't want me to remember that clumsy splash off Buzzard's Neck, but I do, and we don't need a nighttime repeat.

"*Pas*cal Fanning," she's muttering, when I get closer, when

I'm only a few steps behind her, and it hits me all at once, the full force of what I feel for her—one of those big, pounding waves again, right here on the calm shore of the river where I've spent the most settled years of my life.

"Georgie," I say, because it's too big to stay quiet about. Too big to wait for her to work off her anger.

She huffs and turns around. "What!"

Well, I guess she's still mad at me, too. And maybe that means I shouldn't say this next thing, not right this second, but I'm too far gone with it now. I'm pretty sure I've been too far gone with it for a while.

"I love you. I'm in love with you."

"What," she says again, quieter now.

"I'll tell you every ugly thing about me if you want to know it. I'll tell you that I saw you out there with my brother and sister tonight and felt like I was going back to when I was twenty-two years old again, looking at the better versions of me, the ones who always acted right, always fit in. I'll tell you that I saw my brother touch you and all I could think was that I was about to lose you, same as I lost a whole lot of things I loved back when I was young. I messed up, acting how I did, and I know it. But I'm good at fixing things, Georgie, and I'll fix this. I'll do whatever you want."

So you'll stay, I want to add. *So you'll fit here with me forever.* My head echoes with the crashing crest of that wave—every idea I have for keeping Georgie and me together bubbling and foaming in the aftermath.

But I force myself to ignore it. I can hardly believe everything I've already said. Probably bad enough I chose this moment to tell her I love her; I don't want to make it worse by bringing up her future when I know she's still figuring it out.

She's quiet long enough that the back of my neck heats in embarrassment. I shove my hands in my pockets and lower my head, staring down at the straight, sturdy planks beneath my feet.

Until she steps toward me, the toes of her shoes inches from mine.

"You love me?" she asks, almost a whisper.

I look up, meet her eyes. Even in the dark, I can see they're big and brimming wet and beautiful, and I hope that's because she's been hit with the same wave as me.

But I don't need her to say it. Not now, not like this.

I lift my hands and cup her soft cheeks in my rough palms, and I say to her the last two words I've got in me tonight. Two words I've said to her before, and this time I don't mind at all if they sound like a vow.

Because that's how I mean them.

"I do."

Chapter 19

Georgie

Levi Fanning loves me.

It's the first thing I think when I wake up the next morning—my eyes still heavy with sleep, my limbs still pleasantly achy, my heart still full to bursting. Even though I vaguely remember the soft kiss Levi pressed against the top of my head a couple of hours ago before he left for work, it's instinct to roll over and scoot myself closer to his side of the bed, wanting to get close to him—to whatever warmth he left behind. I press my nose into his pillow and inhale the scent of his shampoo and his detergent and *him.*

He loves me.

For long minutes, in the dozing in between my consciousness, I let it sink into me again, flashes of last night coming back: Levi sliding the silky fabric of my top over my head, running his rough fingertips lightly over my shoulders, down my arms; Levi walking me backward toward the bed, his mouth never leaving mine, his manner soft and slow and determined. It'd been perfectly quiet between us—not the heavy, tense silence of the ride back from The Bend, but something weightless and easy, something healing. I lift a hand and settle two of my fingers in the hollow above my collarbone, stroking the spot where I swear I felt a tear slide across my skin last night, when Levi pressed his face against my neck after he came.

I'd held him against me, my own eyes welling in desperate affection for him, for all he'd been through when he'd been young and on his own. I'd felt fierce and overwhelmed and protective, like I wanted to build a wall around him and his broken heart, like I'd wanted to find Pascal Fanning and give him a list of all the ways he'd failed his son. I don't know how long I stayed awake after Levi had fallen almost immediately into a leaden, unmoving sleep, but it must've been hours.

Building my imaginary wall, making my imaginary list.

As I come more fully awake, though, I realize my middle-of-the-night fierceness is now living alongside something else—there's that pressure again, that trying-to-click feeling, a now-narrower sliver of blank space that still won't fill, no matter how happy Levi made me last night, no matter how perfectly we'd come together, no matter how protective I'd felt.

It's because you didn't say it back yet, my brain supplies hopefully in answer, and I'm desperate to listen: It's true that I didn't say it back, true that I'd gone along with what had struck me as Levi's pretty intense need for both of us to say nothing at all. And it's true that it's only a *yet*—that there's no question about whether I love him back. I plan to tell him a hundred times, a thousand times, *infinite* times, even though I think he already knows.

But my brain has nothing on that blank space. I picture it—a small but bright white void, surrounded by its own imaginary wall, miles and miles high. Impenetrable.

So maybe it's only fitting that the next thing I think about is my not-imaginary list.

The notebook.

The fic.

I sit up in bed, shoving a wild tangle of hair out of my eyes, huffing out a sigh of frustration at myself, gusty enough to disturb Hank from his post-breakfast, post-morning walk slumber. He lifts his head and cocks it to the side as he gazes at me, and even though he's probably thinking about food or Levi or whatever he's been sniffing at beneath the old gum tree in the front yard for the last week and a half, I can't help but take his curious stare as some kind of question: *What's that sigh all about?*

And the thing is—it's a good question, actually, even if Hank isn't actually asking it. What's frustrating about waking up and not having every single problem solved by a man being in love with me, by my being in love with him? If anything, I probably ought to be happy about that trying-to-click feeling sticking around this morning; I probably ought to take it as another sign of all the progress I've made. I'm not the same Georgie who showed up here a month and a half ago, lost without a boss to tell her what to do, desperate to find something to fill all my time so I wouldn't have to think about my future. Instead, I'm the Georgie who's been working on it; I'm the Georgie who knows that building a wall around Levi's heart and making a list of grievances on his behalf won't be enough to make me whole.

I'm the Georgie who knows I still have stuff to figure out, and who knows deep down I'm getting closer.

I make my way out of bed, standing on tired legs and crossing the room to stroke my palm across Hank's smooth, flat head in apology. "Sorry about that, little submarine," I croon, using one of the many nonsensical nicknames I have come up with for him over the last several weeks. He lightly thwacks his tail against the floor in contented greeting before lowering his chin onto his paws and falling back into a snuffling sleep.

On the chair in the corner, there's a messy pile of my things— some of my clothes from last night, my robe, my purse, the work shirt I wear for spa shifts, a wrinkled canvas tote bag I bought last time I was at Nickel's. I find what I'm looking for beneath it all, its worn cover more worn now, its softened cardboard cover a familiar texture beneath my palm.

I take it back to the bed, propping up pillows and pulling the covers back over my lap, settling myself in. Levi's dim-display nightstand clock—bright lights and phones in the bedroom are bad for his sleep hygiene, I learned a few weeks ago—tells me it's only a few minutes after eight, so it's hours before I have to show up at The Shoreline and act normal, even after everything I know now. I'm suddenly grateful for the time, for the privacy—for the filled-up feeling this fic still holds for me. Somehow, I still think the answer is in here.

I *want* it to be in here.

It's not strange, given how much he features in this thing, that the first page I happen to open to is one with the wrong brother's name all over it: my fictional prom date, the one who I pictured bringing me a corsage of pale-pink roses, a perfect match to the ball gown-style dress I imagined wearing; the one who would be driving the same car as—wow, this is terrible— Edward Cullen in the first *Twilight* movie.

Any other morning, I'd probably laugh at myself—all these heart *a*'s, God—but this morning, my instinct is to cringe at the sight of it. It isn't that I've made Evan the villain of the story Levi told me—that honor still rests with Levi's dad, and also that guy Danny. If anything, with a few hours of distance, I have almost as much empathy for Evan and Olivia as I do for Levi. I'm sure they've each endured their own share of pain over what happened that night, and probably a bunch of nights before it and since.

Instead, it's that all my girlish imaginings—corsages, cars from *Twilight*, Evan draping his tuxedo jacket over my bare shoulders—are comically shallow after these weeks with Levi, after last night with Levi. I can see, between the lines, what I wanted from that prom date—to feel special, to fit in, to be *adored*—but none of it, of course, translates anymore. None of it feels like someone eating your weird cooking or buying you cans of spray paint; none of it feels like someone showing up to a crowded bar and watching you dance with your pregnant best friend and a pink-haired drunk lady. None of it—

Hank and I both startle at the shrill ring of my phone in the other room, cutting through our cozy silence. I think, fleetingly, of ignoring it—yet another sign of my progress since coming back here, wedded to my phone as I once was—but since I mostly keep it on "Do Not Disturb" these days, it's only those contacts I have marked as "Favorites" whose calls come through with noise. I get out of bed again, smiling with the memory of adding Levi to that list only a few weeks ago. If it's him, I decide, I won't stop myself from blurting *I love you* right when I answer.

When I get to the kitchen counter, though, I see the screen lit up with Bel's name. I should've expected that—not only is it close to the time yesterday's **I'M ALREADY BORED** text came through, it's also the morning after Levi and I left *very* suddenly from a double date that had, up to that unexpected Fanning family reunion, been going great. She's either looking for company or for a full debrief, or both, and when I swipe to answer, I expect her to start yelling at me before I have the chance to say hello.

Instead, her voice comes through small and scared. "Georgie?"

"What's wrong?" My heart's already pounding.

"Okay, well," she says, sounding out of breath. "The thing is, I'm in labor."

IF EVER THERE was a time where my high tolerance for chaos comes in handy, it's in the closest local hospital, where, barely an hour after she first called me, Bel and I arrive with one not-so-neatly packed bag and two not-so-well-hidden expressions of shock. In fairness to me, Bel—she of the many "I can pack for a three-day business trip in a single compact carry-on" boasts over the years—not having a perfectly arranged go bag packed for her labor is a pretty shocking development, which I'm definitely going to ask her about later. But in fairness to her, the harsh reality of having to actually push a baby out of one's vagina seems pretty shocking, no matter how much time you've had to prepare for it.

Also, her water broke all over the passenger seat of my Prius.

Now that we've been here a while, though, I am *in* it—I handled the absurdly bureaucratic check-in with ease; I got Bel changed into the soft, loose nightgown we brought from home; I took out and refolded or laid out everything we'd stuffed into that go bag. I stood by Bel's side when the labor and delivery nurse came to hook her up to a monitor; I took notes on my phone when the doctor on rounds came in to check her. I know that Bel is five centimeters dilated and that her blood pressure is still in a range the doctor is unconcerned about; I also know that it could still be hours before she has to push. I've memorized the names of every person at the nurse's station, conveniently positioned only a few steps outside this room's door, and I've also managed to find the perfect television volume to mostly drown out some very upsetting noises coming from down the hall.

The only problem is, Harry isn't here.

And I can tell Bel isn't okay.

It was only when we were halfway out her front door that she'd said, as casual-as-you-please, "I better call Harry," and I'd shrieked my surprised "*WHAT!*" at her. It'd been bad enough to know that he wasn't home; I'd had no idea she hadn't even *called* him yet. She'd claimed she hadn't wanted to until she was sure this was the real thing, and then—probably when she watched my eyebrows disappear into my hairline in disbelief, worse than when she told me the go bag wasn't ready—she'd admitted that they'd had a fight.

And that she "didn't want to talk about it."

Then she'd had another contraction, right there on her front porch.

In the car—*before* the water breaking—she'd finally called him, her voice strangely, falsely calm, even as Harry grew more frantic. He was already two hours away, snarled in traffic on I-95 on his way to DC, and I'd had to press the back of my hand to my mouth to keep from blurting out ten thousand questions about why he'd go up there in the first place. Hadn't he decided no more work trips, not since the last one he'd taken? Not when the due date was this close?

I know something's happened between them, and I know—I *know*—she's quietly freaking out about it.

From my spot on the chair I've pulled close beside her bed, I turn my head slightly and strain my ears to listen for any of those distressing-down-the-hall noises. When I don't hear any, I lift the remote from the arm of my chair and lower the volume on the television.

"Do you want to talk about it yet?" I say.

"No," she says, plucking at the white waffle-knit blanket covering her lap.

"You're sure?"

She nods miserably, her eyes welling, and my stomach clenches. It's been hard seeing Bel in physical pain over the last two hours, but this is worse, to know she's hurting in this way, too. This isn't how I want this to be for her—I want her filled up with anticipation, with love for the family she and Harry are about to expand.

"Tell me what happened with you and Levi last night," she says, sniffling.

I know what she's doing, know she wants a distraction, and I'd pretty much do anything she asked of me right now. Still, I hesitate. The story Levi told me last night isn't one he'd want me to share, especially with someone he still doesn't know very well. And beyond that—with the way Bel looks right now, I don't know if a story about Levi and me fighting and making up is the best choice for distraction, since she's still clearly waiting on the latter with Harry.

"Georgie, come on. Get my mind off of this. You've probably got six minutes before the next one."

I scoot my chair closer, stilling Bel's blanket-plucking hand with my own. I turn it, palm side up, and start massaging her wrist and fingers. Years ago, before I worked for Nadia, I had a boss who loved hand massages, but who also never had time to actually get them done by a professional. Five YouTube videos later and she'd proclaimed me "better than anyone she'd ever paid." Bel sighs in relief.

I give her the abridged version, the protecting-Levi's-privacy version: the version where I tell her that Levi's reputation for troublemaking was only ever part of the story, that his reaction to his brother and sister last night at The Bend was less about them and more about the man at the head of their family who never treated Levi right. I tell her that he told me so much, things I can't tell her now, but things that made me think Levi Fanning is the strongest, most sensitive man I know.

I tell her he said he loves me.

She interrupts my massage by gripping my hand tightly. She looks at me with a weepy-happy smile.

"You don't even have to tell me if you love him. It's been all over your face for weeks."

"I know. But I—"

"Oh my God!" she blurts, squeezing my hand tighter and stopping me from explaining that I haven't had a chance yet to say it back. "Does that mean you're going to *move* here?" she says, her voice high-pitched and desperate. "Like *forever*?"

"Oh. I mean, we hav—"

"Georgie," she says, and now the hand squeezing is . . . intense. I spare a glance at her belly, though I have no idea what I'm expecting to see there. "You should. You *have* to."

I'm dimly aware of the fact that this conversation—me, moving back here, forever!—would have sounded absurd to me two months ago; I'm also dimly aware of the fact that it doesn't automatically sound absurd to me now. But I'm way more than dimly aware that the look in Bel's eyes has nothing to do with me and what she's asking.

I gently pry her fingers from around the edge of my hand, resituating things so there's less chance of my bones cracking into pieces. I say, "Bel?"

And she bursts into tears.

Noisy, messy, nose-running tears.

I abandon the chair and sit as best I can on the edge of the bed; I lean over to push the hair from her face and to dab my sleeve against her cheeks. It's awkward, clumsy, and I realize that's because I've never seen Bel cry this hard, not even when her mom was at her most ill, not even when she passed, not even at the funeral. Not even in those bleak, sad months afterward, when her tears on FaceTime and over the phone were frequent but soft. Streams, not storms.

"I messed up, Georgie," she finally says, when she can catch her breath.

"You didn't," I say immediately. I know it doesn't make sense, because I don't know what she's even talking about. But when your best friend in the world is this upset, you say *you didn't*, and you mean it with your whole heart. You mean that they've never made a mistake in their whole life that you're willing to acknowledge.

"I did," she sobs, dropping her chin to her chest, and I'm soothing her, cooing to her, telling her to take breaths. It can't be good for her, crying this much when her body is doing what it's doing. I send a worried look toward those monitors, as if I've got any idea what they say.

Eventually, she looks up at me—red-faced, wet-faced, devastated-faced. She takes a big breath and says, "I *hate* it here."

I blink, still too shocked to be anything but foolishly literal. "I mean. It's sterile, sure, but—"

"I hate Darentville. I hate the whole county. I *hate* my house."

"What?"

"I hate it; it's so big and there's carpet everywhere, and you know what? I don't even like that gliding chair in the nursery; it makes me nauseated every time I sit in it. I hate that I have a *yard* and also there's so much *nature* out there—"

"Nature?" I say, confused, but I don't think she hears me.

"And Harry hates it, too, you know. He doesn't want to say, but he does. He's bored and he hates working from home, and last night after you guys left someone spilled a bright blue slushy drink on his back and I think a part of him died on the inside."

Oh no, I think automatically. *Harry wears such nice shirts.*

I don't have time to dwell on it, because Bel is absolutely *unloading*.

"I miss my job. Why did I leave my job? And also, my townhouse; I fucking *loved* my townhouse, Georgie!"

"I know you did," I say, still doing shock-blinks, because Bel never says the f-word.

"You have to *drive* everywhere here. No restaurants serve the food we like. My eyes hurt from looking at the computer all day, and I have to reset my router every two goddamn hours because the Wi-Fi sucks. It's quiet and terrible and *small*. Why did I *do* this, Georgie?"

I'm so stunned I can barely think of anything to say. I cling to the most obvious one, the reason we're here, the reason Bel said she wanted to change her life. "The . . . the baby?"

She wails.

"Oh no," I whisper, fully climbing into the bed with her now, hoping I don't but not really caring whether I disturb the equipment she's hooked up to. I put an arm around her and draw her close to me. Again, it's awkward, unwieldy, too small a space for this sort of cuddle, but it's a necessity. I let her cry and cry.

"I don't think I can do this," she says. "Be a mom, I mean. That's why I couldn't bring myself to pack the go bag, because

I'm not *ready*. I know I've always wanted it, Georgie, but I'm not ready for it yet."

"You are," I say fiercely. "You will be the best mom, Bel. I've never been more sure of anything."

She shakes her head against me. My shirt is wet, tons of Bel's tears and probably a fair bit of her snot. I'm still making out better than the passenger seat of the Prius, though.

"I miss my mom," she whispers brokenly, and my heart seizes with pain. "I think that's why I moved back, because I got pregnant and all I could think was, *I miss my mom so much*. And she would've helped me, Georgie. She would have lived here, too, and she would've helped me with this. She would have taught me how to do it."

"Oh, babe." I hold her tighter, my chest aching. "She'll still teach you how to do this. She will. Because you're hers, and you're wonderful. You're going to be so good, Belly."

She gasps and finds my free hand, squeezing it tight again. "Oh God."

I shift, moving back to the chair, giving her room and letting her crush my hand while she breathes and sweats and still cries, while her body works to do this incredible thing that I know, I *know* she's ready for. I must tell her a dozen times while she makes her way through it; I tell her she's perfect and strong; I tell her how proud her mom would be.

When it passes, she sags back against the pillows, and I'm in awe of her. I'm in awe of anyone who's ever done this, frankly; everyone who has should get a million dollars and also an opportunity to punch someone they don't like in the face. I get her water and a cool washcloth for her forehead, for her tear-streaked cheeks.

"I made him go this morning," she says, once I've gotten her cooled down, though she's still fighting tears. "Harry. There was a quarterly meeting at his firm, and he was going to telecom it, but . . . but I don't *know*. After y'all left last night he hardly talked about anything except my hip and my blood pressure and my swollen ankles, and I'm *sick* of it; I'm sick of this"—she gestures at her stomach—"being the only thing about me, and we had a fight, and then this morning, I—"

She breaks off, shakes her head.

"You what, B?"

"I hassled him so much; I said he should go, said I *needed* him to go, to give me some time alone."

"Bel, there's nothing wrong with needing time alone. I know he's been a lot lately."

"But I think I *knew*," she says, and it's a confession. "I knew today was the day, I had a *feeling* today was the day. But I'm scared, and I know we've made a mistake coming here, trying to reinvent our whole lives, and I don't know how to admit it to him. I've never made a mistake like this, and I don't know how to face the mess I've made, so I sent him away, and now—"

She starts crying again and, honestly, forget about this being more crying than I've ever seen from Bel. This is world-record crying.

"It's okay," I say. "He's coming. He's on his way, Bel, and he'll be here soon."

"I know he will, but . . . but what will I *do*? What will I do with how I feel about my house, and this town, and my job, and . . . everything? What will I do, when I'll have a *baby* to take care of?"

I look long at her—my beautiful, polished, perfect best friend, an absolute mess—and I do the only thing I can think of that might have a chance of helping.

I start talking.

"Well, the first thing is, we're going to let ourselves think of that house you've got as a luxury postpartum retreat. . . ."

I lay it all out for her. I talk about that big steam shower in her master bath and how it'll help her heal; I talk about the cushy carpet that'll pad her bare feet when she's pacing back and forth, soothing the baby back to sleep. I talk about how my parents and I will keep filling her fridge with meals; I talk about how she can flip on the gas fireplace and curl up with Harry on that huge, fancy couch they ordered. I describe how they'll sit together while the baby sleeps and look for someplace new to live, someplace back in the District, or if that's not right anymore, then at least somewhere close to it. I explain that they'll find something better than the old townhouse; I remind her of the drafty windows and the tiny bathrooms there; I tell her that she always wanted to live closer to a Metro station, anyway. I promise that her new house will sell inside of a week, once she's ready; I brag about how much her old job will want her back, and how she doesn't even have to take it, how she can still have her own consultancy business in the District. I describe the perfect daycare I'm picturing, the playground that'll be on the walk home from it, the best babysitter that they're going to hire, easy peasy, and how they'll be able to have brunch dates at a place way better than The Shoreline.

I promise I'll be there for her the whole way.

It takes us through the next three contractions, and she's getting better now—calmer, more focused, her eyes drying and her breaths evening out.

"You're doing so good," I say to her, rubbing at her hand again.

She laughs softly, and I feel like I've hung the moon.

"You know half of that is probably not going to happen, right?" she says, a crooked smile on her flushed face. "The perfect daycare, ha. And I'll probably still have to live in a place with drafty windows and a tiny bathroom. Especially if I live near a Metro station."

I shrug. "Maybe."

"Georgie," she says, her voice serious. "Thank you. Thank you for coming."

I roll my eyes dramatically, a performance to keep taking her mind off everything. "Of course I'd come! What do you think,

I'd let an ambulance bring you here? The costs on those are unreal, you know."

She huffs another laugh. "No, I mean—thank you for coming *here*. Back home. I don't know what kind of shape I'd be in if you hadn't."

Now it's my turn to laugh, a snort of self-deprecating humor. "Are you kidding? You would have been fine. I should be thanking *you*. What would I have done, if I couldn't come back? I'd probably be squatting in Nadia's guest house, eating beans straight out of a can."

"No, you wouldn't have. You would have figured it out."

I wave a hand, scoffing. She still doesn't know about that blank space that's been sticking around.

"Georgie," she says again, and I meet her eyes. They're more than serious now. They're insistent. Almost indignant.

"Yeah?"

"You would have. If I ever made you feel like you wouldn't, I want you to know—that was about me, not you. I wanted you to come back, and I wanted to keep you close. I wanted you to see this big new life I was living. I wanted you to tell me it was okay, the way you did just now. Convince me it would be good, no matter what."

"You never made me feel—" I begin, but this time, when she squeezes my hand, it's gentle and speaking. *You know I did*, she's saying, and I *do* know. *Time to think*, I remember her saying to me, that first day I arrived, her eyes coaxing and sympathetic. Maybe even pitying.

There's a long stretch of silence—or the particular not-silence of hospitals. Strangers' voices and beeping machines and squeaking shoes on linoleum floors, televisions covering up noises you don't want to hear.

"Do you remember why we started the fic?" she asks.

I blink down at where Bel's fingers still squeeze mine, and for a second, there's a strange collapsing of moments in my brain—this morning, the fic laid out on the linens of Levi's bed, and right now, Bel's hand and mine clasped on top of white waffle knit.

"To . . . I don't know. Get ready for high school. Get excited for high school."

She shakes her head. "No. I mean, yes, in general. But do you remember specifically why we started it?"

"I guess not. Was it my mom's idea? You know my mom."

"It wasn't your mom's idea. It was your idea. And you came up with it because of me. Because I was so scared to go to that school."

"Everyone was scared; it was—"

"Not like I was scared. You know that, Georgie. You remember that."

And once she's said it, I *do* remember. I remember the way Bel would ruminate over it, the way she had stomachaches for a year straight. The way she'd talk about what clubs she would join, what AP classes she would take, what GPA she wanted to keep for all four years. I remember the way she'd started to talk about college, even back then—the schools she wanted to apply to, the work she'd have to do to get in.

"You wrote the fic because of me," says Bel. "So I wouldn't be scared. So I would think about the fun things. You used to give me assignments. 'Write about what would happen if the Jonas brothers came to our school,' you said. 'Write about your dream car.'"

It's me who's squeezing her hand now, something tense and scared moving inside me. At first I think it must be disappointment: that notebook I've been hanging all my hopes on, the evidence that I once upon a time thought about my own future, and I hadn't done it for myself at all? I'd been the same back then as I still am now. A puppet. A blank unless I'm filling myself up with someone else, unless I—

Bel breaks the spell by pulling her hand from mine, pressing her palm low on the right side of her belly, wincing. But she breathes deep and slow, and I watch her, realizing I'm not disappointed at all. I'm standing on the edge of a dock, ready to jump in. I'm shaking a can of spray paint. Watching a dance floor fill with people. It's so close; it's about to click.

"Georgie," Bel says, winded now.

"Yeah?"

"That thing you always think is a liability. You not making plans. You not always knowing the exact thing you want for the future."

"Yeah."

"It's wonderful. It's the most magical thing about you, the way you adapt. I think maybe—maybe the world takes advantage of that quality in you, Georgie. I know I have, and I know Nadia did. But it isn't your flaw. It's your gift, and the only reason people don't tell you all the time is because they're too caught up in their own shit."

She presses her hand down again, that little wince, but again she breathes through it.

"They're busy making sure they have a certain job title by the age of thirty. Or that they get pregnant at what they think is the *exact* right time, or deciding to move someplace they take to be better for raising a family. They're buying furniture from catalogs and making their too-big new houses look like no one's ever lived there."

"Bel," I say, scolding her gently, because no matter what she thinks of herself right now, gripped with this pain and fear, I know she's being too hard on herself. I know the most magical thing about her is the way she *doesn't* adapt. The way she holds on to her plans, tenacious and determined. Maybe some of these plans were the wrong ones, made for the wrong reasons, but it doesn't make it any less impressive that she's executed them.

"There's only one person I know who can solve problems the way you can, Georgie, and that's because you've never lived your life ten years into the future. Ten days or ten hours. You've always lived for making things better in the moment. That's why you came up with the fic. Not to plan our future in high school. But to make things better for both of us, in the moment."

I don't want to say it's like lightning, hearing her say it. I don't want to say it's anything bright or loud or shocking. I want to say that it's like the river creeping higher in the rainy season, slow and quiet right up until it's not anymore, right up until it's flowing over everything that's been built to control it. I want to say that the wall inside me is coming down—softening, then crumbling, then collapsing entirely.

That the blank space is finally filling in.

All this time, I thought what I was waiting for was something about my future to fill up that void I've been carrying around from the past: that I'd figure out my future job, that I'd figure out my forever home, that I'd decide whether I wanted to get married or have kids or be a world traveler or whatever. But what Bel has said—that I've always lived for making things better in the moment—I think it means that what I've really been waiting for is something from my *present*.

That I've been waiting to realize I'm okay, and that I've probably always been okay.

That I'm not like Bel or Nadia or Mrs. Michaels or anyone else. That I was good at my jobs not because I didn't know anything about what I wanted but . . . but because I *did*. I wanted to make things better for someone in the moment, and it didn't matter what those things were. That's why I excelled at what I did for Nadia, and all my bosses before her. And if I got lost along the way, too caught up in their lives sometimes, that's okay, because now I figured out the things I want for *myself* in the moment, too: I want friends and colleagues and fun, I want to love Levi and have him love me back, I want movies and making out and swimming in the river, books and knickknacks on shelves, throw pillows a decorator didn't pick out. I want to do projects with my mom and to laugh at my dad and to go out dancing on nights when I've had enough.

I want to be *myself*. The in-the-moment myself.

I've matched my breathing to Bel's; I'm pressing my hand against the fullness that's inside me, too—inside my chest, where my heart beats heavy and steady.

Levi, I think, wanting to call him right now, wanting to tell him every single thing, because I know he'll understand. I think of him that night out by the rock, telling me there's other things in life than clubs and colleges and grades. He's always seemed to understand.

But Bel winces again, this time more dramatically, and I give her my hand again. I hear it before she does—Harry's footsteps coming down the hall, a flat run—and I watch her laboring face, waiting for the moment she realizes he's finally here.

"Annabel," Harry says from behind me, all out of breath, and Bel's eyes open and she raises her head from where she'd pressed it back into the pillow, and then she's crying again—the soft and steady and streamy kind. I back away, Harry's hand replacing my own.

"Annabel," he repeats, bending over her, his face a mask of terror and regret and exhaustion. "I'm so sorry. I'm—I never should have left."

"I made you leave," she says, stroking a hand through his hair, but he's shaking his head.

"I shouldn't have gone. I would've been here sooner, but the traffic. Also, I pulled over twice to throw up. I'm sorry."

Bel meets my eyes over Harry's head and rolls her eyes, but her smile is indulgent and relieved. Henry Yoon, prince among men, who throws up when he's scared. A mess like the rest of us, doing his best in the moment.

I gesture over my shoulder, a question in my eyes. *I'll step out?* I'm saying, and she nods.

"Thank you," she mouths, and I smile, full up. Fully confident in her.

And maybe, for the first time in my life—in myself.

Chapter 20

Levi

I get Georgie's first text not long after 9 a.m., when Micah and I are leaning against the bed of his truck, alternating between sipping the coffees Laz brought us and arguing over whether the property we're working on has enough wind shelter for a floating dock. Micah says yes, that if we do articulating joints we'll be fine. I say no, that the shelter problem's only going to get worse unless a lot more natural cover gets planted for miles down the shore. Laz stays neutral, chewing on his egg sandwich and chuckling when Micah calls me a tree hugger.

When my phone pings, I try to tamp down the smile that pulls at my cheek, since I'm trying to make my position on the wind shelter issue real clear. But when I read it, I know I'm not succeeding.

at hospital with Bel. BABY COMING! definitely need to get my car cleaned <3

The last part is the kind of non sequitur Georgie often offers up in her texts, and that makes me smile as much as the good news about Bel. I think back to last night, before things went to hell, Georgie's best friend out on that dance floor, and I sure do know it isn't my place to say, but I thought she looked ready to pop. I hope she has an easy time of it; I hope I get another text from Georgie soon with a picture of a wrinkled, grumpy-faced baby in one of those hats they always get put in at hospitals.

"Who's texting you there, boss?" says Laz, who definitely uses the term *boss* how Micah uses *tree hugger*. Laz is fifty-eight years old and has been building docks as long as I've been alive, but he freely admits he's got no interest in the business side of things. He can handle himself in a pair of waders like no one I've ever seen, though, moving his body through water as if he was born to it.

"That's gotta be his girlfriend," Micah says, before I can answer. He *tsks* at whatever face I must make at him. "Don't be out here pretending you don't have a girlfriend. I've worked with you a long time, brother."

I tuck my phone away, sip at my coffee to keep my face under control. I'm pretty sure Micah's talking about the fact that more than once lately he's caught me humming along to his music when he's playing it. Last week I asked after those guinea fowl, unprompted, and that's real unlike me.

"'Bout time," says Laz. "I better call Carlos later, fill him in."

I snort, but the truth is, this morning I don't mind too much that Laz—who's been good friends with Carlos for decades, and who saw me down and out way back when—still files these sorts of reports with Carlos. They're never about the business, since Carlos has only ever talked to me about that. Instead they're about me—my mood, my life. It used to make me madder than a wet hen, that watching-over shit, but I find I like the idea of Laz calling up Carlos now.

Telling him I've got someone special.

I get a pang in my chest, thinking about Georgie in my bed this morning, warm and sleeping, murmuring when I bent to kiss her goodbye. *Love you*, I think she said, but I figure it doesn't count, not when she once rolled over in her sleep and told me she "fixed the cat's cassette tapes."

Still, after everything last night, I'm living with a kind of anticipation in my blood, and Georgie's text only adds to it. It's going to be a good day: work on this site, a trip out to see Hedi with some samples, and home to Georgie, where I hope she'll tell me about the new baby, and where I hope she'll say it to me for real.

I felt it in the way she kissed me, the way she held me.

It's a heck of a thing, to have hope over someone's feelings for me—as new as something just born, something just planted. Sure, I know these guys have my back; I know Carlos would do—*has* done—almost anything for me. I know Hedi wants me happy; I even know there's more people around this town than I ever would have thought who want to see me do well. And maybe some of that's love, but if it is, it's not the sort I might get from Georgie.

What I might get from Georgie—I know that'd be like nothing I've ever had in my life.

"Tell him whatever you want," I say, setting my coffee down on the truck bed, and this time, I don't bother hiding my smile. "After we get shit done out here."

I spend a few hours with them, squaring up the site and starting demo of the old structure. Every time my phone pings, I try not to look restless until I can check it, but I doubt I succeed. By early afternoon, when I'm getting in my truck to go see Hedi, I'm up to date on everything from Harry's arrival (**he threw up TWICE!**) to the doctor on call (**drs last name is BOX!!! is that funny or am I stressed**) to the status of Annabel's cervix (**7 cm!!!!!!!!!! btw the health classes at our school were very inadequate about childbirth!!!!**). I try to call her, but it goes to voice mail, and two minutes later, she messages to let me know there's **BIG HAPPENINGS, CALL U BACK <3 <3.**

I don't think I've ever rushed through a meeting with Hedi

so fast in all the time I've known her, and I also don't think I've ever been so good-natured about the shit she gives me over it. She says things like, "You must be too busy for *science* today, young Levi!" and "You don't have time for your old professor, huh?" and "Oh, sure, rush out of here; it's only the future of the *planet!*"

She also tells me I have one month to bring Georgie to meet her, and I get the sense she wants to give me a hug before I go. Instead she pats my shoulder and tells me I did a good job with the samples I brought her.

Halfway home, I finally get another text, and I pull over to look: it's the picture I was waiting on, that brand-new baby's red and wrinkled and grumpy face, its head covered in a pale yellow knit cap, and its tiny left hand curled into a tight fist pressed against its cheek. Georgie's sent a row of heart emojis. **NAME TBA**, she adds. **I'M IN LOVE.**

And then, less than a minute later: **with this baby but also with you. be home soon.<3**

Before, I might've thought seeing it in a text would be disappointing—seeing it when I can't hold her or kiss her or ask her to say it again, say it a bunch of different ways so I can pick my favorite. But now that it's in front of me on the screen, I realize I'm relieved to be alone for this first one. I couldn't explain even to Georgie why this moment is so private to me, why I press the button on the side of my phone to make the screen go dark, why I close my eyes and tip my head back against the headrest of my seat, overwhelmed with relief. I know it's not everything, Georgie loving me back, and I know we've got a lot to sort out between us.

But right now—after what I told her last night—it's pretty much everything to me.

When I get home, I'm still riding high, glad no one but Hank is there to witness the way I'm smiling to myself. I make a bigger fuss over him than usual, getting him real excited and encouraging him when he bolts out the door and runs in tight, joyful circles—a body restless with *Dad's home* celebration. It's good to watch him; it's a kind of lesson. Hank's always been good at reminding me how happiness looks. Once we're back inside, he follows at my heels, hopping and panting, and I tell him about how I'm going to get cleaned up, how I'm going to make a big dinner. I stop myself from saying *your mom's coming home*, but only barely.

In the bedroom, there's signs of Georgie's haste—a bra on my dresser, a pile of stuff she keeps on the chair in the corner mostly on the floor, my old hooded sweatshirt thrown on the end of the unmade bed. I'm used to Georgie leaving things out and around, but it's habit to move straight to the bed to make it up and manage some of the chaos she's left behind.

I don't mean to see it, her notebook open there on top of the sheets, but I also don't think anything of the fact that I do. I've seen Georgie with it dozens of times by now. I've been a *part* of that notebook, even if I've never actually looked inside it.

I don't mean to see it, but I do.

Wide open, packed with her handwriting, taking up every single blank space. Hearts and exclamations everywhere.

My brother's name filling the page.

WHEN SHE GETS home, she's me an hour ago—buzzing with excitement, greeting Hank in a way that gets him riled up and happy.

"Leviiiiiiiiiiiiiii," she calls, in that big, expansive way she has, and I both love the sound of it and hate the way I can't hear it right, hate that I've been telling myself for the last half hour that what I saw in the notebook doesn't matter and hate that deep down, I know I haven't listened.

She finds me in the kitchen, hands stuck deep in the bowl of mash I'm mixing for the veggie burgers I'm making, trying to execute the exact same plan I had before I saw what I saw— make dinner for us, look at the pictures I know she's got to show me, hear all about Annabel and what's happened since I left

Georgie sleeping in bed this morning. But when she flings herself against my back, wrapping her hands tight around my waist and pressing her cheek between my shoulder blades, I stiffen the slightest bit, a bracing against the same pain I felt when I looked down and saw Evan's name everywhere, by Georgie's side for the best date she could have imagined.

I breathe through it, concentrating on letting go of the tension, and I'm grateful Georgie doesn't seem to notice. She presses up onto her tiptoes and smacks a kiss on the skin between the collar of my T-shirt and my hairline and says, "I have ten million things to tell you!"

I clear my throat. "Yeah?" My voice sounds gritty, low. It's not what I want, but it's what I've got to give, this stubborn pain pounding through me, even when I know it doesn't make any sense. Even when I know it's unfair, immature.

Even when I know it's trouble.

But she's too far in it to hear, too unbounded in her happiness. She squeezes me tight again and says, "Ten *million*! I have to go shower, though. You don't want to know why. I'll shower, and then I'll tell you *everything*!"

She kisses me on the back of my neck again, and then she's gone, Hank following, and he's got good reason. He knows my mood doesn't match his anymore. I hear her in there, chatting to him the way she always does, and then she goes quiet, and I go still. I left it there, the notebook, same way I found it, because I didn't know what else to do. I don't want to talk about it, but now I don't know how I'm going to be able to help it.

I step back from the bowl, move to rinse my hands at the sink.

"Levi," I hear her say a few seconds later.

Out of the corner of my eye, I see her standing at the threshold between the hallway down to my bedroom and the kitchen. I keep my eyes down, as if I need to focus on drying off my hands.

I get up the courage to face her full-on, and she has the notebook in her hand now, closed and resting along her thigh. She's got a look in her eyes like she's never been this sorry for someone in her life.

"I figure he's in there for more than the prom," I say, because it gets my back up to see her look at me that way right now. "But I want you to know, I didn't look."

She blinks at me, something mulish crossing her expression, and it's at least better than the pity.

"He is," she says, unapologetic, and that's good, I know. That's how it *should* be. But I've known all my life what was good, what should be, and I spent years choosing the wrong thing anyway. I'm back in those years now. Out of place, out of sorts.

"Great," I say, deadpan.

"Levi." She takes a step toward me, but I can't get open to it, can't do anything but stand here stiff and forbidding.

"That's all teenage stuff," she says. "A crush I had. You have to know that. I would have told you, but it didn't even seem—"

She cuts herself off, probably to stop herself from saying the word *important*. Two months I've been hearing about this notebook, and we both know everything in there is important to her, in one way or another.

And after everything I told her last night, we both know why seeing Evan's name in there would be important to me.

Maybe I'm out of proportion mad.

But I also think she should've told me.

"All the stuff we did," I say, still wiping at my no longer wet hands. "The movie night. The dock. All that, you wrote about doing with him?"

She shakes her head. "No. *No*, Levi. He wasn't the point of it. Bel and I, we—"

She breaks off again, closes her eyes, and takes a steadying breath. When she opens them again, all that earlier mulishness has left her expression.

"I'm sorry for not telling you. I can see how I should have, because I never would have wanted you to find out about it that way. I would never have wanted it to hurt you."

I nod, tossing the towel onto the counter and shoving my hands into my pockets. *Leave it,* I'm telling myself, trying to absorb her apology, trying to let this go. Across from me, she looks tired and ten kinds of messy, her hair falling out of its ponytail, her clothes rumpled. It reminds me of the first day I ever saw her, and what I want is to hold on to how much things have changed since then: I want to get in the shower with her and press her body close to mine. I want to have dinner and hear everything she's got to say. I want her to fall into an exhausted sleep beside me on my couch; I want to carry her to bed and have her murmur nonsense to me when I do.

But I'm still tense, restless. Bruised. I've been hit with that big, pounding wave again, but this time, I'm beneath it, struggling to get air. I remember all the times, over the last two months, where I messed up with Georgie because I panicked— that night she first asked me about my family, and I ran out of that house like I had a hound from hell on my heels. The night her parents found us on their couch. Last night, at The Bend.

I know I can't do that again, don't *want* to do that again. I want to get up to the surface, to get a breath and hold on to something stable.

That's it, I think, a tentative relief spreading through me. I need to be sure of things, sure of her, and it'll be like I didn't see those pages at all.

Make it sturdy, I'm thinking. *Make it stable.*

"Georgie," I say. "What do you want?"

She blinks at me, a look of surprise on her face. "What do I—?"

"With your life," I say, but I can hear already it's coming out wrong. I clear my throat, reaching for that stable thing, somehow. "With us. What are we doing here?"

She furrows her brow, opens her mouth and closes it again, and that delay, that confusion on her face—it's a crack across my sternum. I can't help it: I make a noise, something like a scoff. Impatient and frustrated.

"*What* is your problem?" she snaps now, crossing her arms, the notebook pressing close to her chest. "If it's Evan, you're being ridiculous. It's you I've been with every night, Levi. It's you I—"

She doesn't say it, that thing from her text message. She stops and presses her lips together tight for a second, and the crack gets wider, deeper.

"It's *you*," she finishes.

"It's not Evan," I say, but I know it's a lie, or at least it's not all the way true. It *is* Evan. It's Evan and Olivia and my dad, and my mom, too, and the way I've never fit with any of them. The way I looked down at that notebook and felt, for a long, terrible second, like I didn't fit with her, either.

I'm trying so hard to fix that feeling, to chase it away with certainty. With settling this between us, with getting her to say she'll stay.

"Then what is it?" she says, and it's going too fast—for the first time since I've known her, Georgie's expansiveness is a liability to me, pressing me tighter in my defensive, familiar corner. I can hear Carlos's voice from long ago, one day on the job—when I was young and sad and aching—telling me to slow down while I worked, to be careful not to make mistakes.

But I can't listen. I'm too desperate to get this done.

"I know what I want," I say, and I make my voice sound so confident. I say it as if I've got it all figured out for us: I'm laying planks and hammering them tight into place, sturdy and stable. "I want you to stay here. You can live here, with me."

She's staring at me, her lips slightly parted. Her cheeks pale.

After long, silent seconds, she says, "And what am I doing, in this plan of yours? Beyond living with you?"

My jaw clenches. "You'll be here for your parents. You can help Bel. Work at The Shoreline, if you want. I won't have a problem with it."

She drops her eyes, nods down at the floor. "Huh," she says, and it's the saddest-sounding syllable. *Slow down*, I'm telling myself now, knowing I'm fucking it up but still too defensive, too underwater, to know how.

This is how it used to feel, I think, *to start trouble.*

"I don't need your permission to do a job, Levi."

I swallow. "That's not what I—"

"And my parents do fine without me. They'll be back on the road soon, probably. Also, Bel's moving back to DC."

"She is?"

She nods again. "Turns out, she doesn't even like it here. Some reinventions don't stick."

I know she can't mean me; I know she *wouldn't* mean me. But when I'm this version of myself—when I'm the version of myself that's so close to the boy I've been telling her about, when I'm hurt and desperate—it sure seems like she does, and the temperature inside me turns up.

"Levi," she says softly, trying her best to turn it down. "What are you doing?"

"I'm trying to figure out if we have a chance together," I say, still impatient.

"You're not. Not right now, you're not."

"Don't tell me what I'm doing. *I* know what I'm doing." I lift my chin at the notebook. "There's one of us here who's spent the last two months of their life living according to a fifteen-year-old project, and one of us who has a life here, a house here. A business to run."

She blinks at me in shock, and I know I've hurt her, deep down. Used a thing that was important to her, to us, against her. I'm trying to press her into that tight corner with me, trying to hammer her into place, and I know already it won't work.

It would never work on Georgie. Arms stretched out to the world, expansive Georgie.

I drop my head, lifting my hands and running them through my hair, sick in my stomach and in as much trouble as I've ever been.

"One of us is a mess, is that right?"

"It's not what I meant, Georgie. Let me—"

"No, Levi. I don't think I *will* let you explain this time."

When I look up, she's turned her back on me; she's making her way back to the bedroom. Hank doesn't follow her. He stands in the space she left, looking back and forth between my face and her retreating form.

When I step into the bedroom, she's holding her tote bag from Nickel's, shoving what she can into it—the clothes she's got lying around, her tablet—fuck, her robe that I love so much. I take this opportunity to ask the dumbest question possible. "What are you doing?"

She barely looks up to answer me.

"I'm leaving."

"Georgie. Wait."

She stops, straightening from where she'd bent to pick up a shirt from the floor, her cheeks flushed and her eyes flashing.

"No, *you* wait," she says, her voice loud and hard and unfamiliar to me. "You know what? You are *absolutely* right that one of us is living according to a fifteen-year-old project, but I don't think you know which one of us it is."

"What does that mean?"

It's her who scoffs now, and she packs that sound with more frustration, more derision than I could've ever managed. She stomps into the bathroom, emerging a second later with the two bottles of hair stuff she uses in the shower, and I want to howl in protest.

"What, Georgie?" I ask her, softer now, but she doesn't stop moving.

"Nothing about what you saw in this notebook would bother you if you were thinking about me," she says, jerking the canvas bag open and pulling it out. "It wouldn't bother you because you *know* me, Levi. You know where I've been all these nights, and it's not with your brother, who is nice enough but not for me."

She tosses it onto the bed, almost to right back where I found out.

"You're thinking about you. You're thinking about your family, or your dad, because you've been trying to prove him right or wrong about you for *years*. You're thinking about yourself, going to work and coming home and never being anything but this cleaned-up version of Levi Fanning who won't ever put a foot wrong again, because you won't try anything different. You think *I'm* living according to a fifteen-year-old project?"

"Georgie," I say again, because that temperature in me—it's turned way down now, and I'm cold straight through.

"Stay here, is that right? That's what you want from me?"

"Yes," I say, but I know it's the wrong answer.

Her shoulders sag, her stuffed-full bag nearly touching the floor, and she lifts her free hand to her forehead, rubbing across it.

"I was so excited," she says quietly, "I was so excited to tell you what I figured out today."

"Tell me," I say, desperate now. I'm trying to make a fist around the finest, driest sand. I take a step toward her, and she takes a step back.

"I don't think I will," she says, all the fight gone out of her now. "I trusted you with this, Levi," she says, her voice cracking. She gestures at the notebook. "With my . . . my *mess*."

"I didn't mean—"

"And you threw it in my face. Tonight of all nights." She wipes a tear from the corner of her eye, barely escaped. I want to fall to my knees at her feet, to say something, *anything* to make her stay. Instead I sink down to the edge of the bed and go silent.

It's the same as so many other times I've been in trouble: I'm shutting off from the inside out, trying not to see or hear or feel a thing.

But I could never shut Georgie out that way, and I know it. I know this is going to hurt like nothing else.

"I'm not apologizing for not having it all figured out anymore, Levi. I thought maybe you and I could . . . I don't know. Figure some things out together, a little bit at a time. But maybe you're not ready for that. Maybe you need to do some of that alone."

And yeah, I was right. I can't shut her out, because I see her go—back straight, bag over her shoulder, out the bedroom door and down the hall. I hear her whisper softly to Hank, hear his collar clink in what sounds somehow like confusion.

And when the door closes behind her, I feel it all.

Chapter 21

Georgie

One great thing about finally accepting your present-tense self—your in-the-moment self—is that you are free from thinking about, to give a random example, you and the man you love getting in a big, heartbreaking fight two nights ago. You are similarly free from thinking about, to give another useful and random example, what might happen two nights from now, or two hours from now, or perhaps two minutes from now, in terms of whether that man you got in a fight with might figure his shit out and call you.

You are free to simply be.

Theoretically.

"So I'll go ahead and schedule for next time?"

I blink across the counter at the woman standing in front of me. I can tell from the gentle, somewhat confused smile on her face that this question is being posed as part of a series, as though she has already said at least three other things that I have not heard. Her brown skin is smooth and shiny from her facial, and her eyebrows—done by the aesthetician the spa hired last week—look incredible.

"Oh, I'm sorry!" I say. "Was I spaced out?"

The confused part of her smile fades; it transforms into something more understanding. "Who isn't these days?"

I laugh, a customer-service-type laugh, and move over to the spa's lone computer, pulling up the scheduling program. It's always slow to load, and to prevent myself from using this dead air time to continue to fail at being theoretical, not-thinking-about-Levi me, I decide to launch myself into some customer-service-type chat.

"That's for sure," I answer, falsely cheerful, but I'm convincing. "More than usual for me today." Instead of saying, *Because I wrote this journal when I was in eighth grade that has my boyfriend's brother's name all over it, and my boyfriend found it, and then he panic-offered me a place to live, and also insulted me!* I say, "My best friend had a baby! Yesterday she got discharged from the hospital."

"Oh, isn't that wonderful!"

I nod, finally getting the scheduling program to load. "Sonya Rose," I say, clicking through various tabs. "Seven pounds, nine ounces."

"That's a beautiful name," says the woman, and I nod again.

"After my best friend's mom." I get choked up thinking about it, or maybe it's that I've been getting choked up every ten to twenty minutes for the last two days. Not theoretically.

The client—her name is Tasha, the scheduling program finally tells me—clearly notices my welling eyes but doesn't want to put me on the spot about it.

She says gently, "Do you have any pictures?"

Lucky for her, I have ten thousand pictures. That is maybe a slight exaggeration, but not by much. I met Harry and Bel and baby Sonya at their house yesterday, my parents in tow, and it had been a picture bonanza, even more than at the hospital.

Mostly Sonya didn't do anything but sleep, but it was the most fascinating, beautiful sleeping I'd ever seen, and also, there was something about being around her—being around Bel and Harry being around her—that definitely kept me pretty firmly in the present. Babies and their new parents need a lot to make things better for them in the moment, and I was happy to deliver.

"She's lovely," says Tasha, as I swipe to another photo.

"This one you can see her little fingernails. Have you ever seen anything like that!"

Tasha laughs. "I've got a couple of my own at home." There's a note of patient indulgence in her voice, which means I went too far with the pictures.

I pull my phone from the counter, wincing. "Sorry! I got a little excited."

"You're a great auntie."

I get choked up again over the simple kindness and renew my focus on what she needs—scheduling for her next facial and threading appointment, settling her bill, giving her the small gift bag of samples we hand out to clients after their services. When she tucks it into her purse and thanks me, I'm already restless with the knowledge of what is surely going to be my renewed theoretical failure once she's gone: It's my first shift back at work since Sonya—since Levi—and every time I've had more than five minutes alone I've done the sort of spacing out that Tasha caught me doing. It doesn't help that it's a slow day, not many appointments scheduled, and I'm still here for another three hours before I start a dinner shift over at the restaurant.

But as Tasha's making her way out the door, someone else makes their way in, and for a fleeting second I'm relieved. Maybe this person will look at the 9,775 photos Tasha didn't have time for.

But then I register that it's Olivia Fanning.

I swallow and stand from my chair, smoothing my uniform shirt. I'm unusually nervous in her presence, because I haven't seen her since that night at The Bend, the night I told her and Evan—flatly, sharply—that Levi and I were together. Now it's not even a week later and I not only know something more—something awful—about the Fanning family history, I also don't know what Levi and I are anymore.

"Hey, Georgie," she says, and it's clear she's nervous, too: her cheeks flushed, her hand coming up to pat her already perfect hair.

"Hey," I answer, all my usual enthusiasm muted. Muffled under the weight of my sadness.

She takes a deep breath before she speaks again. "I'm glad to see you here. We were . . . um. We were kind of worried you wouldn't come back."

I furrow my brow, confused.

"You know, after . . ." she trails off, not completing the thought, but I know what it is. *After we saw you and Levi out.* "And then you called off the other day."

"Oh. Well, that wasn't because . . ." Now *I* trail off, not completing my thought, either. "Annabel had her baby," I say instead. "I called off because I was in the hospital with her."

Liv's eyes widen, the awkwardness between us suspended for now. "Oh, *wow!*" she says. "Do you have pictures?"

Olivia is even more interested than Tasha, thrilled at the sight of Sonya's fingernails, and for long minutes I'm in the moment again, telling Liv about every picture as if there's something to explain about an infant at rest. But after a while, Liv's soft, somewhat familiar smile starts to get to me—a reminder of Levi, the person I've missed more than anything over the last two days. The person I'm afraid I'm going to end up missing forever.

I must go quiet, because Olivia sets my phone down on the counter.

She clears her throat. "Are we going to talk about it?"

I raise my eyes to meet hers.

"You and my brother," she adds. "Levi."

"Oh. Well—"

"Because no one is going to make trouble here about you two seeing each other. Being together, or whatever. If you're worried about that. Evan and I, we won't say anything to my dad."

"I don't care if you say anything to your dad." I've kind of— *snapped* it at her, and she blinks in surprise. Here I was, searching my brain for some appropriate response about the status of me and Levi, and now I'm hot all over with annoyance—with *anger*—on his behalf.

"Heck, *I'll* tell your dad. Is he here today? He can *try* saying something to me about Levi."

I punctuate this by shoving the pen Tasha left on the counter back into the cup we keep beside the credit card machine.

"He . . . can?"

I cross my arms over my chest and look at her, her raised eyebrows and bemused expression.

"I'm sure you love your dad, and maybe you two have a nice relationship, but surely you know he's been awful to your brother. And yes, I know about all the trouble Levi got into when he was younger. You don't need to bring that up."

"I wouldn't," she says, still bemused, but I'm not stopping.

"Good! Because he was a *kid*, and now he is a *grown man* who is wonderful and responsible and *nice*, even if it didn't seem that way at The Bend."

Or at his house the other night, my brain nudges, but I ignore it.

"And maybe if your *dad* wasn't such a world-class asshole, you'd actually have a chance to know that about your brother."

She blinks again, the slow and shocked kind. I realize belatedly that Georgie-in-the-moment just called Olivia's father, and also my boss, an asshole, but I'm not going to apologize, because I meant it. Especially because Georgie-in-the-moment is more mad at Cal Fanning than she is at his son. I cringe, thinking of what I said to Levi before I left his house the other night.

You've been trying to prove him right or wrong about you for years.

"Wow," Liv says. "So you two are . . . *together*, together."

For a humiliating second, I think I might cry. But I shove it way, way down. I don't want to lie, so I give her the truth.

"I'm in love with him."

"Wow," she repeats.

"He's a person who is worthy of love."

I'm still . . . I'm still so *mad* at Levi, so hurt by the way he treated me the other night, so frustrated that he took something that should have been wonderful and twisted it into something painful. I'm mad that he stole a perfect, present moment from me and made it about some future he wanted to get settled for himself. Some past he can't let go of.

But I'm also right about what I've said to Olivia.

And it's important for me to tell her why.

"I know you don't know Levi very well now," I say, my voice wavering slightly, losing the battle against the tears. "But you're missing out. He is such a hardworking person, but he's humble about it. And he's also—he's really gentle. I'm sure you don't remember him that way. But you should see him with his dog. Or with my parents. Or if you ever like . . . make him a pretty unsuccessful dinner. He also cares about a lot of things. Big things. He reads all the time about climate change and about the bay and . . . I don't know. Everything having to do with plants and water."

I'm on a roll now, though the stuff I'm saying gets increasingly chaotic, disjointed. A Georgie-in-the-moment mess.

"He keeps his house clean and he cooks and he has throw pillows and also . . . knickknacks?" I make a clutch decision not to mention the Pinterest. "He would give anyone money for a milkshake. He hardly ever laughs, but he does have a good sense of humor, kind of a silly one. He really . . . he pays attention. You can be talking to him for such a long time about all sorts of stuff, but he keeps track of it all. He pays attention."

"I remember that about him," she says quietly, quickly, right in the moment I'm taking a breath to gear up for more of my messy speech.

It's enough time for me to see the wetness that's gathered in her eyes.

"He always listened to me talk about movies," she says. "When he was around."

In that small addition, I hear a world of pain that takes some of the fight out of me. I don't regret anything I've said to Olivia, but I also can see the way she must hurt over this, too. In a different way than Levi, I'm sure, but I don't think it's any less valid. There's no doubt in my mind that having your older brother get disowned—on a night where something scary happened to you—would be pretty traumatizing, and that's to say nothing of the years before, when I'm sure the Fanning household was tense with constant battling between Levi and Cal.

I press my lips together, finally uncrossing my arms. At the moment, the only thing I feel free to be is sad and tired and in desperate need of a hug, but I don't think it'd be right to ask Olivia for one, not after all that.

"Georgie," she says.

"Yeah?"

"I'm going to—" She gestures over her shoulder, vaguely indicating that she's going to go—maybe to her office, maybe outside, maybe to phone a friend to talk about the employee who insulted her dad straight to her face.

"I hope you won't quit here," she says. "I like you. Everyone likes you. You've helped us so much."

"Oh," I say, caught off guard by this turn to professional matters, even though we are literally in a professional environment. But looking at Olivia, I can tell something; I can *recognize* something. Something she has in common with the brother I've tried to re-introduce her to with my spontaneous speech. I think of the night I first brought up Evan to Levi, standing in my parents' house and cleaning up after that first mess of a meal. I think about the night he first kissed me back on their couch, the way he bolted at the first opportunity.

She's being nicer about it, but what she's looking for is a way out of this for now. An escape from something hard, something that hurts.

My heart swells with affection for her.

"Thanks," I tell her. "I like you, too. I like working here."

I don't make any promises beyond that, because I have no idea if I'll keep working at The Shoreline. But I know for sure I'm not going to quit because of what happened with Levi.

She nods and gives me a small smile, doing that *I'm going to go* gesture again, and I smile back at her, trying to make it apologetic and understanding. I'm wrung out, relieved when she's almost to the door. I have to try—theoretically—to put Levi out of my head for the rest of my workday.

But before she pushes it open, she pauses and turns back to me.

"I'm glad my brother has you," she says.

Then she goes, and I know I'm not even going to bother trying now.

By THE TIME I pull up to my parents' house later that night— after having gone straight from my spa shift to a dinner shift in the restaurant, where I know I did not put on a good show of being my normal self—I am almost amused at how colossally I have failed at not thinking about the past or the future, at how I spent nearly all of my workday either replaying my fight with Levi or rehearsing different ways I might reach out to him, or, better yet, ways he might reach out to me. I must've checked my phone every fifteen minutes, hoping for one of those clumsy *Come over* texts.

I wish I could say I'm glad to see my parents outside on the patio, my dad strumming at an old banjo he usually keeps in the RV, my mom gazing at him dreamily. But the truth is, I have to drag myself out of the Prius and over to the citronella-candlelit table, because the whole scene makes me ache for Levi.

I slump inelegantly into a seat next to my mom, groaning out my fatigue.

"Tough day, Foreman Grill?" my dad says.

I can't help but laugh. I haven't heard that one in a while.

"Long day. Stressful day."

"Want a gummy?" my mom offers cheerfully.

She's one hundred percent serious, but this makes me laugh, too. Maybe I am glad to see them out here.

"Not tonight, Mom," I say.

"Suit yourself. I always take a gummy when your dad and I have a fight."

My dad snorts. "We haven't had a fight in a decade."

"I know," she chirps. "That's because I take a gummy!"

Now they both laugh, my dad playing a jokey-sounding jig on his banjo. I'd join in, except that behind this teasing exchange is something real: My parents know about me and Levi not being right.

"Who said I had a fight?" I ask.

My mom points a slightly hooked finger at me. "Your face says."

My dad makes a noise of agreement. "Wanna tell us about it?"

I sigh and tip my head back to look up at the clear sky, the pinpricks of starlight I can see through the gently fluttering leaves. My first instinct is to say no—to say that I'm too tired to tell them, or that I don't want to talk about it. After today's scene with Liv, I probably can't be trusted to say anything about it that would make sense. Maybe I'd end up doing that whole speech again, but this time with the details about Pinterest included.

But then I remember where I am, and who I'm with—my kind of nonsensical childhood home, with my kind of nonsensical parents. I feel the same wave of comfort as I did when I first drove up to this house all those weeks ago, the fic on the seat beside me, my head swimming with thoughts about Nadia and Bel and the blankness that had been overwhelming to me.

This had been a good place to end up, and there's no reason to think it won't be a good place now.

So I tell them everything. Nadia, Bel, the fic. The big blank and the way it got smaller and smaller while I was here. Nickel's Market and Mrs. Michaels and those milkshakes. Hank falling in love with Rodney, and how the citronella candles on the table remind me of the best pizza I ever ate. Sott's Mill and spray painting and the water off the Buzzard's Neck dock. Horror movies and how good Levi is at making out. Harry's overprotectiveness, Bel's grief, my fear and insecurity and what Bel called my gift.

Levi, Levi, Levi: I tell them so much about Levi, the stuff I haven't wanted to tell anyone else but that I know I can trust them with. The trouble he was in, the school where he was sent. The night he lost it all.

The things he said to me, once he saw the fic.

The things I wanted to tell him, before he did.

When I'm finally done, the citronellas are burned way down, and my dad's set his banjo on the chair beside him. It could be four in the morning or midnight; I'm not sure. I'm more tired but less overwhelmed.

"Talk about a long, strange trip!" my mom says.

"Peach, I gotta tell ya!" Dad adds. "You've been through a lot!"

I nod seriously, taking a sip out of his mug to moisten my now-parched throat. It's long gone cold and will probably give me dreams about talking clouds or animals with human feet, but I'm too thirsty to care.

"So what now?" says Mom, and maybe it's the tea at work already, but the phrasing strikes me as important. It's different from Levi's tight, forceful *What are we doing?*—a demand for the future. My mom says *what now?* because my mom is a lot like me.

What's for the moment. What would make things better in it.

I learned it from her. From both of my parents.

"Maybe I *should* call him," I say, because wouldn't it make things better to hear his voice, to make sure he's okay? To tell him I'm mad, but not forever mad; to tell him that we have a ton to talk about? To tell him—

"I don't know about that, Georgie," my dad says, and since he's not used a nickname I know I definitely should be listening.

"No?"

He shakes his head, folds his hands over his belly. He's wearing a Legend of Zelda T-shirt and I don't think he's showered yet today, but somehow he looks to me like the smartest person in the world.

"Now I understand that Levi hurt your feelings with what he said. And of course I don't like that one bit, no, I do not."

"No," echoes Mom.

"But from what you've said, Levi has also done a lot of stuff to recommend himself to you these last couple of months."

Mom again with the needless but comforting refrain: "True, true."

"And you *did* tell him he has some stuff to figure out."

"Hmmm, you did," says Mom.

I look back and forth between them. Since I have only had one sip of tea and zero gummies, I'm being left out of the cryptic realization circle they seem to be participating in. I spread my hands, palms up, in what I hope is a clear gesture for "*And?!*", as in, *And what am I supposed to do now?*

My dad smiles. "You said you love him?"

"Yes," I answer. No question.

"You want to be with him?" says Mom.

"Yes."

Dad shrugs. "Then maybe the best thing you can do for him—for you both—is to give him some time to do the figuring you told him he had to do."

Again I'm stuck staring back and forth between them, and for a few seconds I'm pretty sure they're waiting on me to make the connection on my own. But it's either midnight or four a.m.

and actually, this time, I need someone to make something better for *me* in the moment.

"Georgie," Mom finally says, "from what you're saying, it took you two months to figure—"

"Well, Shyla. Longer than two months! She's telling us she's been bothered by this blank feeling for years!"

Mom nods, waving that crooked finger along with her head's bobbing movement. "That's right, years! It took you years to figure out what that was all about. Took you finding that fic and having a whole two-month hiatus from the life you'd been living!"

My heart sinks.

Years?

"Now we're not saying it'll take Levi years," Dad says.

"No," Mom adds again, and I cling to this particular echo like it's a lifeboat.

Not years, I tell myself.

Then Dad leans forward, unclasping his hands and putting one over mine. "I don't know Levi as well as you do, but I've lived around here long enough to know how tough he is. And you know why he's so tough?"

It's the kind of question he doesn't want me to give an answer for.

"He's tough because he's never had a soft place to land," Dad says. "Not a lot of kindness offered to Levi Fanning around here, for a long time, and I bet that makes it pretty hard for him sometimes. Especially when he needs to figure the soft things out."

I blink through another sudden rush of tears. *I* want to be Levi's soft place. Maybe I should have been, that night he saw the journal. He said those things that hurt me; he handled it all wrong. But should I have stayed anyway? Should I have been soft instead of hard, even if it would have cost me something?

I know Dad can tell I'm restless—that I want to get up and make it better right now—because he pats my hand again, stilling me.

"Around here, everyone thinks it's pretty lucky to be born a Fanning. That family's awful classy. Got a lot of money, a lot of history. Heck, from what you're saying, two of those kids never even had to think about what kind of job they'd need to get some day! That's really something."

I swallow thickly, knowing already where he's going with this.

"We never gave you a life like that, Georgie, and we didn't intend to. We tried to give you a life with different kinds of advantages."

Two months back here, two months poring over that notebook and being with Bel and falling in love with Levi, and I can see all those advantages clearly now. They encouraged me to make friends, to try new things, to make mistakes. They gave me the space to be a blank, a mess; they never treated me like their puppet. They gave me what I needed but never told me what I wanted. They made sure I had a place to come when I was finally ready to figure it out.

They *loved* me, no matter what. No strings attached.

I wipe at the tears rolling down my cheeks, mumbling my messy, inadequate gratitude. My mom scoots her chair closer to mine and puts her arm around my shoulders, squeezing as best she can.

"You can't be everything to Levi, Georgie, same as your dad and I could never be everything for you," she says. "You were right to give him that time. You've got to let him take it for a few days."

"And be there for him when he's ready," Dad says. "Have faith."

He picks up the banjo again, strums a gentle tune. Mom leans back in her chair again, and it's as though they've reset themselves, right back to the way they were when I got home.

"Anyway, you've got plenty to do," Mom says, breaking the silence.

I look over at her, raise my eyebrows.

"All that stuff you figured out you wanted, right? It wasn't all about Levi." She waves a hand. "We'll do some crafts together. Go see that precious little baby. You can help your dad with the shutter out front. Go dancing, if you want."

My heart fills, *aches,* at what she's giving me.

Something she and my dad have given me all my life. Something I've always taken for granted.

She's giving me something for the moment.

A soft place to land.

Chapter 22

Levi

The first time I ever got in trouble—real trouble, outside-of-the-house trouble—I was eleven years old. It was a Saturday, and back then Saturdays were important days for my dad when it came to the inn. When the weather was good, like it was that day, he'd be out on the golf course, playing rounds with important guests, glad-handing and finding ways to talk about his plans for the future of the property. A few times, I'd been on the course with him, dressed in stiff pants and uncomfortable shoes, a shirt to match his, meant to be looking like one of those future plans. But Dad learned pretty quick I was too sullen to be out there, too uninterested in shaking hands and smiling, and on that day, he'd taken Evan in with him.

On golf Saturdays, it wouldn't ever just be golf—it'd also be dinner later at the inn, the whole family dressed nice and being seen by the guests. My dad would order for the table—one of the specials for each of us, so the dishes would come out and be seen, too, no matter if what was put in front of us was anything we'd actually want to eat. Good manners. Pleasant smiles.

Frequent, welcome interruptions from people coming by to say hello, to shake my dad's hand and compliment him.

A happy family, a successful family.

I hated those dinners.

That Saturday, I'd resolved not to be there; I'd been on fire with the idea of not being there. The week before, my dad had locked up my bike in the back shed, a punishment for coming home from school with a note from my teacher about my refusal to participate in some classroom activity or another. But I wasn't going to let not having my bike stop me. Probably I would've busted open that shed and gotten it out, except that'd only prove he'd taken something from me that mattered. So I got out there on my own two feet that day, leaving the house while my mom was in the shower and the nanny was tied up with Olivia. I'd walked three and a half miles to the Food Lion that sat right on the border between Darentville and Iverley; I'd swiped a handful of plastic bags from an unmanned cashier's station. Then I'd started filling them up with everything that struck me as the opposite of a special from The Shoreline's kitchen. Doritos. A plastic tray of cupcakes, almost all frosting. A block of cheddar cheese. Bags of candy.

In the end, it was clear I didn't expect to walk out unnoticed. I made it as far as the first automatic door before the store manager—who'd been watching me the whole time, it turned out—caught me by the collar of my T-shirt and led me back behind the customer service desk, where a couple people waiting in line to cash checks or buy lottery tickets tried not to stare. I sat in a plastic chair and calmly gave the manager the number of the front desk of The Shoreline.

I'd felt huge. Satisfied. Successful.

But I had to sit in that chair for a long time, as it turned out, and even an eleven-year-old will get to thinking after a while. I did miss my bike a whole lot, was the thing. I didn't like cupcakes. The nanny we had at home was an all right person, and now she'd probably get an earful from my mom. Whoever answered that front desk phone, they probably hated having to go find my dad, having to tell him who was on the phone and why.

It'd be nice if all that thinking had stopped me from making trouble going forward, but the thing is, it's not as if an eleven-year-old comes to the right conclusions all the time. Instead of stopping myself from making trouble, mostly what I did from that point on was figure out a way not to do any sort of thinking at all about what I'd done.

But over twenty years later, I know I've lost that particular talent.

Because once Georgie's gone, all I do is think.

About how I hurt her.

Hurt her because I was hurt.

It's three nights since she walked out, and I've spent every one of them in the same spot I'm in right now—out on my dock, facing the water, Hank lying with his chin pressed hard against my booted foot as though he's weighting me to the ground. Making sure I don't up and float away.

She told me I needed to figure some stuff out, and I think the problem is, I already have. I've turned that night over and over in my mind, and what it boils down to is this: I saw the inside of that notebook and a hole yawned open inside of me, then I took it out on her. I made her feel messy and small. I made her an offer, but it wasn't a real one. It was me trying to fit her into a place that'd fill me up again. That'd make *me* feel better, safer. More stable.

I think what I've figured out is that I don't deserve Georgie Mulcahy at all.

Hank lifts his chin from my foot and peers back toward the yard, his ears perking. He's done that a lot the last three nights, waiting for her to come back.

"Settle in," I tell him, same as I have every other time he's done it. His naked, relentless hope is almost as painful as every other part of this.

I wait for him to sigh and set his chin back down, but this

time, he doesn't. Instead he stands and wags his tail, and a few seconds later I hear a car coming down the way. It's too loud to be Georgie's, not that I had any hope of it. I sit forward in my chair, scrubbing my hands through my hair and over my beard, knowing and not caring I probably look awful, tired and untended. It's probably Laz or Micah coming to check on me, since I bailed on a site today. If I had any interest in being polite right now, I'd get up and turn around, make my way up and greet whichever one of them it is. Put on a show that I'm fine.

But since I don't have any interest in that, I stay where I am, expecting any second to hear one of my coworkers gently rag on me for being lazy.

Instead, I hear a once-familiar phrase.

"Hey, Lee."

Hank comes over, nudging at my hand, trying to jolt me out of my temporary paralysis at the sound of my brother's greeting, sounding exactly the way it had all those years ago.

When I finally stand and turn to face him, though, he's still all grown up, same as he was at The Bend the other night. He's dressed more casually now—jeans and sneakers and an old UVA T-shirt, a ball cap pulled low over his eyes. Dressed this way, standing that way—hands in his pockets, shoulders braced—he and I look so much alike it makes my chest ache.

Get gone, I hear myself saying, years ago, and I realize I'm not going to say anything like that now.

Because he looks so grown standing there. So separate from my dad and so close to me.

For the first time in years, it's perfectly natural to greet him.

"Hey, Ev."

MY BROTHER LOOKS at me for a long time, and I wonder if he's doing the same thing I am, in a way. Looking into something that's not quite a mirror, but damned close. Trying to do something different from what we did when we saw each other the other night.

He clears his throat. "Nice place you got here. I heard you took it over."

I nod, watching him take the property in. "Thanks. I got lucky."

We lapse into silence, and Hank . . . well.

Hank farts.

I lower my chin to my chest and sigh.

Evan laughs. He always had the easiest laugh.

"Good boy," he says, crouching and welcoming Hank into his open stance. "I don't know how we woulda got through that moment without you."

He's rubbing at Hank's ears and chest, letting him lick at his chin, and all his cheerful openness with my dog gets my brain back online enough to wonder why he's come. It can't be anything too bad, what with the way he's acting, but after all this time it can't be anything too good, either.

"Everything all right?"

He nods once and stands, tucking his hands back in his pockets. "I thought I'd come by. After running into you the other night."

I lower my head and scratch the edge of my thumbnail over my eyebrow, hoping he can't see my face redden.

"I ought to apologize about that. I mean, I do apologize. About the way I acted."

He blows right by that, as if I didn't even say it. "Pretty unexpected, finding you there. We never see you around."

That's on purpose, I don't say, but I'm sure he figures it anyway. I wonder, fleetingly, if he's come to warn me, if what he's telling me with that *We never see you around* is a gentle *Don't let it happen again.* But if that's what it is, he doesn't have to worry. I don't expect I'll have a reason to let it happen again.

I see some things, I remember saying to Georgie, weeks ago, when I was telling her about the life I'd made for myself here. Jobs, my house, Hank. That's what it'll go back to now.

"It was nice," he says.

I swallow reflexively.

"Pretty awkward, but nice. Liv wanted me to tell you hi."

"She didn't have to do that," I say automatically, as if saying hi is some kind of chore, or a favor. I blow out another breath, shaking my head. "Sorry. I'm not—"

"Used to talking to me?"

"I don't know if you should be coming around here, Ev," I say, but I make sure it's gentle. I make sure there's no *Get gone* about it this time. After Georgie, I'm soft all over, my shell peeled right off my skin.

"Because of Dad?"

I lower my chin in a quick, abbreviated nod.

He shrugs, casual as you please. "I think I'm done with that."

I blink up at him. "Done with Dad?"

He shrugs again. "Not the way you are. But done doing everything he says, I think. Done being under his thumb."

I don't see as how that'll work, what with how involved my brother is in the business, and the iron grip my dad keeps on it. But I also don't see as I have a right to ask. Instead I look out toward the water and say, "He won't take well to that."

Evan snorts, a real *I don't give a shit* sound if I ever heard one. "Well. My wife left me because of him, so."

I snap my head toward him, surprised by the anger that surges inside me—a fire banked for all these years, and I've been waiting for someone to toss a log onto it. To give it a little air.

"What?" I say, not bothering to hide any of the word's sharp edges in my mouth.

"That's probably an exaggeration," he says. "Really she left me for some guy from her high school. But she never liked it here, never wanted to work for him. She always told me I was too wrapped up in the path he'd set for me. We argued about it a lot."

I'm quiet for too long, but it might be a necessity—I'm still getting over the shock of me and him standing here together, and now after ten years of never talking to each other he's told me something personal about him and his ex-wife.

That openness—I admit it reminds me of someone, and that hurts like a punch to the gut. I think of their names paired together, *Georgie and Evan*, and hate how I'm betraying her all over again with the thought.

It's you, she'd said.

"Sorry to hear it," I finally say, hoping he doesn't hear the rawness in my voice.

"She's happier now. She deserves that."

I know how you feel, I think, but I can't bring myself to say it. Can't bring myself to be open with him in the way he is with me.

"Sucks, though," I manage, and he chuckles, then goes quiet again.

"Look, Lee," he says, lowering his eyes to the dock. "I can tell you'd rather I go, and I get it. I'll say my piece and leave."

I blink at him, confused. Do I seem like I want him to go? "I didn—"

"First, I came to apologize to you. For how things went down that night, with Danny."

"Jesus Christ, Evan," I say, my voice coming out harsh. "Don't apologize to me."

He furrows his brow, and there it is again: his confusion a mirror of my own. "Why not?"

"You've got nothing to apologize for. I brought him there. I was . . . I was who I was back then. It's me who's sorry. I messed up everything for you."

"Why, because I broke my collarbone? Who cares? I hated playing football anyway."

"No you didn't," I say, but I realize as soon as I do that I have no idea what he hated, what he loved. I didn't know him at all, except as an extension of my dad.

"It doesn't matter," I correct. "It was my doing, that night. I never should've gotten you or Liv into that situation. Or Mom and Dad. I shouldn't have come around, especially with how I was at that time."

"Well, I shouldn't have swung on that guy the way I did," says Evan.

"You were protecting Liv."

He shrugs, this one looking less casual and more strained. "He backed off as soon as I came out. I took the bigger risk, starting a fight, with him holding a gun. Something worse could've happened."

He might be right, but I don't see how it matters now. "You don't have to apologize to me for that. I don't give a shit that you fought with him, except that you got hurt. He had it coming. I would've done it, too."

"I know," Evan says. "That's what I'm saying. I did it because it's what you would've done."

If that's somehow supposed to make this apology make more sense, I'm not following.

"I'm not going to say I looked up to you. That's too simple. I did, when we were younger, but once you . . ."

He trails off, unsure. But I can help him out with this one.

"Started being a little punk."

He huffs a laugh. "Yeah, I guess. Once you started being like that, I don't think I understood you."

"That's because you knew how to act right. You always did."

He shakes his head. "I know how to act like everyone else. Like Dad. I've always been good at that."

"That's not—"

He holds up a hand to stop me talking, and I do. I owe him that.

"But that Thanksgiving, man—I hated school. I hated being on the team. I was nothing there, and—" he breaks off, laughs at himself a little. "I wasn't used to being nothing. And then you came home, and you looked so different. Living your own life."

"I wasn't. I wasn't in a good place. I wasn't really living."

"I can see that now. But back then, I . . . I don't know. I was angry. At Dad, at myself. At you, for being gone. I saw that guy out there with Liv, and I thought, *fuck this guy*. Fuck everything."

It's so much of the mirror feeling now I can hardly stand still. I shift my feet against the boards beneath my feet, hardly believing the way I understand him.

Fuck everything: it's what I thought back then, all the time.

"I get it," I manage.

"And I heard what Dad said to you, after." He shifts now, too, looks toward the water. "I know you thought Liv and I were back inside, but I wasn't. I heard him tell you to go."

Heard him call me poison, I'm sure. Heard him tell me to never come back. I don't know why it should embarrass me, to know Evan heard it, but it does. I make a noise, a grunt of acknowledgment.

"I think what I'm sorry for is that I didn't come out. That I didn't try to help you the same way I tried to help Liv."

That forces a constriction in the back of my throat, a press of wetness at the backs of my eyes. I have to breathe through my nose to contain it all before I can speak again.

"You couldn't have," I say, meaning it. Back then, the only thing that could've helped me was getting clean. Getting therapy. Getting on with my life.

"Maybe. But I wish I would've done it differently. I was weak back then." He pauses, reaches down and pats his leg, waits until Hank comes over to him so he can rub his ears again. "I'm still pretty weak now."

"You're not," I protest, but he doesn't let me keep going.

"You're the strongest person I know, Lee. I know I don't ever see you, but I keep tabs. You're strong."

Too bad about that constriction again. This is pretty much the weakest I ever felt.

"Dad told you to go and you went, but you did it on your own terms. You made your own way. You showed him."

He offers it as a compliment, but I don't hear it that way. Not with his words and Georgie's clattering around in my head together: Evan's *You showed him* and Georgie's *You've been trying to prove him right or wrong about you for years.*

I think I might get sick.

I take a step closer to the edge of the dock, setting a hand on top of one of the pilings. Strong and sturdy, the way I built it, but I don't know if it could hold me at all.

"You're still my big brother, Lee," Evan says quietly from behind me. "I still admire you a lot."

I lower my head, dangerously close to tears. "Ev—"

"Up until you let Georgie Mulcahy go, that is."

It flips a switch in me, hearing her name, and I turn to face him again. "What do you know about me and Georgie?"

"Well, after The Bend, I thought I knew you were with her. I gotta admit, I was disappointed to know she was taken."

"She's not taken. Don't talk about her like that, like she's a thing."

Something sparks in his eyes, and I recognize that look, too: He's trying to start trouble.

I just don't know why yet.

His mouth quirks. "No need to get pressed. She has no interest in me. Believe me, I tried."

I narrow my eyes at him. "You hit on her?"

That casual shrug again, easy breezy. But I can tell he's walking a line. "Sure, she's gorgeous. I don't know how I didn't notice her in high school."

"Me neither," I snap. "You're a tool."

"I'm saying," he says, laughing. "She didn't have the time of day for me. Anyway, my heart wasn't in it. I'm still torn up over Hannah. I wanted something easy."

"Georgie's not easy," I growl. "You have any hope of staying dry out here, you better watch—"

His smile's big now, broad and satisfied.

I answer it with what I hope is a fierce frown.

"I thought you came here to apologize," I say.

"I did. Now I'm on to the second thing. Telling you how fucking stupid you are."

"Brother, I already know," I say, without thinking. Then I slow down enough to realize that if he's here knowing something's gone wrong with me and Georgie, it must be because she said something to him. "Is she all right?"

He waits a long time before he answers me, a punishment. It's not cruel, though. It's . . . *knowing*.

"She's all right," he says, and something loosens in my chest. "Not herself at work, though. She doesn't talk half as much as usual. Barely smiles, or if she does, it's the kind that looks wrong on her face."

I turn back toward the water.

"Plus, she told Liv she's in love with you."

Man, he's not laid a hand on me. But I'm getting my ass kicked all the same. He doesn't let up.

"She also called Dad an asshole for what he did to you. Not to his face, but still. I'm pretty sure she's going to quit over it, but you know Georgie. She'll want to wait until we're not short-staffed."

"I don't want her to quit," I say, more to myself than to him.

"Doesn't seem you get a say."

"Yeah, well. That's okay, because I'm pretty sure I don't deserve one."

I don't deserve anything.

"You mind turning around?"

Of course I mind. Because I'm about four seconds from a full-on cry out here, and I don't want to do it in front of Evan, who said I'm the strongest guy he knows.

But at the same time, it took a lot of strength for him to come out here and tell me about how weak he feels. The least I can do is show him he's not alone.

I turn to face him, and yeah. He's not alone, because I can see it in his eyes—the same strained, vacant look I've seen in my own every time I've brushed my teeth or washed my face over the last couple of days.

This is how it looks to be without someone you love.

"I'd like to get to know you again, Lee. And Liv would, too, even if it causes trouble with Dad. If you don't want to give us that, I get it, because I'm sure it'll be a mess."

This cleaned-up version of Levi Fanning, I hear Georgie say, sharp and scornful. Not running from her mess. *Proud* of it.

Evan doesn't stop, not even to let me respond.

"But there's one thing I can give you other than my apology, and it's a piece of advice."

I manage a nod.

"If you're letting Dad get in the way of what you have with Georgie, don't. I told Hannah for years that I worked the way I did at the inn because it's what I wanted, but the truth is, how can I ever know if I meant it? I was doing what Dad expected of me. Leaving her on her own here, not supporting her the way I should have. Not listening to her when she said she wasn't happy."

It isn't like that, I almost say, but I stop myself, hearing Georgie again. *You've been trying to prove him right or wrong about you for years.*

So I guess it is sort of like that.

"I don't know what happened with you and Georgie," Evan says. "Maybe it's not anything you can fix. But—" he pauses, and lowers his head, his mouth turning down as his chin quavers.

It's pretty much the strongest thing I ever saw. I take a step closer to him, wait while he gathers himself.

"That stuff I heard Dad say to you that night—I know it's not even the half of it. I know he said that kind of thing to you all the time. And I bet it's pretty hard not to let that get in your way sometimes."

I nod again, unable to speak. I'm busy borrowing some of his strength for myself, letting my own tears gather. Letting them come out. I watch one drip onto the dock beneath me.

"I don't think you're poison, Lee. Not to me and not to our sister, and I bet not to Georgie, either. I wanted to tell you that, in case you were thinking any different."

All these years since that night, and it's the one thing I've never been able to tell anyone about what my dad said to me. Not Carlos, not that therapist I went to, not even Georgie. I'd told them he sent me away for good, threatened me and my siblings if I ever came back. But for some reason I didn't ever want to think about, I've never told anyone the part about me being poison.

Hearing my brother say it now—hearing my brother say the opposite of it now—it hits me fully, how hard I took it.

How much I've carried it.

How much I've *believed* it.

All the efforts I've made to keep myself sturdy, stable, routine. *This cleaned-up version of Levi Fanning.* So much of it was good—healthy and smart and necessary at the time when I first rebuilt my life, when I was desperate to simply keep my head above water.

But maybe some of it wasn't, eventually. Maybe some of it, I was just trying to keep myself contained. Keep the poison from spreading. To Ev and Liv, to the people I work alongside, to the few folks in this town who didn't write me off.

To Georgie.

I'm pretty sure I . . . yeah. I *sniffle.*

"I was," I say, not hiding the way my voice is all wet and choked. "I was pretty much thinking that."

Evan moves to put a hand around my shoulder, and I don't know how, but it feels perfectly natural. Like we've done it a hundred times, fitting together the way I think siblings should.

It feels like an antidote.

"I get it," he says, an echo of my own words.

We stand together that way for a long time, Ev's arm around me and Hank coming to lie at our feet, probably wondering how come he keeps getting drops of water on his back when it's not even raining.

I go back to thinking, but it's different this time: I think about how I got hurt and how I hurt Georgie, but that doesn't mean I'm poison. That only means I could use some help, and it isn't as if I haven't needed help before.

I've just never needed it for this. For making my life bigger instead of smaller, for expanding it in the way I deserve to— making it more than a job and a house and the best dog in the world. Making it friends and maybe even some family. Some fun.

I need help for loving someone the way I want to love Georgie. The way she deserves to be loved, forever.

And it's a good thing my little brother's here right now, because I'm pretty sure the help I need is going to have to start with him.

Chapter 23

Georgie

"Is that Georgie Mulcahy I'm seeing?"

Halfway through my dinner shift at The Shoreline on Saturday night, I go still in the middle of the act of setting down a plate of tonight's appetizer special—lemon garlic scallops—in front of a polished, elegant couple at table six who seem to have absolutely zero things to talk about with each other, if the last half hour is any indication. I straighten my wobbling smile and set their plate down gently, hoping I've heard that voice behind me wrong.

"Georgie?" I hear again, trilling and musical, and since I cannot stand here with this weird wince-smile on my face and watch this possibly unhappy couple of out-of-towners eat their scallops, I say a pleasant "Enjoy," take a deep breath, and turn around.

To face the music, again.

Mrs. Michaels and her husband—the wrestling coach at the high school, if I remember right, who has a head in the shape of a lantern—are being seated by our recently hired hostess at table nine. That is mercifully not in my section, so at least I'll be spared serving someone who already looks like she's eaten a full plate of this-is-exactly-what-I-expected-of-Georgie-Mulcahy pie.

But I know I can't be spared at least some conversation. Not without being rude.

I start to make my way over, lifting a hand in greeting. Remy passes me on their way to the bar and whispers, "Oh Christ, it's Mrs. Michaels! Watch your posture," in a tone that's so knowing and sarcastic I have to suppress a laugh.

It's such a small moment, but it's hugely helpful as I approach the table—joking, casual snark with a friend and co-worker, someone who's on my team and who I know will have my back if I need them. But after the initial cringing surprise of once again running into Mrs. Michaels, I find that I'm pretty sure I won't need anyone's protection. I find I don't care if Mrs. Michaels eats twenty of those this-is-exactly-what-I-expected pies, because tonight I'm perfectly happy to be working at The Shoreline, chatting with customers and commiserating with staff, pulling in good tips already.

All right. Maybe not *perfectly* happy. Maybe *pretty much* happy, except for the big, impatient hole in my heart.

The one that gets bigger every day that I don't hear from Levi.

But my old music teacher doesn't need to know anything about that.

"Hi, Mrs. Michaels," I say, my wince-smile transforming into something that I hope looks broad and genuine. "Mr. Michaels, nice to see you."

"Georgie Mulcahy," he says, pointing a meaty finger at me and narrowing one eye. "Didn't you used to cut holes in your gym uniform?"

"Sure did!" I say, and he laughs.

"I didn't know you'd taken up waitressing!" Mrs. Michaels says.

I wave a hand, then set it comfortably on the spare chair at their table. I set my other hand at my waist, cocking my hip out in a posture I know she hates, but one that conveys my comfort, my total confidence in standing here for a catch-up.

"Oh, I was a waitress for *years*," I say. "It's nice to be back at it!"

She raises her eyebrows. "Is that right?"

"Mmhmmm. How are things going for you? Getting ready for the new school year soon, I bet!"

"Oh, well . . . yes. Yes, I am." She's clearly caught off guard by not leading the conversation, and I have to admit: I love catching her off guard.

"You know who I ran in to not long ago? Melanie Dinardo! I know you remember her. She had such a great voice. I always wanted her to learn my special 'Circle of Life' lyrics. Do you remember those?"

Mrs. Michaels clears her throat.

"I remember Melanie," she says, through pursed lips. "And I remember you saying you'd come home to spend time with Annabel."

I do a dramatic gasp. "Have y'all heard about Annabel? She had her baby! I'll come by and show you pictures later. Sonya Rose Reston-Yoon, if you're wondering."

Probably she wasn't wondering, plus, I bet she hates the hyphenate. But at this point I will use any excuse to bring up Sonya, who I've made a major feature of my days lately, while I work so hard to be patient. To give Levi his space.

"Well, that would be nice," Mrs. Michaels stutters, smoothing her napkin over her lap. But this is a lady you could never keep down for very long; once she fell off the makeshift stage in the cafeteria while she was leading the choir through a version of "Lean on Me" and she hardly missed a beat. A second later, she's changing tactics.

"Does this"—she gestures up and down at my uniform, a dismissive gesture if I've ever seen one—"mean you actually *are* moving back?"

I shrug casually, keeping my smile firmly in place, even

though this is pretty much a direct hit, and not because I believe—the way I did a couple of months ago—that moving back to Darentville for good would be some kind of failure. No, it's a direct hit because I've thought and thought about exactly this question over the last couple of days, and I only want to talk about my answer with someone specific. Someone who is not my ninth-grade music teacher.

But it's been a whole week now—a whole week of doing crafts and holding baby Sonya and helping my dad fix that old shutter, a whole week of keeping myself busy—and I'm starting to wonder if it's time to take matters into my own hands.

"We'll see," I say lightly, but inside, I'm not light. Suddenly, seeing Mrs. Michaels here strikes me as the sign I've been waiting for—that I've given Levi enough time, enough time that I've even run into this lady who was there on the very first day he and I met. My mind races ahead to what I might do after my shift tonight. Would Ernie Nickel's place still be open? Could I get a couple of milkshakes and go over to his house, barge in there and rescue him in the same way I was planning on rescuing Bel when I first came to town?

Though it took about two months for Bel to need any kind of rescuing, and that was something she had to do for herself, and—

I'm suddenly aware of having gone too quiet, or . . . or actually, maybe the restaurant has gotten quieter? There's still the sound of conversation, of silverware clinking on plates, but I do think the volume's been turned down in here.

"Ow," I say, feeling a not-too-subtle jab at my back, and I turn to see Remy there, who clearly does not realize the strength of their own elbow. This is a pretty aggressive rescue from Mrs. Michaels, if you ask me, since I was doing fine over here—

"Oh," I say, because Remy was *not* elbowing me about Mrs. Michaels.

"Holy shit," Remy whispers. "Look who it is."

And yeah.

Look who it is, indeed.

Levi Fanning.

No ball cap, hair and beard tidy. Gray T-shirt, but with a casual button-up over top of it, untucked and with the sleeves rolled back. No battered jeans, but jeans still: dark and newer-looking. No dirty work boots, but a freshly brushed pair. In his left hand, he's holding a small black gift bag.

"Holy shit," I echo.

The hostess crosses to the restaurant's entrance to greet him, and because she's new and also not Fanning family, she has no idea that there's anything unusual about this man, in this restaurant, looking like this. I can see her greet him with a big smile, and I can see that he seems totally taken off guard by her presence, as if the farthest he'd gotten with thinking about this trip to The Shoreline was getting inside the door.

He looks over her head, and immediately—unerringly, *perfectly*—meets my eyes.

"Is that Levi Fanning?" I hear Mrs. Michaels ask from behind me, but I don't bother answering. I weave through the tables toward Levi, my eyes on his the whole time, my heart pounding in thrilled relief.

I'm almost there when I see Cal Fanning enter the restaurant right behind him.

No, no, no, I'm thinking, my heart pounding with something different now.

Levi steps to the side, obviously sensing someone at his back, probably simply trying to clear a path, but I can tell the moment the hostess greets Cal, too, can see the way Levi stiffens when he turns. I'm almost there, and I am *braced*. I haven't seen much of Cal in the time since I told Olivia I thought he was an asshole, but I swear I'll say it to his face now if he even thinks of kicking Levi out of—

"Hello, Dad," Levi says, and I stop moving. Two steps behind the hostess, holding my breath. *Hello*, he said, which means he's nervous, and oh my God. Oh, this is about the bravest, strongest thing I've ever seen this man do.

Cal stares at him. Long and hard and obviously unsure. "Hello," he finally replies.

"I won't stay long," Levi says to his father, an assurance. Cal's throat bobs in a swallow, but I can't tell if it's relief or regret.

"I came to give something to Georgie," Levi adds, and then he turns his eyes back to me, and the look he gives me . . . well, I can tell *everything* about this. It's a mess of relief and regret and nerves and fear and *pride.*

And also love.

So much love I have to hold my body stiff, Levi-like, so I don't simply fling myself into his arms.

I know that would be the wrong move. I know as well as I know myself that he's come here to show me something specific— that he's not trying to prove anyone right or wrong anymore, that he's not making trouble, but that he's also not afraid to put a foot wrong, coming somewhere where he knows he's not been welcome in years and years.

I step past the hostess.

"Hi, Levi," I say, making sure Cal hears it, the casual cheer in my voice. No hesitation, no concern, no heavy weight that would show the way I've been waiting for Levi for days. I make it sound as if Levi is the most regular, welcome customer we've ever had at The Shoreline.

"Georgie," he says, warmth in his eyes, because he knows what I'm doing. "Hope I'm not troubling you too much at work, but my brother let me know you'd be here tonight."

That, too, is calculated—I can sense Cal shifting, can sense how cut out he feels.

Good, I think, but I keep my eyes on Levi.

"Oh, it's no trouble," I say, trying not to moonbeam all over his face. Trying to keep it casual, the way I can tell he wants this to be.

He nods. "I wanted to stop by to ask if you were free after your shift?"

"Oh, hmm," I pretend, as though I haven't been developing an entire milkshakes plan to show up at Levi's house and beg him to hurry up with his figuring. It's all part of the act, and his mouth quirks at the corner. A small expression that strikes me as hugely courageous.

Levi, with an almost smile, when his father is standing right there.

"I think I could be free."

"Okay," he says. "Okay, that's good. Do you think you could stop by my place?"

"Yeah." I'm pretty breathless now, but I'm trying hard to keep it together. "I can swing that, I'm pretty sure."

His mouth is more than a quirk now. "You can change before if you want, or not," he says, and then he lifts the bag he's holding, pulling from it a square, clear plastic container. "But either way, maybe you could wear this."

I take it from him with shaking hands, unsure at first what it is I'm looking at—it's all bold, bright colors inside there; it looks like—

"It's a corsage!" blurts the hostess.

Levi smiles at her, and I'm pretty sure I can hear the crush she forms right in that second. Like a semitruck of tall, hot, bearded man just ran right into all the places her hormones come from.

I relate.

"I made it," Levi says. "With your mom. They're tissue paper."

"Oh," I whisper, *hugely* unable to seem casual anymore.

But Levi saves me from myself. He says, "I'll see you in a bit," and then he gives a short, curt nod to his father before turning and walking right back out the door.

And I'm left standing there with the corsage I'll be wearing later.

To prom with Levi Fanning.

* * *

OF COURSE it's not a *real* prom.

An hour later—Remy made me leave early, as long as I promised to tell them everything at my next shift—I'm outside Levi's house, sitting in my Prius, my hands trembling with anticipation while I carefully take out the corsage he brought me. The band that goes around my wrist is made from a scrunchie, a dark purple velvet that contrasts with the bright marigolds and reds of the tissue paper flowers. It's pretty much exactly the opposite of the pale-pink roses I imagined receiving from Evan Fanning way back when, and for that, I love it all the more.

It suits me all the more. The me I am right now, the me I've always been.

The me Levi has always seen.

I'm careful with it as I open my door and step out, hit with a new wave of nervousness about my attire—I'm hoping I read the situation right, read that look in Levi's eyes right, and I fiddle nervously with the tie at my waist, shaking and smoothing out my garment as best I can. Then I hear the scrabble of Hank's nails hitting the front porch, his happy bark, and the excited clink of his collar.

I'm crouching to greet him, arms open, when the yard illuminates, hundreds of tiny white twinkle lights strung across the porch, across the yard, all the way down and around the dock. Hank leaps and turns in front of me, celebrating them, and I calm him enough to press my cheek against his head, a steadying greeting that I need if I don't want to turn into a sobbing mess before this prom even gets started.

Of course then I realize Hank's wearing a bow tie.

I wipe my face of the tears that are already falling.

"Hey, Georgie," comes Levi's voice, and I stand from my crouch, taking him in, relieved that I did, in fact, read the situation right. The button-up is gone; he's just in the T-shirt now, and he's swapped the stiff-looking jeans for a familiar pair.

He looks perfect.

"I like your dress," he says, that quirk of his mouth back, and I fiddle with the tie again, looking up at him through my wet eyelashes and trying to harness some flirty teasing.

"This old thing?" I say, twirling once in my soap opera robe, wrapped and cinched at my waist over a pair of old cutoffs and a tank top.

Levi's favorite outfit of mine.

When I face him again, the quirk is gone—instead, he looks serious, solemn, full of the overwhelming emotion I was doing my best to hide against Hank's big head.

"Thanks for coming," he says softly.

"Thanks for inviting me."

"You got here sooner than I expected. Dinner's not ready yet."

"That's okay. I can go drive around for a while if you want. It might look suspicious, though. Obviously I don't want to get pulled over in my robe."

He smiles again. "No. But maybe you wouldn't mind a dance before dinner?"

"I wouldn't mind at all," I say, as if I'm not bursting with happiness and relief and excitement.

He takes my hand and guides me across the yard, down to the lit-up dock, and even though he doesn't quite seem ready to talk yet, I can't help myself.

"This looks so pretty, Levi."

He nods as we step onto the first plank. "I had some help. Your mom, obviously, with the flowers," he says, touching lightly at my corsage. "And your dad, he's the one who told me a tuxedo would be a bad idea."

I can't help but laugh. "You were going to wear a tuxedo?"

From his back pocket, he pulls out his phone, swipes and taps until the low, soft sound of a country ballad pipes through speakers I can't see.

"That was when this idea was in the early stages," he says, turning me to face him, and I step easily into him—one of his hands coming around my waist, the other that's still joined with mine now lifting while he begins swaying to the music. I press close to him, breathing in his perfect, familiar smell. Soap and salt water. *Levi.*

I missed him so much.

He clears his throat. "And my brother and sister," he says, his voice rough. "They came over and helped with the lights."

I tip my head back, looking into his eyes. In them I see all the emotion he attaches to this—all the meaning behind his brother and sister being here.

"How many stages were there?"

He quirks his mouth, a self-deprecating smile. "Kind of a lot," he says, and I know he's not talking about corsages and tuxedos and twinkle lights. I know he's talking about his siblings. About that moment he walked into The Shoreline.

"I'll tell you about all of them," he says. "But I wanted to tell you some other things first."

"Okay," I whisper, but he doesn't start right away. Instead he pulls me closer, and for a few seconds he simply moves with me, his beard tangled in my hair, his soft shirt against my cheek. It's exactly what I wanted for myself that night at The Bend, but better.

That's always how it is with Levi: what I want, but better.

"Georgie," he finally says, low and quiet, and then he leans back to look down at me, to adjust the way he's holding me. He puts one of his warm palms against the side of my neck, and I slide both of my arms around his waist.

"This night," he says, then he pauses and clears his throat. "This . . . uh . . ."

He pauses again, a sheepish look on his face that makes me tighten my arms around him.

"Prom?" I prompt, a gentle tease in my voice.

He offers another of those devastating self-deprecations with his mouth and nods before speaking again.

"I want you to know, I didn't do it because of what I saw in your journal about Evan—"

"I know," I blurt, a knee-jerk reaction, an unthinking desperation to put distance between this and that: hearts for *a*'s, the wrong guy at what would have surely been the worst prom. But Levi's palm against the side of my neck must have been strategic, because it lets him easily stroke his thumb across my chin, pressing the pad of it softly against my bottom lip, a pleading request.

"Wait?" he asks, and I nod, grateful for his intervention. After all, I don't really want distance between this and that. I want it all—the notebook, the mess, *me*, as part of the story of how I got here.

Of how *we* got here.

And Levi—what Levi says next tells me he wants it, too.

"I did it because that notebook—you letting me go back to the things in that notebook with you—that changed my life, Georgie. You were right about what you said. About me and my dad."

I think of it again, that careful *Hello* at the entrance to the restaurant. I tip my head down and press a kiss to his chest before looking back up at him, mostly to stop myself from blurting out a dozen other things—*you were amazing in there; he looked like he swallowed a frog; I think the new hostess is in love with you.*

"And you were right about how I've been living. Trying to prove something to him. Trying to never put a foot wrong. Living my life small and stable and real contained, and still telling myself that all the good things I have were things I didn't deserve anyway."

Down the dock, Hank barks excitedly at the splash of a fish in the river, and Levi and I both smile.

"I saw you that day in Nickel's Market needing money for a couple of milkshakes and right away, my life got a little bigger. More complicated. And then being with you at your parents' place, doing your notebook with you—even bigger. Even more complicated. Chaotic and fun. The kind of trouble I wish I would've been getting into all along."

I make a face of mock offense, even though my voice is watery with emotion. "Levi Fanning," I say softly. "Are you calling *me* trouble?"

He lowers his mouth to kiss me, slow and perfect. When he lifts his head, his face is serious, his eyes on mine.

"I'm calling you the best thing that ever happened to me," he says.

I squeeze him again, so tight it makes my arms ache, so tight he makes a noise. *Ooomf.* My heart is so big and bursting with feeling that I have to bite the inside of my cheek to keep from interrupting him.

"I'm sorry for what I said to you that night. I'm sorry I tried to make this thing between us small and stable. As contained as I've been trying to make myself all these years. That was my fear and my past talking. The wrong kind of going back."

He moves again, brings his other hand up so he can cup my face in his palms. His breath smells like peppermint candy, like the nervous prom date I never had. I'm crying again.

"The truth is, Georgie, the way I love you—that's the sort of love I don't ever want to contain. That night, I asked you what you wanted, but I need you to know that I love you no matter what the answer is, no matter if you've got no answer at all. I'll love you if you want to go back to LA, or if you want to go somewhere else. I'll love you if you decide you want a whole new job or if you want to set on doing whatever gets you enough money to get by, if you want to make marks out there or you don't. I'll love you if you want to get married tomorrow or you never want to get married at all, if you want kids or you don't. I'll love you if you want to leave your stuff all over the place, wherever you're living. I just hope I'm living there with you."

I unwind my arms from his waist, bring my hands up to cover

his. I press them against my wet cheeks more firmly, memorizing the feel of this as much as I want to memorize the words he's said to me.

This is what you've always wanted, I think. *But endlessly, perfectly better.*

"I hope that, too," I whisper. I press onto my toes and kiss him once, hard.

"I know I've got to work on it, Georgie. Making space, I mean. I'm going to do that. That's what having Ev and Liv over was about. And asking your parents for help. I've got other ideas, too. Make more space in myself so I can love you the way you des—"

I stop him this time, pressing two of my own fingers against his lips.

"Levi," I say, because I can't *not* say it anymore. It's that full feeling again, everything opposite to a blank. "I *love* you."

His lips curve beneath my fingers and I drop my hand so I can see that perfect, grateful smile. He takes a deep, shuddering breath, lets it out slowly.

"I'm glad you'll love me no matter what the answer is to all that stuff you said, because the truth is, I don't really know about most of them yet. But I know what I don't want, and that's to spend another day without you."

"Yeah?" he says, and I know he believes me. But because I know Levi, I also know there's still a note of surprise there, a question about what he deserves, and I'm determined to settle it for him.

I get my palms on his face now, that somehow-soft scratch of his beard a comforting texture on my skin.

"It's *you,* Levi," I repeat to him, the words he couldn't hear the last time I said them. "The person I want most in the world. The person I want to figure out all the blanks in both of our lives with. It's you. No strings attached."

He moves to pick me up then—arms around my waist, lifting me from the dock and turning me in a circle, restless and joyful, relieved and celebratory. I recognize it: something finally filling him up, clicking into place. Hank's nails clack closer, and he offers a happy yelp of commiseration that has Levi and I both laughing again.

When he sets me down, he clasps both of my hands in his, ducking to set his forehead against mine.

"It's you, too, Georgie. You're the one for me. I'm pretty sure you would've been the one for me back then and you're the one for me now and I know you're going to be the one for me forever." He takes our clasped hands and spreads them out wide, kisses me, and then smiles. "*Expansive* Georgie," he says.

I smile back, not totally sure what he means, but I can tell from the look in his eyes that it's something good, something about making that space he needs. Something deep and rich and infinite.

We slip easily back into our swaying dance, and for long minutes we stay that way—Hank lying at our feet, lights twinkling above us, little ripples and splashes from the river punctuating the perfect silence. I think of the promise I made to myself minutes after I first met the man holding me right now—that I wouldn't let that feeling of blankness chase me anymore.

That I'd figure it all out.

And it's funny how I feel now. Not like I'm being chased, but like I'm being wrapped up—in Levi's arms and in this moment, where every page in front of me is somehow both beautifully blank and comfortingly full up. Bel and Harry and Sonya, my mom and dad. Hank and this river, and I hope Evan and Olivia, too.

Me, making things better in the moment, in whatever way ends up making sense.

My name and Levi's, side by side.

Forever.

Chapter 24

Levi

Georgie's made the sort of mess I haven't seen in months. Maybe ever.

In fairness, it's not just Georgie who's responsible—I'm pretty sure Bel is the guilty party behind the confetti poppers that have left tiny, shiny squares of multicolored paper all over the counter I'm leaning against. And the gigantic piece of heavily iced carrot cake I'm only halfway through eating was brought over by my brother, who maybe did not anticipate how clumsy Natalie and Micah's daughter could be once she got a good few bites of her own slice in. There's a big blob of cream cheese frosting over there on one of the throw pillows, and I bet the crumbs situation is worse. This is to say nothing of what Hedi's sort-of step-teenagers have done to the shelves in the last hour in their apparent quest to read the back cover copy of every book Georgie and I own.

I scan the room for Hank, taking in more of the scene—the homemade HAPPY BIRTHDAY, LEVI banner that Georgie and her dad hung up a half hour before this party started, the bright yellow balloons that Shyla blew up haphazardly dotted around the floor. Harry—he's got on a tie, which makes no kind of sense—is sitting cross-legged in front of the bookshelves with Sonya in his lap, tapping one of the stray balloons high in the air and smiling like a guy who doesn't wear a tie to a birthday party every time Sonya giggles with delight as it descends. Micah's in the corner talking to Hedi, and it's got to still be about guinea fowl, a big topic since I introduced them a couple hours ago. Evan's coming in the back door with Paul, Hedi's husband bringing up the rear. By the looks on their faces, if they weren't all out there getting stoned, I'll eat my shoe. I catch Liv's eye near where she stands by the door and she wrinkles her nose, which I guess is confirmation. Good thing she drove today instead of Evan, but I can't begrudge him. He's laughing with Paul, the kind of laugh I love to see on him, and anyway, Paul's a good kind of trouble for Ev, the sort we needed more of in our lives every once in a while. Liv smiles at me and shrugs, and then she's caught by Bel, who shows Liv something on her phone that makes them both burst into laughter.

This is the best birthday I ever had.

The only birthday party for me I can even remember.

I'm shoving another bite of cake in my mouth when I spot Hank, his tail bobbing through the crowd as he makes his way toward me. He's got that slobbering grin on, his tongue lolling as he pants happily. It's been a big day for Hank, this many people in the house, more full than it's ever been, and he's been a champ. I pat my thigh and scratch at his ears when he gets to me, praising him, setting my plate on the counter and letting him lick at a stray drop of frosting on my index finger.

"Pretty different around here these days, huh, pal?" I say, and he wags and pants and then turns, tapping his way over to the front door and looking back at me in invitation. I bet him wanting to go out is the same as me coming over to the kitchen to eat my piece of cake kind of quiet-like. I didn't have to blow out candles or anything, but there was singing, and I'm surprised my beard didn't melt off my face from all that attention. Georgie had been moonbeaming as bright as I've ever seen.

She's at the table with the cake, sitting with Shyla and Remy, and when I look over at her she seems to sense me immediately, raising her eyes to mine and smiling big. I'm close to crying from all the gratitude I feel for her right now, having this party for me. I fought her on it at first, told her that the house was too small, that the occasion didn't matter to me, that the quiet celebration we had last year, only the two of us—and mostly in bed—was what I'd want again. But Georgie said I just had to trust her, that this party would be *great*, and like with most things she was right. It's made something better inside me, this birthday. Opened up another one of those spaces I didn't even know I had locked tight away.

Instead of crying in front of her mom at my own dang birthday party, though, I return Georgie's smile and then nod my head toward the door where Hank stands wagging, letting her know I'm taking him out. She blows me a big, noisy kiss and my face heats up again, hoping we'll get some of that birthday bed time later once everyone leaves. I don't even care if the house stays a mess.

I duck away before I get any more emotional or wound up.

I let Hank out the front and follow, getting greeted by a big shout of "There's the birthday boy!" from Carlos, who showed up as a surprise yesterday. He's leaning against the railing with Laz having a beer and they both toast me. Carlos and I had a long catch-up last night out on the dock, and I'm still recovering from all the nice things he said about how I've been doing with the business. How I've been doing with my life.

I make my excuses and take Hank around the house to the back; he's trotting ahead and happily stretching his legs, taking in the open air. He stops to do a big bark of greeting at my birthday present, the one Georgie and Paul and Shyla presented to me before the party, and I can't help but chuckle. A big metal rooster, nearly the same as the one on the Mulcahy property. It looks about as silly as anything, especially since un-like the Mulcahys, I don't have any other lawn ornaments, but even after a few hours it's my favorite thing in the yard. Georgie says she's going to give me the wooden sign she had made for around its neck later, but I already know what it'll say. In the meantime I've got to think of a name for him, make him an of-ficial part of the family.

Once Hank's done his business he comes back to me, and we make our way out to the dock. I won't stay away from the party for too long, but it's good to have the planks beneath my feet, to get that sturdy sense I still need. In the fourteen or so months since Georgie and I stood out on this dock for that prom I put together, I've come out here a lot—sometimes with Hank and Georgie, sometimes by myself. A few months back, I spent almost every night out here for weeks in the dead dark cold of January and February, trying to get my mind right while Georgie was away—a whole month and a half she spent out in California, a favor for one of her PA friends who was going on a temporary family leave and trusted only the famously unflap-pable Georgie Mulcahy to fill in.

"Jade and I have a similar style," she'd told me when she'd filled me in about the offer. "And Lark is pretty easy to work for."

I'd blinked and swallowed and nodded, names like Jade and Lark sounding so far away to me, so separate somehow from Georgie. But after she'd finished telling me, I'd waited until she was on her weekly FaceTime with Bel, and then I'd come out here on this dock and tried to settle myself, to remember everything that I'd said—that I'd *meant*—on prom night: that I'd love her no matter whether she stayed here or went back to LA or anywhere else. That what I wanted was to figure out life with her.

Still, it was scary to see her go, to wonder—in spite of her assurances that this was all temporary—if she'd get back there and remember a life she was used to once, if she'd eat at restaurants we don't have around here and like them better, if she'd do work that she wanted more than the shifts she was still taking at The Shoreline.

If she'd get near that big, loud ocean and find this quiet river wanting.

It was scary not to know what might be coming.

But in the end it was good for both of us. Good for Georgie to get some West Coast sunshine and time to catch up with old friends, good for her to do work I could tell she still liked. Good for me, too, to fill my days without her in ways that were different from what I mostly did before I met her—good to help out over at Paul and Shyla's, to sign up for another class Hedi suggested I try, to help Evan finally move out of my sister's place and into a rental not that far from me. It was good to text Georgie throughout the day, good to talk to her every night, good to get up the courage to go out there and visit her one long weekend, in case California was about to become a bigger part of our lives.

By the time Georgie's gig was up, she was clear on that not being the case, though. She'd cried big, messy tears when she saw Hank and me waiting for her in passenger pickup at the Richmond airport; she'd wrestled herself into the extra coat I brought her and made sure she was touching me for the whole drive home. She said she missed the house, missed our bed. Missed the river and Hank and her parents, missed Nickel's Market and everyone she worked with at The Shoreline. Missed being only a three-hour drive from Bel and Harry and Sonya.

Missed me most of all.

She'd done more than missing things during that time she spent away, though, and since she's been back she's put all her efforts from her time in California to work here at home. Right now she's mixing her shifts at The Shoreline with remote work for some of the contacts she has in LA, people she's built trust with for all the years she worked as an assistant. She can do it easy now that I—well, I ought to give Evan most of the credit—got her set up with a better Wi-Fi signal in the house. She does the kind of admin stuff that doesn't mean she needs to be in front of anyone—meal delivery orders, travel arrangements, online shopping for stuff like terrier-size sweaters and special edition skin care packages that she has to set an alarm on UK time for. On her busy days I don't know how Georgie makes it without screaming at that phone pinging in her hand, but she always handles it. Then when her day is done she turns it to silent and tells me and Hank all about it, laughing and decompressing in the way she says she never knew how to do before.

"Leviiiiiiiiiiiiiii," I hear her say now, her footsteps on the wood following her voice, my favorite sounds. I turn to her and catch her up in a hug, spinning her again like I did on prom night, and she laughs against my neck.

"Happy birthday," she says, for probably the hundredth time today. When I set her down I realize she's got carrot cake on her face, but maybe for a few seconds I'll stay quiet about it. I love the way she looks, messy and happy and fun.

"Thanks," I tell her, lifting her hand to my mouth and kissing her palm.

"Got to be too much in there for ya, huh?" she says, teasing.

"Crowded," I tell her.

"Another reason to get started on that extra room, am I right?"

Since she's been back, Georgie and I have been talking about making some more space in the house, an office for her work and mine, a place where we could have Bel and Harry and Sonya stay when they come down from DC to visit. A place for whatever the future might hold for me and Georgie, too. At night we look up ideas on the Internet, and Georgie still laughs every time I add one to my Pinterest.

"Anyway, I told my parents to start wrapping things up in there," she says. "So, you know. Probably in another two hours they'll get going on that."

I laugh, pulling her toward me so I can kiss her. It's quicker than what I want, but for now it'll have to do. "Thanks for the party," I tell her, and she beams at me again.

"You liked it?"

"I loved it."

She shuffles her feet in excitement, in happiness. This party was for me, but it was for Georgie, too. It's the sort of thing that makes her happiest. Makes her who she is.

"One more present, though," she says, stepping back from me.

"You weren't even supposed to get me anything."

She rolls her eyes. "Like I'd listen to that. Anyway, that rooster is really for Hank."

I fold my arms across my chest, making my expression mock stern. Georgie calls it my milkshake face.

"Close your eyes," she says, and I narrow them at her instead. She narrows hers right back, because she knows I'll end up doing what she says.

I close my eyes.

"Hand out," she adds, and I huff a big sigh like Hank does.

"This better be good, Mulcahy."

I bet she's blushing to hear that name. She loves when I call her that.

I put my hand out and wait.

After a second I feel a warm, light weight of plastic in my hand, a familiar shape my fingers close around immediately. If I was capable of beaming, I'd probably be doing it right back at her when I open my eyes.

"Had it right here in my pocket the whole time," she says, patting the front of her overalls.

I look down at the Sharpie, remembering the day we dove into this river together, the start of our going back and going forward, all at the same time.

"Better dock than Buzzard's Neck," she says, repeating my long-ago words back to me.

"What about the party?" I ask her, but the truth is, I don't think I care about the answer. I'm making a wish and getting in that water with her, one way or the other.

Georgie shrugs. "We'll keep our clothes on this time," she says. "It'll give people something to talk about."

"Hmm." As if I'm thinking about it. She knows I'm not.

She knows I'm always game for trouble, when it comes to her.

I uncap the Sharpie. I think about that day again, when I was the one handing over the marker, trying to get Georgie to forgive me. I think about the spirit of Buzzard's Neck, the small wishes we were all supposed to write on our arms while we waited for a new school year to start.

I don't have to be any kind of small, not anymore. Not even with my wishes.

Georgie watches me with anticipation while I turn my arm up, ready to write. I'm pretty sure she knows what I'm thinking. I'm pretty sure she knows I can do this by heart.

I look up at her and set the marker against my skin.

And I write the wish I wanted to make all along.

Acknowledgments

Georgie, All Along is the seventh book for which I have written acknowledgments, and when I sat down to compose them this time around, I had the sudden concern that readers would notice that I always seem to have the same set of people to thank. But then, of course, I realized that I am so lucky to have that same set of people to thank, so lucky to be surrounded by loyal and longtime support that makes it possible for me to write these books. I hope you'll indulge my gratitude for some folks who may be familiar to you if you've read one of these pages before.

The first group should be absolutely familiar because it's you—readers and reviewers and bloggers and booksellers and librarians. Your support of my writing, your messages of excitement and kind encouragement, your book recommendations and your passion for the genre—they are a gift. I started writing romance because of the comfort and joy romance brought to me, and my hope has always been to give some of that back to the world. Thank you for all the ways you remind me why it matters.

My agent, Taylor Haggerty, and my editor, Esi Sogah, always deserve such a lion's share of my gratitude that I hardly know how to articulate it fully. What I can say is that every writer should be so fortunate to have a team that pays such good attention to what the author needs during the drafting stage, even when said author does not always know it herself. I thank you both, as ever, for this attention—and for your belief in me, even when I am sure I am testing the limits of it. As I approached the final stage of revisions for *Georgie*, I was thrilled and fortunate to enlist the editorial services of Jennifer Prokop, who helped me see clearly how to craft and polish an ending that would truly shine.

The team at Kensington Books has worked tirelessly during a time of great pressure on the publishing industry, and I thank everyone there for the work they have done on all of my books, including this one. I owe special thanks to Michelle Addo, Lynn Cully, Jackie Dinas, Vida Engstrand, Norma Perez-Hernandez, Lauren Jernigan, Alexandra Nicolajsen, Kristine Noble, Jane Nutter, Shannon Plackis, Adam Zacharius, and Steve Zacharius. I also thank Kristin Dwyer and her entire team at LEO PR: Kristin, I cannot count the ways I was lost before you—you are a ray of sunshine in my life and an absolute powerhouse in publishing.

In the years since I began my publishing journey, the most profound lessons I've learned are about vulnerability in the creative process—how to share my own and how to be open to others'. I am grateful to so many people who have been willing to brainstorm and commiserate about writing, but I owe special thanks for *Georgie* to Lauren Billings, without whom I would not have had the courage to begin or finish this story: Lo, thank you for letting me be the mess I'm afraid to be and for loving me anyway. I also thank two marvelous early readers, AJ and Amy, who were willing to look at bits and pieces of this as I shaped it into something book-shaped. Your patience and enthusiasm saved me at so many points during the writing of this book. Sarah MacLean, thank you for always picking up the phone and saying, "Let's talk it out." You all make a lonely process feel so much less so.

Speaking of loneliness: there are many to thank for helping to keep it at bay as I wrote this book. Some are people, like my beloved family (all of you, I love you so), my dear and longtime friends (your names are written on my heart, always), my coworkers and extended community members, all of whom contributed to the vast and difficult project of fostering a sense of togetherness during a time when we have had to stay so far apart. Some are animals, like my sweet dog, by my side for every word I wrote of this manuscript. Some are things—things that have, during these last couple of years especially, been lifelines: books and puzzles and music and crafts; great TV series and films and funny videos on the Internet; soft pants and blankets and endless cups of tea; an exercise bike and coaches online who somehow managed to bring energy to the basement; every piece of technology that allowed me to see someone's face and hear their voice, and every piece of technology that let me settle for typing out my *hello*s and *how are you*s and *can you help*s some days. I thank every creator who stared this period of history in the face and said, *Let me make something that brings someone else comfort, or laughter, or joy.*

I believe that all of us, no matter how we have spent our time over the last couple of years, owe a massive debt of gratitude to anyone working in a healthcare environment—research scientists, physicians, nurses, first responders, medical assistants of all kinds, hospital house staff at every level, public health workers and communicators, and more. I want to add here a particular thanks to the healthcare worker with whom I share my life, whose stoic and patient approach to these very difficult times has been nothing short of inspiring. I know you don't like when I say it, but . . . you are, in fact, a genuine hero. Thank you for always making space for me, especially during a time when the world has allowed you so little.

Georgie, All Along

Kate Clayborn

The following discussion questions are included
to enhance your group's reading of *Georgie, All Along*.

Discussion Questions

1. Early in *Georgie, All Along*, Georgie comes face-to-face with a former teacher who remembers her as flighty and disorganized. What do you think the teachers from your past remember about you from when you were young, and do you think they judged you fairly back then?

2. Georgie and Levi spend a lot of their time together revisiting some of Georgie's old adolescent dreams from her teenage years. What moments from your teenage years do you wish you could relive, and why?

3. One thing Georgie struggles with in this book is the feeling that she never really knew what the "plan" for her life would be, especially because everyone around her always seemed to have goals for the future. Do you relate to this about Georgie? Do you think our society places too much emphasis on the kinds of plans that Georgie never seemed to be able to make?

4. Throughout this book, Levi feels an incredible amount of guilt about who he used to be when he was young. Did you feel empathy for what Levi went through, and do you think there's a chance he'll ever have a relationship with his parents?

5. Levi's dog, Hank, is an important part of revealing who Levi is as a character. What qualities do Levi and Hank seem to share, and how are they different?

6. Bel and Georgie are unlikely friends in terms of their personalities. Do you have any close friendships with people whom you're very different from? What makes those friendships work?

7. Bel and Georgie each have different impressions of Darent-ville, the small town where they both grew up. Do you re-late more to Bel's or Georgie's views of their hometown? Do you think of yourself as a city or small-town person, or somewhere in between?

8. Where do you see Georgie and Levi in ten years? Will they have their happily ever after?

9. If you could have a separate book about any of the second-ary characters in *Georgie, All Along,* whose book would it be and why?

10. Time for some fan-casting: Who do you think should play Georgie and Levi—and their friends and family—in a movie of their story?

Visit us online at
KensingtonBooks.com
to read more from your favorite authors,
see books by series, view reading
group guides, and more!

BOOK **CLUB**

BETWEEN THE CHAPTERS

Visit us online for sneak peeks, exclusive
giveaways, special discounts, author content,
and engaging discussions with your fellow readers.

Betweenthechapters.net

Sign up for our newsletters and be the first
to get exciting news and announcements about
your favorite authors!
Kensingtonbooks.com/newsletter